MY LADY
BELOVED

LAEL ST. JAMES

MY LADY BELOVED

SONNET BOOKS
New York London Toronto Sydney Singapore

This book is a work of fiction. Names, characters, places and incidents are products of the author's imagination or are used fictitiously. Any resemblance to actual events or locales or persons, living or dead, is entirely coincidental.

An *Original* Publication of POCKET BOOKS

 A Sonnet Book published by
POCKET BOOKS, a division of Simon & Schuster, Inc.
1230 Avenue of the Americas, New York, NY 10020

ISBN: 0-7394-1781-9

SONNET BOOKS and colophon are trademarks of
Simon & Schuster, Inc.

Front cover illustration by Alan Ayers; tip-in illustration by Sanders and Cherif Fortin

Printed in the U.S.A.

for Diane Hollis,
the courageous crusader,
with love and admiration

My Lady
Beloved

1

⚜

Late summer, 1369
St. Swithin's Abbey,
Devonshire, England

 Uhe uppermost branches of the oak, a gnarled and venerated tree, ancient of days and fully grown long before the first stones of the abbey's foundation had been laid, rustled beneath the bare and somewhat grubby feet of nineteen-year-old Gabriella Redclift, soon to be Lady Avendall. She peered into the distance, squinting a little, and held her breath, glad her expression was hidden from her sisters, standing below on the path.

"Can you see Sir Avendall and his men?" called Margaret, her twin, who grew vexed if addressed by any name save 'Meg.' Her voice floated up through the green, bristling leaves, high and eager, for she, like everyone else at St. Swithin's, believed the fiction that Gabriella truly wanted the marriage arranged for her, long ago, by their late father. None must ever suspect that she was merely pretending to be pleased, for the sake of her mother and sisters and the crumbling old manor house, Redclift Hall, two days' journey north of the abbey, that was her heart's home. Her body and soul, indeed all she had, were her dowry; Avendall's gold, of which there was a surfeit, would assure Meg and Elizabeth's futures, whether they chose to wed or to take holy vows and remain at the abbey, and Ariel, their ever-fretful mother, would know security and peace at long last.

"In the name of the Holy Mother," lamented sixteen-year-old Elizabeth, no doubt crossing herself as she spoke, for she, with her gentle nature and devout ways, was almost surely destined to take the veil, "*do* come down, Gabriella, lest you fall . . ."

Ignoring Elizabeth's plea—dear Elizabeth, she was forever apprehensive about *something*—Gabriella gazed into the distance, beyond the walls of the abbey, at once comforting and confining, searching the horizon for any sign of her bridegroom, come to claim her. Although the weather was already growing cooler, the days moving inexorably toward autumn and then the bitter cold of winter, the late afternoon sun was dazzlingly bright, the sky a heart-pinching blue. Gabriella tried not to think of Redcliff Hall, with its fields and meadows and streams shimmering with trout, a place she would most likely never set eyes upon again. Instead, she must fix her thoughts on what lay ahead, forsaking all that lay behind.

"I think I see just a flicker of color on the horizon," she called down to her sisters, clinging to the tree trunk with one arm and shading her eyes with the opposite hand. "Still, I can't be certain—"

"*Come down,*" Elizabeth reiterated, striking a note of clear desperation. " 'Tis sorrow enough that you're leaving us—I should not be able to bear it if you landed at my feet in a heap of broken bones!"

"Do be still," enjoined Meg, ever impatient with any sign of trepidation, either in herself or in others. She would gladly have climbed to the top of the oak tree personally, if Avendall had been her bespoken husband instead of Gabriella's. It was a bitter if private irony: unlike Gabriella, who wanted only to live at Redclift Hall and cause the place to prosper once more, Meg yearned for romance, adventure, and travel.

"I won't be still," argued Elizabeth, who was a Redclift, after all, and not without spirit, for all her prayers and piety. "I'm the only one here with a grain of common sense!"

It was then that the speck Gabriella had glimpsed on a distant hilltop resolved itself into four horsemen, clad in red and gold—Sir Avendall's colors.

"There they are," Gabriella said, trying to sound pleased. Instead of the wild, heady delight Meg would have exhibited, she felt a sting of poignant sorrow. Probably before she saw another sunrise, she would be a married woman, and on her way to live out her days on Avendall's Cornish estate. Redclift Hall, her sisters, the abbey—everyone she loved and everything she knew—were already slipping away, soon to be lost.

She swallowed hard, and blinked back tears.

"Hurry, then," Meg called up to her, breathless with anticipation. "I shall brush and plait your hair—I'll weave the crimson ribbon through—and Elizabeth will lay out your good velvet gown."

"We shall have to do something about those feet," Elizabeth said plaintively, as Gabriella began making her way back to the ground, moving deftly from branch to branch. "And I'm sure your kirtle is covered with wood sap—"

"Don't fuss," scolded Meg, but good-naturedly. "After all, this may be Gabriella's wedding day, and we should all be positively delirious with joy—shouldn't we?"

As Gabriella dropped from the lowest limb to land on her feet, facing her sisters, she saw, with dread, that Elizabeth's wide brown eyes were brimming with tears. "I know I should be happy," the youngest sister blurted out, "but I'm not. Gabriella is going away. Far away."

"Goose," Meg said affectionately, putting an arm around Elizabeth's fragile shoulders and giving her a quick squeeze. "You know Gabriella will send for us, once she's settled in her new home. She'll see that you and I have husbands—just like we planned. Mine will be an adventurer—perhaps a seagoing man—and yours, Elizabeth, a gentle scholar. You'll see."

Looking at her sisters now, her beautiful, destitute sisters, Gabriella once again felt like weeping. It had been easy enough, these seven years since they'd come to the abbey, to lie in their cots in the cell-like room they shared at night, spinning dreams of wonderful futures for all of them; rich visions, they'd been, filled with love and laughter, children and sunlight.

The reality was that they were penniless, that they had been admitted to this secluded convent only because the abbess was a distant cousin to their father, Sir Alexander Redclift. Alexander had died young, and in poverty, having spent both himself and his modest fortune in service to Edward III. His widow, Ariel, had been overwhelmed by the loss of her husband, the great love of her life, and like a bird taking shelter in a storm, had remarried at the first opportunity. Hugh Mainwaring, Gabriella, Meg, and Elizabeth's stepfather, though of benign temperament, was even poorer than his wife, and no better at managing the family's meager resources than Alexander had been. As a result, he and Ariel were forever on the verge of penury.

Having three unmarried daughters, intelligent, personable, and accomplished though they were, had only compounded the problem.

Sir Cyprian Avendall's claim on Gabriella had come as a vast surprise to everyone. A year before, he had descended upon St. Swithin's Abbey unannounced, with a company of five men-at-arms, and requested an audience with the dour abbess, Mother Mary Benedict.

They had met in Mother's study, the men-at-arms standing guard outside all the while, as though expecting an attack, and during their lengthy conference, the entire abbey had been abuzz with speculations as to why such a man should venture into the Devonshire countryside to consult with a nun.

In due time, Gabriella and Meg had been called to Mother Mary Benedict's rooms, there to be presented to Sir Avendall like petitioners at court.

A handsome man, broad shouldered and strong from many years of wielding a sword in the king's service, Avendall greeted the sisters with a curt nod and then proceeded to study them as if they were horses to be sold or bartered at market. Or so Gabriella had thought; Meg had not seen the encounter in the same way at all.

Gabriella had disliked the visitor readily, and bristled during the whole of the interview, but Meg, the most impressionable of the three sisters, had been intrigued by the towering, dark-haired man, even though he did not smile once during their time together. For her, his appearance at the abbey was a wish granted, a prayer answered, an event to be passed down in legend and story. Apparently, she had paid little or no heed to mundane details, such as his hard, rather grim countenance, or the cold and measuring look in his eyes.

Presently—though not soon enough, by Gabriella's lights—Sir Avendall had departed, leading his weary men through the open gates of the abbey and out into the twilight. She'd been relieved to see him go.

After the evening meal, however, Mother Mary Benedict had again summoned Gabriella to her quarters, this time instructing her to come alone. There, the abbess announced that Sir Avendall wished to take Gabriella to wife in the space of a twelve-month. In his generosity, he was willing to overlook the fact that she could bring nothing to the marriage beyond her fair person, a worthy name, and excellent virtue. He'd produced a document, signed by Gabriella's father when she was but a babe in arms, agreeing to the marriage, in return for a sizable amount of gold. Gold Alexander had certainly squandered, for the barns and cellars and granaries at Redclift Hall had long been empty, as had the coffers. Avendall, in a grand and, in Gabriella's view, rather high-handed, gesture, had settled an ample sum upon the abbey, in compensation not only for his bride's upbringing, but for the care and keeping of her sisters as well. From the day proper vows were exchanged, he decreed, Ariel and Hugh Mainwaring would want for nothing. A river of florins would flow, benefiting everyone concerned.

Gabriella had never considered refusing Sir Avendall's suit; even if she had had that option, she would not have taken it. Too much depended upon this marriage, and it was her duty as the eldest daughter and the only sensible person in the entire family, to shoulder this particular yoke and carry on.

As Avendall's wife, Gabriella would live in a grand keep in Cornwall, very near the sea. She would be addressed as Lady Avendall, and could rightly expect her own palfrey to ride, and probably several servants to attend her. She would wear beautiful gowns and mayhap even jewels, and always have plenty to eat, even in winter. In time, she would bear children, and her sons and daughters would be her solace, her joy. Too, Avendall was a soldier, surely away fighting for years at a time.

Now, faced with the actual arrival of her betrothed, with the exchange of sacred vows in the abbey's main chapel, then having to bid farewell to Meg and Elizabeth, from whom she had never been parted, even for a night, Gabriella's firm resolve wavered a little. She did not allow her thoughts to stray quite so far as the threshold of Sir Avendall's bedchamber, where the mysterious rites of marriage would inevitably take place, once they reached his holding in the west.

Meg caught her hand in a brief, reassuring grasp. Although she and Gabriella were not alike physically, Meg's hair being a rich shade of chestnut, while Gabriella's was fair, her eyes a vivid green, as opposed to the changeable hazel shade of Gabriella's, they were so close that they could often communicate without speaking. It had not been easy for Gabriella to deceive her twin.

"Come," Meg said quietly. "We must prepare you for your bridegroom."

"And if Mother Mary Benedict sees you barefoot, wearing that old kirtle, with your face smudged and your hair in such a frightful mess," Elizabeth said, already moving resolutely toward the part of the abbey where their room was, along with those of the other gentlewomen, impoverished and otherwise, who made their home within the walls of St. Swithin's, "she'll make you pray on your knees for hours, in the hope of redeeming your immortal soul."

Meg sighed. "Sometimes, dear sister," she told Elizabeth mildly, "you are a trial, with all your talk of souls and saints." Meg had a distinct inclination toward irreverence, a fact that gave poor Elizabeth frequent nightmares, in which her sister was engulfed in hellfire and tormented by devils and invariably unrepentant in the face of it all.

Elizabeth linked her arm with Gabriella's, ignoring Meg's remark. "I shall say a novena for you—nay, *two* novenas—one that you might endure your—your—" here, she lowered her voice to an awestricken whisper, "wedding night." Clearly, she saw this prospect as the earthly equivalent of purgatory, and Gabriella secretly agreed. Elizabeth paused again, swallowed, and then went bravely on, her tone exceeding cheerful. "And one, of course, that you will reach Cornwall without being set upon by brigands and murdered in the road."

"Thank you," Gabriella said circumspectly, and gave the grinning Meg a fierce glance of warning, over the top of Elizabeth's head. "It is a comfort to know you will be petitioning the Holy Mother on my behalf."

Elizabeth bit her lower lip and looked longingly in the direction of the chapel, a white stone structure on the other side of the vegetable garden. "Perhaps I should get started right away!" she confided, her dark eyes wide and luminous.

Gabriella patted her younger sister's hand. "Yes," she agreed. "I'm sure there's no time to waste."

Elizabeth nodded and rushed away, fairly floating between the rows of pumpkins and squash as she made her way toward the tiny church where everyone at St. Swithin's gathered for prayer on a painfully regular basis.

"Little ninny," Meg said fondly, watching Elizabeth go.

Gabriella stiffened slightly. "She's doing what she

can," she replied. She loved her sisters desperately, and the imminence of their parting made her peevish.

"Gabriella." Meg spoke with a firm solemnity that made Gabriella turn to face her. Meg gripped both her hands and squeezed them tightly. "Do you truly want to do this? Marry Avendall, I mean? I know he chose you for a bride, but you could feign some sort of fit, and I could offer to go in your place—"

Gabriella freed her hands, cupped Meg's cheeks in them, kissed her sister's forehead. "Silly creature," she said, smiling through tears she made no effort to hide. "The abbess would surely see through such a ruse and, besides, I *do* wish to marry. Who wouldn't want such an advantageous match?"

"You, I think," Meg answered sadly. "You're doing this for Elizabeth and me, for Mother and for Redclift Hall. Don't you think I know that?" She took a breath, then launched a new volley of words, rapid and obviously well rehearsed. "Think of it, Gabriella—if I were the one to marry Avendall, then you would be free to return to Redclift Hall. You could take things in hand, plant crops, buy cattle and pigs and horses with Avendall's gold—"

"No," Gabriella interrupted, her palms still resting against Meg's face, which was now wet with tears. "It is decided."

"But—

Gabriella stood firm. Duty was duty, and honor was honor. This lot had fallen to her, and as much as she wanted to shrink from it, she knew her conscience would give her no rest if she allowed Meg to rescue her. "No," she said again, and let her hands drop to her sides.

A number of fiery emotions flared in Meg's green eyes, despair among them, and pride. "Must you be so bloody

noble?" she hissed. "This is a sacrifice for you. For me, it
would be a boon, a chance to *do* something with my life."

Gabriella smoothed her sister's chestnut hair, always
a little tangled, but she did not relent. If she'd truly believed that Meg would be happy as Lady Avendall, she'd
gladly have stepped aside, but she knew otherwise.
Avendall, for all his impressive appearance and fat
purse, was not the prize Meg fancied he was; Gabriella
had quickly discerned, despite their brief acquaintance,
that he was a humorless, unimaginative man, and quite
possibly ruthless. "Your time will come," she said, and
then, to let her twin know the matter was closed, she
turned and walked away without looking back.

Sir Cyprian Avendall, as it happened, was not among
the arriving riders. He had not deigned to attend his own
wedding, it seemed, and for the briefest, most fleeting
ghost of a moment, Gabriella hoped he'd changed his
mind entirely. This thought was immediately followed
by a raging storm of guilt, for without Avendall, there
would be no gold to restore Redclift Hall and its lands to
former glory, no quiet, scholarly husband or place in the
church for Elizabeth, no auspicious marriage for Meg.

"What do you mean, 'milord could not make the
journey himself?'" Meg demanded, nearly two hours
after the confrontation at the garden's edge, standing
beside Gabriella in the abbess's study. Elizabeth hovered nearby as well, having interrupted her prayers, it
would seem, stricken to silence and pale as milk.

A short time before, when Gabriella had been
brought to that plain and homely room, with its one
desk and a single hard bench to accommodate visitors,
its cold stone floors and tiny, ash-filled fireplace, Meg,

though still flushed from their earlier disagreement, had insisted on accompanying her. Elizabeth, as stalwart as she was reluctant, had been alerted by one of the novices, and hurried to be present.

The leader of the four men-at-arms Sir Avendall had sent from Cornwall to fetch Gabriella tried to daunt Meg with a level, lingering gaze. When that necessarily failed, the large, battle-scarred and generally graceless man cleared his throat and replied, "My lord Avendall has many responsibilities. He did not think it prudent to abandon his holdings just now, and therefore sent myself and these good men to fetch his bride home to Cornwall."

Mother Mary Benedict, a tall and slender woman who never seemed to age, interceded. "Surely you do not expect me to send an unmarried girl traveling through the countryside, alone but for a company of rough fighting men."

Gabriella felt a swift, dizzying flood of relief, and was immediately ashamed of her weakness, however fleeting. Her course was set, and she would not step aside from it. Meg and Elizabeth moved closer, one at her left side, one at her right, and she was deeply touched by their devotion, sustained by their courage.

The burly man stood straighter. "My lord anticipated your concern," he told the abbess, "and has asked that I serve as a proxy for him. The ceremony must take place as planned."

Gabriella raised her chin. "I will stand before the altar of God with no man but my rightful husband," she said. Meg and Elizabeth both drew even closer to her.

Mother Mary Benedict looked at Gabriella. As the young woman's guardian, the abbess had the authority to override any protest, and there was Avendall's settlement to consider. If Gabriella did not go through with the marriage, the gold would have to be returned, and furthermore, even though Gabriella's talents for planning and managing had benefited St. Swithin's, she was really just another mouth to feed. Another indigent gentlewoman, with nowhere else to go.

"Proxy marriages," the abbess said, "are neither uncommon nor improper, Gabriella." The older woman stood, impassive, her hands folded inside the wide sleeves of her habit.

Meg slipped an arm around Gabriella's waist from one side, Elizabeth from the other. Neither sister spoke.

"I do not even know this man's name," Gabriella said evenly.

The soldier, already ruddy from long exposure to the wind and sun, reddened slightly. "I am called Halsey," he said, ducking his head with a sort of desultory deference. "Begging my lady's pardon, but I do not think she understands. Her lord husband has commanded that she offer her vows before setting out for Avendall Hall."

"Avendall is not yet my husband," Gabriella pointed out, with an slight toss of her head. Then she turned an imploring but still proud gaze upon the Abbess. "Please, Mother," she said, with quiet dignity. "Let me travel to Cornwall, and be married there."

Mother Mary Benedict smiled gently. "I am sympathetic to your position, child," she said, before turning her attention from Gabriella to Halsey. "There was nothing in my original agreement with Sir Avendall that allowed him to send a surrogate bridegroom. His request is therefore denied. Moreover, I cannot permit this young woman to leave the abbey in your charge without a proper chaperon."

Gabriella held her breath, her heart pounding beneath the fabric of her one good gown, a threadbare garment of dark blue velvet, given to her by a more prosperous resident of St. Swithin's.

"What say you to this?" Mother Mary Benedict asked of the escort, when he stood speechless.

Halsey inclined his head a little. "We will not take the woman by force," he said, "but neither do we dare return without her. Can you offer an acceptable companion for the lady?"

Mother nodded. "Our own Dame Julianna would well serve in this instance," she said. "I will ask her to prepare for a journey."

Halsey bowed. "With your permission, Mother, we must needs set out on the morrow, at first light. My lord Avendall is most eager to begin his marriage and sire an heir."

Gabriella, a silent witness to this exchange, was struck by such a wave of panic that she nearly swooned— she, who had never fainted in her life. Still, she could scarce afford to back down. "I will be ready," she said, hoping that her voice did not quaver too much.

Mother Mary Benedict dismissed Gabriella, Margaret, and Elizabeth with a kindly gesture of one hand and a murmured, "You may join the others in the chapel for vespers."

Gabriella was determined to play out the role fate had thrust upon her, without flinching. "Yes, Mother," she said, and lowered her head, lest the abbess catch even a glimpse of fear in her eyes.

"Mother—" Meg began.

"Yes, Margaret?"

Gabriella took a painful hold on her sister's arm and

half dragged her toward the door. "We must not be late for vespers," she said, and pinched Meg, hard, when she would have balked.

"Indeed not," the abbess agreed, rather dryly.

Gabriella fairly shoved Meg over the threshold, then, after stepping aside for Elizabeth, she pulled the heavy door closed and stood in the corridor with her hands on her hips. "Not another word," she told Meg, before letting her stern gaze slide to Elizabeth's wan face. "From either of you."

Elizabeth swallowed, and Meg looked miserable as well as angry, but both of them held their tongues.

The churning clouds of an approaching storm made a dark and ominous fringe on the horizon. By morning, Morgan Chalstrey thought with grim satisfaction, the king's roads would turn to muddy bogs, his forests, surrounding Morgan and most of his men at that moment, to dripping curtains of green.

The perfect setting for an ambush.

Leaning against an oak tree, braced by one arm raised and bent at the elbow, Morgan surveyed the abbey, St. Swithin's, huddled at the base of a distant hill. He had been watching Avendall's men, as had a small detachment of his own forces, ever since they'd left Avendall's gloomy keep on the rugged cliffs of Cornwall. Watching and waiting.

Soon, very soon, he would avenge an old and well-fermented grievance. He wondered why, now that the moment was almost upon him, he felt no elation, no sense of a wrong about to be righted, a cause about to be well served.

"You look thoughtful," remarked his best friend and

most trusted officer, Gresham Sedgewick, in a damnably cheerful tone. "Is it possible that my devout prayers are finally heard and you mean to turn from this foolish course?"

"You've never uttered a prayer in your life," Morgan challenged, "devout or otherwise. And no—nothing's changed. I still intend to carry out my plan."

Gresham sighed. He was a tall man, as big as Morgan himself, with fair hair and a face as beautiful as any woman's, with his blue eyes and patrician features, and he was bold enough to shame the very devil. "Better to go back to the Levant and do battle with the Turk than to stir the embers of an old feud," he remarked. "Let this thing rest, Morgan. Let Rebecca rest."

Morgan thrust himself away from the tree, scowling. The mere mention of Rebecca was like a blade, plucked from a forger's fire and pressed against tender flesh. Even Gresh did not, could not understand the extent of his animosity toward Avendall, much less the true reasons behind it. "You need take no part in this enterprise if you are so opposed," he said. "Is it possible that you sympathize with our old friend? Or mayhap, in your advancing years, you are afraid?"

Color surged up Gresham's neck to pulse at the base of his jawline. No one, including his multitude of adoring mistresses, could irritate Sedgewick with quite the same ease as Morgan. "You know I'd sooner see Avendall burn by inches than spit on him to put out the flames," he growled, "and you mislead yourself sorely if you think I'm afraid of him or anyone else. Including you, *Lord Chalstrey.*"

Morgan grinned at the scathing emphasis his friend

had given those last two words. "I never mislead myself," he answered. He had not thought about his appearance in years, but now, suddenly, looking at Gresham, seeing the fury in his eyes, he wondered what he had become. What the old and cherished hatred he bore Avendall had made of him. His mirth faded as he shouldered past his friend, moving toward the waiting horses.

What would Rebecca see if she looked at him now? The same rugged, determined features? Was there a coldness in the pale blue eyes she had once described as merry, gray in the deep brown hair she had run slender, impertinent fingers through?

He gave himself a mental shake. He was thirty-three—too old for such vain and fanciful thoughts. His looks didn't matter, hadn't for a long time. Rebecca Sommerville had languished in her grave these five years, buried in unhallowed ground because of the great "sin" of her despair.

Rebecca, Morgan's first and only love, had died by her own hand. He bore her no grudge, of course, but he would never absolve the monster who had driven her to take her life.

He untethered his horse, a spirited stallion called Nimrod, and swung up into the saddle with an ease fostered by years of practice. Morgan, like Gresham and everyone else in the private, twenty-man army, could not remember a time when he did not ride.

"Morgan," Gresham reasoned, mounting his own charger, "what of the girl? She is certainly innocent. She'll be ruined by this."

Morgan wheeled Nimrod toward the trail descending the back side of the knoll from which they had watched Avendall's men-at-arms approach and enter St. Swithin's

Abbey. Their camp, not far away, was deep in the forest, at the edge of a hidden meadow, and he spurred the stallion toward it before answering. "The girl will not be hurt," he said tersely. "Do you think I plan to ravish her, or toss her to the men like a scrap to dogs?"

"You might as well," Gresham said, with a patience that was obviously hard-won. "Her reputation will be compromised—I needn't tell you that. Avendall will surely discard her, fearing that you've taken her to your bed and gotten a child on her. What will be left to her, save whoring?"

Morgan ground his teeth. They had been over this ground before, he and Gresham. "The lady will be returned to St. Swithin's, once her purpose has been served, as virginal as ever. Surely there are worse things than living out one's days among nuns, though I can't honestly say what they would be." He spared a scalding glance for his friend who, never good at subjugating himself to a superior officer, rode stubbornly beside him. "If you are so concerned with the lady's welfare, Sedgewick, mayhap you should wed her yourself."

Sedgewick offered no response; Morgan had known he wouldn't. Beloved of many women, Sedgewick had no desire to confine himself within the boundaries of holy matrimony, however flexible they might prove to be after the fact. Still, he did not allow his horse to fall so much as a pace behind Morgan's as they rode in uncomfortable silence.

Behind them, two men lingered to keep watch on the abbey and the unsuspecting prey within.

Vespers proved a trial to Gabriella, and she did not attempt to join the others in the refectory afterward, for the evening meal. She simply sat on the edge of her narrow cot, hands folded in her lap, partly to control their trembling, awaiting her fate.

Meg and Elizabeth, having gone to supper at Gabriella's insistence, soon returned, one bearing a bowl of barley soup, the other, a heel of brown bread.

Numb to the center of her bones, Gabriella ate, not because she was hungry, but to keep from frightening her perceptive sisters further. Surely, too, she would need strength to face the inevitable separation from Meg and Elizabeth, the long journey to Cornwall, and then the marriage itself.

How grand the idea of becoming the mistress of a castle had seemed, when she and her sisters were children, dreaming aloud, in the drafty nursery at Redclift Hall, of gowns and minstrels' music, palfreys white as alabaster, and plump babies. Now, it seemed she could think, with any constancy, only of the sorrows of leaving her family and, from a very real standpoint, her home. She, with Meg and Elizabeth, had been at St. Swithin's for a long while, and as much as she had yearned to return to her family's holdings, Gabriella now knew she would miss the abbey.

Here, she had discovered mathematics and astronomy, learned to speak and write passable Latin, as well as proper English and a smattering of French. One of the other residents, a widow named Katherine March, had shared volumes of romantic poetry with Gabriella, and the abbey's atmosphere of reverence, the constant prayers and rhythmic plain chant, had nourished her spirit in ways she had neither comprehended nor appreciated until now.

Elizabeth sat beside Gabriella, when she'd taken all she could of the broth and bread, and took her hand.

"Are you terribly frightened, Gabriella?" she asked, with a tenderness that nearly broke her elder sister's heart.

"Of course she is," Meg burst out, before her twin could speak a word in reply. Standing nearby, hands on her hips, she went on in a rush of frustration and fury. "Gabbie, you needn't go to Cornwall. We'll run away, the three of us, before the moon rises—"

Gabriella smiled, in spite of her sorrow. "And where would we go?" she asked reasonably. "Back to Redclift Hall, where there is hardly enough bread to feed the mice, let alone our mother and stepfather?"

"We'll become mummers," Meg suggested, still quite carried away by the vision. "Take to the roads, make our living amusing the rich."

"Methinks we might find ourselves reduced to amusing the rich in most deplorable ways," Gabriella said, clasping Elizabeth's small hand in both her own. Then she shook her head. "No, Meg. I shall go to my husband, as I have promised to do, there to make my vows and to honor them, all my days."

An uncommon fire blazed in Elizabeth's normally saintly eyes. "It is unfair, the lot that falls to women! What can God have been thinking of, to leave us all in such a plight?"

Meg's smile was bitter, utterly lacking in mirth. "God has, from the creation, shown His preference for the male gender. Do men bleed? Do they die in the throes of childbirth? No, they but enjoy the pleasures of spawning the babe in the first place—"

"Meg!" Gabriella scolded.

"Heresy," murmured Elizabeth, equally horrified. "Besides, what do you know of childbirth, and of the making of babes, Margaret Redclift?"

Meg had the good grace to blush. "I've heard things," she said defensively, folding her arms. "After all, not everyone at St. Swithin's is a nun."

Suddenly, Gabriella was fair to bursting with a shameful and desperate curiosity, and she longed to question Meg on everything she'd learned. It would help so much to know precisely what she was facing, what was expected of her, as a wife and, eventually, as a mother.

Elizabeth, on the other hand, looked up at Meg with a plea in her eyes. "Pray, Margaret, do not burden our ears with tales of agony—I cannot bear to think of our Gabriella suffering!"

Meg made a sound too much like a snort to be proper in the least. "Most everyone agreed that giving birth was pure torture. But to hear some of the widows talk, it wasn't all suffering. Being bedded by a man can be pleasant—or a few of them hinted as much, anyway."

Gabriella's face flamed. "Margaret!" she protested, but she was even more curious than before. Why hadn't *she* been present when these scandalous topics were raised? More importantly, why hadn't Meg confided what she'd learned, long ago? As much time as Elizabeth spent praying and tending her various gardens, the twins could surely have found an opportunity to speak in private, thereby sparing their younger sister's delicate virtue.

"You mustn't go," Elizabeth cried, clinging to Gabriella now, as if to hold her back. "Sir Avendall will surely get a babe on you, and you will die as horribly as any of the martyrs!"

"Nonsense," Gabriella said, trying to comfort Elizabeth while shooting an arrow-sharp look at the recalcitrant Meg. All the while, she felt like running out into the courtyard and vomiting from pure terror. "Bearing children is quite natural, and women survive the experience all the time. Our own mother, for example. She brought us into the world, did she not, and lived to tell the tale?"

Meg rolled her eyes. Any mention of the frail, meek Ariel Mainwaring annoyed her. She had often said she must surely be a changeling, so unlike her mother was she. Gabriella knew the rumormongers said something much worse—that Lady Mainwaring, having produced more than one child in a single pregnancy, had most surely been unfaithful to her gallant first husband. The belief that two babes, when born together, must needs have two fathers, was a common one, though Dame Johanna, who had taught Gabriella the fascinating alchemy of numbers, among other things, said that was ignorant superstition.

"Our dear *mama* has never ceased to wail of her pain and travail in childbed, and you well know it," Meg said uncharitably.

"Poor Mother," said Elizabeth, with a beneficent sigh.

Meg turned the subject back to Gabriella's impending departure. "You do not have to do this, Gabriella," she insisted, with uncommon gentleness. "We *can* flee now, tonight—"

Gabriella shook her head, straightened her shoulders, managed a convincing smile. "I do not want to escape my marriage," she lied. Her life would be what she made of it, and she meant to make a brilliant success of the enterprise before her. She would come to love Sir Avendall, she decided, and he would care for her in return. She would have everything she had ever wanted and so, through her, would her sisters. "Let us put out the lamps and take our slumber, for I must rise at cock's crow."

They were each allotted one oil lamp, like the twelve virgin brides in the parable, and with no more ado they extinguished their separate flames, climbed into their narrow cots, and, as they had been taught since childhood, wriggled out of their clothes.

"When I am wed," Meg announced in the darkness, when they had all settled in for the night, "I shall undress standing up, with my lamp still burning, instead of squirming under the covers like a worm caught beneath a wet leaf."

Elizabeth gasped, but Gabriella laughed. The sound was soblike.

A silence descended, blanketing the night with the soft weight of new-fallen snow. Then, in that strange, inadvertent wizardry that so often occurred among the three of them, Meg and Elizabeth spoke the same words at the same time.

"You won't forget us?"

Gabriella took a moment to control her tremulous vocal cords, then replied. "As the Holy Mother is my witness," she vowed. "I shall not pass a single day, a single hour, without thinking of you. Immediately upon joining him, I shall petition my husband to bring you both to Cornwall, there to abide with us until you also are wed, with fine homes of your own."

She was young. She could not know that some promises, even the most heartfelt, are all but impossible to keep.

2

Gabriella hoped the cold, drizzling rain greeting her at sunrise was no portent of things to come. Her throat ached with the effort to choke back sobs as she stood under a stone archway at the edge of the abbey's main courtyard, watching numbly while Halsey and the rest of Sir Avendall's men prepared the horses for the day's travel.

Because Gabriella owned so little, there was no need of a cart to carry her belongings; everything she possessed fit easily into one small bundle—her velvet gown, a spare chemise, her prayer book, with a dried flower from Elizabeth's summer garden pressed between its pages, and Meg's treasured ivory comb, bought long ago at a fair.

Dame Johanna, the small, round woman chosen for her unflappable practicality to make the journey to Cornwall with Gabriella, waited at a discreet distance from the place where the three young sisters stood, all but clinging together. The nun held the reins of Zacheus, the white mule, a most intemperate creature.

"I vow I have not felt so wretched since the day we left Redclift Manor to come here," Elizabeth whispered, unable, in her purity of spirit, to hide her true feelings. "Oh, Gabriella, what shall we do without you?"

Meg spoke in a sharp whisper, meant, Gabriella knew, to hide her own dismay and, at the same time, distract both her siblings from theirs. "We shall fit ourselves for the day when we too are brides, that's what," she said sturdily, her arm linked with Gabriella's.

Torches flickered and snapped in the rain, their light making jagged crimson gouges in the darkness. Halsey approached, halted a small but still respectful distance away, and bowed.

"I trust milady has broken her fast?" he asked.

Gabriella, still not trusting herself to speak, merely inclined her head in a slight nod. As a child, she had dreamed of being addressed as "milady," and not once had she imagined that the term could ring so hollow.

"Then bid your farewells and be done, I pray you," Halsey went on briskly. "We must make haste, for the weather is uncertain, and Sir Avendall awaits his lady wife most anxiously."

Gabriella knew that the journey to Cornwall required several days' hard and perilous travel. Worse, upon her arrival in that far place, she faced a lifetime as the chattel of a stranger, a man she had mistrusted on sight. Nonetheless resigned, Gabriella turned to face both her sisters, standing forlornly in their plain convent garb. She kissed each of them tenderly upon the forehead, first Meg, and then Elizabeth, and their flesh felt chilled against her lips.

"It will not be long," Gabriella promised, in a brave and quiet voice, playing the role that had sustained her thus far, "until I send for you. Be strong in the meantime, and serve God and the Holy Virgin well, for we all depend upon their grace."

Embraces were exchanged, hurried and frantic. When Gabriella made herself turn away, Elizabeth was weeping softly, while Meg stood, pale and proud, with a supportive arm about their younger sister's shoulders.

Gabriella knew that image of them would haunt her until they were reunited, and vowed that that blessed day would come sooner, rather than later, no matter what she had to do to make it happen.

With no further word, Halsey took her light bundle and bound it to the saddle of the plain gray mare they had brought for her, then lifted her up by the waist, setting her upon the horse's broad back. She arranged her skirts, and sat with the dignity of a queen about to depart for her coronation.

Mother Mary Benedict came to stand looking up at her erstwhile charge with a benevolent and placid expression. "Be of good courage, my child," she said. "The Holy Mother journeys with you. Say your prayers faithfully, and cultivate a docile nature, for this quality in a woman pleases the Lord greatly."

"Yes, Mother," Gabriella mumbled, grateful that she and the abbess and all the nuns and other inmates of St. Swithin's had already said their good-byes, after prayers and the usual light morning meal of bread and milk. At that moment, "cultivating a docile nature" was the least of Gabriella's ambitions.

The ancient gates of the abbey creaked open, signaling Halsey's eagerness to depart, and Gabriella turned her face to the adventure that awaited her, not daring to look upon her sisters again. Then, surrounded on all sides by her future husband's men-at-arms, she rode through the yawning chasm and out into the awakening world.

Word of the departure of Avendall's bride and her pitifully few protectors reached Morgan Chalstrey, camped several miles distant, within the hour. It had not been a restful night for him, and almost before his own men had opened their eyes, he gave the order to ride.

Sleepy squires scrambled to douse fires and saddle horses, while their equally befuddled seniors hurriedly relieved themselves beyond the edges of the light, pulled on their boots, and mounted. None dared grumble that there had been no time to gulp down a scrap of bread, empty though their bellies were; Chalstrey was a hard master, it had ever been so, and he would suffer no semblance of weakness in his men.

Only Sedgewick, riding beside him as usual, had the gall to lodge a protest. "You are obsessed," he said. "I warn you once again, Morgan—this idea is unsound. Give it up now, while you are yet able. Return to the king's service—we are surely needed in France—and let Avendall have what is his."

Chalstrey sighed. "You know my feelings on the matter. If you no longer wish to serve with this company, you are free to leave."

Sedgewick shook his head in exasperation. His mane of golden hair was rumpled from a night passed on the hard ground, a soldier's usual bed, his blue eyes fierce. "Aye," he said. "Yet I fear to turn my back. We all have our gifts, Chalstrey, and yours is finding trouble. I swore a vow to your lady mother that I would keep you alive as long as possible and by God, I will honor it."

Chalstrey hid a smile and spurred Nimrod down the muddy hillside, moving away from the clearing and into the dense woods beyond. Indeed, Sedgewick was a nursemaid at heart. "Go or stay," Morgan told his friend lightly. "The choice is yours."

Gresham muttered a curse and kept pace with Chalstrey, seething all the while.

Dame Johanna, riding beside Gabriella, within the circle of four men-at-arms, shivered visibly. It had been at least an hour since they had left the abbey, and the sun was up, but it spared them little warmth, so gray and clouded were the skies.

Gabriella wanted to ask if her teacher shared the distinct uneasiness that troubled her, but she dared not speak and disturb the hushed aspect that had overtaken the small party almost immediately after their departure from the abbey. The members of the escort seemed especially watchful; each rode with a hand resting on or near the hilt of his sword, repeatedly scanning their surroundings.

The path was narrow, and so muddy that the horses' hooves made a rhythmic, sucking sound with every step. Giant oaks towered on either side, their limbs forming a canopy high above and sprinkling the sojourners with a cold and invisible mist. The birds were silent, and the hares and hedgehogs that normally would have skittered through the deep grass were apparently in hiding as well.

A slow shudder moved up Gabriella's spine, and she exchanged sidelong glances with Dame Johanna, who was of uncommonly grim countenance that morning.

When the attack came, it was so sudden that even in their vigilance, Sir Avendall's soldiers were taken by surprise.

The outlaws dropped, powerful, scruffy creatures, shrieking like the heathens they undoubtedly were, from the very limbs of the trees, dragging Avendall's men to the ground before they could draw their swords. Still others blocked the path, afore and behind, mounted on great, nickering chargers, blades gleaming ominously even in the gloom.

Gabriella was too startled to scream; by the time that option occurred to her, the skirmish was at an end.

Indeed, it was Dame Johanna who broke the terrible silence. "I pray you, sirs, do not harm us or these men. We are poor travelers, and carry nothing of value."

Gabriella's attention was fixed on the obvious leader of the band. He was at the forefront, an impossibly big man, with broad shoulders, dark, shaggy hair and eyes the soft blue of a summer sky. He wore a battered tunic, a chain mail vest, plain, undyed leggings and worn leather boots, and held a sword easily in his right hand.

The look on his handsome face was so ferocious, so utterly unyielding, that it sent a chill coursing through her blood. Even in her profound innocence, Gabriella realized that here was a man who would not be turned aside from any purpose he might set for himself.

His gaze locked with Gabriella's all the while, he answered the nun's petition with surprising cordiality. "I fear I must differ with you, good sister. You carry a cargo that is most precious indeed."

Color suffused Gabriella's heretofore pale flesh. At her feet were sir Avendall's trusted soldiers, sprawled on the ground and disarmed, while outlaws held daggers to their throats. "You will suffer for this outrage, Sir," she said boldly.

The knave threw back his head and laughed. His

eyes sparked with amusement and something else that eluded Gabriella and, at the same time, stirred a pleasant discomfort in places she had rarely even thought about before.

Still watching Gabriella, he gave an order to his men. "Bind them, hand and foot. We'll keep their horses for spoils."

Halsey growled with rage as he was hauled upright, only to be restrained with lengths of thin rope. "You would do well to heed the lady, Chalstrey," he growled. "My lord Avendall will have your eyes for this."

Gabriella bit her lower lip as a renewed awareness of what she and Dame Johanna might be facing washed over her.

"Tell Avendall he is an even greater coward than ever I thought," Chalstrey replied, clearly undaunted. "It is a great disappointment to find him missing; I had looked forward to cutting his throat."

Gabriella gasped, more offended than frightened— for that moment, at least. "Sir, you are a brigand."

Chalstrey laughed again. "Oh, that and more, milady. That and more." At last, he broke the spell that had held her gaze fixed to his and turned to speak to the man beside him. "You are the most noble of us all, Sedgewick— therefore, I put the ladies in your charge. See that they are brought to camp and made comfortable. If they attempt to escape, we shall take harsher measures."

The man called Sedgewick made no reply to his master, but simply came forward to take the bridle of Gabriella's mare in one hand. With his fair hair and finely chiseled features, Sedgewick looked, she thought, like a fallen angel, or one of the old gods, wooed back to life by some pagan priestess. Chalstrey, though equally

impressive to look upon, seemed more the product of
hell than heaven.

"We will not harm you or your companion, milady,"
Sedgewick said quietly, flinging another furious look at
Chalstrey. "And despite all appearances to the contrary,
we are king's men, not outlaws."

"Pray, do not credit the words of these rogues,"
Halsey cried, red with indignation. " 'Tis plain enough
what they are. Avendall will find you, milady, and bring
you safely to his side."

"He's made a fine job of looking after the lady so far,
hasn't he?" Chalstrey asked, riding close to the man to
place one booted foot in the center of his chest and
send him sprawling backward into the mire. With that,
he wrenched something from round his neck and tossed
it onto Halsey's heaving chest. "When Avendall asks
where to seek his bride, give him this. It will answer all
his questions."

Gabriella glanced down at the object; it was a simple
talisman, a tarnished medallion of some sort, its chain
woven of faded blue ribbons.

Before she could hear any more of the exchange, she
and Dame Johanna were removed from the scene, and
clung helplessly to the pommels of their saddles as
Sedgewick and another man took them off the path and
into the thick and fragrant wood. Behind, a clamor rose
as Sir Avendall's troops were tied, wrists to ankles, as ordered by Chalstrey, and probably relieved of any gold
they might be carrying, as well as their weapons and
fine, grain-fed horses.

The trip through the forest was not an easy one;
branches hung low and nearly brushed the two women
from their mounts on several occasions. Their gowns

and thin cloaks were wet through, and it seemed as though hours had passed when they finally arrived at a well-guarded outpost, built of timbers and nestled deep in the woods.

Beyond its seclusion, the bandits' quarters revealed no effort at secrecy. Several large fires blazed in the dooryard, and smoke curled from the stone chimneys. A number of tents shivered in the breeze, and the carcass of what was probably a wild boar roasted fragrantly on a spit. There was a large stable, and many horses—no doubt stolen from other unfortunate sojourners—grazed in the tall grass. Half a dozen boys played some rough-and-tumble game in the relative shelter of a huge birch tree, and paused in their sport to study Gabriella, who returned their gazes with a stubborn directness.

Sedgewick, who had not spoken since the abduction, a good hour before, dismounted and beckoned for one of the boys to come and attend to his mount. The silent order was obeyed instantly, the horse led away to be groomed and fed. After looking up at Gabriella for a few moments, he dismissed the other man who had ridden with them. The fellow turned his horse toward the stable.

Gabriella and Dame Johanna sat in silence, privately terrified, the reins of their mounts dangling into the sweet, damp grass. Gabriella's attitude was one of cold disgust, crafted to disguise her fear, while Dame Johanna's was pensive. Hers was a logical mind, given to weighing and measuring, assessing and calculating. Gabriella hoped the nun was hatching some brilliant plan of action.

Just then, Chalstrey and his marauders arrived, having stayed behind to deal with Avendall's men-at-arms. Chalstrey immediately joined Sedgewick and the two women, smiling, his great horse prancing beneath him, no doubt as insufferably proud as his master. Though mud-splattered and wet, with a new beard darkening his jaw, Chalstrey seemed to exude heat; Gabriella could feel it, even from a distance, and against her will, she was drawn by it.

"Again I am disappointed," he said, leaning on the pommel of his saddle addressing Gabriella with a smile that appealed to her and, at one and the same moment, made her long to slap him with all her strength. "No rebellion? No attempt to flee? Can it be that Avendall has chosen yet another meek woman?"

The words "yet another" troubled Gabriella, and she wondered, only momentarily, if her intended husband's heart would be out of her reach. In the circumstances, the matter seemed trivial. She would be fortunate indeed to come out of this situation alive, and with her virtue intact. Sedgewick's relatively polite handling of the ordeal notwithstanding, Gabriella sensed that Chalstrey, by himself, was more dangerous than every man in his company put together.

For all of that, she was suddenly more furious than afraid, and without giving it a thought, she prodded her tired mare with the heel of one sodden slipper, drawing close alongside Chalstrey. Then, her eyes flashing with the fire that burned, oft hidden, within her, she spat. Though aiming for his insolent, rakish face, she missed and struck the center of his chest.

He merely grinned and, oddly, it was only then that Gabriella considered what he *might* have done—drawn his sword and cut her down, for example. Or backhanded her, as her true father had done to her mother, shamed because she had borne him twins and brought scandal upon Redclift Hall.

"Gabriella," Dame Johanna said sharply, and she realized that it was not the first time the nun had addressed her.

Chalstrey made a reassuring gesture with one hand. "All is well, good dame. I have never harmed a woman, and I do not intend to begin now." His eyes danced as he regarded Gabriella, who would happily have spat upon him again, if she'd trusted her aim. "Mayhap I misjudged Avendall's choice in wives. Sedgewick, take this *ill*-mannered wench inside, along with her much wiser companion, and see that they are given blankets and food."

Having issued his command, he calmly turned his charger and rode away, toward the encampment of tents.

Gabriella, who was by nature neither bold like Meg nor sweet-tempered like Elizabeth, but instead steady and sensible, was left to grapple with a nearly ungovernable urge to fling herself upon her captor from behind, scratching, kicking, and biting. Never, in all her admittedly sheltered life, had she encountered anyone who roused her to such hysterical irritation. But then, she'd never been waylaid in the woods before, and abducted.

"No more, Gabriella," Dame Johanna said quietly, but with the firmness of spiritual authority. "There is naught we can do until our captor sets us free or Sir Avendall undertakes to rescue us. To do battle now would be a foolish waste of strength we may need later."

Utter despondency weighted Gabriella's heart, but she knew Dame Johanna was right. Far better to conserve what vigor she possessed, that she might strike when the bandit Chalstrey least expected a reprisal. Then, God willing, she and her sensible chaperon might hope to take successful flight.

She allowed Sedgewick to lift her down from the

mare's back, and almost liked him for loosing the bundle containing her belongings from the saddle and handing it to her. Almost, but not quite. Well-mannered as he was, this man rode with highwaymen and was, therefore, surely of the same tawdry ilk.

She waited, head high and proud, shoulders straight, while Dame Johanna was helped down from her mount—the abbey's only mule, the fiend Zacheus.

The two women were led, with some ceremony, into the long, low-slung timbered structure in the center of the holdings, a lodge of some sort, rustic but spacious. Gabriella, though full of renewed fear, walked with her back straight and her head high. The many elaborate games of pretense she and her sisters had played as children stood her in good stead under these new and sorely trying circumstances.

Dame Johanna, no doubt comforted by her abiding spiritual beliefs, walked sturdily behind.

Gabriella's imagination raced as they crossed the high threshold and entered the smoky, dimly-lit interior. Low fires burned on hearths at either end of the single long room, and there were lofts overhead, in the rafters, probably used for storage. The windows were high and narrow and void of glass, and the floor was hard-packed dirt. There was a large dais, rather than a bed, bedecked in animal hides, and she made out the shadows of crude berths affixed to the far wall. Mice skittered in the gloom, and Gabriella suppressed a shiver.

Sedgewick, their escort, closed the heavy door behind them, then stood with his arms folded, his expression quite unreadable.

Gabriella swallowed. She had not failed to notice this man's reluctance, and she dared to hope he might be chivalrous enough to come to Dame Joanna's aid and her own. "Will you not help us, sir?" she asked, interlocking her fingers behind her, lest she make some imploring gesture. "I can see that you mislike injustice."

He smiled; she saw the flash of his white teeth. "Oh, I do," he agreed, "as does Morgan Chalstrey."

Gabriella felt color surge into her cheeks, and stiffened her spine slightly. "Then surely—"

He held up a hand to silence her and, in the same instant, the smile vanished. "The harm is done, milady," he said. "Avendall's man, Halsey, is well on his way to Cornwall by now, carrying the tale of your capture. There is nothing to be accomplished by taking you back to the abbey now."

Gabriella's mouth fell open, and the pit of her stomach dropped like a stone tossed from a high place, for there had been an unnerving note of finality in Sedgewick's words, as well as his tone and countenance. "What do you mean?" she asked, though she feared she knew Even if she managed to return to St. Swithin's, nothing would ever be the same after this wretched, dismal day. There would always be gossip and speculation with regard to her virtue, even though her innocence was still intact.

And perhaps that was only temporary.

Dame Johanna drew near and put one arm around Gabriella's waist. "If there is any honor in you, sir," she said evenly, "and I suspect there is, you will allow no hurt to come to this young woman."

"You are both quite safe, for the time being at least," Sedgewick answered, with what sounded like weary resignation. He went to the nearest fireplace, added wood from a pile on the hearth, and prodded the flames to life with a poker. "Chalstrey, though misguided, is no spoiler of damsels and nuns." He leaned the iron rod against the wall and turned to look at Gabriella and Dame Johanna again. "If you would fear someone, fear Avendall. He will not soon forgive this day's misadventures."

Of course Chalstrey was a cruel and ruthless man, whatever Sedgewick's protests. How could he be otherwise? He had taken two law-abiding women captive upon the road, after all, overcoming their guards, binding those luckless men, and leaving all but one afoot, without defenses against wild animals, roving criminals, and the elements themselves. Indeed, he might have murdered them all, if he hadn't wanted Sir Avendall to know his bride had been taken, and by whom.

"What," she demanded, "does Chalstrey hope to gain by this outrage?"

"Revenge," Sedgewick answered flatly, and thrust a hand through his fair hair. "If you want to know more than that—and I'm sure you do—you will have to ask Morgan." He indicated the room with a gracious gesture of one hand. "In the meantime, I would suggest that you take your rest where you find it. Food and hot water will be brought to you. When you've eaten and washed, you would be wise to sleep if you can."

Dame Johanna held her peace, but Gabriella was determined to pry some sort of explanation out of *someone*. "What is this place?" she asked, looking around her. "Are we to be held here indefinitely?"

Sedgewick made no reply, and the door creaked open on its hinges.

Gabriella froze, one hand raised to her chest, and Dame Johanna's grip on her forearm tightened in warning.

Chalstrey himself loomed in the chasm, insolently masculine, Lucifer disguised as a being of light. Head inclined to one side, he regarded Gabriella with quiet amusement. "So many questions," he said. "Methinks the lady has a lively mind, as well as a most comely appearance."

She felt hot color surge beneath the surface of her skin in a violent flood as she took a step forward, a female Saint George, challenging the dragon. "Return us to the abbey at once," she ordered.

"To be promptly apprehended by the sheriff's men and hanged?" he asked, in a low, teasing voice. "I think not, milady."

"Hanging is what you deserve!"

He laughed. "Perhaps that is so," he agreed mildly, folding his arms and watching her as he might the antics of a tinker's trained monkey, "but I should like to live a little longer, if it's all the same to you."

"What did you do to Avendall's men?" she persisted. "Are they dead?"

He raised his dark brows and drew back a little, as though she'd tried to hurl hot water into his face, though that irritating mirth still danced in his eyes. "What an imagination you have," he said. "They're in a crofter's barn, under guard. In a few days, they'll be released."

Dame Johanna had evidently been holding her breath, and she crossed herself hastily at this news.

Gabriella would be appeased by nothing short of full reparation for all that had transpired, even though she knew that was impossible. She fumed as Sedgewick crept out, leaving the door gaping behind him. Coward.

She set her hands upon her hips. "What are your intentions?"

Again, Chalstrey's brows rose. "My intentions, milady?"

"Will you hold us for ransom?"

He smiled. "I have lands and gold aplenty," he said with a dissolute shrug, spreading his hands. "Besides, Avendall wouldn't pay so much as a farthing to get you back. Not now."

"Morgan," Sedgewick protested, from somewhere near the door, but plainly without much hope of dissuading his overlord. Gabriella, still reeling a little, caught a glimpse of him, out of the corner of one eye, holding what looked like a large trencher in both hands. With him were two squires, one bearing a bucket of steaming water, the other carrying woolens of some sort.

Just then, thunder rent the sky, seeming to shake the very rafters above their heads. Chalstrey bowed, straightened, dragged his brash gaze from Gabriella's head to her feet and then back to her face again, all at excruciating leisure. "Good night," he said, at last, and strode out.

Gabriella would have followed him—spoiling for a fight, she was—if Dame Johanna hadn't caught hold of her arm and restrained her. With the greatest of effort, Gabriella held her tongue and sheathed her claws.

The food—succulent meat from the roasted boar they'd seen on the spit outside—water and woolen cloaks were left upon the dais, and Sedgewick and the two squires made haste to leave.

Dame Johanna was tight-lipped when she turned on Gabriella, almost the moment the door was closed, and gripped her shoulders in hands made strong from years of hard work in the abbey's gardens and fields. "You have been reckless!" she flared, her usually mild eyes flashing with a fury Gabriella had never seen in her before. "Chalstrey is a scoundrel and an adventurer at best, and there is every likelihood that he can be named worse things, into the bargain. We are his *prisoners,* Gabriella, and if you persist in baiting him, we may both suffer very grave consequences!"

Dame Johanna spoke the purest reason and naught else, and yet Gabriella still lusted for Chalstrey's blood. She had never had such an intense reaction to another person, but then, she had never been abducted before, either.

"I am sorry, Dame," she said, lowering her eyes so that the nun would not see that her words were at least partially a lie. Her heart was still pounding, and she pressed her fingertips to her temples in a vain effort to calm herself.

The nun sighed and then began pushing up the sleeves of her robes. She poured part of the bucket of hot water into a crude basin and began to wash, and when she was finished, Gabriella did the same. They were both ravenous, but Dame Johanna offered a seemingly endless prayer of thanks before they began consuming the contents of the trencher. There was wine, too, and they drank. Only when the warmth began to spread through Gabriella's system did she feel truly grateful.

"I am much vexed," she confided, when she had eased her hunger and sated her thirst and stopped her shivering, "to find my temperament so changed by this man, Chalstrey. He has shaped me into a common scold, and I mislike giving such power to a common churl."

The nun had eaten with as much composure as if they'd been in the refectory at St. Swithin's, instead of a timbered lodge somewhere in the dark heart of a forest.

"God will sustain and guide us," Dame Johanna said, pouring more wine into her cup and taking a deep draught. "We must trust in Him."

Gabriella was impatient with talk of God. Where had He been when Chalstrey's men swooped down on them from the branches of trees, like so many vultures?

"What will happen to us?" she asked.

Dame Johanna sighed. "I do not know, child," she confessed. "We've been well-fed, and while we would rather be elsewhere, of course, we have not been harmed. We have wine and a fire and a roof over our heads, and what would seem to be clean garments to keep us from the chill. You may do as you wish, but I intend to lie down and rest. There can be no guessing what the morrow will bring."

Gabriella cast a nervous glance toward the bed, with its piles of furs. "Do you suppose *he* sleeps there?"

The nun yawned. "What does that matter?" she asked, somewhat impatiently.

Gabriella couldn't say. She only knew that the idea of sleeping in Morgan Chalstrey's bed filled her with all manner of conflicting emotions, every one disturbing. She needed to relieve herself, though it seemed that Dame Johanna had been granted divine dispensation where such small indignities were concerned.

She looked around for a chamber pot and saw no sign of one.

Dame Johanna stretched out on the bed with a sigh and closed her eyes. Within moments, she was snoring.

Gabriella sat still as long as she could, biting her lower lip, then made her way to the door, opened it, and peered out. Twilight was falling, and guards stood on either side of the lintel posts, eating roasted meat with their bare hands. They'd been laughing at some jest, but when Gabriella appeared, they were instantly sober of countenance.

"What is it, milady?" the older one asked.

Her face flamed; she had no idea how to answer. The guards peered at her.

And Morgan Chalstrey appeared, seeming to take shape from the dusk itself. His smile flashed, bright as sunlight on clear water, and he inclined his head slightly, his gaze intent upon her face.

"Methinks the lady wants a walk," he said, and offered his arm.

Gabriella hesitated, then accepted.

3

❦

The sky was a dark canopy, prickled with stars, and there was a biting chill in the air. Morgan stood with his back pressed against the trunk of an enormous birch tree, arms folded, ignoring the boisterous activities of the encampment itself, and waiting for Cyprian Avendall's purloined bride to come out of the bushes. Though he'd laid the plans to kidnap the wench months before, and never doubted his purposes for a moment—until he'd gotten his first glimpse of his quarry, earlier that day, that is—he was surprised to find himself in a state of amazed uncertainty.

He heard the underbrush rustle behind him, smiled, and shook his head. Until he'd actually encountered Gabriella Redclift, she'd been little more than a symbol to him, an image, a pawn in a game. But of course the reality was a great deal more complicated. She was a woman, flesh and blood and spirit, full of passion and temper and, unless he missed his guess, intelligent as well.

"You wouldn't try to escape, would you, milady?" he teased. Even as he spoke, he heard the not-so-distant howling of a wolf pack, probably drawn to the fringes of the camp by the sounds and scents, not only of men and horses, but of wild pig, roasted the whole day over an open fire.

In a trice, Gabriella was beside him, shoulders back, chin high, kirtle in proper and decorous order. "Indeed I would already be miles from here, sir, if I thought I could succeed," she replied. "No doubt an opportunity will present itself, if I but bide my time."

He laughed, raised a hand to touch her face before he realized what a mistake that would be, and dropped it to his side again. "Where would you go, milady?" he asked, in what seemed to him a reasonable tone of voice. "Back to St. Swithin's? You could never gain the gates of the abbey before I or my men caught up with you."

The bewilderment in Gabriella's hazel eyes affected him in a way a display of temperament would not have done. " 'Tis plain enough," she said, "that you hate my intended husband beyond all sense and reason, but I confess I am confounded, sir, by the malice you bear me. After all, are we not strangers to each other?"

His position seemed indefensible, in the face of her tranquil inquiry, and the fact annoyed him vastly, for he was not a man to follow foolish notions, and he had worked through the scheme in his head time and again, coldly and logically, and found nary a flaw. "All my spite is reserved for Avendall," he said evenly. "It was—unfortunate—that you and Dame Johanna had to be involved."

" 'Unfortunate?' " she echoed, and though she spoke moderately, there was an undercurrent of quiet fury in her voice. "You make it sound as though it was some kind of accident, your snatching us from the road the way you did, and dragging us to this—this place, whatever it is."

They were almost to the door of the lodge, and the two guards on duty there ignored them studiously, staring straight ahead as though fascinated by the darkness itself. Morgan hated carrying on such a conversation in their hearing, but there was nothing for it. He was undone, too weary by half to wage the battle he knew would ensue.

"It was no accident," he replied grimly, "but you have my promise that you will not be harmed."

"Your promise," she scoffed, with a sweet smile, "is of no more import to me than that of any other highwayman. You are quite without honor, and God Himself will call you to account for what you've done."

Morgan started to speak, then stopped, realizing he had no viable answer at the ready. Gabriella Redclift vanished inside the lodge and shut the door smartly in his face. He thought one of the guards chuckled, or coughed, but couldn't be sure which, in that poor light. He scowled at each of the men in turn, just in case, and then started back toward the main camp fire, aware, suddenly, that he was furiously, ravenously hungry.

A squire brought him a trencher without being asked, along with a flagon of wine, and he sat down on a moss-chilled stone, a few yards from the fire, to eat. His thoughts were full of Gabriella: in his mind's eye he saw her ride over to him, still flushed from her capture, and spit upon his chest.

The almost Lady Avendall, for all her delicate beauty and fine breeding, was fashioned of the sort of fire that can consume a man's reason like so much dry tinder.

Morgan's mirth subsided. He wanted this woman, and that hadn't figured into his plan at any time; indeed, he hadn't even considered the eventuality. He was still trying to come to grips with this discovery when he saw

Sedgewick coming toward him. He pretended not to notice, hoping his friend would go on past and leave him alone, but that was not to be.

The other man paused a few strides away, a trifle unsteady on his feet, it seemed to Morgan. Sedgewick took a long pull of wine, and when his thirst had been slaked, or at least eased a little, he stoppered his flask, slipped it under his belt, and assessed Morgan with narrowed eyes. "Second thoughts?" he asked, slurring his words a little. Poor Sedgewick; he had a delicate conscience, for a soldier, and when it bothered him too much, he tended to overindulge.

There were times when Sedgewick's ability to read him proved trying. Chalstrey tossed away the last of the pork and set the trencher aside. "About what?" he countered, though he knew full well.

Sedgewick merely waited, seething. He could be as stubborn as a he-goat; it was one of his best qualities— and one of his worst.

"Yes," Morgan conceded gruffly. "I may have made one or two errors in judgment, Saint Gresham. I admit it. Are you satisfied?"

Sedgewick wavered slightly, or so it seemed in the unreliable light of the campfire, but held his ground. " 'Errors in judgment?' " he marveled. "You've abducted a *nun*, Chalstrey. That ought to condemn you to hell, if your history with women hasn't already won you a place in the heart of the flames. And Avendall will spare no effort to avenge this."

Morgan felt his face harden. "We've had this conversation," he said. "Besides, you are assuming he cares for the girl. The man has never cherished a tender sentiment in all his bloody life!"

"Avendall's affections are quite beside the point," Sedgewick insisted. "Damn it, Morgan, the affront to his pride will be all the cause he needs to run you down like a fox in the field and tear your throat out."

"Let him try," Morgan responded. He welcomed the idea of a confrontation with Avendall; that, after all, was the reason he'd abducted the girl and her companion in the first place, to force his enemy's hand. He sighed. As much as Sedgewick irritated him at times, the two had been raised together, like pups from the same litter, and both men were accustomed to thinking aloud in each other's presence. "I had not expected to find the wench so fetching," he confessed at last.

Just when Morgan was beginning to think he had forgotten how, Sedgewick smiled. "The lady is past fetching," he agreed. "And she has a temper to rival your own. Mayhap you should make Gabriella your wife, since you've gone this far, and fill Edgefield Keep with babes."

The suggestion roused a raw and unexpected longing within Morgan. "You've taken leave of your senses," he said. "Even if I wanted to get a child on that little chit— which I do not—she would have none of my attentions, and you know it. I should have to force her into my bed, and such is Avendall's custom, not mine."

"It is as I thought, then," said Sedgewick, with satisfaction and no little amusement. "Bedding the lady is much on your mind. And you fear all the fair Gabriella has made you feel, if not Avendall's sure and certain reprisals."

Morgan said nothing. It would be useless to deny his friend's allegations, but neither was he about to confirm them.

Sedgewick arched an eyebrow, and another grin

quirked the corner of his mouth. His friend was, Morgan thought, drunker than he'd guessed, and he wondered what was chewing on him, besides his excessive sense of chivalry. "If I am wrong, and you have no interest in our lovely guest, say so now. I should like to pursue her myself—no doubt the role of noble rescuer would suffice to win so innocent a heart."

Morgan caught himself just as he was about to surge to his feet, fists clenched. He interlaced his fingers and spoke in a rasp. "Pray, do not underestimate the lady, Gresham. Gabriella's heart may be innocent, but it is that of a lioness, not a dove." He paused, and a short, charged silence flashed between the two men, like invisible lightning. "And if you dare to woo her, friend or no, I shall drag you from here to London town behind my horse."

Sedgewick threw back his head and laughed. When he regained his composure and met Chalstrey's impatient gaze, his eyes glittered with anguished good humor. "You are in grave trouble, my friend, as am I."

Having made that pronouncement, Sedgewick turned and walked away, and only someone who knew him well, as Chalstrey did, would have known that he'd had too much of the drink.

Chalstrey muttered an oath, for he knew Sedgewick was right. They were bound to come to grief, both of them.

Gabriella awakened, feeling chilled in the scratchy woolen garment Sedgewick and the boy had brought to her earlier. The lamps had burned out, or been extinguished, and the embers in the fireplaces and the braziers glowed a dull crimson, doing naught to push back the darkness.

The recollection of where she was and how she had

reached this place were slow in coming, so weary was she, and so distracted by the cramps in her arms and legs. When it came to her that she was in an isolated holding, the prisoner of an unprincipled rogue, her eyes flew open, and she sat bolt upright with a groan of misery.

Gabriella's problems were immediately compounded by the realization that she was alone in that dark, musty den. Dame Johanna, snoring beside her when she finally lay down and closed her eyes, was gone.

Crossing herself frantically as she offered up a wordless prayer, Gabriella scrambled to her feet and nearly went sprawling before she righted herself. She called for the nun, and was not surprised when she received no reply. Used to living in a community of women, she'd sensed her state almost as soon as she'd awakened.

Fear seized her as the fog of sleep began to clear from her head. The nun would not have left her willingly, which meant she'd been taken, or spirited away on some ruse. . . .

"Dame Johanna!" she cried in a panic, groping her way to the door and flinging it open to the frigid night, only to collide with something as hard as one of the abbey's venerable stone walls. Strong hands gripped her shoulders and stayed her from falling backward, as well as from moving ahead.

She looked up, frightened, and, in the gold and crimson light of a nearby torch, made out the rugged, implacable face of Chalstrey, her tormenter.

"Where is my friend?" Gabriella cried, squirming in his grasp. "What have you done with her?"

"Calm yourself, milady," Chalstrey instructed, his voice taut as twine stretched to the breaking point. "One of our lads was taken with a fever, and the good dame has gone to look after him. She was escorted by the two guards who've been standing watch outside your door."

Gabriella could have sobbed in relief. Her face worked with emotion; she tried to hide what she felt and knew all along that she had failed. "She is safe then?"

He frowned. "Of course she's safe," he said, sounding affronted. His hold on Gabriella's shoulders did not slacken, and she found to her chagrin that she didn't mind so very much. Her knees had turned to water, and she wasn't sure she could have remained upright on her own. "God's blood, what a fanciful little fool you are," he went on indignantly, giving her a little shake. "We are not the sort to rape nuns, let alone kill them!"

The floodgates opened. Entirely against her will, Gabriella began to cry. She commanded herself to stop, but to no avail, and then wept in earnest, so overcome was she by the accumulated events of the day just past.

Chalstrey, looking both bewildered and pained, stared at her in consternation for a few moments, then whisked her up into his arms, without so much as a by-your-leave, and carried her back into the lodge. There, to Gabriella's helpless horror—and, if she were to confess the secrets of her soul, an equally powerful sense of glorious anticipation—he tossed her onto the bed of furs, in which she had passed most of the night.

It was extraordinarily soft, that bed, a luxury Gabriella, raised in the spare accommodations of Redclift Hall and a longtime resident of an impoverished convent, had never experienced before. She almost wished that decency, not to mention pride, did not demand that she rise immediately. "I would go and help Dame Johanna," she told him.

Chalstrey sat her firmly down again. A disgusted expression crossed his face when she flinched. "Have no fear, milady," he said mockingly, "I am not about to rob you of your virtue. There is sickness abroad and the night is wet and cold. Since Dame Johanna is otherwise occupied, it falls to me to see to your welfare, and by God's red leggings I shall succeed if it takes the rest of this woe-begotten night!"

She struggled to rise, and he rewarded her efforts by cocooning her so tightly in one of the fur wraps that she could barely move. Gabriella squeezed her eyes shut, braced to be ravished.

She was confused and, yes, oddly disappointed when Chalstrey merely placed her firmly beneath the soft, warm covers, then stood glaring down at her. A muscle along his jawline bunched briefly. "Mayhap I did Avendall an unwitting service by stealing you," he observed, a little breathless from their mild tussle. "It does seem that the task of taming such a wife would have been a fit recompense for his many sins."

Gabriella's heart was beating so hard and so fast that she feared it would shatter against her ribs. Her eyes were wide open, though every part of her craved sleep. "Why are you doing this?" she whispered, yet again. "Why?"

She knew Chalstrey was looking down at her, although she could not make out his face, for the moon had gone into hiding and the room was in full darkness again.

"Once—as recently as this very morn—I could have answered that question easily. Now, I am no longer sure of anything." He was silent for several long moments, as though reflecting with some amazement upon his own words. Then, incredibly, he sat down on the bed and wrenched off his muddy boots, tossing them aside.

"You can't mean to lie here, with me?" Gabriella asked, her terror renewed in the space of one wretched instant.

"It is my bed," Chalstrey responded, as though that settled the question.

Gabriella made to skitter away, only to be pressed back down again in a single, easy gesture.

"Pray, my lady, do not take to flailing about again," Chalstrey said, betwixt expansive yawns. "I grow weary of the struggle. Moreover, I have no desire to avail myself of your favors, appealing though they are."

Gabriella flushed in the darkness, torn as before between a woman's natural indignation at such a rebuff and maidenly gratitude for her deliverance. "You have ruined me, sir," she fretted softly, wanting to weep again but too worn out to manage it. "I am fit to be no man's wife, and I have you to thank for my eternal shame and disgrace."

Chalstrey lay stretched out beside her, atop the covers and at a narrow distance. He sighed deeply and cupped his hands behind his head. "Were you better acquainted with your chosen husband, my lady, you might indeed wish to thank me for all I've spared you. Cease your prattle and sleep."

Prattle indeed, Gabriella thought, insulted. She waited, lying stiff as a corpse on a funeral pyre, for him to ravish her. When he rolled onto his side, giving her his back, she allowed herself to relax a little. An instant later, she tumbled headlong into the consuming, silent oblivion of utter exhaustion.

She awakened well after dawn, afraid to move a muscle lest she inadvertently touch Chalstrey and rouse him to unseemly passions. Her mother had once warned her that a woman could get a babe planted in her belly by sharing a man's bed.

Gabriella's eyes opened wide, and she pressed both hands to her flat stomach. Daring to turn her head, she saw that Chalstrey had left the bed, and she was at once relieved and deflated. His distinctive scent—cloth rinsed in a stream of clear water and dried in the morning sun—lingered among the covers, and the pillow beside her own bore the imprint of his head.

The door opened, and Dame Johanna came in. The nun knelt before one of the fireplaces and added wood to the embers, and soon a delicious, fragrant warmth arose from the crackling flames. Dame Johanna turned, smiling, and got to her feet. "I am much heartened," she told her charge. "These are not cruel men, Gabriella. If that were so, they would not have taken me to young Blodwen's side, when he fell ill last night." She smiled again and gestured for Gabriella to join her beside the fire. "Look. Someone has brought bread and fruit and even goat's milk. Come, child, and break your fast. You will be the better for a good meal."

Gabriella was hungry—she was, for all her willowy slenderness, *always* hungry—so she arose and went to the rickety table, which was nothing more than a board suspended between two tree stumps, and peered at the foodstuffs arrayed upon it. It unsettled her more than a little to realize that there had been so much coming and going while she slept, dead to the world.

Only when she'd eaten her fill did she make her confession to Dame Johanna. "Chalstrey passed the night here," she said dismally. "If I was not ruined before, surely I am finished now."

Dame Johanna seemed remarkably unruffled. "What are you saying, child?"

Gabriella's face felt hot, and not because of the

comfortable fire dancing merrily on the nearby hearth. She averted her eyes, unable to face her friend and companion's inevitable look of sorrow and reproof. "He lay beside me," she whispered. "Upon the bed there."

"That is all?" Dame Johanna prompted gently, when Gabriella fell into a miserable silence.

Her gaze flew to the nun's face, wide and full of shock. "What do you mean, 'that is all'? Whatever honor was left to me is surely gone. No man will want me for a wife, and what fate is left to me, if I do not marry?"

Dame Johanna smiled, and Gabriella realized that she had spoken thoughtlessly. When she started to apologize, the nun took one of Gabriella's cold hands into both of her own and squeezed reassuringly. "It is all right, child," she said kindly. "Now, tell me. What else happened last night?"

Gabriella considered. "Well," she said, at some length, "nothing."

"Nothing?"

"Chalstrey slept, and so did I."

"You are—intact, then?"

Gabriella frowned and looked down at herself, like one searching for something gone missing. The question baffled her.

Dame Johanna laughed and kissed Gabriella's cheek. "How guileless you are," she said. "Pray, do not worry the matter further, lass. You are still unspoiled."

Gabriella did not see the situation the same way. Her dreams, modest as they had been, were dashed. While it was true that she hadn't wished to marry Avendall in the first place, she would have made the best of things, forged some sort of life for herself and her sisters. Now even that chance had been taken from her, and she would be fortunate if she did not end by selling herself on the streets of London town.

The nun made everything worse by laughing, the sound as joyous and musical as the peal of the little bell outside the abbey gate. "Oh, child, do not fret so. You are a lovely creature, and you will have your choice of husbands if Lord Avendall decides to spurn you."

"But I am irretrievably damaged," Gabriella protested.

Dame Johanna sighed, still holding Gabriella's hand in an effort to calm her. "It is true that another woman's reputation might be sullied, but you are very beautiful, Gabriella, and of good breeding. Quite accomplished, too, although I have often despaired of your impatience and your temper. You have all the qualities that most men seek in a wife."

Gabriella was silent, absorbing the nun's words. "There is hope, then," she said, more to herself than to Dame Johanna.

"There is always hope," the nun replied quietly. "Now, the man Sedgewick has given us permission to venture out and walk within the perimeters of the camp, that we might take the air and exercise ourselves. Let us take full advantage of this opportunity, lest it prove rare."

Gabriella hurried to find her slippers. If she and Dame Johanna were to be allowed this freedom, it was entirely possible that they might find a means of escape. She had quickly discerned that Sedgewick was a reluctant jailer, and he might even turn a blind eye if they fled into the woods.

The sun was quite high and the sky, soggy and gray the day before, was now sweetly blue. Gabriella calculated that about half the men of the camp had ridden out with

Chalstrey, to abet him in the day's chicanery, no doubt, and those that remained behind were hard at work.

Several were grooming horses, while others carried wood and water and prepared an enormous hart for the spit. The boys, playing like children under the birch tree when Gabriella and Dame Johanna had arrived, were mending bridles and other such equipage, stirring pots at the fireside, fetching tools for a burly man engaged in removing a broken wheel from one of several carts.

Sedgewick, overseeing all this, and periodically making notes upon a wax tablet, turned to greet the women with a half bow and a cordial smile. "I bid you good morning," he said, joining them.

"I would look upon young Blodwen," Dame Johanna announced, after inclining her head in prim response. Then, without awaiting permission, she trundled off toward one of the other tents.

Gabriella was busily assessing the tall man before her, wondering if he was friend or foe. She decided, despite his pleasing manners, to be cautious. Though Sedgewick might well prove to be their salvation, there were obviously strong bonds between him and Chalstrey. If that were not so, he would have interceded at the beginning, or found some opportunity to set her and her companion free, mayhap even to escort them safely back to the abbey.

"You do not seem fitted to the life of an outlaw, sir," she remarked.

Sedgewick laughed. "I am no outlaw, milady," he protested, though good-naturedly. "As I believe I've already told you, I am but a simple soldier, serving the king these many years, mostly in France, but among the infidels, too."

If Sedgewick had done battle against the Turk, so, most likely, had his captain. She felt a chill, just to imagine the things these men had seen in their travels, and done.

"If you defended the faith in foreign lands," Gabriella reasoned, when she had taken a few moments to think, "you must be a man who reveres God. Why, then, have you taken part in this scurrilous plot to thwart my marriage to Sir Cyprian Avendall?"

The smile left Sedgewick's eyes as well as his mouth. "There is much you do not know, milady," he said flatly. And then he turned and strode away without another word, bearing all Gabriella's fragile hopes of freedom along with him.

She was still standing there, staring after the vanished Sedgewick, when Dame Johanna rejoined her, beaming with pleasure.

"The Lord is good," the nun enthused. "Blodwen is much improved from last night!"

Gabriella was glad the boy was recovering, of course, but it amazed her that her companion could be so joyous while being held prisoner in a barbarian's camp, with God only knew what terrible fate awaiting the pair of them. Lifting the hems of the oversized robe she'd been given soon after her arrival, Gabriella marched determinedly toward the edge of the encampment.

If nothing else, she would have the promised walk.

Dame Johanna joined her, managing to look both amused and holy, with her gracefully folded hands.

How long would it be, Gabriella wondered, until word reached Sir Avendall, far off in Cornwall? Moreover, would he trouble himself to ransom or rescue his impoverished bride, or simply throw his hands up and turn elsewhere for solace? Surely there were many

women who would be pleased to wed such a man—
women with dowries and even titles.

She frowned as she stomped through the wet grass at
the edge of the camp. Not for the first time, Gabriella
wondered why Cyprian Avendall had chosen a woman
such as herself for a wife, however taken he might have
been with her appearance and manner during that single visit to the abbey. The heartrending songs of wandering troubadours and the magnificent poems of the
bards notwithstanding, marriages were generally made
for practical reasons involving property and political influence. Gabriella had little of the first and none at all of
the latter.

She dared not dwell too long on her situation, and
gave an exasperated little huff, frustrated beyond measure. She had pinned her paltry hopes on the union betwixt herself and Avendall, reluctant as she'd been to
undertake the match. She had dared to dream of children, a home and, maybe, if she was very, very fortunate, the sort of rare and lasting love that sometimes
grew between a man and woman when they were well
suited. She'd imagined similar blessings for her beloved
sisters as well. Now, despite Dame Johanna's reassur-
ances, Gabriella feared that all was lost.

"He has laid ruin to all I cherished!" she muttered,
thinking of Chalstrey.

Dame Johanna kept pace, still smiling serenely.
"Mayhap God has taken a hand in the matter," she said.
"It could be that you were never destined to be Aven-
dall's wife."

Gabriella marched furiously along. "Would that God
had 'taken a hand in the matter' *before* we set out on
this adventure."

At this, Dame Johanna laughed aloud. "What an impertinent minx you are," she said presently, when her amusement had subsided. Tears of mirth glimmered in her eyes. "Surely God tolerates you only because you are such a delight."

At the sound of horses approaching through the trees, Gabriella stopped. Listened. "Chalstrey," she said.

"Yes," Dame Johanna agreed mildly.

Gabriella stood, angrily entranced, as Chalstrey rode into camp at the head of a band of men. She found it galling that he did not so much as glance in her direction, but instead dismounted and immediately engaged in an animated discussion with Sedgewick and several others.

"There, it may well be, is the mate God has chosen for you," Dame Johanna remarked.

"You cannot mean Morgan Chalstrey," Gabriella gasped, whirling on her friend. "He is an outlaw—a savage!"

Dame Johanna was gazing toward Morgan and the other men. "I think not," she said simply, and continued her stroll.

Gabriella was impelled to follow or be left standing there like a dunce, gaping at a man she had every reason to despise. Burning to approach him, to challenge him, to do anything to get his attention.

She was enraged with herself as she stumbled after Dame Johanna, who walked in long, confident strides.

"There can be no possibility of a union betwixt myself and Morgan Chalstrey," Gabriella hastened to point out, as though there had been no lapse in the conversation. She bit her lip, forced to unburden her bruised heart, at least a little, and then admitted very softly, "He finds me wanting, you see."

Dame Johanna did not slow her pace. "Does he, now?" she asked.

"Yes," Gabriella whispered sorrowfully. "He told me so, last night, as he lay down to sleep."

"Mayhap he lied," Dame Johanna suggested, in blithe tones.

That thought confounded Gabriella, and made her feel as though a small bird, roosting within her bosom, had just taken flight. Before she could summon up a response, however, she caught a glimpse of Chalstrey out of the corner of her eye, striding grimly toward them, and was instantly paralyzed.

Dame Johanna stood calmly at her side, waiting.

Chalstrey came to a stop before them, still unsmiling. His clothes, a chain mail vest, plain brown tunic and leggings, sword belt and boots, showed the ravages of hard use. "Dame," he said to the nun, in greeting, tilting his head respectfully, before turning his gaze upon Gabriella.

She would have curtsyed to another man, but glared into this one's face, her back rigid. "We take horse for Cornwall tomorrow at dawn," he said, with all the grace of a king uttering a decree. "Prepare yourself for the journey."

"Cornwall," Gabriella repeated. "You are returning me to Sir Avendall, then?"

Chalstrey's smile was cold and bitter. "No," he said. "I am taking you to my keep, which stands some ten miles south of Avendall's. There, my lady, we will wait patiently for him to come to us."

An awful prescience came over Gabriella. "And when Lord Avendall does as you say, you plan to kill him."

The diabolical smile did not waver. "Indeed, milady," Chalstrey affirmed. "That is exactly what I intend."

4

※

Gabriella was stunned by the calm way Chalstrey stated his plan to murder Avendall, if not by the plan itself. "I will not allow you to kill the man I am pledged to marry!" she burst out.

Chalstrey was cool, immovable. Mayhap even amused. "How," he countered smoothly, "do you plan to stop me?"

As easily as that, he goaded her to the very brink of mayhem; Gabriella was about to fling herself on the man in a frenzy of rage when Dame Johanna stepped between them, ever the peacemaker.

"Sir Chalstrey," the nun said intrepidly, "you are deliberately baiting this young woman and I must say I find such behavior contemptible as well as callous."

Gabriella was about to gloat when the crusading bride of Christ turned on her. "As for you, Gabriella Redclift, you *will* control your temper from this moment forward or I shall give a full report to Mother Mary Benedict as soon as I return to the abbey. She, in turn, will almost certainly send word to your benefactor immediately!"

Both Chalstrey and Gabriella listened to the diatribe in

silence, and when the good dame realized what she had inadvertently revealed, she turned an unholy shade of red.

As one, her hearers chorused, "Benefactor?"

"Do you mean Avendall?" Gabriella demanded. "I know he has contributed—"

Dame Johanna gazed heavenward for a few moments, as though imploring every saint and angel to forgive her blunder, then shook her head.

"Tell us, good dame," Chalstrey said, quietly but with no less interest than Gabriella had shown. "If not Avendall, then who?"

The nun crossed herself rapidly. "I cannot."

"Someone *has* been paying for my place at St. Swithin's all these years—and mayhap for my sisters' as well. And we've thought ourselves paupers, objects of pity, every moment of that time!"

Dame Johanna's eyes were compassionate, and her straight shoulders stooped with chagrin. "Have we ever been unkind to you, Gabriella?" she asked gently. "Or to Elizabeth or Margaret?"

Some of Gabriella's shock subsided, and with it a little of the injury the revelation had done her. It was true that Mother Mary Benedict and everyone else at the abbey had made the allegedly indigent Redclift daughters feel welcome from the day of their arrival.

"Who?" she pleaded. "Who could—or would—pay for our lodging, our food, our learning?"

Dame Johanna pressed her mouth into an implacable line and shook her head. "I cannot say," she replied. "Forgive me, Gabriella—I have taken a vow. The few of us who know have long since given our solemn promise, and dare not break our word." She fell silent, and tears welled in her eyes. "I must go now, and see to poor

Blodwen," she said, and hurried away, toward one of the tents.

Gabriella watched her companion's retreat with mingled betrayal and confusion.

Surprisingly, Chalstrey made to comfort her. With an unusually awkward gesture, he reached out to touch her arm. "My father served the king alongside yours," he said. "The Redclift name is a proud one— mayhap you will take some solace from that."

Gabriella looked up at him, forgetting, for the moment, that he'd vowed to kill the man who was to be her wedded husband. Forgetting that he'd taken her captive, along with her friend, Dame Johanna. "You are overgenerous, milord," she said, raising her chin. "My father was a spendthrift, a wastrel, and a brute, as was his sire before him. And you, it would seem, are no better."

Having made this pronouncement, Gabriella lifted the skirts of her gown and would have hastened away, but for the fact that Chalstrey took a painless but unbreakable grasp on her wrist and stayed her.

"Don't you ever grow weary," he asked, "of all this— all this *emotion?*"

Gabriella tried to pull away. When the effort failed, she let out a rush of breath and straightened her spine. "I am ordinarily a practical person," she responded, measuring the words as though doling them out to an idiot, who could comprehend them only by piecemeal. "However, I find that being kidnaped, forced to share a bandit's bed, and then told that my betrothed will be lured into an ambush and murdered, has had an unfortunate effect on my disposition!"

"I do not plan to ambush and kill Avendall, deserving

as he is," Morgan told her. "I was merely trying to vex you, and it worked too well."

"And now you are remorseful?" Gabriella taunted, tapping one foot.

"I didn't say that. God's blood, Gabriella, you could drive a saint to violence!"

"As there are no saints near at hand, we shall not have to test the theory." She gazed at him, pondering.

"Do not dare to spit upon me, if that's what you're considering," Morgan warned, tightening his hold on her wrist for a moment. "For by all that's hot in hell, I swear I will give you cause to regret it if you do!"

When, in instinctive response, she again moved to free herself, Morgan let go so suddenly that she nearly toppled to the ground.

"Now," Morgan growled, before Gabriella could get herself into more trouble, "prepare yourself for long and hard journey. As I said before, we will be on our way at first light."

She rubbed her wrist and gave Morgan an insultingly wide berth as she moved around him and proceeded toward the tent.

Watching Gabriella march off in the opposite direction, Morgan gave a ragged sigh and thrust one hand through his hair. They were poison to each other, he and the lady, and just then he devoutly wished Avendall had chosen one of her sisters as his bride. The sweet and docile one—if indeed such a creature existed. Of course, there was every likelihood that the other two were as stubborn and volatile as their sibling.

The idea offered little comfort, after a hard day of scouting the surrounding countryside for any sign of the sheriff's men and making sure Avendall's pathetically inept guards had managed to make their way back to the abbey or the nearby village of Upper Gorse.

By now, Halsey was well on his way to Avendall Hall in Cornwall, bearing ill tidings indeed, with his troops a day behind him. Avendall would be furious when they arrived empty-handed, and downright apoplectic when he learned that Gabriella was with Morgan.

He was greatly cheered, imagining his foe's reaction to the news that his nubile young intended had been spirited away to Edgefield Keep. Then he realized that every man and boy in the camp was looking at him, had probably witnessed the whole embarrassing encounter with Gabriella.

Silently daring anyone to offer a comment—including Sedgewick, who, like some maiden aunt, felt called upon to give his opinion in almost every instance, whether anyone sought it or not—Morgan strode into the middle of the fascinated crowd and swept the lot of them up in a look fit to roast a man in his armor.

When he had their sober and undivided attention, he began issuing orders. The tents were to be taken down before dawn, and the carts loaded. A handful of men would travel slowly back to Morgan's holdings in Cornwall, accompanying the two-wheeled wagons. The rest were to form an escort for the women, and the unlucky fellow who failed in his duty and caused the girl Gabriella to be lost, be it by treachery or mishap, would feel the bite of the lash.

Until the whip was mentioned, the soldiers and their youthful squires had been amused, though they'd made a creditable effort to hide the fact. Now, because they well knew that Morgan meant what he said, their mood was universally solemn. He was a fair master, they knew that as well, but each man had vowed to accept his authority in all matters when they joined the lucrative company, and harsh discipline was the rule in every such enterprise.

Only Sedgewick watched and listened without any semblance of fear, though even he was subject to the rules, despite his lifelong friendship with Morgan. Very little, including the lash, frightened the man, and that made him the fiercest and best soldier of all. On the most accursed of days, Morgan would have trusted Gresham Sedgewick with his very life, and that had not changed, even though there was a subtle strain between them.

When Morgan had given the necessary commands, in his usual thorough way, the men scrambled to carry them out. Except for Sedgewick, of course, who had been sent to earth, it often seemed, to get under Morgan's skin like a burr at every opportunity.

From the days of their boyhood, Sedgewick had served as Morgan's better nature, and now that Gabriella Redclift was a part of the equation, it was worse than ever.

"You forgot to outline my tasks," Gresham pointed out, with an arrogant inclination of his head. He showed no sign of his intoxication the night before except, perhaps, for the slight furrow between his brows, most likely an indication of an aching head.

Morgan, who had been crouching, drawing makeshift maps and diagrams in the dirt for the benefit of the others, rose to his feet with a weariness that had never afflicted him before, even in the lulls following their bloodiest skirmishes with the Turk.

"On the contrary," Morgan replied, "I've saved the most important duty for you. I would have you return Dame Johanna safely to the abbey."

Gresham's mouth dropped open, and though he recovered quickly, he was plainly displeased. "Did I mishear you?" Sedgewick rasped, his eyes glinting with fury.

Morgan wisely suppressed a laugh. "No," he said, facing his friend. "Your ears are as trustworthy as ever, my friend. But I'll repeat the order if you'd like."

"Damn you, Morgan," Gresham protested, moving closer, so that their words would not be overheard. Discord between a captain and his second in command was poor soldiering, and both were mindful of that. "You'd better be about to tell me that you're returning the girl as well."

So it ran as deeply as that, did it, Morgan reflected. Gresham wasn't just taken with Gabriella; he had appointed himself as her champion.

Morgan gave a long-suffering sigh. Both men kept their fists from clenching and their stances easy and relaxed, for they were surely being watched. "You were standing here when I explained my plans. Gabriella goes to Cornwall, and to Edgefield Keep, there to await her aggrieved husband-to-be."

"He will come for your blood," Sedgewick spat, "not for Gabriella. For God's sake, at least allow the good dame to accompany her to Cornwall in the guise of a chaperon!"

"The nun's presence will make no difference to Avendall," Morgan pointed out reasonably. He was getting tired of bickering with Sedgewick on the matter of Gabriella Redclift and would be more than passing glad of a few weeks' respite from his friend's incessant nattering. "As you well know— but I shall remind you, since you seem unable to retain the simplest thought—the presence of the Virgin Herself would not keep Cyprian from tossing Gabriella aside like a stained tunic now that she's traveled with me. Once he's met me on the field, of course, and sundered my arms and legs from their sockets with his sword, which he will naturally attempt to do, he will cast her out. The chit's protests that I have not lain with her, in the purest sense of the word, will amount to neither tittle nor jot by Avendall's reckoning, should he survive our private contest. There will always be doubt in the minds of everyone who hears the tale, and Cyprian could not bear that."

"What of Gabriella? Will you simply abandon her when this is over?"

"Of course not. I will send her back to the abbey, with gold enough to keep her for life."

Gresham spat. "I will have no part in this."

"I fear it's a little late to decide that," Morgan said. "You are still a part of this company, and subject to my command. Therefore, you will either take to your horse or consign yourself to the whipping post, like any other man who fails to obey an order."

Sedgewick looked furious enough to kill, but he did not lose his composure. That would come later, probably, when the two of them would have the luxury of settling their differences with their fists, in the dooryard of some seedy tavern, unobserved by the fighting men in their charge.

"Before you decide," Morgan went on, seeing that Sedgewick was yet too angry to speak, "bear this in mind. Who else, besides you, is fit to escort the good dame back to the fold? Would you entrust a bride of Christ to any of this lot?" He cocked a thumb toward the others.

Gresham drew deep, rapid breaths. His sun-browned skin was tinged with pink, and his eyes flashed with a rage only barely contained. Finally, he ground out, "I will take Dame Johanna back to St. Swithin's—

not because you've commanded it, but because it is the only decent thing to do—and then I shall rejoin the company in Cornwall. But mark you these words, Morgan: friend or no friend, when this piteous business is ended, I intend to thrash you so thoroughly that even your horse won't know you! That done, I will take my leave from you and your bloody army, for good."

"Fair enough," Morgan replied cheerfully. Not for one moment did he believe that Gresham, closer to him than a brother, would actually turn his back on their friendship. "Of course that means you might have to save me from Avendall, before you can have the pleasure of bludgeoning me into unconsciousness."

"Who said I would stop at unconsciousness?" Sedgewick muttered, calmer now. There was even a glimmer of humor in his eyes, though his countenance was still ruffled. "In truth, I would prefer any punishment, including the lash, to telling the Lady Gabriella that you mean to separate her from her trusted companion."

Morgan turned thoughtful, considering the exchange between the two women, only a few minutes before, when Dame Johanna had misspoken and revealed what was apparently a well-guarded secret: Gabriella and her sisters had a patron, besides Avendall, probably a very highly placed and powerful one, with sound reason to keep his identity secret.

Tomorrow, during the long ride, he decided, he would permit himself the pleasant distraction of working through that particular puzzle, and thus keep his mind, at least part of the time, from Gabriella and all her charms.

Gabriella was shaken awake at dawn, not by Dame Johanna, who was absent again, but by Morgan Chalstrey himself. He had stayed mercifully away from her bed the night before, but now he thrust a heel of bread and a wedge of cheese into her hands and told her to be ready to ride within a quarter of an hour.

She got up when he'd gone, shivering because no fires had been lit, splashed her face with water, and hurried through the doorway into the misty gray-pink light of a newborn day. Although she saw Zacheus, the demon mule, despised at the abbey for his recalcitrant nature, saddled and standing with the horses, there was no sign of Dame Johanna.

Gabriella felt shame; she had been angry with the nun, when she learned of the benefactor, and had ignored her throughout the evening. Now, she wanted to apologize. Dame Johanna had taken a vow never to tell, and a promise was a promise, especially one made by a member of a holy order. Though she still resented the secret, and all those who had kept it, she knew that being unkind to a friend would not serve.

Since Morgan had already walked away to confer with one of the carters, she stopped a boy hurrying by with an armload of rolled blankets.

"Pray—where is Dame Johanna?"

The freckled lad spared her hardly a moment's pause, so intent was he on the tasks that were his to perform. "The nun, milady? Why, she's there—" he gestured toward a small band of horses and men, "with Sedgewick. They're making ready to leave for the abbey, I think, and Blodwen with them."

Gabriella felt as though she'd been slapped. Dame Johanna had been her only protection, her only comfort, her only true hope. And now she was *leaving?*

She drew a deep, steadying breath, tucked the

cheese and bread Chalstrey had given her earlier into the pocket of her cloak, and ordered herself to be calm. Another tantrum would not serve, and besides, she was weary of anger; until she had encountered Morgan, that particular emotion had rarely plagued her. She waited until her heart had stopped racing and then approached Sedgewick and Dame Johanna. Blodwen, the sick boy, was already mounted, looking wan.

Gabriella came to a stop a few yards from where Dame Johanna stood. She would not weep, Gabriella decided firmly; she would not be a weakling. She must try to restore her former sturdy nature and behave reasonably and with restraint, if she wished to prevail in this wicked game. Mayhap God, at least, had not abandoned her, and she might still find a way to save herself.

"Gabriella," Dame Johanna said softly.

"You're going?" Gabriella heard herself say. "Why?"

The nun's gaze was direct, unflinching. "Lord Chalstrey has given an order. There seems no choice but to obey."

Gabriella swallowed, blinked rapidly.

Dame Johanna took a step closer, and lowered her voice. "This boy, Blodwen, will die if he does not get proper rest and care, Gabriella," she said. "He needs to be at the abbey, where there are beds, and medicine."

Gabriella nodded, biting her lower lip, still not trusting herself to speak.

"Be strong," the nun went on quietly, evenly. "When Sedgewick returns, I shall contrive to come with him. In the meantime, Gabriella, mind your tongue and do not attempt to strike out for the abbey on your own. Hear me, now. It is most important that you stay within Chalstrey's protection."

Chalstrey's protection, indeed, Gabriella thought, despairing. Had this most intelligent of women gone soft in the head? "Were—were you going without even saying good-bye?" Gabriella managed.

Dame Johanna kissed Gabriella's cheek. "That might have been the better course," she said gently. She squeezed Gabriella's chilled hands. "Fare-thee-well, Gabriella, and remember, be brave. I will find a way to come back to you, and I will bring help if I can."

Gabriella clung a moment longer, when Dame Johanna would have released her fingers. "My sisters," she said quickly. "Tell them not to fret about me. Tell them—tell them whatever you must."

Dame Johanna nodded, then turned and walked away, toward Sedgewick and Blodwen and the waiting horses. Gabriella watched her for a few moments, then turned herself, and strode in the other direction, head held high. She must appear resigned to her situation, but all the while she would be planning and scheming and watching, ever watching, for her chance. She was alone in the world, for all practical intents and purposes, and despite the nun's insistence that she stay with Chalstrey, she must look out for herself.

Even Morgan Chalstrey had to sleep, didn't he?

One of his aides, a pleasant-looking, rumpled man who might, at one time, have been a friar, approached her, leading the mule. She yearned for one last look at the departing Dame Johanna, her teacher, her erstwhile friend, but she didn't dare permit herself even that much. She might lose her composure if she did.

"Milady," the man said, with a little bow, interrupting her thoughts.

She gave him her hand, and he helped her into the

saddle. Gabriella would have preferred to mount the beast herself, but there had been no opportunity to ride during the years at the abbey, and she was yet awkward at it. No matter, she thought grimly, smoothing her skirts and wrapping herself more tightly in the cloak, she'd be getting all the practice she required.

Chalstrey rode up beside her, and the mule twitched its great ugly ears nervously at the proximity of the master's stallion. "We will not be stopping to rest the horses for several hours," he informed her tersely. "I hope you have attended to any personal needs."

Gabriella met his gaze. Her temper, quelled by cold determination, remained firmly under control, and she spoke moderately. "You need have no concern for my comfort, sir," she said, and was pleased to note that he had not missed the irony in her words.

His brow knitted as he frowned. "I expected you to harangue me about Dame Johanna's return to the abbey."

"No doubt you are disappointed," Gabriella said sweetly, as she tucked away this new insight into his nature, to examine later. She would decide, in good time, how to use it to best advantage. In the meantime, she must not let him see how frightened she was, with Dame Johanna going away.

She smiled with all the false warmth she could muster. "Certainly my dear friend will be better off at St. Swithin's. Would that I were going there, too."

Chalstrey did not return her smile. "The men are waiting. Try to keep the pace and, pray, spare yourself the humiliation of attempting to flee. These men have done battle with the best horsemen in the world, and prevailed. They will have no trouble overtaking a wench mounted on a mule."

With that, Morgan reined his great stallion around and shouted a command to the assembled company. Gabriella was glad, for she would not have had him see the fury and trepidation that surely slipped past her resolve to flash in her eyes.

Mounted men closed around her, Chalstrey riding at the head of the group with all the confidence of Alexander the Great or one of the Caesars. Gabriella had to admit, in the privacy of her thoughts, that he was well suited to either role.

A light rain began to fall as they left the carters and squires behind and wended their way into the forest. Gabriella raised the cloak of her hood and reconciled herself to the certain miseries of a long and trying day mounted sidesaddle on a mule. She could only hope that Zacheus, renowned for his nasty spirit, would mind his manners for once and not add to her trials.

As she rode docilely along, surrounded by guards, Gabriella indulged herself by imagining Sir Avendall's rescue.

He would appear wearing full armor, gleaming, of course, in the sunlight. Riding bravely through Chalstrey's guard on an enormous, snow-white charger, he would battle his way to her side, wielding a dazzling sword with a jeweled hilt. The air would be filled with the clanking of steel blades, striking so hard that blue sparks flew.

Reaching her, Sir Avendall would curve one arm around her waist and haul her from the mule's back to settle her safely before him on his own gold-inlaid saddle. Strong arms shielding his beloved from all harm, he would ride away, leaving Chalstrey and his men behind, defeated.

But not dead, of course. It would not be Christian to wish Chalstrey dead.

She frowned. The image of Morgan Chalstrey sprawled on the ground, bloodied and bruised and utterly defeated, brought her no solace. No, the thought stirred something very like pain in Gabriella's breast, and she turned her attention firmly toward the future, and proceeded to spin shining dreams. Like the ones she and Meg and Elizabeth had shared, in their chilly cell of a night.

She tried to picture Avendall Hall. Surely it was grand, with glass in its windows and bright flags of red and gold flying from its many towers, like the castles in stories she'd heard from childhood. In Gabriella's daydream, her intended husband carried her to that splendid place; she felt his armor pressing against her back, his fragrant breath upon her nape. She actually heard the clatter of his charger's hooves as they crossed the drawbridge, passing over a moat brimming with crystal blue water, and entered the stronghold inside the towering stone walls.

There, a crowd of happy vassals greeted them, as well as neighboring nobles who had gathered to celebrate Sir Avendall's triumph over the evil Morgan Chalstrey.

Inside the great hall, lined with exquisite tapestries and furnished with cushioned chairs as well as benches and long, gleaming trestle tables, a horde of smiling servants waited, in a tidy line, to greet their new mistress.

There was food, and music, and dancing, and Gabriella smiled, envisioning herself clad in a glorious gown and bedecked in precious jewels, presiding over the festivities at Sir Avendall's side.

She had a good imagination, and ventured further

into the mental milieu, enjoying it thoroughly. In the charming, candlelit chapel of Avendall Hall, Gabriella stood before a priest, with the man she would surely address as "Cyprian" when that intimate juncture was reached, and modestly murmured her vows.

Finally, gloriously, she was Sir Avendall's true wife, for all time and eternity. He took her hand and, unable to look away from her face, led her under an arch of glimmering swords, held high by his men-at-arms, through the broad courtyard, and into the keep itself.

They moved as one over the fresh rushes strewn across the floor of the great hall, amid the cheers of nobles and servants alike, and proceeded up the broad staircase.

Gabriella's heart began to beat faster, in the daydream and in real life, as she watched the vivid scene unfold in her mind. At the top of the stairs, in the sheltering shadows, Sir Avendall, her lord, would draw her swiftly into his embrace and gently press his mouth to hers . . .

Except that the kiss was hard and demanding, and so heated Gabriella's blood that she gasped and drew back, only to see that Avendall, without a by-your-leave from her, had turned into Morgan Chalstrey!

"What ails you, my lady?" a male voice intruded. "Are you ill?"

Gabriella was both startled and annoyed to open her eyes and find the man of her nightmares, not her dreams, riding easily beside her.

"Indeed not," she replied, but she felt warmth climbing her neck, flooding her face.

Chalstrey grinned. "I would give much of my hard-won treasure to know what you were thinking just now," he said.

Dear heaven, the man was all but insufferable. It required the forbearance of a saint to speak civilly to him, and Gabriella Redclift was hardly that. She skipped mass whenever she could and rarely remembered to say her prayers—which was probably why she was in this dreadful coil now.

She fluttered her eyelashes and smiled as witlessly as she could. "I was dreaming," she confessed, in all truth, "of my marriage to Sir Avendall." Not for all the riches of the Turk would she have admitted that the fiery imaginary kiss that had nearly melted her bones had been his, not Cyprian's.

"I see," said Morgan. As though he truly did.

The track they'd been following had narrowed to a strand of muddy loam, twisting and turning between two banks that sloped downward into birch trees and gooseberry thickets. Thus, it was necessary to ride single file.

Morgan moved ahead, turning in his saddle to look back at her with a maddening expression of speculation in his blue eyes, while the others straggled behind, silent and watchful.

She recalled the food squirreled away in the pocket of her damp and smelly cloak, and pulled out the substantial slice of cheese. It was while she was occupied with that that Zacheus, for reasons known only to him, undertook to revolt.

Between one moment and the next, the mule brayed loudly, balked at Gabriella's startled attempts to subdue him, and then bolted down the bank on the right-hand side and into the trees.

Inexperienced as she was, Gabriella dropped the wedge of cheese and grappled with the reins, too shocked even to cry out.

Branches whipped at her face and snagged in her clothes as the mule dashed through the dense thickets, carrying on as though someone had touched a hot coal to his flank. Gabriella gave up trying to stop him and hung on, bending low over the saddle's pommel in an effort to shield herself from some of the grasping vegetation. Behind, she heard Morgan's stallion crashing through the trees.

Suddenly, the woods gave way to the largest bog Gabriella had ever seen, and Zacheus plunged in and somehow flailed his way to the middle before the thick stuff brought him, at last, to an ignoble halt.

Gabriella, splashed with sticky mud, her heart beating hard enough to make her temples bulge, turned and glared at Morgan and his magnificent horse, who had stopped short of the snare.

Morgan leaned on the pommel of his battered leather saddle and smiled broadly. "As an escape attempt, milady, I'd say that was a spectacular failure."

Gabriella seethed. She'd be damned if she'd tell him she hadn't meant to flee—not yet, at least. A number of the other men had followed, lining the bank of the mud pit, and while some watched Morgan worriedly, others seemed to share his amusement at her predicament.

"If there is a gentleman among you," she said evenly, "which seems doubtful, I should appreciate some assistance."

For a seemingly interminable interval, Morgan simply sat there, plainly enjoying the sight of her, foundering on the back of that wretched mule, but at long last he turned to the man at his side. "Jocko," he said merrily, with a little flourish of one hand, "a rope, if you please."

5

The process of removing Gabriella and the mule from the mud was a lengthy and humiliating one, and when it was finished, much time was forfeit. For that reason, Morgan seemed more determined than ever to push on, to wring the last possible mile out of every man and horse.

Gabriella had no opportunity to wash, or even to don the single threadbare gown knotted at the back of her saddle, miraculously unharmed. She herself was covered in sludge, one of her slippers was forever lost, and she was cold to the bone. On top of all that, she harbored in her heart a wholly unrepentant hatred for a certain white mule.

It was well after sunset, and growing darker by the moment, when Morgan finally gave the command to halt. His men-at-arms immediately began setting up camp in the center of a small clearing. Watchmen were posted on all sides, and the fire was fed slowly, so that it would not rise great and crimson in the gloom, and serve as a beacon to anyone who might be abroad.

Gabriella huddled close to the blaze, seated on the

saddle that had been removed from Zacheus's back, her pitiable bag of belongings lying near at hand. Shivering, she nibbled at the piece of bread, now stale, kept all this while in the pocket of her cloak.

Chalstrey crouched beside her. "I've made a shelter for you, there, past yonder trees," he said, with surprising gentleness. "Go and lie down, Gabriella."

She stared at him, confounded by his kindly manner. After the incident in the bog, which he had initially found amusing, his mood had grown more and more remote, and he did not confide his thoughts in Gabriella.

"Ah," she said, having worked the puzzle through. "You fear that your bait will take a chill and perish before you can spring the trap on Avendall."

"There are bears and wolves in these woods, along with a number of other perils," Morgan said, looking baffled. "Why did you try to run away like that?"

Someone approached and handed a cup to Morgan. He passed it to her, and she took a sip of the stout wine before replying. "It was the mule's idea," she said.

Morgan laughed, though whether he believed her or not, she could not guess. "What a sight you made."

She scowled at him, but took another, deeper draught of the wine. It warmed her insides and sent a delicious torpor stealing through her sore muscles. If she took enough, mayhap she could forget, for a little while at least, that days might pass before she had a hot bath and a roof over her head. Too, she was concerned about her sisters—what torments of worry would they endure when Dame Johanna returned to the abbey without her? The nun had promised to return, it was true, but from Gabriella's viewpoint, such a feat seemed impossible.

"How long will it be," she ventured cautiously, "before we reach Cornwall?"

Chalstrey considered. "A sennight, if there are no mishaps along the way. Twice that if we, say, are forced to elude a band of sheriff's men or deal with bandits." He paused, grinned. "Or if you have to be hauled out of another bog."

She found herself smiling, but in a moment, she was serious again. Word of her capture would surely reach Avendall soon—Halsey, traveling alone, could cover much more ground than a company of men and horses—but would he still want to marry her? Gabriella's lovely fantasy of being rescued and properly wed had less substance than the shifting blue-gray smoke of the campfire; while she had been comforted by all her pretty imaginings, she knew they were nothing more than that.

She blinked back weary tears.

"Come, Gabriella," Chalstrey urged, in a gruff voice, unfamiliar because it lacked its usual arrogance. He rose gracefully and extended a hand to her. "You're shivering."

Defeated, for the time being at least, Gabriella finished her wine in a few unceremonious gulps and, after grabbing her bundle, laid the palm of her free hand upon Chalstrey's calloused one, allowing him to draw her easily to her feet.

A tarp made of tautly drawn deer skin had been erected between two small trees, and beneath it lay several thick, warm-looking blankets, carefully spread over another hide. Gabriella yearned to wrap up tightly in the scratchy woolen covers, turn her back on the dismal world, and lose herself in an exhausted sleep.

But she dared not indulge this whim, for she was alone, an unmarried woman in a camp full of rough and unprincipled men. She must be vigilant, must guard her virtue and the tattered shreds that remained of her reputation.

No doubt seeing a thousand and one misgivings in her face—she was too spent to dissemble, verbally or physically—Chalstrey gave a ragged sigh and rubbed the back of his neck with one hand. "Your garments are wet through, Gabriella. You'll catch your death if you don't change."

She retreated a step, set her jaw. Sneezed ingloriously.

He took a blanket from a bedroll, shoved it at her, along with the bundle containing her other gown. "Change your clothing," he commanded, "or I will do it for you."

She looked at him in bleak disbelief. "There are *men* everywhere," she pointed out.

"None within sight of this place," he reasoned. "We are alone."

Gabriella realized that he'd spoken true; she could hear the men and the tired horses, but the shelter was entirely shielded by trees and the brittle foliage of summer's end. "Turn away, then," she commanded, watching Chalstrey warily.

He proved malleable and, folding his arms, gave her his back. "When you're settled," he said, "I'll bring you more wine."

Gabriella waited a few judicious moments to see if he would turn again, in the hope of catching her unclothed, but he remained steadfast. Indeed she was chilled to the bone, and her teeth were chattering. Moving quickly, she shed her cloak and mud-stained, sodden kirtle, and pulled her gown from the bundle. When she'd shimmied into it, she crawled into the shelter and covered herself with the blankets.

"I am finished," she said, only then, her tones regal.

With a low chuckle, Morgan rounded and looked down at her. "So you are," he replied. "I'll fetch your drink. Will you take food, as well?"

Gabriella was wildly hungry, but her eyelids were already drifting down. "I should like plenty of wine, warmed over the fire," she said. "Bread, too, and cheese, if you have it."

He laughed again. "Done," he said, and vanished into the twilight.

A savory smell brought her, unwilling, out of the cozy depths of sleep, some time later. Her eyes widened when she saw Morgan sitting cross-legged beside her, beneath the hide shelter, a small lamp burning low at his side, a cup and ewer nearby. On his lap was a trencher, holding slices of some succulent meat.

"Hare," he said, before she could ask. "I fear the cheese and bread are gone."

Gabriella sat up and yanked the trencher out of his hands. The food was still warm, with skin that crackled pleasantly, like that of a well-roasted fowl, or the pork they'd eaten at the lodge.

Morgan watched in admiring silence, one corner of his mouth tilted upward, while she consumed every bite, then set the trencher aside on the grass with deliberate dignity.

He smiled and shook his head. "What manner of woman are you, Gabriella?" he asked, as though he were truly bemused. "One moment, you're ordering me about like a dowager duchess instructing a servant—'bring me more wine.' 'Turn away while I change.' The next, you're gobbling down a platter of meat that would have satisfied three of my men."

Gabriella felt no remorse. She was only glad the three men hadn't gotten to the plate before she did. "If I may say so, my lord," she said, giving a wry note to the last two words, "you are of a most confusing temperament yourself. You are a kidnapper, and you plan to murder my chosen husband. You force everyone in the company, including me, to endure a grueling ride through miserable weather. Yet for all of that, you bring me sustenance and provide a warm, dry place to sleep. And so I turn your own question back to you. What manner of man are you, Morgan Chalstrey?"

He stretched out, deliciously, uncomfortably close, bending one elbow and resting his head in his palm. "Oh, the usual sort," he said huskily, and his blue eyes glinted with mischief. "I like the way my given name sounds when you say it. Pray, milady—call me Morgan, if you will."

The idea was entirely too appealing. Gabriella scooted back, away from him, and came up hard against the trunk of one of the trees that supported the improvised tent. "You may leave now. I'm ready to sleep. Nay, I am *past* ready."

Chalstrey smiled, revealing those straight white teeth. "But I cannot leave you unprotected, my lady," he protested. "There are outlaws in this forest, as well as boars and wolves." He bent and blew out the oil lamp he'd lit for her earlier, then casually arranged himself beside her. "You will share the blankets, won't you? It's starting to rain again, and the night air has sharp teeth."

Gabriella's first instinct was certainly to protest, but before she could do so, it occurred to her that there were indeed wild animals in the forest, not to mention

the occasional cutthroat and thief. While she supposed
the man beside her fit into either of the latter cate-
gories—mayhap into all three—she did not choose to
be alone in such an isolated and dangerous place. It was
a case of the devil she knew being preferable to the un-
known variety.

Fussily, she attempted to settle in, squirming and
wiggling in an attempt to keep her distance in a narrow
space, and inadvertently making matters worse with
every shift of her body.

Chalstrey, who had been lying on his side, with his
back to Gabriella, was moved to turn and face her.
"What *is* the matter?" he demanded, rather testily, for a
man who had just insinuated himself into a lady's bed.

"I have to—I have to do something," Gabriella admitted, mortified.

Muttering, Chalstrey sat up beside her. "Well, go and
do it, then," he said. "I should like to close my eyes for a
few minutes before dawn is upon us again."

Gabriella scrambled out of the blankets and ventured
a little way, though not far, into the bushes. When she
returned, Chalstrey was sitting with his back pressed
against one of the trees that supported the shelter,
knees drawn up, hands dangling loosely between them.
He made room for her, in a rather desultory fashion,
and she took her former place on the inside of their cozy
nest, glad to be shielded by Chalstrey's powerful body.

He did not turn away this time, but lay facing
Gabriella, his breath settling into a deep and even
meter as he closed his eyes and slept.

Gabriella, aching in the very marrow of her bones,
and more tired than she had ever been before, found
herself wide awake. She burned with a new and unset-

tling awareness of Chalstrey's unseemly proximity, of his unique scent, of his formidable masculinity. She was filled with an unchristian longing to touch him, to explore the magnificent contours of his face with her fingers and, Holy Mother forgive her, the remainder of his person as well. His chest, for instance. His lean waist and muscular thighs.

And still other things.

Tentatively, she reached out and laid the tips of her fingers against his leather jerkin, in the place that sheltered his heart. She felt it beating, felt that steady *thump-thump* meld with the rhythms of her own body, then quicken every part of her.

Gabriella was stricken, in that private and daring moment, with a plethora of strange new sensations, some searingly pleasant, some very troubling indeed.

Emboldened, Gabriella traced the lines of Chalstrey's breastbone, and growing more brazen still, his midsection, which proved to be as hard as the white mule's head.

Gabriella's courage failed her, so awed was she, and she would not have dared to go farther, much as she longed to do just that. Just as she went to draw back, however, Chalstrey took so sudden a hold on her wrist that her stomach leaped into her throat and she gasped.

"If you would have chivalry from me, my lady beloved," he ground out, "you must not play the temptress. It is hard enough, I vow, to lie still beside you."

Gabriella was instantly motionless. A sensible woman would have been afraid, but Gabriella was not, at that moment anyway, a sensible woman. She simply stared, eyes stretched wide open, into Morgan's shadowed face.

After some inner struggle, which Gabriella felt coursing through the sinews of his arm and into her every pulse, he leaned forward and, with only a raspy sound from deep in his throat for a warning, pressed his mouth to hers.

At first, Gabriella tensed, for she had been kissed, heretofore, only in her imagination, and the sweet, jarring impact of it stunned her. That the contact was whisper soft, at first, made no difference. Then, conversely, as it deepened, as Morgan intensified the kiss, skillfully causing her lips to part for him, it did seem that Gabriella's very bones had dissolved. She went slack, with a little sound that might have been a moan or a sigh, as his tongue moved upon hers in a prelude she instinctively associated with another sort of joining entirely.

Unschooled as she was in matters of lovemaking, Gabriella was a creature of instinct, and she slipped her arms around Chalstrey's neck.

He moved over her, and she felt the wonderful, hard strength of him, pressing upon her own softness, imprinting itself there. She would surely have surrendered, had he not drawn back from her, as swiftly as he had descended, and muttered a string of curses fit to redden her ears.

Still grumbling, Morgan scrambled to his knees and then his feet, and began to pace back and forth, in only his leggings and jerkin, over the damp leaves that carpeted the forest floor.

Gabriella was disappointed and stung, but common sense, having taken flight when she dared to touch Morgan in the first place, was slowly returning. How odd that she did not welcome it more. She did not speak because she feared she would either weep with humiliation or rant in frustration and fury if she did. Where this man was concerned she was, in so many ways, a stranger to herself. Mayhap, in light of this latest encounter, even an enemy.

Morgan's mutterings assembled themselves into more sensible ravings. "God's blood, Gabriella," he sputtered at last, still striding to and fro, "did I not warn you? Do not plague me so again, or I shall surely dishonor us both!"

She watched him, sitting up now, her teeth sunk into her lower lip, her arms around her drawn-up knees. "How did I plague you, my lord?" she asked, with no touch of sarcasm and so softly that the chilly night breeze all but carried her words away.

Morgan came to an abrupt halt and stood looking down at her, his face illuminated by the light of a foundering moon. His was a warrior's stance; feet apart, hands resting on his hips. "You really do not know," he marveled, in an undertone. "Did the nuns tell you nothing of the ways of men?"

"How could they?" Gabriella reasoned, with a little shrug. "They themselves are ignorant of such matters."

He sighed, thrust a hand through his hair, and came back to the bed he'd just flung himself out of, kneeling on the blankets and gazing into Gabriella's face with an expression that could only be called consternation.

"There are other women in the convents—widows, ladies put aside for treachery to their husbands. Do they never speak of—of—"

"Of love?" Gabriella asked, in a wistful, dreamy tone. "Aye, they do—my sister Meg has told me things she heard, but they cannot be true, for they are more than passing strange." She frowned, remembering. Then she beamed at Morgan, who still looked flummoxed and quite unsettled. "I am very glad you kissed me, my lord. I have learned something."

Morgan's eyebrows, frosted with moonlight, drew together. "What have you learned?" he asked, with a moderation that seemed to cost him dearly.

"That I shall probably like being married, after all," Gabriella said, with rising good cheer. "I hope my lord Avendall will kiss me like that every night and every morning—"

Chalstrey spat out another oath.

"This does not please you?" Gabriella asked lightly, with an innocence that was, unlike her earlier artless words and actions, wholly false.

"No," he growled, tossing back the blankets and arranging himself beneath them with a great deal of ado, "it does not."

Gabriella smiled to herself as she lay down beside him. A delicious sense of triumph filled her, as though she had bested a formidable rival in some contest of wills and wits. She had a certain power over Morgan Chalstrey, though tenuous, and that knowledge soothed a thousand unnamed fears and as many grievances.

Morgan was careful to keep his distance, but she was warmed by the heat of his body and knew that he must needs feel the sumptuous suffering that afflicted her.

She closed her eyes, still smiling.

It was not in Dame Johanna to do violence, and yet she knew there were times, in the service of the Lord, when one must choose between one evil tool and another, laying hold of that which was the lesser.

They had taken a circuitous route since leaving the outlaws' camp, she, Sedgewick and the lad, Blodwen, mostly, Dame Johanna suspected, to confuse her, so that she could not lead the sheriff and his men back to it. If she were to do that, it would naturally be an easy matter to pick up Chalstrey's trail.

Dame Johanna, the daughter of a gamekeeper, possessed numerous virtues, but one was sterling: she had a sense of direction to rival that of any falcon, and she had memorized every inch of the way back to the place where she and Gabriella had been made to part.

At eventide, of the second day's travel, Gresham Sedgewick brought their little party to a halt beside a stream, still some miles from the abbey. Dismounting, the soldier instructed Blodwen to spread out his bedroll and lie down, while he went down to the bank to spear several trout for them to sup upon.

Studying her escort, as she had been throughout the two grueling days since they had parted with the rest of the company, Dame Johanna deduced that young Sedgewick cared not at all for this mission. Indeed, he was disgruntled and petulant of countenance and manner, though he always spoke kindly to her, when he had cause to speak at all, and even attempted to smile now and then.

Blodwen helped Dame Johanna down from her horse and then went off to gather wood for a fire, disregarding Sedgewick's order to take his ease, but he was soon back in camp. They cooked the trout, and ate heartily, and the boy rolled up in his blankets, beneath a nearby tree, and dropped into an exhausted sleep.

It was when Sedgewick crouched to stir the blaze, sending a plume of crimson sparks rising toward the night sky, that Dame Johanna picked up a large, flat rock, crept up behind and, closing her eyes tightly and murmuring a prayer, struck him smartly over the head.

Guilt assailed Dame Johanna as her victim toppled to one side, and she crossed herself and offered yet an-

other prayer—this one of penance—as she knelt hastily
to examine the wound and then laid her head to his
chest, listening for the sound of his heart, and was relieved to find it strong and steady. She glanced back
over one shoulder, saw that Blodwen had not stirred,
then returned her attention to her victim.

Long experience told her that poor Sedgewick was
not badly hurt; he would awaken in a little while, suffering from a headache fit to finish a weaker man, and
surely give chase. With a bit of consideration from
heaven—to be expected only if none of the saints had
been angered by this sinful but patently necessary act—
he would expect her to go on to the abbey and follow, if
only to make certain she'd arrived safely.

After unrolling a blanket and spreading it tenderly
over the man she'd just rendered senseless—his silver-
gold hair was already bloodstained, but then, that was the
way of head wounds—Dame Johanna broke the eighth
commandment and stole the best of the horses, Gresham
Sedgewick's powerful stallion, which bore the pagan
name of Mithras. She had contrived to leave the mule,
Zacheus, with Gabriella, because he was slow and stubborn, and might impede Chalstrey's progress toward
Cornwall, thus allowing her to catch up to them quickly.

Grateful that Sedgewick had not yet unsaddled the
beast, she mounted and, riding astride for the sake of
speed, spurred the animal across the grass and down
through the birch and oak trees to the king's road, in the
hope of confusing anyone who might give chase. When
she was satisfied that she'd given the appearance of
striking out for the abbey, Dame Johanna sent the great
Mithras bounding up a hillside, toward the trail they'd
followed earlier.

Like the wise men setting out to mislead Herod, she traveled by another way, but there was never any doubt of her direction. Dame Johanna did not take her responsibilities lightly, and she would not rest until she had found her charge. While there was little she could do to protect Gabriella, she was determined to be at her side, lending what encouragement she could.

Mother Mary Benedict was sure to understand the demands of duty and expediency. Dame Johanna could only hope that God and Gresham Sedgewick would take the same generous view.

Even though Gabriella awakened promptly at dawn, she found herself alone in the tangle of dew-dampened blankets; Chalstrey had been gone long enough that the place where he'd lain was cold to the touch.

Although she had been almost exultant the night before, Gabriella was disconsolate as she peered out at the drizzling rain—would it never stop?—and smoothed her rumpled gown. Her feet were bare, as she'd lost one slipper in the bog the previous day, and thrown the other one into the woods in a temper. Thanks to Zacheus, her toes were certain to freeze in the endless hours of travel that lay ahead. Chalstrey, no doubt, would drive them all on as relentlessly as ever, until every one, mortal and beast alike, was ready to swoon.

Coming to the swift conclusion that it would do her no good at all to sit there under that deer hide, upon blankets smelling of a man who both infuriated and fascinated her, wishing things were otherwise. Reality, unfortunately, was all she had at hand.

She crawled out and, wearing the thin cloak in a vain attempt to stay dry, rustled into the bushes to do necessary business. Heaven knew, it would be the only chance she had all day, for Chalstrey certainly did not pander to such lowly requirements. How he and his men managed to hold their water for hours on end was a riddle to her.

She had returned, and was rolling the blankets, when Chalstrey came striding through the brush, looking harried. There was, sadly, nothing whatever in the man's bearing to indicate that he had kissed Gabriella in the night and, in doing so, made it abundantly clear that he wanted her.

She might have imagined the whole experience. Except, of course, that she hadn't.

"I am ready," she said, lest he have the small but singular pleasure of commanding her to mount that bloody mule.

"You do not wish to break your fast?"

Gabriella shook her head. She was cold, she was barefooted, and she was traveling with men who probably had prices on their heads. Moreover, one of those men had kissed her, and she had responded without reservation. In such circumstances, she could barely stand to think about eating.

Morgan approached and felt her forehead with the back of his hand. Upon deducing that there was no fever—Gabriella was rarely ill—he pronounced her fit and proceeded to dismantle the makeshift tent he had erected for them.

Perhaps that night, Gabriella mused, they would again lie down together.

A sweet shiver of anticipation pulsed just beneath the surface of her skin.

"Mayhap we could sleep at an inn tonight," she said. "I am in sore need of a bath."

He gathered up the hides and took the blankets from her arms. Then, with an impudent grin, he asked, "Shall I give you one?"

Gabriella felt her advantage in their secret game slipping as an involuntary flush hurried to her face. Not daring to say anything, lest he best her again, she moved around him, picking her way toward camp on her bare and tender feet.

Morgan himself helped her onto Zacheus's mud-stained and quivering back—he knew, that cursed beast, that she bore him no gentle sentiments—and then kept her close by his side throughout the morning. Gabriella could not discern whether this was because he did not trust her, or because he enjoyed her company.

Mayhap it was a bit of both.

They traveled at a brutal pace until midday, when, to everyone's surprise, Chalstrey called the troops to a halt. In the shelter of a copse of oaks, just beginning to lose their leaves, they rested and took a meal of cold meat and brown bread, bought from a crofter's wife along the way. The men stretched their legs, and rough-housed like boys, while Gabriella perched in the fork of an ancient tree, nibbling at her food and doing her best to ignore the thoughtful, even brazen glances that came her way.

Every man in the company knew, of course, that she had lain with Morgan Chalstrey on two occasions. No doubt they had named her harlot, and why should they not? The insight roused her ire toward Morgan, and made her long to avenge her lost honor.

The problem was, a part of Gabriella wanted more from this enigmatic man. Much and scandalously more.

They had been at rest for perhaps a quarter of an hour when Morgan came to her, moving as confidently as if he'd had the right to share her bed, and handed her a pair of small leather boots.

"These belong to young Kettleburn, there, the lad with the bright red hair. He's lending them to you for the length of the journey. They're his best, I might add."

Gabriella accepted the shoes, since her feet were now numb to the ankles, and pulled them on. "Thank you," she said wryly, looking past Morgan for the boy in question. Chalstrey stood very near, and at an angle, so that she could see his profile clearly.

Kettleburn favored her with a bold glance and smirked.

She made to remove the boots instantly, her cheeks burning, but Morgan stayed her hand.

"What is it?" he demanded, frowning, looking into her face.

Gabriella struggled not to weep with mortification "These men believe I am your whore," she said softly. Miserably. "And who can blame them, when you insist on lying with me every night?"

Morgan's face darkened ominously, and he turned to sweep the assemblage up in a single glance.

Smug expressions turned solemn, all around.

"To your horses," Morgan said coldly, in a voice no one but the devil himself could have equaled for sheer menace. "I do not pay you to frolic under trees like maidens on May Day."

After lifting Gabriella onto the mule's back, Morgan mounted the stallion Nimrod and rode close alongside young Kettleburn. An exchange passed between the two men that Gabriella could not hear, strain though she might, and when it had ended, Morgan rode away without so much as a glance in her direction. A gray-haired man came out from among the others to travel beside her.

Gabriella hoped this man was to be her escort; if he were, there was hope of carrying out a successful escape.

The man laughed good-naturedly. "I can guess what you are thinking, milady," he said, "but I'll advise you not to attempt it. He has eyes in the back of his head, milord has, and a better horseman never lived. While you might well leave me behind in a trice, you could never elude Morgan."

Gabriella, irritated that she had been so transparent, was also intrigued. "Why did you call him 'milord?' " she asked.

The older man spurred his muddy horse, and they took their places in the middle of a long, winding strand made up of subdued men and laboring, damp-smelling horses.

"Because that is his proper title," her companion replied. "Has Chalstrey never told you that he is the duke of Edgefield?"

6

Cyprian Avendall knotted his burly right hand into a fist and slammed it down hard on the tabletop. Halsey, head of the small company he had sent to St. Swithin's to fetch back his bride, quailed before him, pale of flesh and unsteady of countenance. He reeked of ale; no doubt he'd tarried along the way, reluctant to return with such news. At Halsey's back, in various states of panic, waited the men-at-arms, three fidgeting, one gone rigid with fear.

"God's eyeballs!" thundered Cyprian, half rising from his chair and then, at the dizzying surge of blood to his head, lowering himself again. "You allowed Chalstrey, that thieving whoremonger, to *steal my bride!* By the saints, I cannot credit such stupidity—"

Halsey swallowed, his Adams apple bobbing the length of his throat. "We were but a few men, my lord, and there was more than a score of them. There was no warning, for they were upon us, Chalstrey and his band, dropping from the trees—"

Cyprian spoke in slow, carefully measured tones, lest he lose his temper and not regain it before the whole of

Avendall Hall was laid waste in the wake of an almost ungovernable wrath. "Had you been vigilant, as I warned you to be, not even Chalstrey could have taken you unaware. Where is the cur now?"

"On his way to Edgefield Keep, surely," Halsey answered quickly, anxious to please, to restore himself to favor. How stupid he was, not to know that that was impossible—Cyprian was not a man who gave second chances. "That being but ten miles from here, my lord, we could intercept the wastrel, give him the thrashing he requires, and reclaim the lady. A fair one she is, sir— aye, you've chosen wisely and well."

Avendall ground his teeth until his jaws ached. The thought of Chalstrey, of all people, traveling with his chosen wife, galled him as little else would have done. "You have proved yourself to be no match for the likes of Edgefield," he bit out. He sent his gaze slicing to the towering bailiff guarding the chamber door, and instantly that door was opened, admitting half a dozen more men of equally impressive size. To them he said, "Take these mewling wretches below, and see that they are soundly whipped, one after the other."

"Please, my lord—" one ill-fated soldier burst out, only to earn himself the promise of another ten lashes and a cuff from one of the guards before he was dragged away.

Halsey struggled in the grasps of two of the others, his eyes blazing with a mingling of fear and indignation that almost made Avendall rescind his disciplinary commands. Almost, but not quite.

"This is unjust, my lord," Halsey protested. "If there is one who wants whipping, it is that devil Chalstrey, not I!"

Cyprian permitted himself a small, tight smile. "Do not trouble yourself on that account," he said, in a tone of acid indulgence. "Chalstrey will scream aloud, begging the heavens for mercy, before I've had done with him." He waved a dismissive hand and scowled. "Remove this vermin," he commanded. "The mere presence of such cowardice and ineptitude sours my stomach."

When the great portal of his private chamber had closed, leaving Avendall alone at long last, he spat another curse and thrust himself out of his chair to pace the long, homely room. The knowledge of what Morgan Chalstrey had taken from him chewed at his gut like a litter of half-starved foxes, and the simple act of containing his emotions was almost beyond him.

He had had his choice of the Redclift women, and he'd made the decision carefully. The youngest, though fair to look upon, was rather too timid for his liking, and too fragile to bear the half dozen sons he wanted. The one with the chestnut hair— Meg, she called herself— had shown a fondness for him and, perversely, he had chosen the fair sister, the cool and distant one, knowing that winning her allegiance would be a challenge.

He wrenched a sword down from a rack on the wall and sliced the air with it, in a vain effort to spend some of his rage. Instead, the familiar feel of the hilt in his right hand made him yearn to cut his enemy down, and the bloodier the encounter, the better.

Again, the image of Gabriella Redclift, the chit so carefully nurtured these many months, at his behest, swelled, voluptuous and tauntingly sweet, in his mind. A terrible wanting swept through him, like a fire racing over dry grass, out of control and voracious. God's blood, he had not bought the wench to see her end in Chalstrey's bed!

Avendall made another swipe with the broadsword and severed a chair leg in twain, sending the whole thing toppling to the floor with a crash. Then, remorseful, he forced himself to draw slow, deep, even breaths, until the desire to pillage like a Norseman subsided a little. Then, without warning, the wave crashed over him again, crushing him beneath its great weight.

He flung the sword away, and it clattered against a stone wall before spinning to a stop on the floor. Avendall strode to the window behind his table and braced himself against the ledge, glaring out over the rugged countryside, which speared and jutted its stony way along the coast of an angry sea and then met with Chalstrey's land, and once again he attempted, without notable success, to quell a fury as old and as elemental as the sea itself.

"This time, Morgan," he vowed, fixing all that he was, all that he'd ever hoped for and been denied, on the thriving estate he could see only in his mind, "I will kill you."

Directly below, in the main courtyard, the first of the miscreants was dragged into view, screaming and fighting, and bound fast to the whipping post. Avendall leaned against the sill and waited.

"Chalstrey a *duke?*" Gabriella scoffed, as the cursed mule Zacheus plodded along beside the old soldier's own squat and humble horse. "Sir, you trifle with me— he is but an outlaw."

The aging soldier smiled. Earlier, he'd given his name as Will Bible, and explained that he'd served with Chalstrey's father. "As you like, milady," he responded, with a smug note.

Gabriella's gaze sought Chalstrey, riding as always at the forefront of the company, and she frowned. "But the duke of Edgefield is among the king's favorites. I have heard songs and poems about him—he battled the Turk and fought in France with the Black Prince—"

"Aye," Bible agreed, at once earnest and complacent, a state which did little to reassure Gabriella. "He did at that. And may well do so again, should His Majesty demand it of him."

"But Chalstrey is a *brigand.*"

"Think you His Majesty and the Black Prince are not more ruthless yet?" He nodded toward Morgan's imperious back, turned to them all this while. "These are harsh days, milady, and harsh men are required to set wrong matters aright."

Gabriella was vastly confused. "Why would such a man trouble himself to steal the bride of another Englishman?"

Will sighed, watching Chalstrey not speculatively, as Gabriella had done, but with a certain alert caution, as well as admiration. It was clear that he, like all the others in the company, with the notable exception of the departed Sedgewick, feared Morgan as much as they respected him.

"Not even for one so fair as you shall I risk the whipping post, milady. If you would know Lord Edgefield's reason for most any endeavor, you must ask him yourself. I would not see him wroth."

"Surely Morgan—Lord Edgefield would not actually whip anyone?"

"He would bind his own mother to the post and flay her, were she under his command and foolhardy enough to flout an order." He paused, arched one gray and bristly eyebrow. "Shall I show you the scars I got from his father, when I was young and wont to be rebellious?"

Gabriella, privately horrified and not a little disbelieving, was quick to shake her head. She'd been raised in a convent, had never witnessed violence of any sort. The thought of a man being whipped for any reason sickened her, filled her with dread, and yet she knew a soldier's life was indeed a harsh one. Knew that her own father had disciplined his men with the lash when he deemed it necessary.

The conversation lapsed, and Gabriella, vastly unsettled, fixed her attention on the road ahead, which twisted and wound through another gloomy, dripping, and eerily soundless forest. To herself, she recited an epic poem, one she and Meg and Elizabeth had spent the best part of a year memorizing—a tragic but beautiful tale of a Celtic warrior and his lady. This pursuit helped a little, in taking her mind off her damp, soiled clothes, her tangled hair, her unwashed flesh. And, most of all, the immediate future, which seemed less promising with every passing moment.

Toward sundown, the rain ceased and, almost simultaneously, they left the dense woods for an open, windy place, where a good-sized stone cottage stood behind toppling fences, with a stable and a granary and other equally decrepit outbuildings teetering around it. Their roofs, all made of dirty thatch, were caving in.

The air, Gabriella thought, tasted faintly of salt. She frowned. Surely they were still miles from the sea—or were they? She had become disoriented; time seemed but a muddy strand woven from the hoofprints of the horses at the front.

Like the others of the company, she drew up on the reins of her mount and waited for Morgan Chalstrey's inevitable commands.

He dismounted before the cottage's gaping door, drew his dagger, and ventured inside. Moments later, he emerged, sheathing the blade in a worn scabbard on his belt.

A duke? Gabriella marveled to herself. Morgan certainly had the presence for such a title, and he did not want for arrogance, either, but surely a man of such eminence had better things to do than harry innocent women and nuns!

"The horses are weary," Morgan announced. "We will pass the night here, and press on in the morning."

"The horses," complained Will Bible, under his breath, still close by Gabriella's side. "Never mind the men—"

Gabriella barely heard him, for she was thinking of Dame Johanna, as she had oft done since Morgan had so callously dismissed that good woman to return, with Sedgewick, to the abbey. Had she arrived unharmed? Were poor Meg and Elizabeth distraught, even now, having finally learned of their sister's abduction?

Perhaps Mother Mary Benedict had already summoned the sheriff, and sent him to find and rescue her.

She sat still and fretting upon her mule while Morgan assigned half a dozen men to make camp here, and half a dozen there, and still more in other parts and places. When he had arranged them in vigilant groups, all around the cottage, only he and Gabriella herself were left.

Morgan strode over, reached up to grasp her round the waist, and lifted her down. She slid along the imperious, unyielding length of him, though whether by accident or by his design she could not say, before her feet touched the ground.

Oddly, the chill, with her all the day like a stubborn

specter, indeed penetrating her very bones, vanished in an instant.

"Where shall I sleep?" Gabriella asked, though she knew, and was terrified by the certainty, and exultant as well. At some point, she had acquired wanton inclinations and, for the sake of her immortal soul, must somehow put a finish to the wicked yearnings this man stirred in her. Her gaze caught on the coiled whip affixed to his saddle, and the effect was like a face full of cold water.

"You will sleep where I do," Morgan answered, looking, for a moment, as utterly befuddled as she felt. It was as though his own decisions—at least where she was concerned—came as a surprise to him. "Inside the cottage."

Gabriella swallowed. "There is already unworthy talk, my lord."

He grinned in that endearing, crooked way that lifted only a corner of his mouth and made him look more like an angel gone astray than a valiant duke and friend of the king. "Indeed," he said. "Mayhap I should send a man ahead, to make sure the news reaches Avendall's ears as well."

Morgan might have slapped Gabriella, so sharply did his words sting. Not for any treasure of earth or heaven, however, would she let him know what injury he had done her. If he moved her to lose her temper, it would mean she had given her power over to him, and the idea of that was abhorrent.

"I see," she whispered tautly, folding her arms. "That, no doubt, is why you kissed me, whilst sharing my bed. So you could plague your old enemy with the tale of my inconstant virtue!"

"He will mislike it, methinks," Chalstrey said, with a nod and a false air of chagrin, spreading the splayed fin-

gers of one hand upon his chest in a mockery of despair.
His eyes danced with merry mischief all the while. "I
confess I shall contrive to make matters worse before
this journey is at its end."

Gabriella longed, with all her being, to strike Chalstrey a blow that would send him reeling, but she refused to rise to the bait.

"You will need my help, sir, in making a harlot of me,"
she remarked, as a chill wind rushed over the land, hardly
slowed by her gown, and bit at her smudged and gritty
flesh. "And I do not intend to aid you." With that, she
moved to sweep past him, for she had glimpsed a stream
flowing like a dark ribbon beyond the cottage, and she
wished to investigate. Perhaps she might launder her
gown and enjoy at least the illusion of being clean.

He caught her arm as she reached his side, and drew
her back to face him. "You will go nowhere except in my
company, Gabriella," he said.

She raised a mocking eyebrow. "Do you mistrust
your own men, milord?" she asked, putting a disdainful
emphasis on the title.

Morgan's fine jawline tightened. "Mayhap it is you I
mistrust, milady," he replied. Then he relaxed both his
grasp and his hard expression softened, though only
slightly. He seemed more perturbed than angry. "I do
not mean to be unkind."

Oddly, Gabriella believed what he said. Again, she
wondered what, in his past and in Avendall's, had driven
Morgan Chalstrey, Duke of Edgefield and heaven only
knew what else, to carry out such a desperate and reckless deed.

"Will Bible says you would whip your own mother,"
she said, raising her chin. "Is it so?"

"My mother," Morgan said, releasing her with a quick gesture that might have been contained fury, "is dead of the plague these ten years past, may God have mercy on her gentle soul. See if the cottage is to your liking, milady, while I have a word with certain of my men."

It was Gabriella's turn to grasp Chalstrey's arm as he turned to walk away from her. She had spoken recklessly, and now she feared that Will might be sorely punished for her thoughtless words. Morgan's flesh felt ominously hard beneath her hand, and she believed his heart must be very like it.

"It was I who would bait you, my lord," she said hurriedly. "Please do not place blame on another."

Morgan looked down at her hand, then returned his gaze to her face. He seemed amused, but coldly so, in a way that gnawed more deeply than the cruel teeth of the wind. "My men do not need you to beg mercy for them, Gabriella. Nor would I heed you if they did."

Gabriella's cheeks ached with color. "Go then," she hissed. "Whip the lot of them to bloody shreds, for all I care. But pray, do not presume that I will forgive your barbarism when I am reunited with my lord Avendall, for I shall not!"

For one terrible moment, she thought he was going to laugh. Instead, he sighed. "Avendall is not your lord," he said. "For the time being, I am. And I do not need your intercession with him, though you seem to have appointed yourself as intermediary to half the world. Furthermore," he went on, looking her over pointedly, "I had not planned to whip anyone. Not at the moment, in any case."

Gabriella curtsyed briskly and then turned from him with a whirl of ruined skirts, for he had bested her in this round of play and she had no choice but to sound retreat. Temporarily.

She thought she caught the sound of a low masculine chuckle as she stepped gingerly over the threshold of the cottage—as commanded by her lord. Only the stiffening of her shoulders might have revealed that she'd heard, and she did not look back to see if he'd been watching.

The inside of the little house, long empty, was hardly fit for a rat's nest, let alone for two human beings to pass the night. Nothing of use had been left behind—nary a kettle nor a cot—but there was a loft and a firepit against one wall, with a large hole cut in the thatch overhead to let the smoke escape.

Gabriella went back out to Zacheus, who stood, long ears quivering, in the dooryard, and removed her canvas bag from behind the saddle. "You are a reprehensible beast," she told him pleasantly, "and if there is any justice in creation, you will be struck by lightning."

"Most unkind, milady," remarked a voice from behind her.

She turned, holding her things, and saw the red-haired lad, Kettleburn, standing nearby. His gaze was brazen and mildly contemptuous as he appraised her like a calf at the fair.

"There are creatures," she said evenly, "who seem born to suffer unkindness. In fact, if they do not encounter disfavor by chance, they seek it out deliberately."

Kettleburn was clearly not a quick-witted man, but he knew he had been insulted, and he was not pleased.

"A kiss for the loan of my good boots, my lady," he said, in an oily voice that caused Gabriella's skin to crawl. "Surely that's a just price?"

"I would sooner walk barefoot from here to London town," she answered, and, leaning against the mule for balance, raised one foot to remove the first boot. She meant to fling both of them into his spotted face.

There was no divining what prompted the lad to do what he did then; indeed, the moon had not yet risen, so it could not have been an enchantment of that sort. Whatever the reason, with Morgan Chalstrey somewhere nearby, though not in Gabriella's sight, young Kettleburn lunged at Gabriella, his grubby hands curled to grasp her shoulders and wrench her forward into his kiss.

Zacheus, frightened by the sudden move and never of sublime disposition anyway, brayed loudly and skittered back. Gabriella, who had been leaning against him to remove her borrowed boots, toppled into the mud that rolled like a black, gummy sea in the dooryard. Kettleburn lost his balance and fell squarely on top of her, an accident of fate, certainly, but one of which he took full advantage.

Gabriella squirmed, kicked, and clawed, but still Kettleburn pressed his wet mouth to hers, and her revulsion was such that when the boy was suddenly pulled off her, she retched once, twice, a third time.

"God's blood, lad," Morgan rasped, grasping Kettleburn by the back of his jerkin and wrenching him to his feet, "you've got gall to spare." He flung him aside, to be caught and steadied, though not in a kindly way, by Will Bible. "Take him to the stables and bind him like a pig balking at the chopping block. I'll see to him later."

Having regained her breath, if not her composure, Gabriella struggled to rise and failed. Morgan offered a hand and pulled her, with a great and humiliating sucking noise, out of the mud and onto her unsteady feet.

"What happened here?" he demanded. The men who had stood gathered at the scene only moments before were now gone.

Gabriella looked down at her unspeakably dirty clothes and barely contrived to hold back a sob of utter frustration and despair. Her gaze fell to his belt, where he carried the whip she'd seen earlier, fixed to his saddle. When her eyes met Morgan's, she knew that her own expression was one of pleading, but she did not care. If he had sought to humble her, he had done so.

She could not look away from the lash. "Do you—do you mean to use that? On the boy, I mean—?"

Morgan folded muscular arms. His expression was unreadable. "Mayhap I will," he said. "Kettleburn leaves me little choice."

Gabriella swallowed hard. She had no love for Kettleburn, of course, nor was she especially inclined to turn the other cheek, given what the man had done. It was the prospect of bloodshed, and Morgan's apparent willingness to engage in brutality, that fair stopped her breath. "Do not be hasty—"

He was obviously not moved by her plea. In fact, there was something unrelenting in his countenance. Something fierce. "Pray," he countered, "do not tell me how to manage my company." He made to turn away.

Gabriella stepped forward, grasped the sleeve of his tunic. "Mayhap it was my fault," she said, desperate to prevent what seemed an inevitable savagery. "Aye. I wanted—I wanted to see if I could make him kiss me—"

Chalstrey plainly did not believe her. "You tell an untruth," he accused, and if anything, he was even angrier than before. "I saw what happened, Gabriella. So did half the company."

She dragged in a deep breath and let it out in a slow, forlorn sigh. "If I can forgive him, can you not do the same?"

A muscle jumped in Morgan's jaw, which had begun to show the rough beginnings of a beard, causing Gabriella to wonder how his face would feel, against her flesh . . .

"No," he spat. "I cannot."

Gabriella swallowed, still struggling not to break down and weep with weariness and confusion and a thousand other emotions. She had come to the end of her personal resources, and though she would surely rally, it would take time, and peace. "Then you are a brute."

Morgan muttered a curse. "Sedgewick was right," he railed, under his breath, looking around the dooryard as if to discover help. There was only the mule. "I have brought this upon my own head." He spread his hands, let them slap against his sides in irritated dismay. "May God turn the breath in my lungs to fire if e'er I court such a mad plan again—"

Gabriella stared at him, at once confounded and hopeful. Was he going to release her, send her home to the abbey, or on to Avendall Hall? "My lord?"

"What?" Morgan nearly yelled.

The courage to ask his intentions deserted her in that moment, and she cast about for something, anything, to say. "May I—may I go inside and—and change my gown?"

Morgan tilted his head back and scanned the heavens. Evidently, they were of no more help than the mule had been. "Do as you like," he hissed. He was furious, though she could only speculate as to the reason. He misliked her pleading for clemency for the churl, Kettleburn, she guessed. Or perhaps it was not herself that had roused his temper at all, but events, and other people, both present and absent. "I had not thought, my lady, that letting Avendall have you would have been a far better punishment for his many sins than keeping you from him!"

Gabriella snatched her bundle from the mud and hurried into the cottage, there to cry quietly, in private.

She had barely slipped out of her gown and donned the other, hardly cleaner, when Morgan came in again, bearing an armload of twigs and branches found, no doubt, in one of the outbuildings. He hurled the light burden onto the hearth and crouched before it, producing a tinderbox from inside his jerkin.

"What has happened to Kettleburn?" she dared to inquire, though in a small and tremulous voice.

Morgan turned and looked up at her. "Mayhap it is better not to ask, my lady," he said, and went back to lighting the fire.

Gabriella closed her eyes, swaying slightly on her feet. "How could you? How could you be so cruel?"

The blaze caught and Morgan rose, dusting his hands and moving to face her. "Cruel? Do you know what can happen to a soldier on the field of battle, indeed to an entire army, when one man—just one—fails to follow orders? Have you any idea, even the vaguest comprehension, what the Turk will do to a prisoner, taken because he was undisciplined or cowardly and fell behind or tried to flee the field?"

Gabriella held up a hand, bidding him to silence, and closed her eyes. "I have heard," she whispered.

"You have not *dreamed*," Morgan said fiercely. "And I am not 'cruel' enough to tell you. Suffice it to say, my lady, that in a company such as ours, obedience is everything and insubordination is exceeded only by treason as cause for the severest punishment. If I allow one man to step out of line with impunity, I will soon have chaos."

She pressed her fingers to her mouth, and tears sprang to her eyes, though she willed them back with all that was in her. "I am not a soldier," she pointed out brokenly.

Morgan grew gentler then, though only a little, and reluctantly at that, and moved in a stiff and ungraceful way to take her into his arms. She did not resist, but only sank against him, trembling with exhaustion and sorrow and a need for comfort of which she had never known the like.

"You are so cold," he said, as though informing her of something she had not suspected until then. "Come—stand by the fire. I will bring food and blankets and you can rest—"

"I would rather have water," she replied, looking up at him with all her fragilities plainly visible in her eyes because she could not hide them. "Hot water. Rivers of it."

Morgan laughed hoarsely, then kissed the tip of her nose. In spite of everything, she felt a frisson of warmth rush through her, as if she'd just taken a draught of mulled wine. A glint of passion flashed in his eyes. "Will you accept that as my penance?"

She hesitated, then nodded. "What of Kettleburn?" she dared to ask. "What will happen to him?"

"That is not your concern," he said.

She bit her lower lip. "It is," she insisted.

"You will mislike the answer."

They stood in silence for a time, staring at each other, gauging, measuring, evaluating. Then, for a reason she could not have explained to save herself from purgatory, Gabriella stood on tiptoe and kissed him, lightly, briefly, on the mouth.

Startled, Morgan threw back his head and laughed outright. Then, eyes sparkling with mischief one moment, and dark witchery the next, he leaned down and took Gabriella's mouth with his own. The kiss was tentative, teasing at first, as hers had been, then powerful and commanding, robbing Gabriella of all balance and good sense.

"Mayhap," he said, at long last, when he'd finally broken away, "kissing you is worth a few lashes."

She hoped he was jesting, but dared not pursue the matter of Kettleburn's punishment any further, lest she make matters worse. "You may certainly kill the mule," she suggested, on a bright impulse, "if you must do violence to something."

He laughed again. Then, with resolution, he left her, and did not return for so long that Gabriella began to despair of him, and even more of the promised hot water. At least an hour had gone by, she estimated, when he finally returned, appearing in the cottage doorway, a wooden bucket steaming in either hand, and watched Gabriella in a strange, fascinated way as she turned, having glimpsed him at the edge of her vision, from feeding the fire, to meet his shadowed stare. It was almost as though he didn't recognize her, was indeed bemused to find her there.

"You have supped?" he asked, his words rough and barely audible.

Gabriella felt an unaccountable thrill. Surely there was nothing of her girlhood fantasies in this—a little hot water, a bandit duke, a night that would surely be spent lying on a deer hide in the center of a dirt floor.

"Aye," she answered softly. Mayhap the autumn moon, full and golden, had enchanted her, she reasoned. "Will brought bread and stew. I am all but restored."

Morgan entered the room at last, as though having just burst through some invisible restraint, and set the buckets down on the hearth. "Here," he said. "Have your bath, milady, such as it is. And make haste, for I cannot swear these pails will not leak. One of the men found them in a shed."

Gabriella wet her lips nervously, and clasped her hands together. She was, after all, a virgin, late of St. Swithin's, and not half so daring as her sister Meg, though she wished she could be. "You can't mean to—to stay?"

"Of course I mean to stay," Chalstrey replied. "Who will stand guard over you, if I am not here?"

And who, Gabriella wondered, would guard her from him? Nay, more, from herself?

"Will you not leave the cottage?" she asked, glancing at the water with yearning. Even then, the precious stuff was cooling, perhaps seeping between the slats of the ancient buckets to be wasted on the floor.

"Aye," Morgan answered, with a long-suffering sigh. "But pray be quick. I am weary and I have not yet had a meal."

Gabriella watched, wide-eyed, as he made a great matter of going out. She heard him outside the door, talking quietly with another man, and feared he might return at any moment. Because she was utterly desperate to wash, however, she tore off her clothes, grasped the cloth she had torn from the hem of her chemise for the purpose, and began what passed for a bath. It was bliss, feeling the warmth of the water, the emerging smoothness of her skin.

No more than a few minutes had gone by while she indulged in these ablutions, she was sure, and yet her heart raced throughout and her chilled flesh burned with the heat of a peculiarly delicious shame. She had barely finished, and pulled her chemise back on, when he stepped inside, bringing a rush of cool evening air with him, causing her to tremble.

Chalstrey bore a haunted expression as he studied her, and rubbed the back of his neck in a gesture she had come to recognize as a sign of tension. "God in heaven, Gabriella, why must you be so fair to look upon?"

She was flattered, although all good sense dictated that she should accept no compliments from such a scoundrel as the duke of Edgefield.

Gabriella passed over his remark, because she did not know how to respond to it. "I am most grateful indeed for the water you brought, my lord," she said.

Morgan groaned. "Gabriella, Gabriella," he lamented gruffly. "Pray, do not say such things lightly. You cannot know how a defenseless man might take such a remark."

She smiled tentatively, thinking she understood but, as always with this man, uncertain, and began to spread the deer hides on the cleanest part of the filthy floor. "I shall sleep well tonight, I think," she said.

He watched her intently, even somberly, for a few moments. "Gabriella—do you know—do you even imagine—?"

"What?" she asked, peering at him. Genuinely confused.

"The sight of you. Doing that. Looking the way you look. God's blood, Gabriella, if this is revenge, it is a torment worthy of the Turk!"

Gabriella ceased her bedmaking and approached the man who so confused her, who so delighted and infuriated her. "Revenge?"

"If I lie with you—" he broke off, spun away in

undisguised agitation. "My grievance is with Avendall, not with you." Making a great and almost comical effort not to look at her, Chalstrey bent to snatch up one of the deer hides and a woolen blanket. "I'll sleep there, by the door. You may rest here, next to the hearth. But pray, do not settle in too close, lest a spark—"

Gabriella was amused by this usually able, usually articulate man's struggle to deal with a perfectly normal situation, but she had the good grace not to show it. She owed him that much, she reasoned, after he'd saved her from Kettleburn, and brought her water for a bath.

"Will you not sleep beside me tonight, my lord, as you have before?"

Chalstrey shoved splayed fingers through his hair which, like his beard, was badly in need of a barber's attentions. His back was rigid under the jerkin and chain mail he wore, and his sword, even then, was still in its scabbard at his waist. "I dare not," he answered wretchedly, and at great length.

Before Gabriella could taunt him further—in truth she did not want Morgan to leave her or to make her his own, but simply to lie beside her, a strong comfort in the cold and frightening darkness of a land that was not her home—there arose a great din outside. In the space of a heartbeat, Chalstrey sprang through the doorway, sword drawn.

Gabriella followed, frowning, and saw that the dooryard was awash in the dancing crimson light of numerous torches. For one horrible, wonderful moment, she thought Avendall had come at last, with many men, to save her.

Instead, two of Morgan's own soldiers rode out of the

frigid gloom, leading the horse of a third rider between them.

Gabriella recognized the stallion first; it was Mithras, Sedgewick's treasured mount. But astride the beast's broad back was Dame Johanna, looking rumpled, exhausted, and politely triumphant.

Sagging in the saddle, her robes wet and every bit as soiled as Gabriella's own, she smiled down into Morgan's upraised and no doubt incredulous face.

"We found this woman on the forest trail, my lord," one of the men told Chalstrey. "What would you have us do with her?"

"I dare not answer that question for fear of being struck dead by a vengeful God," Morgan replied tersely. "Be gone, back to your posts."

The two guards immediately rode away, abandoning the renegade nun to her fate.

Morgan spoke in careful, measured tones as he helped Dame Johanna down from the saddle. "Where, pray tell, is my most cherished friend, Gresham?"

"No need to worry about young Sedgewick, my lord," Dame Johanna responded confidently, studying Gabriella, still poised in the doorway, with thoughtful, knowing eyes. "He'll be fit as ever, once that head wound heals."

7

As the travelers drew nigh to Edgefield Keep, the scent of the sea came forth to greet them, robed in a salty mist. Gabriella was mounted behind Chalstrey on the stallion, Nimrod, and clinging for dear life, while Dame Johanna perched upon the fractious mule. A full sennight had passed since the initial abduction, and Gabriella was numb with exhaustion, floating through the corridors and passages of her life like a ghost, sleepwalking.

Sometime before—was it three days, four, even five, mayhap?—Dame Johanna had boldly returned, riding Sedgewick's horse, catching up with Chalstrey's party on the road, her clothes disheveled and soiled, her wimple askew. Immediately after extracting an explanation, Morgan had dispatched two men to ride back to the abbey to collect Sedgewick, leading the charger behind them. There had been no sign of them since, or of his friend, and there were whisperings in the company that Gresham Sedgewick, vexed with Chalstrey, had decided to go his own way. The men sent after him, it was said, were the sort to go along with just such a plan.

Gabriella thought back to the night at the cottage, when she had come so close to surrendering her virtue to Morgan Chalstrey. It was providence, she reflected, with glum relief, that Dame Johanna had found them when she did, or the deed might have been done. Instead, when the women were settled on the deer hides before the fire in that decrepit little cottage, Dame Johanna having been given a hasty meal, Morgan had stretched out on the cold dirt floor, just inside the door, without so much as a blanket to warm him.

Gabriella, sharing the nun's cover, had sneaked over in the night and draped the spare carefully over Morgan. Every night since, she had slept the sleep of the innocent, and she wasn't entirely pleased about that, though of course she was almighty glad that Dame Johanna had come back.

Now, riding behind Chalstrey, Gabriella did not allow herself to think how much she enjoyed being in necessarily close proximity, having her arms round that lean waist and her legs pressed against his. There were moments when she was certain she could hear the strong, steady beat of his heart through his thick leather jerkin.

Inwardly, she sighed. She should despise this man, she knew, but a part of her longed for him, and besides, the harm to her reputation and prospects for marriage had surely been done. If she was to suffer the consequences of lovemaking, should she not also know the joy? She would tuck the memory away in a corner of her heart, to remember for all her life.

In point of fact, Gabriella cherished a secret and guilty regret that Dame Johanna had not arrived a few hours later, or perhaps not even until the morning, but she did not allow herself to reflect upon that overmuch

either. There were times when it was better to think of
other things . . . her sisters, for example. The potato
patch at St. Swithin's, where she had worked so many
hours, planting and weeding and watering, hating every
moment of it. The summer and autumn fairs that
Mother Mary Benedict sometimes allowed her to attend, in the village, with Elizabeth and Meg, there to
watch the mummers, and hear the songs of wandering
troubadours and the tales of seedy bards. To hold the
squirming piglets brought to market from some outly-
ing farm and, if there was a coin to spare, to buy a sweet
and eat it slowly, that it might last.

Why, Gabriella wondered, had she not appreciated
those times more? Why had she never guessed how
fleeting such uncomplicated joys could be, how precious?

"I am certain your sisters are well, Gabriella," Dame
Johanna said. She had, of course, been watching her
charge's expression and manner of countenance, in that
careful, discerning way of hers. "You will wish to write
to them, and when I return to St. Swithin's, I shall carry
your letter myself."

The idea cheered Gabriella immeasurably, and she
smiled. "Surely my lord Sedgewick will find his way to
the abbey, and Meg and Elizabeth will learn that I am
well." She sensed that Morgan was listening, although
he gave no sign of it, and added for his benefit, "Considering the trials I have suffered of late."

Her reward was a slight stiffening in the muscles
banding his torso; she felt it against the undersides of
her forearms.

Dame Johanna's eyes held a merry light. "Aye," she
agreed. "But you mustn't worry them with complaints,

Gabriella. That would grieve them sorely, since they are in no position to come to your aid."

"Mayhap Sedgewick will take it into his head to bring them back, as a special favor to me."

Morgan turned and looked down at her. "Sedgewick will have one thing on his mind when he returns, and one thing only," he said seriously. "Removing my hide in payment for leaving him to be bested by a treacherous nun."

The nun in question smiled placidly. "I am certain he will forgive me," she said.

"You are certain, it seems to me," Morgan retorted, "of a very great deal. Mayhap you will suffer me to observe, good dame, that you and that mule of yours are by nature well suited to one another."

Dame Johanna's smile broadened. "You speak true, Lord Edgefield," she answered. "Zacheus is not easily turned from any course he sets for himself, and neither am I."

Morgan inclined his head, in silent concession to a worthy adversary, but Gabriella caught the faintest twitch of his lips before he turned his attention back to the barren track ahead.

The sun was high and bright when, after hours of travel, Edgefield Keep loomed before them, at long last. Welcoming flags of blue and white fluttered on the points of several towers, caught in the salty breeze, and the whispered song of the sea teased the ear, like a tune played low, and far off. The drawbridge was lowered, and the walls of the castle were high and sturdy, with guards walking the parapets. The windows, out of range of all but the swiftest arrow, glittered with glass.

Gabriella drew in a sharp breath and let it out audibly. "My lord," she whispered, thunderstruck.

Morgan turned to grin at her. "Not so terrible a prison, methinks," he said.

Gabriella's exuberance immediately waned, at the word "prison," while Dame Johanna stared in disbelief, first at the castle, and then at its lord and master.

Then, at last regaining her equanimity, the nun crossed herself hastily and murmured something about the ways of the Almighty being past finding out.

Morgan cast a sidelong glance at Dame Johanna, but he did not tender a reply. Instead, he spurred Nimrod toward the base of the drawbridge, compelling Gabriella to hold on more tightly or tumble off into the path of the horses bringing up the rear.

Keeping pace, Dame Johanna gave her a reassuring look and even contrived to reach out and touch her arm with steadying fingers.

Within the walls lay a village, packed with cheering, smiling people, and Gabriella was reminded of her fancies, early in the journey, in which she'd imagined herself in just such a place. The difference was, of course, that in her private visions, the castle had been Avendall's, the villagers *his* vassals and servants, not Chalstrey's.

Still, she permitted herself to pretend, to enjoy the festive welcome as though it truly included her, and not just Morgan and his road-weary men-at-arms, who were even then being greeted by bright-faced women and children bounding and skipping with excitement alongside their horses.

Gabriella could not fail to notice that more than a few of the females studied her with speculative and less-than-friendly glances, and that unsettled her a little. She straightened her shoulders and assumed a haughty attitude as a means of defense, glaring back at the women.

As the drawbridge was raised behind them, Morgan dismissed the company of men, with the exception of poor Kettleburn, who rode in disgrace, his hands bound to his saddle horn, his face sullen and set. Gabriella had often watched the young man, surreptitiously, trying to determine whether or not he'd been whipped for his transgression, but she could not tell, and nothing was ever said about the matter, in her presence at least.

"What of me, my lord?" Kettleburn asked, glowering at Morgan, and though his words were proper, his tone was bitter, and dangerously brazen.

"Bless your saints that there are women here," Morgan answered smoothly, "for if there weren't, I should send you sprawling off that horse with the back of my hand. You will pass a night in gaol, there to ponder the error of your ways. Then, if you are fortunate and I happen to be in a malleable state of mind, you will be turned out."

Kettleburn flushed at having been set down so smartly, and cast a hateful look at Gabriella, as though she were at fault for all he now faced, and what he had already endured. He opened his mouth to speak again, apparently thought better of it, and fell into a prudent if belated silence.

Morgan called to one of the villagers, a smith if the man's brawny build and soot-stained apron was any indication. "See to our court jester, if you will," was Chalstrey's offhand reply. "I would have him treated as well as one of our stubbornest horses, but no better."

"Aye, milord," agreed the smith, tugging with one blackened hand at his forelock and then wrenching poor Kettleburn from the saddle in a single motion and flinging him over a massive shoulder in another. "And where might I tether this misbegotten colt, my lord? In the dungeon?"

"An offense to a lot of innocent, hardworking rats," Morgan responded. "Take him to the old granary, give him water and a bit of food, and bolt the door."

Kettleburn, carried in such an ungraceful fashion betwixt a great many laughing men, who took the opportunity to swat him with their gloves or a length of rein as he passed, uttered not a word.

Too late, he had learned that, with such as Chalstrey, judicious speech was indeed a virtue. Gabriella made due note of the lesson, and resolved to deal carefully with the duke of Edgefield.

Gabriella had never been inside a castle of such splendor and space. Indeed, by comparison, Redclift Hall, her childhood home, a cramped and drafty place built of creaking, worm-eaten timbers and crumbling stone, was hardly fit to serve as a dovecote.

Morgan vanished almost immediately—Gabriella felt a pang of unfounded, unaccountable jealousy, and hoped there was not a woman waiting to greet him in private—and then silently reprimanded herself for a fool. Chalstrey did not care for her, she fretted; he meant to use her to obtain vengeance against an old enemy, and she would be wise to remember that.

The task of showing her and Dame Johanna through the keep was left to Chalstrey's manservant, Ephriam Frame, a tall and spindly man with coarse features and a friendly face.

Gabriella soon learned, under Frame's tutelage, that the lower floor of Chalstrey's stronghold was given over to kitchens, servants' quarters, and storerooms. Above was the vast counsel chamber, where Morgan conferred with advisers in matters of war and finance and general enterprise. There also was the great hall, where formal meals were taken and occasional feasts and other festivities were held. Minstrels' galleries looked down from either end, and Gabriella could easily imagine merry music, prompting gentlefolk in jewel-colored clothing to dance.

A great stairway rose straight from the passage outside the great hall, and Ephriam trudged up it, clearly expecting Gabriella and Dame Johanna to follow. Which, of course, they did. As they progressed through the castle, Gabriella added detail after detail to the letter to her sisters that she had been composing in her mind ever since Dame Johanna had suggested the project. Having thought the missive through these many times, she had only to set it down on parchment.

The manservant passed several enormous doors, all with iron keyholes, pausing at last at the end of the corridor. With an inclination of his head, Ephriam opened the chamber, and the sound of the sea rose to Gabriella's ears.

With a little cry of pleasure, she hurried over the threshold, setting aside, temporarily at least, the inherent difficulties of her situation, and stood in the center of the room.

It was an enormous chamber, with two huge beds, plump with cushions and covered in shimmering golden velvet. A pretty desk graced one wall, and there was a terrace, open that fine and temperate day, to the ministerings of the nearby sea.

Gabriella, who had only read about the ocean, and heard tales of it, was fascinated. She went to stand on the balcony, watching the waves strike the stony shore and rise spraying against the Cornish sky. Tired though she was, a prisoner though she might be, Gabriella was enchanted.

"Have you ever known the like of it?" she whispered, when Dame Johanna came to stand beside her.

The nun laid a gentle hand upon Gabriella's. "God's world holds many wonders," she said. "And no, I have never looked upon the waters of the deep. Come inside, child. There is time to watch the sea when you have rested, and taken sustenance."

Reluctantly, Gabriella followed her chaperon back into the bed chamber. There, serving maids were filling a copper tub with warm, scented water, while still others set a meal of quail pie, boiled turnips, and fruit upon a table before the fire. Ephriam oversaw the whole undertaking, giving quiet orders to this lass and that one.

"His lordship would have a word with you in the counsel chamber when you have eaten and deem yourself ready," he said, addressing Dame Johanna, while politely leaving Gabriella uninvited.

She did not care, for she had not tasted quail pie since Christmas, and she was wildly hungry. Besides, she wanted to step into that bath and soak herself clean before the water turned cold.

"I would see Lord Edgefield now, if you please," Dame Johanna said. "I, too, have matters I wish to raise."

Gabriella barely paid any mind to the exchange. "I shall save you half the quail pie," she promised.

Dame Johanna chuckled and shook her head. "Eat your fill, child," she said. "I do not have your appetite."

With that, Ephriam ordered the serving wenches out, and he and Dame Johanna followed. The great door closed with a clatter behind them, and only later did Gabriella pause to think that there had been a disturbing finality in the sound.

Morgan rose from the chair behind his work table as the nun swept into the counsel chamber, just behind Ephriam. A platter of cold fowl, thinly sliced in the way he preferred, had been set out for Chalstrey, along with a ewer of elderberry wine, but he had yet to touch either.

"You have taken refreshment?" Morgan asked, noting the fire in Dame Johanna's eyes and marveling that she was not clad in armor and leading armies to defeat the French and drive back the ever-encroaching Turk. He was very careful not to smile.

"I have need of none," the good dame replied. She turned her formidable gaze upon Ephriam. "You may go," she said, as though he were in her service, rather than Chalstrey's own.

Chalstrey did not protest. No, indeed, he was far too busy trying to marshal his expression into something properly solemn to engage in trifling arguments.

He gestured to a chair, once the great door had closed behind a startled Ephriam, and the nun crossed to it and sat herself down with all the dignity of a monarch assuming her rightful throne.

"This present situation will not serve," she announced.

Morgan slid the platter toward her. "Restore yourself, dame. I fear you have not taken the time to do so before this." He paused, studied her wryly. "No doubt assaulting my captain and stealing his horse took its toll on your strength."

She looked at the food, and a look of longing flickered in her eyes, then was quickly mastered and put aside. Plainly, Dame Johanna was a person to put first things first. "What, exactly, do you intend to do with Gabriella?" she asked.

Perched on the edge of the desk, Morgan picked up a slice of roast fowl and nibbled at it, puckering his brow into a pensive frown. "How do you mean?" he countered.

"You know very well what I mean," replied the nun, in brisk and un-nunlike tones. "Gabriella is an innocent girl, barely more than a child. Hers is a good, if impoverished, family. She has a fine mind, a brave heart, and a noble spirit. Sir Cyprian Avendall may well have represented her one chance to marry well, prize that she is, because she can bring no dowry to her husband. You have most likely ruined any hope she has of becoming Lady Avendall, and I should like to know what you propose to do in reparation."

Morgan took time to chew and swallow, to pour himself a cup of wine and take a leisurely sip. He enjoyed sparring with Dame Johanna—indeed he did not doubt that she was made of sturdier stuff than any of his men save Sedgewick—and wished to prolong the exchange.

The nun folded her arms and sat calmly, and it was plain from her manner and the look on her unremarkable face that she would not be moved until all pertinent questions had been answered to her satisfaction.

"What would you like me to do?" he asked reasonably, spreading his hands in a receptive gesture.

"Have you no wife, then?"

Morgan flinched. "None," he admitted. "Nor do I wish to acquire one."

"I am quite certain," Dame Johanna replied, unruffled, "that Gabriella never wished to be abducted, and have her reputation spoilt."

He set his jaw. "I had a reason for what I did."

"Yes," the intrepid nun agreed, "revenge for some transgression of Avendall's."

"A transgression you know nothing about," Morgan pointed out.

"Mayhap you would care to enlighten me."

He shook his head, intertwining his fingers. "I cannot," he said, and it was true. He had not been able to speak of Rebecca even to Sedgewick, his most trusted friend, except to relate things that didn't matter.

To Morgan's abject surprise, Dame Johanna rose from her chair, walked over to him, and covered one of his hands with her own.

"I believe you," she said quietly, and with a degree of kindness that was nearly his undoing. "But there comes a time when, however grievously we have been wronged, we must turn from what belongs to the past and embrace the present. You are an uncommon man, Morgan Chalstrey, but like so many brave fools, you fix your thoughts upon the horizon and fail to notice what is already within your grasp."

The reminder of Rebecca, and what Avendall had done to her, raised a cold sweat on Morgan's flesh. Although he had awakened in such a state, trembling and sick in the grasp of a nightmare, on more occasions than he could count, he had never experienced the phenomenon in daylight.

He turned his back on Dame Johanna and strode to the window, there to look out over the treacherous sea that had held a strange sort of sway over him all his life. "Go now," he said hoarsely. "I am not fit company."

Without another word, the nun left the room.

✳   ✳   ✳

Gabriella lay sleepless upon her vast feather-stuffed mattress, staring at the shadows on the ceiling, while Dame Johanna snored daintily in the other bed. Far beyond the closed doors of the terrace, the sea murmured and crashed, and Gabriella fancied that the sound was the pulse of the very earth itself.

She sighed. It was positively ungrateful to be lying there, cosseted in silk and freshly bathed, with a stomach full of savory fare, longing all the while to sleep on a deer hide instead, beside a certain man. Yes, Gabriella marveled to herself, she would gladly have traded all the unfamiliar comforts that surrounded her now to be back in her mud-splashed gown, barefoot and cold, hair trailing and all atangle, with only the food the soldiers could carry, shoot, or snare to eat and naught but the sky for a roof over her head.

Gabriella shifted to her right side and closed her eyes tightly, but it was no use. She had slept deeply, and for hours, after eating and washing herself clean, and she simply wasn't tired. She could think of nothing but Chalstrey —the way he looked when he smiled, and when he scowled. The way she had felt when he kissed her in the cottage that night, just before Dame Johanna's timely return.

She trembled as a wave of heat rolled through her, and flopped from her right side to her left in an effort to shake it off. Mayhap even now, while she lay there alone, Morgan was with a woman. A laughing, worldly woman who knew what to do and say, how to please him, how to kindle his desire and then to slake it.

Gabriella stifled a moan of frustration. If only she had never met that wretched man! She would be duly wed by now, and know at last the forbidden secrets of the marriage bed. Perhaps her sisters would even then be on their way to Cornwall, never to be parted from her again.

She groped for an image of Avendall, the way a victim of a shipwreck might reach for anything afloat, and found that his features would not come to her mind.

Chalstrey had stolen even that from her, she thought angrily.

Unable to stay abed a moment longer—she would certainly scream if she did—Gabriella rose quietly and pulled on the embroidered woolen gown one of the servants had brought to her earlier. She had not asked to whom such a fine garment might belong, and she did not permit herself to wonder even now.

Careful not to awaken Dame Johanna, who was clearly exhausted by adventures of her own, Gabriella crossed the moonlit chamber with a light step. Reaching the door, she opened it an inch at a time, grimacing all the while, lest the hinges creak and give her away.

Squat tallows sputtered and flared in metal sconces along the passage wall, smelling of grease and producing an unsteady glow. The corridor was chilly, and Gabriella shivered, silently naming herself a fool. She had no business creeping about in the dark, she fretted. People who did such things deserved whatever unpleasantness they might encounter along the way.

"Gabriella?"

The voice startled her so that, for the beat of a hummingbird's wing, her heart stopped. She squinted, peering into the gloom, stricken to an uncharacteristic silence.

Morgan took shape, shadow by shadow, in the faint glimmer of a candle, reaching up to remove the tallow from its sconce. He held it out, spilling light over her.

"What are you doing?"

Gabriella wished she had not given in to her own impetuous nature and ventured outside her bedchamber. A part of her, the romantic part made up of dreams and wishes, had undeniably hoped to encounter Chalstrey, but the reality was unsettling indeed.

She thought rapidly, desperately. "I was making an escape," she lied, in a burst of inspiration, and saw straightaway that Morgan did not believe her.

That familiar crooked smile lifted a corner of his mouth, and was quelled so swiftly that she couldn't be certain it had ever been there at all. "Tell the truth, Gabriella. To lie is to endanger your very soul."

Gabriella bit her lower lip, gazing woefully at Morgan. "Then I must confess, my lord," she said softly. "I hoped to find you."

"And so you have. Now, what do you want?"

She swallowed, and gathered all her courage. "I want to lie beside you again, and have you kiss me."

8

"**H**eaven help me," Morgan said, as though uttering a prayer, watching Gabriella with an expression of awed dismay. The passageway seemed to yawn around them, dark and cold.

Gabriella held her tongue, and waited.

He took a step toward her, still grasping the guttering candle in one hand, and then halted himself by means of some inner force that seemed barely strong enough to restrain him. "Gabriella," he rasped. She saw then that his face was ravaged by an almost intolerable emotion, one she couldn't begin to comprehend, and caught the smell of rum on his tunic and his breath. "You must not ask this—it is beyond me to hold you and kiss you, and then turn away. Were I to lie with you, this of all nights, I should trust neither myself nor my honor."

The candle Morgan held went out, and he tossed it aside with a murmured imprecation. The darkness seemed to swallow them both, for the other tallows were burning low as well, and giving only a faint specter of light.

"Dear God, Gabriella, do you understand what I'm telling you?"

She swallowed and raised her chin. "Yes," she replied evenly. "I believe that I do." Having spoken so, she extended a hand, and met with Morgan's chest. In an instant, he had grasped her wrist, rather, it seemed, like a seaman anchoring himself in uncertain waters.

Chalstrey uttered a low sound Gabriella could not put a name to, and then, as swiftly as he'd taken hold of her a moment before, swung her off her feet and into his arms. There, in the middle of that deserted corridor, he kissed her, not gently as before, not teasingly, but with a demanding hunger that stirred her very soul.

"If you would remain as you are, Gabriella," he told her, his breath ragged, as if torn from him, "tell me now, and I shall return you safely to your own door."

Gabriella knew what she was doing was rash and probably foolish, as well as sinful, but she didn't care. A moment ago, an eternity ago, she could not have said when, she had come to care for this man in a way beyond explaining. "No," she said simply. "I will not leave you."

Still carrying Gabriella like a prize taken upon a battlefield, Morgan proceeded to a nearby door, which he pushed open with one foot.

Inside, a fire burned low on the hearth, but Gabriella could see naught else. She cared little what manner of room it was; it mattered only that, for a time, however brief, Morgan would belong to her, and she to him. She had decided not to think beyond that single, glorious fact, and it was her own strong will, rather than any unworldly notion, that prompted her choice.

Morgan mounted several steps, onto an unseen dais, and laid Gabriella gently upon a bed as large and soft as

the one she'd left a short while before. After a moment
of utter stillness, on both their parts, he struck a spark
from a flint and lighted a single oil lamp on the night
table.

Gabriella flushed, not from shame but from pride, as
he took long moments to admire her. She was comely of
face and form; this man, standing over her, had taught
her that.

He smiled. "You do not shrink from the light." It was
a comment, not a question.

"I have naught to hide, my lord." In her innocence,
she was like Eve in the garden, with no concept of
shame, though she suspected she might come to know
that emotion intimately as time passed. For now, she
simply didn't care.

Morgan placed one hand on either side of her head
and bent at the waist, so that his face loomed only
inches above hers. The glow of the lamp seemed to ignite something in his eyes, something both primitive
and infinitely tender. "No doubt you speak true, milady,
but I shall have to see that for myself."

Gabriella trembled as Morgan undid the laces at the
bodice of her gown, but there was no modesty in her then,
only a strange, fiery wantonness. She watched him, unblinking, as he spread the garment like the cover of some
great oracle, and gazed in wonder upon her bare breasts.

Then, looking into her eyes, he laughed, low in his
throat. She suspected he was at least partly intoxicated—
she had not seen him so before—and while she supposed
that should have mattered to her, in truth, it did not.

Tenderly, but with a telling skill that could only
have come from much practice, Morgan undressed
Gabriella, and she lay willing and pliant, even eager, be-

neath his hands, well aware that she was teetering on the threshold of the great and mysterious secret that had eluded her for so long.

He sat down on the mattress beside her, still fully clothed, and gathered her breasts against his palms, chafing the nipples with the sides of his thumbs.

The sensation rushed through Gabriella, so exquisite that it made her gasp and arch her back slightly. Her body seemed to know what to expect, to seek it out boldly, in fact, but her mind was full of curiosity.

Morgan chuckled, and bent to nuzzle the peaks of her breasts, first one, and then the other.

Gabriella made a whimpering sound at this, so acutely sweet was this new sensation, and then cried out in stunned delight when Morgan took her into his mouth and suckled.

Instinctively, she plunged splayed fingers into Morgan's hair and held him to her, tossing her head from side to side all the while, certain that such wanting could not long be borne by a mere mortal woman.

When Morgan had taken suckle at both her breasts, with rising greed, he drew back, and began kissing the underside of her jaw, the length of her throat and the thundering pulse at its base, the edges of her collarbone. Every part of her was attuned to him, like a lute to a minstrel, and she tried to guide him back to her nipple.

He laughed, the sound quivering against the flesh at the curve where her neck and shoulder met. "Oh, there is more, my lady, so much more that I must show you."

With that, Morgan began nibbling his way slowly down her breastbone, and every time Gabriella thought he must surely stop, he went further. When he circled her navel with a light pass of his tongue, she gave such a lusty cry that he reached up and laid a hand to her mouth.

Perspiration dampened Gabriella's body, causing her hair to cling to her cheeks and temples and neck, making her belly slick where Morgan tasted it.

He raised his head, drew a deep breath, and let it out. "I am about to have you, Gabriella," he warned gently, "in much the same way I might enjoy a peach at summer's end, or a sweetmeat. You will want to cry out, but you must not, lest you bring the wrath of a certain avenging nun down upon both our heads. Do I have your promise?"

Gabriella nodded, strangely and deliciously frantic and, after a slight hesitation, Morgan removed his hand from her mouth.

In almost the same motion, he burrowed through the silk that sheltered her woman-place to feast there, and Gabriella forgot her name, let alone the promise she had just made. Raising her hips high, in an offering as old as time, she dug her heels into the depths of the bed, tilted her head back upon the pillows, and out of her mouth came a throaty, triumphant, animal sound that she had never dreamed was in her. Her fingers were locked around Chalstrey's head in an instant and purely desperate hold, for if he withdrew, she would not be able to bear it.

His chuckle reverberated through Gabriella from the apex of her femininity, but he did not punish her by pulling back. Indeed, he drew harder upon her, adding intensity to the wonderful, ferocious crescendo building within her, staying with her as she writhed upon the bed, taking more and more until finally the shattering explosion came. Caught in its throes, Gabriella keened with pleasure, like a she-wolf with her mate.

Morgan lifted his head only when she had stopped straining in release. He did not speak until he'd risen, removed his clothes, and allowed her to see him, through half-closed eyes.

"There is more, my lord?" she whispered, disbelieving.

He grinned, but then, just as quickly, grew somber. "Aye, milady." He lay down beside her, gathered her close, brushed musk-scented lips across her temple, which still throbbed in the aftermath of her passion. "I will go slowly, Gabriella," he told her, "but there will be pain."

She pressed strong hands to either side of his face and looked deep into his eyes. "I want to feel it all," she told him fiercely.

"You do not know—"

Gabriella laid a fingertip to the sensual mouth that had given her such astounding pleasure. "Is not the pain a part of the pleasure?"

Morgan sighed, but then he kissed her, very gently but very deeply, and caressed her with his hands. As easily as that, he made her want him again, in a quieter but no less desperate way than before.

He spent a long time preparing Gabriella, and she was touched, for even in her relative innocence she knew this forbearance cost him dearly. She felt his need in every line of his powerful body, saw it in his face, in his eyes, but he would not be hurried.

When at last Morgan parted Gabriella's legs and mounted her, she was dazed, almost delirious with renewed need.

"*Slowly*, Gabriella," he pleaded, his manhood hard and insistent at the portal of the place he would soon conquer.

Gabriella would hear none of caution; if there must be suffering, then she wanted to plunge through it, put it behind her. She wished to please Morgan as thoroughly as he had pleased her, so she slid her hands down his tense back and boldly grasped his buttocks in an attempt to thrust him toward her.

With a long moan every bit as primitive as her own cries had been, Morgan lost control at last, and surrendered to her urgings. He plunged deep into her in one thrust, and breached her maidenhead. The tearing sensation Gabriella felt was swift and severe, but she was hurled far beyond it in the next heartbeat, when something greater took her over. As Morgan moved upon her, Gabriella moved with him, rising and falling as he rose and fell, meeting him stroke for stroke.

This magical exchange went on and on, forever and ever, or so it seemed to Gabriella, but even eternity was not long enough or large enough to contain the unutterable power of the cataclysm that finally engulfed them both

Morgan threw his head back and gave a low shout when the end came, while Gabriella sobbed and clawed at his bare back like a falling climber trying to catch hold. She felt his seed spilling into her even as something clenched over and over again, far inside her, producing a pleasure that was almost too great to endure.

At last, spent, Morgan collapsed beside her, gasping for breath, holding her to him as he turned onto his side. Gabriella clung to him, shuddering as smaller releases caught at her, held her in their grip, and let her go.

"I have surely won damnation this night," Morgan

said haltingly, after a long time, "if I had not earned it already. And it was worth every lick of hellfire."

Gabriella was profoundly aware that they were still joined, and that his staff was growing within her, becoming hard again. She could not help a low, crooning sigh of contented anticipation. "You should not jest about such things, my lord."

Idly, Morgan began to move, grasping her hips to secure her, making long, leisurely thrusts.

"There are matters in this life, Gabriella," he said, "that can only be borne by making jests."

She groaned softly as Morgan drove her slowly toward another storm of sensation, already half swept away, and had neither the strength nor the words to answer.

"Gabriella," Morgan gasped. "Gabriella. What witchery have you worked to render me such a fool?"

"None, my lord," she whispered, and sought his mouth, brushing her lips against his. "I can cast no—ooooh—spells—"

Morgan silenced her, and his kiss was as thorough as his possession of her body. His muffled shouts of pleasure echoed through her, and hers through him, and when, in a burst of fire, they had satisfied each other, they slept.

The sharp whisper of her name brought Gabriella out of the depths of slumber with a jolt. She opened her eyes and saw Morgan smiling down at her, his features rimmed by the first fragile light of dawn.

At first she was dumbfounded, but in the next moment she remembered everything, and her face throbbed with sudden heat. When she would have looked away, Morgan caught her chin in his hand and stayed her.

He smiled at all he read in her eyes and gave her a

quick, mischievous kiss. "Hurry and dress yourself, before Ephriam arrives with my customary razor and pitcher of hot water and sees you lying there, looking sweet and rumpled and very, very beautiful."

Gabriella did not quite know whether to be indignant or flattered, and she wasn't about to linger while deciding. Morgan extended her chemise and gown, which he had so deftly removed the night before, and she snatched the garments from his hands, jumped off the bed, and began wriggling into them.

Handsome as ever, for all his want of barbering, as utterly immodest as a pagan god, Morgan sat in the center of the bed, watching her with an expression of amused appreciation as she struggled with the knotted laces of her bodice.

Finally, he came to the edge of the mattress and, kneeling there, caught hold of Gabriella's hand. He pulled her close, untangled the laces and, before tying them, opened the front of her gown, tugged down her chemise, and teased each nipple into a hard point with the tip of his tongue.

Gabriella, for all her pride, stood trembling during the brief and excruciating, exultant ordeal. Her color must have heightened further still, for she felt as though she'd been taken with fever, and she could not help a soft cry of ecstatic dismay.

She had barely had time to collect herself when, just as quickly, Morgan replaced the top of her chemise, closed her dress, and tied the laces into a swift and tidy bow.

"Go," he said. "Ephriam has attended me for five and twenty years, and he has never tarried a moment in all that time."

Taking care not to tumble off the dais, which would

have been inglorious indeed, Gabriella descended the steps provided and dashed for the door. Footsteps echoed on the stone floor of the corridor, and she looked back at Morgan in horror.

He gestured toward a carved and painted screen in a corner of the room, and she had barely ducked behind it when there came a perfunctory tap at the door, followed by the click of the latch and the creaking of hinges.

Gabriella, huddled behind the folding screen, held her breath and squeezed her eyes shut. The humiliation of discovery loomed, and she did not even dare to pray, for she was in no position to enter a divine petition.

"Did you sleep well, my lord?" she heard Ephriam ask, as he had probably done every morning since his first day in Morgan's service.

"Oh, very well indeed," Morgan replied easily, and there was a certain subtle note in his voice calculated, Gabriella knew, purely to nettle her. She listened, face flaming, as the master of Edgefield Keep moved about the room, no doubt unabashedly naked.

Peering through one of the cracks between the three sections of the screen, Gabriella watched in breathless, unblinking panic as Ephriam mounted the dais and tossed the covers aside, with the obvious intention of tidying the rumpled bed.

"I see you have entertained a guest recently," the servant remarked dryly.

Mortified, Gabriella held her breath, lest she erupt into wild hysteria and give herself away.

She could not see Morgan, but the sounds of splashing water reached her ears, along with his completely arrogant response.

"Aye," he said, in cheerful tones. A faint rasping

sound indicated that he was shaving, and Gabriella harbored a fleeting wish that he would cut his throat. "A ripe and saucy little wench—from the kitchens, I think."

"Indeed," said Ephriam, without conviction, bundling the bedclothes and proceeding to the door, which he opened with apparent ease.

Not until she'd heard the latch snap did Gabriella come out of her hiding place, fuming.

Morgan stood before a small mirror affixed to the wall, razor in hand, face half shaved, clad in naught but a green woolen tunic that made a fetching contrast to his blue eyes. He grinned cordially. "Did I rouse your temper, milady—referring to you as a ripe and saucy wench?"

"Yes!" Gabriella gasped, still stricken almost breathless. Ephriam had nearly seen her, and she was far from convinced that the elderly servant had not suspected something.

The smile broadened. "Good." Morgan turned back to the looking glass and resumed his barbering. "Passion of any sort becomes you. Pray, take your leave, milady, before I woo you back to my bed and raise a scandal fit to blister the chapel walls."

Gabriella could not afford to challenge him, not then, in any case. She flung him a poisonous look, gathered up the skirts of the embroidered gown, and marched to the door. There, after grimacing at the squeal of the hinges, Gabriella peered carefully down the corridor, in both directions, then made a dash for the chamber she had been meant to sleep in.

Dame Johanna had risen, Gabriella saw, with a sinking heart, as she fairly hurled herself into the room. The nun had donned her spare habit and wimple, and stood gazing out the window.

Gabriella stood perfectly still in the center of the floor, at once mortified and quietly defiant. She was nearly twenty, an age when many women had not one child but several, and even though she had hoped her return would go unmarked, she did not regret giving herself to Morgan the way she had.

Dame Johanna turned, regarding her without expression. "Will he marry you, child?"

Gabriella had not thought to inquire, so anxious had she been to flee Morgan's bedchamber without being seen. She bit her lip as a great sorrow filled her. "I do not think so," she said, in a wholly wretched whisper.

"Would you take Chalstrey for a husband, should he offer for you?"

Because she had no dowry, Gabriella had never been called upon to accept or refuse a suitor. And she could make no demands upon Morgan's honor, for she had gone to him willingly, had indeed placed herself in his path and *asked* to lie with him. "He will not," she replied, more forcefully, with her chin set at an unrepentant angle.

"You did not answer my question," Dame Johanna pointed out firmly, taking up her missal. Already the bells in the chapel tower were ringing, though it was not yet light outside, to herald the mass.

Gabriella swallowed the great lump of misery that had swelled in her throat, and blinked back foolhardy tears. There would be no profit in weeping for a circumstance she had brought upon herself. "If I were entitled to choose a husband," she said, "I would want none other than Morgan Chalstrey."

Dame Johanna considered in silence for a long mo-

ment, then nodded and swept toward the door, causing
the flames in the oil lamps to bend in the draft and then
flicker wildly. Only when the nun had gone did
Gabriella allow her tears to flow.

Avendall was alone in his private chambers when the
churl Kettleburn was brought to him and flung without
ceremony over the threshold. The boy was red-haired, a
sure sign of an intractable nature, and late of Edgefield
Keep, which might prove to be a useful thing.

"You are Chalstrey's man," Cyprian said, tossing a
well-chewed chicken bone into the cold grate of his
fireplace. "Pray, do you bring some message, or are you
simply weary of life?"

Kettleburn drew himself up, but it was a wasted effort. "I've left the duke's company," he said, in barely
civil tones.

Cyprian tolerated the impudence only because he
suspected this spot-faced cur could tell him things he
very much wanted to know. "Thrown out, I'm told," he
said, watching the boy through his lashes as he pretended to concentrate on selecting another morsel of
boiled fowl. He waited for Kettleburn's face to blaze
with the same horrendous color as his hair, and then
spoke again. "He's a hard master, is Chalstrey."

Kettleburn said nothing, but he was crimson behind
those spots of his.

"Come, come," Avendall remonstrated, in a cool and
quiet voice, chewing. "You are wasting my time and that
is an offense I do not suffer lightly. Tell me what you
want or get out."

"It's about the woman," Kettleburn allowed, grudg-
ing. "The one we stole."

"Gabriella," Avendall said softly. His whole being was centered on the little traitor now, but he schooled himself not to show interest, and was, as always, successful. He had spies inside Edgefield Keep, and he had been duly advised of Gabriella's arrival, and her formal status as a prisoner. What he had not yet learned, and was desperate to know, was whether or not Edgefield, a legendary seducer of women, had got the chit onto her back.

Avendall's hand tightened convulsively and, he hoped, imperceptibly, around his wine cup. "What do you know about the lady?" he asked, in the smooth, almost cordial fashion that usually served with idiots, snarling hounds, and women.

"That she is more than passing fair," Kettleburn said, eyeing the chicken carcass on Cyprian's trencher. "And that Chalstrey fancies her."

Cyprian took a long time to answer, for he did not trust himself to speak at first. "I see. And does she fancy him in return?"

Kettleburn actually dared to smile, the insolent whelp. Cyprian would have had him whipped for two notes of song from a mule's throat, and he pondered this indication that Edgefield had turned careless in matters of discipline. Perhaps his old enemy had grown lax, upon his belated return to England.

"The lady is as spirited as any mare not yet broken to ride," Kettleburn answered.

Cyprian's right hand ached to clasp the handle of his lash, but because so much was at stake, he controlled every muscle, large and small, in the whole of his body. He knew his face showed not so much as a twitch, his eyes neither flickered nor blinked.

"Not yet broken to ride?" he echoed, as though he did not understand the lad's lewd simile.

"Your lady is well guarded, my lord. By a nun. For all Chalstrey has lain beside her, it was to no purpose but to keep her from the rest of us."

Could it be? Cyprian was hardly able to credit the possibility that Edgefield had left Gabriella untainted— it would be a point of honor, after that disagreement, years ago, over poor Rebecca. Still, might it not be that he, Avendall, had underestimated his chosen bride's moral constancy?

He found himself smiling—the first breach of self-control he had permitted himself throughout the interview.

"Why do you bring me this news?" he asked, reaching for a piece of bread and breaking it between his hands. "What do you hope to gain by betraying your master?"

"I have told you," Kettleburn said coldly. "Chalstrey is not my master. He sent a man to turn me out just after cock's crow, and give me a message as well—if I ever set foot on his lands, he'll spare me no punishment. I didn't even get a chance to bid farewell to a lass or two in the village, I was out that quick."

Avendall considered, hiding his glee behind a passive expression, and called to his bailiff in a deceptively idle way. When the man appeared, he spoke to him quietly.

"Direct this man to the kitchens, where he is to be given a meal. Then send a messenger to Edgefield Keep, bearing my colors. Relay to the duke that I expect him to deliver my bride to Avendall Hall, forthwith, and see that he is advised of my terms: if he fails to comply with my demand, I shall bring an army against him."

Kettleburn beamed, obviously pleased at the prospect of bloodshed. "Chalstrey is weary of war," he said, his pleasure fading to a look of uncertainty. "But he is as proud as Lucifer himself, and he will not receive your words kindly."

"When you've had your bread and wine," Avendall went on, as though Kettleburn had not spoken, "get out and do not show your wretched face within my walls again."

Kettleburn looked stunned, then angry, but he followed the bailiff out, and when the door had closed, Avendall got up to pace.

Gabriella had heard, as had everyone else in the keep, of the approach of a party of men from Avendall Hall. Thus, she contrived to be nearby when the outer gates were opened and a single, expressionless rider passed beneath the portcullis.

Morgan awaited him, and accepted the scroll handed down from the horse without comment of any kind. The combined populace of castle and village watched his face for any hint of the news Avendall's messenger had brought.

At last, Morgan looked up from the parchment and smiled, narrowing his eyes against the bright dazzle of the autumn sun. He held the missive out, as if to hand it back. "Here," he said, "is my reply." With that, he released the heavy paper, and before it could reach the ground, he had drawn his sword and sliced it in twain.

The rider scowled, and raised his voice, that all might hear. "It was my lord Avendall's vow that, should Edgefield refuse to heed his wishes, he will come, with soldiers, and raze this keep, with all who defend it, to the ground."

Morgan's men-at-arms scoffed at this announcement, laughing and elbowing each other, and the children, especially the lads, seemed to think it was all a grand game. There were scattered twitters among the women, but some of them looked as Gabriella felt—terrified.

"They must not take up arms," she whispered to Dame Johanna, standing beside her. "Not for so frivolous a cause!"

"But I fear they shall," the nun replied. Her face was drawn and waxen.

Gabriella knew better than to plead with Morgan; he had not spoken to her, or even looked in her direction, since sending her from his room that morning, while her body still thrummed from his attentions. He may have wanted her in his bed, but he would not hear her counsel.

She slipped away, hurrying unnoticed through the foolish, jovial throng, a frantic and reckless plan forming in her mind.

9

❧

Two hours after Sir Avendall's ultimatum was delivered, Gabriella left Edgefield Keep with a band of pilgrims, who had taken shelter within the castle walls the night before. Wearing Dame Johanna's spare robe and wimple, her pale-gold hair covered and her eyes properly lowered, she walked over the drawbridge and out into the open countryside.

When the small party reached the road, the pilgrims set themselves toward far off London town, while Gabriella made for Avendall Hall. The fresh hoofprints of the messenger's horse, and those of his men's mounts, were all that told her which direction to take, for of course she had not dared make such an inquiry of anyone inside Edgefield Keep.

Walking fast, oft looking back over one shoulder, lest anyone inside the castle had taken notice of a lone sojourner scurrying along the empty road, Gabriella rushed headlong toward her fate.

At twilight, with no sign of Avendall Hall on the horizon, a man appeared, wearing a peasant's coarsely woven clothes and driving a cart pulled by a single gray ox. Gabriella considered running away, but when the carter hailed her as "good dame," she recalled her disguise and inclined her head circumspectly, as she had seen Dame Johanna and the other nuns of St. Swithin's do.

"Will I come soon to Avendall Hall?" she asked, eyeing the hay-filled cart with longing. Her legs were aching with fatigue, her feet burned, and she was filled with misgivings.

The carter gave her a cordial and, at the same time, pitying look. "Nay, good dame—that place is yet seven miles off." He gestured toward the back of the little wagon. "I'm bound there myself, it happens, to fetch back my girl Bess. I can do with some company, if you'll accept a ride?"

"Oh, aye!" Gabriella cried, forgetting to be nunlike, and fairly bounded onto the back of the cart. Feet dangling, she attempted to assume a more pious countenance. "Thank you," she said demurely. "You are very kind."

The old man smiled and swatted the ox with a long stick, and they were moving, jostling and rattling over the rutted track that led to Avendall Hall.

For a time, they talked, mostly about the carter's daughter, a pretty vixen of a decidedly wayward nature, who worked as a kitchen maid and had gotten herself into trouble with a lad from the stables. Avendall's housekeeper, a Mistress Cooper, had no patience with such indiscretions and had given the girl notice to leave or be thrown out with the slop. Word of their daughter's plight had reached Bess's parents by way of a roving peddler, and because the meanderings of such men in-

variably took a very long time, there was no telling what
fate might have befallen the poor creature by then.

Gabriella tried her best to be reassuring, though the
effort did little to distract her from her own problems.
She had left a man she loved for one she was wary of, all
in the hope of averting a battle that was sure to end in
needless bloodshed and, most likely, the death of one or
both men. Mayhap she could reason with Avendall, or
even win his affections.

She had no idea how she would be received, a terrifying prospect in itself, and even if Avendall accepted
her, indeed welcomed her with open arms, she still
faced a grim future. While it was certain that Chalstrey
did not care for her in any lasting way, she certainly
loved him, and would, she suspected, for all the days,
months and years left to her.

If Avendall still wanted her for a wife, Gabriella
would wed him, and suffer the rest of it with all the patience she could muster. If he did not, he would surely
turn her out, leaving her destitute.

She must not think of that possibility yet, she decided
firmly. All that truly mattered was that Avendall's demands
be met, and a bloody conflict avoided. When placed beside that, every other concern seemed small indeed.

Full dark had long since overtaken the travelers when
the ox and cart trundled through a postern gate and
came to stop in a torchlit courtyard of Avendall Hall.

Gabriella thanked the carter, gained her feet, and
squared her shoulders. Then, like a martyr determined
not to tremble before a hungry lion, she started toward
the hall itself, which loomed cold and unwelcoming
against a festive sky, spangled with stars.

After only a moment's hesitation, Gabriella gathered

all her considerable courage and approached the main entrance, where guards were posted, ominous and unsmiling in the stark light of still more torches.

Before she could be challenged, indeed, even before she could explain her identity and her purpose, Sir Avendall himself appeared in the high stone archway. The instant she saw him, she remembered all the disturbing impressions she'd formed when they first met, more than a year before, at the abbey.

He paused on the threshold, assessing her, from head to toe, with a quick, unreadable glance.

Gabriella was not certain that he recognized her, and executed a respectful bob. Then she said clearly, "I am Gabriella Redclift, my lord."

Avendall descended the half dozen broad steps nimbly, but he tendered her no smile of greeting, no romantic kiss pressed to the back of her hand. A muscle in his square jawline bunched and, not for the first time, Gabriella felt not only sorrow and reluctance, but a very great uneasiness as well.

Here was a man who, for all the fine appearance he made, seemed to have no trace of humor or merriment in him. That thought, more than any other, caused Gabriella to wish she had not been quite so hasty in carrying out her plan to set matters aright. It wasn't his barely bridled fury that stunned her—that was natural, given that Morgan had kidnaped his intended wife. No, looking upon Avendall now, Gabriella realized that the poisonous rancor he exuded had little or nothing to do with her.

And everything to do with Morgan.

Gabriella had feared, in her rashness and vanity, that she was a reason for war. In truth, she knew now, she was but an excuse.

"What are you doing, wearing those ludicrous garments?" he demanded, taking a bruising hold on her upper arm.

Afraid before, Gabriella was consumed by indignation now. "Release me at once," she said, digging in her heels when he would have propelled her up the steps. "You are hurting me!"

Avendall glared at her for what seemed a long time, then relaxed his hold. "Do not make a scene," he warned, in a low voice, and the way he spoke was far more threatening than his hurtful grasp had been. "I am the master here, and you will be wise to remember it."

Gabriella subsided, not because she regretted her behavior, but because she knew she couldn't win. Not then, at least.

"Yes, my lord," she said, feigning timidity.

Avendall pressed a hand to the small of Gabriella's back and steered her past the guards and into the vast, echoing chamber that probably served as a great hall. A fire burned low on a hearth in a far corner of the room, and Gabriella longed to stand before it a while, warming her hands as well as her soul, but that was not to be.

Avendall did not slow his pace and, accordingly, she was given no opportunity to dally. As they mounted the main staircase, Gabriella felt cold horror settling over her. Perhaps Avendall was taking her to his bedchamber—it had not occurred to her that he might take such a liberty, so soon—there to claim her as Morgan had done. Only this time, she knew well, the experience would not be so pleasant.

Gabriella considered making a dash for the door, but she knew she'd never get to the base of the stairs, let alone across the great hall and past those grim-looking guards outside.

"Where are we going?" she asked, speaking with all the moderation she could summon, given the fact that she was sure she was about to vomit or swoon. When he didn't answer immediately, she added a tremulous, "My lord?"

"I would examine you," Avendall said, as calmly as if he'd told her his name, or remarked that it was a fair night, or mentioned the color of his favorite horse.

They had gained the top of the staircase, and Gabriella whirled, though with caution. "*Examine* me, my lord? To what purpose—in what way—?" She watched a storm gathering in his face. "Do you mean to count my teeth?"

There was no inflection in his voice, despite the terrible wrath flashing in his eyes. "I am not concerned with your teeth, Gabriella. It is your virtue I should like to assess."

Gabriella felt her eyes widen. Her stomach pitched itself upward into her throat. "God's blood!" she cried, a phrase she had learned from Morgan, but heretofore used only in her head.

Avendall's gaze narrowed, but he let the exclamation pass. "It is not uncommon," he said, very reasonably, but his expression was savage. "I am told you have had bed sport with Chalstrey, at his whim."

Color flooded her face and immediately subsided again, leaving her light-headed. She tried to slip past her tormenter—no attempt to escape seemed too desperate now—but he caught her easily, hooking an arm around her waist and raising her, kicking and struggling, off her feet.

"What is the matter, my lady?" he breathed, close to

her ear. "If you are yet a maiden, you have no cause to fear."

Gabriella did not waste her breath screaming; there was no one to come to her aid. By force of will and no other means, she ceased struggling, as well, in order to conserve her strength for the battle to come.

Avendall carried her into a large, sparsely furnished chamber, set her on her feet, and locked the door behind them.

His captive used that time to look around for a weapon, and found naught. The poker was too far away, and there were no ornaments or small pieces of statuary. Only a chair, too heavy to lift, a table, and, God help her, a bed.

Avendall turned, leaning against the door, and assessed her once more. "Remove that wimple," he said tersely. "It hides your hair."

Gabriella dared not disobey, though she still had no intention of surrendering. In stony silence, she tugged at the plain veil, and her profusion of bright fair hair tumbled free, falling well past her waist.

For the first time in her presence, Avendall smiled. "Beauty makes recompense for so many sins," he said.

Gabriella shivered and then raised her chin. "Whose sins, my lord? Mine or yours?"

"Oh, yours," he replied, with a sort of bitter pleasantry. "Everything short of fornication with Edgefield, that is. That I could not forgive."

Gabriella had never heard the word "fornication," but it was no feat to guess what it meant. When Avendall took a step toward her, she retreated precisely the same distance. "And if perchance I had given myself to another man, besides Chalstrey?"

Avendall made an impatient gesture. "Silence!" he

hissed, and Gabriella's heart fluttered with fear. "There is one way you might spare yourself—and me—the ordeal, of course. You could simply tell me the truth."

At that point, Gabriella decided she had nothing to lose. Either way, Avendall would discover that she was impure, and either way, he would exact revenge. At least if she admitted what she'd done, there would be no reason to "examine" her.

"Very well, then," she said, after drawing a deep breath and letting it out slowly. "I spent the whole of last night in Morgan's bed."

The ensuing silence was worse than shouting, more fearsome than threats. Gabriella stood utterly still, while pride and terror did battle within her, and Avendall stared at her with the eyes of a demon.

When he spoke, his voice was soft. Lethal. "He seduced you, then."

Gabriella's besetting sin was an impulsive nature, and she had yet to overcome it. "No, my lord," she said, just as softly. "I sought him out, and asked him to lie with me."

The instant that foolish admission had left her tongue, Gabriella regretted it, but it was too late. Avendall advanced on her, in a blur of anger, and backhanded her across the face, sending her stumbling backward. She nearly fell, but regained her footing at the last moment.

"I am sorry, my lord," she said, but her contrition was for the heedless words she had spoken, not for the night spent with Morgan, and he seemed to know that.

Seething, Avendall grasped Gabriella by the back of the head, his fingers digging into her skull, and half pushed, half hurled her toward the door.

In the corridor, he grasped her arm, and though the pain made Gabriella wince, she dared not speak. Avendall's rage was such that he might fling her headlong down the great staircase, to lie broken or dying at its foot.

When she could not move fast enough to suit him, he grasped her round the waist again, and carried her the rest of the way. Then he strode across the great hall in the same fashion, and outside, to where the guards stood, pretending not to see what mischief their master was about.

"My horse!" Avendall bellowed, so loudly that Gabriella, still pinned against his side, squeezed her eyes shut. "Now!"

One of the men scrambled to obey his lord's command, and Avendall went on holding Gabriella. It was almost as if he'd forgotten she was there.

She, meanwhile, was trying not to think of all the chastisements he might devise for her, in his wild fury.

Hardly more than a few minutes had passed when the second guard returned, leading an impressive gray stallion.

Avendall tossed Gabriella up into the saddle, then mounted behind her. He was probably an expert horseman, and she had already learned firsthand that he was fearfully strong. If he meant to avenge himself against Morgan, he would make a ferocious opponent.

The stallion's hooves clattered over the paving stones of the main courtyard, and at Avendall's shouted command, the heavy gates swung open.

Gabriella closed her eyes again, and the wind buffeted her face and stole her breath, so rapidly did Avendall drive the enormous horse over the black, winding ribbon of a road. Silently, because she was certain she was going to die, she asked the Virgin to intercede for her, that she might be forgiven for all her sins and re-

ceived into heaven. Or at least spared the singular torments of hell.

When Edgefield Keep came into view, after what
seemed an impossibly long time, Gabriella was at once
relieved and frightened. Would Avendall challenge
Morgan this very night?

She shuddered at the prospect. If that happened,
and Morgan perished at the point of Avendall's sword,
the greater measure of the fault would be hers. She had
come to this place in the hope of making peace between
Avendall and Chalstrey. How had such fine intentions
gone so far awry?

At the base of the drawbridge, which had not been
raised, Avendall reined in the stallion with such force
that it screamed and pranced backward in an attempt to
slip the bit.

"Chalstrey!" Avendall roared. "Come out. I have
brought back your warm-blooded wench!"

"What do you mean, *she's gone?*" Morgan demanded, forgetting, for a moment, that the woman who
had addressed him was a nun.

Dame Johanna stood solidly before him, there in the
great hall, looking unusually ruffled. "I should have suspected," she fretted. "But one of the villagers broke a
leg today, whilst pruning a tree, and there was a babe to
be birthed below stairs—it was only a little while ago
that I returned to our chambers and found the habit
and wimple gone. I suspect that Gabriella put them on
and sneaked out of the keep."

Morgan felt sick, and quietly furious as well. It was
dark, and there were perils abroad—wolves driven out
of the forests by hunger, to stalk sheep and other easy

prey, as well as smugglers and highwaymen and cutthroats of every kind.

He closed his eyes for a moment, fighting to stay
calm. If any harm came to Gabriella, he feared he
would lose his sanity.

"How could she have gotten away?" he murmured,
more to himself than Dame Johanna. He was reeling,
and could not seem to think straight, an alarming devel-
opment in its own right. After all, Morgan was a seasoned soldier and strategy was his greatest gift. "I've
had every gate watched since we arrived."

The nun looked impatient. "Did I not say, my lord,
that my spare habit and wimple are gone? Gabriella
must have left with that group of pilgrims, wearing my
garments. I'd say she's gone to Avendall Hall."

The horrible truth of Dame Johanna's words satu-
rated Morgan's flesh and seeped into his bones. "God's
blood—she wouldn't!" He forgot himself, gripped
Dame Johanna's shoulders, and shook her. "Would she?"

Dame Johanna sighed. "I fear so, my lord. She was
there when the message came, and witnessed your response. I'm certain Gabriella believes herself to be the
cause of the trouble, and therefore the solution, as well.
She hopes to prevent your death, sir, and Avendall's as
well."

Morgan felt the blood drain from his face as he considered all the things Avendall might do to Gabriella, especially if he suspected that she'd shared another man's
bed. And Gabriella was just forthright enough, just
gullible enough, to admit the truth, if Cyprian asked.

He shouted a summons to the guard outside his
counsel chamber, and when the man appeared, gave a
terse order that his horse be saddled immediately.

Dame Johanna grasped his arm with both hands. "My lord, you must see reason—Avendall will not admit you, unless to do murder! But I would surely be received—"

"And what would you do then?" Morgan rasped, wrenching free of her hold. "Preach a sermon? I know Avendall as you do not, dame, and I give you my vow— he will not heed the gentle reproaches of a nun!"

"You are overwrought—"

"Aye," Morgan hissed, striding toward the open doorway. "I am that and much more."

Dame Johanna squeezed past and stood before Morgan, arms outflung, a determined barrier. If the circumstances had not been so dire, he might have laughed at the bold spectacle she made.

"I beg of you, my lord," she cried, "do not be rash— seek counsel with your best men—"

Morgan made a scathing bow. "Due to your own rash nature, good dame, the ablest and most valuable man in my company is probably lying in the infirmary at St. Swithin's, if the wolves haven't already devoured him, if thieves didn't set upon him before he could even reach the abbey gate, and *if* you didn't kill him with that stone!"

Dame Johanna winced at his words, but she stood her ground. She might have mentioned the persistent rumors that Sedgewick had deliberately chosen not to return to his employ, but she was too wise for that. "As Avendall will surely kill you!" she replied.

Morgan set her aside forcibly and strode past. He had gotten no farther than the courtyard when a lad of eight or nine years came running up from the village, gasping for breath.

"My lord," the child cried, flinging himself against

Morgan in his panic. "My lord, it's Avendall—I'm to tell you he has brought the woman Gabriella with him!"

Morgan steadied the boy in a distracted motion, then broke into a run himself. A small crowd had gathered before the gates, but they were still shut fast.

"Open them!" he shouted to the gatekeepers.

"It may well be a trick, my lord," one man offered tentatively, but the gates were already creaking on their enormous iron hinges.

Morgan bounded through the opening and stopped cold at the top of the drawbridge. At its base was Avendall, mounted on a lathered charger. Gabriella was there as well, hair loose and windblown, eyes wide with fear in the thin light of the stars and the red glimmer of the torches carried by the men gathered behind Morgan.

"I was beginning to think you weren't interested," Avendall taunted, wrenching Gabriella out of the saddle with one arm and holding her by the waist, suspended several feet off the rough timbers of the drawbridge. If he dropped her, she might easily fall into the empty moat, which was treacherously deep and littered with sharp stones, or be trodden upon by the fitful stallion. "Do you not want her, Edgefield? Mayhap you have found other amusements, now that your true purpose has been met?"

Morgan was a soldier, and his long experience served him well, in that situation. If he lost his head, Gabriella might so easily lose her life, or be grievously hurt.

He spoke quietly. "Tell me what answer you want to hear, Cyprian," he said, "and I will render it gladly."

Avendall threw back his head and laughed, and the stallion nickered and danced, straying dangerously near the edge of the bridge. To her credit, Gabriella kept her peace, staring mutely at Morgan, and clinging to Aven-dall's imprisoning arm with both hands.

Cyprian stopped laughing as suddenly as he'd begun—he was mad with jealous fury—and growled, "Did you think I'd be content with your leavings?"

Morgan took a cautious step forward, one hand rest-ing lightly on the hilt of his sword. "Have you become so poor a fighter, since last we met, that you must use a woman as a shield?" he countered evenly. He must speak neither too loudly nor too softly, must issue nei-ther a challenge nor a concession.

Avendall cursed and then, without warning of any kind, hurled Gabriella away from him. She went sprawl-ing on the timbers, and Morgan approached her calmly, offering her a hand without looking at her.

Indeed, his gaze was fixed on Avendall, and he ut-tered just one word.

"When?"

Avendall understood readily, as Morgan had known he would. "Tomorrow at midday," he answered. He drew his dagger and pointed toward the half-opened gates at Morgan's back. "Lances, in your own lists. I should not wish there to be an inconvenient distance between the place where you fall and your grave, my lord Edgefield."

Gabriella stood beside Morgan, saying nothing, but he felt her trembling, her innate nobility, and her fear. Out of the corner of his eye, he saw a tear trickle down her cheek.

Morgan would not be baited; this, among other things, was his advantage. "So be it," he agreed, his fingers open-ing and closing idly, and with longing, over the sword hilt.

With a nod and a long, inscrutable look at Gabriella,

Avendall reined the horse away and rode off into the darkness.

Gabriella was indeed wearing Dame Johanna's robe, though her trailing, starlit hair was evidence that she'd lost the wimple somewhere along the way. She looked up at Morgan with an expression of such abject misery that the blistering lecture he'd drawn breath for dissolved in his throat.

"Did he hurt you?" he asked.

"He handled me roughly," Gabriella acknowledged, with a typical mixture of truth and pride, "but it is no matter—I am safe now."

Morgan gestured toward the gates with a mocking grandeur, and Gabriella preceded him inside, her chin high, her spine straight.

Behind her, Morgan shook his head. Tomorrow, or the day after that, he would instruct the Lady Gabriella on the finer points of prudence, humility, and feminine obedience. Just then, however, he wanted only to attend to any wounds Avendall might have inflicted and, should Gabriella prove willing, make love to her so tenderly, so thoroughly, as to drive the trials of this night from her thoughts.

Gabriella paid no mind to the villagers who stood watching as she and Morgan passed. Nor did she concern herself with the soldiers in the courtyard or the servants inside the keep itself. She was bound for Chalstrey's bed; she knew it, and so did they. And Gabriella did not care.

She had but one desire, and that was to lie safely in Morgan's arms. She would not think of tomorrow, she promised herself, until it was upon her, with all its terrible danger.

When they had reached Morgan's chamber—what a contrast it made, with its blazing fire, its colorful tapestries, its rugs and splendid furnishings, to Avendall's spare cell—Chalstrey settled her in a chair and handed her a cup brimming with wine.

As she sipped, holding the drink in both hands lest she drop it due to trembling, he touched her tangled hair once, gently. Almost reverently.

"I'll only be away a little while," he said.

Gabriella wanted to beg him to stay, but she was too proud and too weary. She nodded and lowered her eyes, so he would not see how much she needed him.

True to his promise, Morgan was back only minutes later, carrying a gown of blue silk, embroidered in gold thread. He laid the wondrous garment across her lap and crouched before her, to look up into her face. Setting aside the wine cup, which she had filled and emptied twice already, he took her hands in his.

"You are so cold, my lady," he said, with a concern she found almost unbearable for its beauty, and because it was so at variance with his normal cunning and his fierce strength.

Gabriella blinked back hot tears. She was used to being scolded, and nearly impervious to it, but she had no defense against tenderness. That had been a rare thing in her life, except with her sisters, and they, for all their devotion, had been as lost as she was.

"I am sorry, my lord," she fretted. "I but wished to help, and instead, I made everything worse."

Morgan laid a fingertip over her lips. "Shhh," he said, with a smile. "I will say all the things you're saying to yourself another time. Leave them to me. For now, I would look after you."

Gabriella sniffled, and another tear raced, unchecked, down her cheek. "I think I should find it easier, my lord, if you ranted and raved, and named me all manner of fool."

Morgan rose to his full height, a faint smile resting briefly on his lips, and then several servants came in, keeping their eyes averted and carrying a round tub fashioned of copper and brass. After setting their burden down before the hearth, they hurried out again.

Gabriella's eyes widened; she had never seen anything so sinfully alluring as that bathtub, glittering in the light of the fire.

Morgan busied himself with minor tasks, such as unfastening his swordbelt, kicking off his boots, taking a portion of wine and sipping from it in reflective silence.

Presently, the same servants returned, as circumspect as before, bringing buckets of warm water. They filled the beautiful tub and swiftly took their leave.

This time, Morgan closed and locked the door, and Gabriella's heart, already overworked that night, picked up an extra beat.

Morgan came to her, knelt again, and tugged off her leather boots. Then he stood, and pulled her to her feet in a careful motion, to strip away her stolen robe, and the chemise beneath it.

In the light of the fire, he went over every inch of her skin, searching out bruises, kissing each one. She was shaking, and not with cold, when he stood her in the lovely, warm tub.

Using a soft cloth and perfumed soap, that rarest of luxuries, Morgan bathed Gabriella, and then she sank into the water, to soak, and he brushed her hair until all the snarls were gone, and it glistened.

When that small ritual had been completed, Morgan

raised Gabriella upright again, and dried her in a caress-
ing way that drew her blood surging to the surface of
her flesh and set her every nerve to ashiver. Just when
she was sure she would not be able to stand on her own
feet for another moment, but must surely swoon, he
lifted her easily into his arms and carried her to his bed.

"The choice is yours to make, Gabriella," he said,
when he had laid her upon the smooth, warm sheets. "If
you prefer it, I'll sleep in a chair, next to the fire."

She shook her head. "I would have you here, my
lord," she whispered. "Beside me."

10

❧

Gabriella lay sleeping next to Morgan, a pagan god-
dess as yet unaware of her singular powers. Her face,
though bruised where Avendall had struck her, held
that look of serene triumph only the recent and thorough adoration of a lover, indeed a worshiper, could inspire. The well-shaped, slightly swollen mouth, so ready
with an impertinence when Gabriella was awake, was
curved into the faintest, most mysterious of smiles.

Lying on his side, propped up on one elbow as he ad-
mired her, Morgan felt a helpless wrenching sensation,
brutal and quick, in the deepest and most private region
of his soul.

The smile that touched his own lips was bitter and
fleeting. *But you have no soul, Chalstrey,* he reminded
himself, *and no heart.* Rebecca had taken both of those
things with her when she died. Too, he was a soldier,
and not given to sentiment. When the king beckoned, as
he inevitably would, Morgan would have to go.

Gabriella stirred and made a soft sound, something
between a whimper and a very intimate sigh. The

moonlight played over her bare breasts, and Morgan's groin tightened almost painfully as he recalled the delight of suckling her, feeling her hands moving, frantic, in his hair, hearing the pleas he suspected no torment on earth could have caused her to utter, in any other circumstances.

Morgan traced the fine aristocratic line of her perfect nose with the lightest possible pass of a fingertip. Even as he named himself a rogue for using the little minx the way he had, and an idiot for being used in return, he wanted her again. Desperately.

He bent and nibbled at the peak of one breast, and then the other.

Gabriella moaned and her heavy lashes fluttered. "Morgan," she whispered, and sighed. It was not a reprimand, but an invitation, soft and sweet and too tempting for a mere mortal to foreswear.

Morgan mounted Gabriella, rested upon her lightly, smoothing her wild, silken hair back from her forehead. And then he uttered words he had never said to another woman, though he had had many.

"I need you," he admitted, with a difficulty that surprised even him.

She opened her wondrous chameleon eyes, made a crooning sound that was his undoing, and raised her hips to welcome him.

Morgan surged inside her, with a low, grateful cry, and she received him eagerly, moving with him, her body as supple and graceful as a willow branch in a spring breeze. She murmured tender words as he rode her, his pace slow and measured at first, then faster, deeper, more demanding.

When at last she wrung his seed from him, in a series

of ecstatic bursts so intense as to sunder soul from body, Gabriella met him boldly in the midst of the fire, straining and sobbing in release beneath him.

He collapsed beside her, at long last, utterly depleted, satisfied as he had never been before this one particular woman had come into his life. As he tumbled helplessly into sleep, his last grasp on a crumbling and slippery ledge of thought was to wonder how he would endure the inevitable leave-taking when it came.

Gabriella rose and dressed hastily the following morning, upon finding herself alone in the master's bed, for the din of an army preparing for battle seemed to echo off the cold stone walls of the castle. Whilst winding her troublesome hair into two plaits and then weaving both into a coil at the crown of her head, she stood at the window, watching servants scurry back and forth across the main courtyard on urgent and wholly mysterious errands.

Morgan's chamber was highly placed, and Gabriella could see the main gates from where she stood, as well as the lists, where the joust would be held. Men were already busy there, preparing the field, while others swarmed over the rickety seats reserved for important spectators. Still others made mock war with swords and poles, and the archers, not to be outdone, erected their targets and were even then at practice. Clearly, the planned duel between Chalstrey and Avendall had grown into a full-fledged tournament.

A rush of dizzying fear fairly swamped Gabriella as she imagined the multitude of horrors this acursed day might hold, and her fingers were white where she grasped the window casing when Dame Johanna entered. Mercifully, no mention was made of the obvious fact that Gabriella had passed the night in that room.

"Look—there in the distance," the nun said, taking her place beside Gabriella.

It was a bright, chilly morning, and Gabriella squinted against the blazing dazzle of the sun. Then, far off, on the road she had traveled herself only a day before, she saw an approaching procession—Avendall, mounted upon that demon horse of his. A contingent of men-at-arms followed close behind, some wearing armor, some carrying red and gold banners that fluttered in the bracing wind.

Gabriella shivered, and brought her gaze back within the castle walls, searching for Morgan. "Where is he?" she fretted, and was not aware that she'd spoken aloud until Dame Johanna answered.

"Edgefield is in the great hall, where his armor is arrayed for his inspection. Quite a display it makes, too—the squires have been up all the night, rubbing a shine onto the stuff."

"I am sore afraid," Gabriella confessed, turning to her friend.

"Then you are a sensible young woman after all. You do not always comport yourself so."

Gabriella lowered her eyes for a moment, before meeting Dame Johanna's gaze. "I am most sinful," she blurted miserably, "and I shall surely burn in hell for brewing this trouble between Chalstrey and Avendall!"

"Child," Dame Johanna reprimanded gently, "you cannot be blamed for that. You must know that the enmity here took root long, long ago."

"What if Morgan is killed?" Gabriella could hardly bear to consider the possibility, but it was very real. She, after all, had seen the true scope of Avendall's rage, had experienced it firsthand. She touched the bruise that marked her right cheek—the hurt Morgan had kissed in the night, and sworn to avenge.

"We must pray that he is spared," the nun said. She was paying no attention now to Avendall's promenade, just reaching the base of the drawbridge, but instead watching Gabriella. "Indeed, we shall make petition that, if God wills, both men shall live to look back upon this day and shake their heads at the price they might have paid for their arrogance and pride." She paused, plainly reluctant to go on and, at the same time, determined. "We shall not speak of sin, you and I, for it is a natural thing for a man and a woman to lie together. But what of your future, Gabriella? What if Chalstrey gets a babe on you?"

Gabriella turned from the window, but not before seeing the gates of Edgefield Keep swing open to admit Avendall and his finely dressed entourage. Avendall, who contrived even then to bring death within those seemingly inviolate walls, to strike down the man who was the heart of Gabriella's soul.

"If I carry Chalstrey's babe," Gabriella said, quietly fierce, "I shall count myself as blessed, whether I am wife or mistress."

"And what of the babe? If a lad, will he honor you, when he's grown to manhood and must stand by helpless while other sons, born within a marriage, claim Edgefield's lands, his name? If a woman-child, will she be wed to a noble husband, or used as a pawn in some political gambit or given away for a courtesan?" When Dame Johanna saw that her questions had struck their target, she went on, more gently. "In any case, Gabriella, you are not suited to be a mere ornament, a partner only in bed sport. No, my child, not you. Your passions are too fierce, and your pride too great, for such a frivolous and empty existence. You require a man who will give you a firm place in the center of his life, and you will never be content, no matter what you may be thinking now, with anything less than the whole of his devotion. Have you forgotten why you were so eager to come to Cornwall in the first place?"

Gabriella stared at her friend, stricken. There could be no denying Dame Johanna's words: while Morgan's lovemaking was indeed magical, and able to transport her well beyond the bonds of earth, she knew that, alone, it would not be enough to sustain her. She was strong, and possessed of a good mind, and since the beginning of her adventures, that day on the king's road, she had known that she needed to use those attributes, and others, to their fullest.

"You cannot mean to suggest that I should wed Avendall?" she whispered. "He has spurned me—did you not see him fling me at Morgan's feet last night?"

Dame Johanna compressed her lips into a line, as she was wont to do when vexed or troubled. "Avendall is a fiend, and I would not see you tied to one such as he. But you court disaster, Gabriella, by sharing the bed of any man who will not take you to wife."

Tears stung Gabriella's eyes. Even if Morgan survived today's melee, the day would soon come when she would be forced to bid him farewell. It would be better to return to faraway Redclift Hall, and take up the management of her mother and stepfather's failing estate, than to remain at Edgefield Keep without him.

Bleakly, she nodded, to let Dame Johanna know she understood. Then, together, they left the bedchamber and made for the great hall.

Morgan barely acknowledged Gabriella's presence, so caught up was he in the preparations for that day's blood sport. This from a man who had shuddered in her arms only the night before, and confessed that he needed her.

Gabriella was too proud by half to demand his attention; she might not have seen Morgan standing there for all the notice she paid him. Instead, she swept haughtily past, toward the outside stairway, on her way to the lists, where she meant to examine the benches where the spectators would sit.

Morgan brought her to a dignified halt with a single good-natured, "Gabriella!"

One would not have guessed, from his tone, that he might be mere hours from a grisly death—indeed, he sounded hardy, even cocky. Incensed that an otherwise ingenious man could be so thickheaded, Gabriella turned, cheeks warm, to face him. Dame Johanna paused beside her.

Gabriella inclined her head in the fashion convention demanded, for Morgan was, after all, master of Edgefield Keep and liege lord to all who lived within its walls, but stopped short of the deep curtsy she would have made for any other man of his rank. Nor did she utter the expected, "Yes, my lord?"

Morgan approached her, frowning slightly, and to Gabriella's private chagrin, the mere proximity of the man caused her pulse to quicken. When she did not lift her eyes to meet his—she viewed him through her lashes—he curved a finger under her chin and made her look at him. Heat surged through her, so sudden and so consuming that it took her breath away.

"Where are you bound, my lady, in such a grand hurry?" Morgan inquired, not unkindly.

"I am restless this morning, my lord," Gabriella replied hesitantly. "I mean to inspect the lists."

At this, a low ripple of masculine laughter swelled behind Morgan, making it plain that the two men-at-arms and four squires in attendance had been listening to the exchange. Morgan quelled their amusement by turning his head to sweep them up in a brief glance. Then he was looking at Gabriella again, but mercifully he was no longer touching her, and she could breathe properly once more, and trust her heart not to pound its way through her chest and fly off like a falcon taking wing for the hunt.

"The lists?" Chalstrey inquired.

Gabriella was red with an agitation she understood only too well—it had naught to do with indignation now, and everything to do with the violent passions Morgan stirred in her with such damnable ease. "Actually, it is the seats for the spectators that interest me, my lord," she said awkwardly. "I glimpsed them from my windows, and it seems they might be unstable, and cause injury to those who sit upon them during the—during the confrontation."

A slight smile raised one corner of the mouth Gabriella had kissed with such abandon in the hours just past, and the memories caused a delectable discomfort in the region of her body Morgan had conquered so masterfully.

"That is your greatest concern?" he asked softly.

Gabriella met his gaze at last, and let all her misery and all the resultant ill temper to show in her face. "No, my lord. I fear, instead, that you will be skewered on the point of a lance like a skinned hare on a spit."

The low, nervous sound of mirth rose from the small gathering at the trestle table where Morgan's armor lay, like the gleaming, sundered parts of some manlike

creature forged of metal, but this time he did not reprimand the men. Instead, he glared at Gabriella, his eyes
like blue flint.

"Do not fear for me, my lady," he said, in a soft and
yet scathing tone, measured out to her word by word. "I
am an able soldier, and can acquit myself with honor
against the likes of Cyprian Avendall."

"Oh," Gabriella replied, matching him look for look
and tone for tone, just as she had matched him for
thrusts and stamina in his bed the night before, "then it
shall be Avendall who is skewered instead. I am much
comforted by this news!"

Morgan's nose was an inch, mayhap less, from hers. "As
you should be, given what that whore's whelp did to you!"

"Aye, 'tis true that I have no liking for Avendall. But I
would not repay him with a vengeance that is God's alone
to bestow! Now, if you will kindly give me leave, I will
make for the field, as I had intended in the beginning."

"Go!" Morgan growled, with a furious gesture of one
hand.

"Mayhap you should give the wench a sword and
armor, my lord," remarked one of the men-at-arms. "I
vow she could hold her own against Avendall's forces
with no help from any of us."

"Silence!" Morgan bellowed, and Gabriella, instead
of retreating, stood toe to toe with him.

"I would ask you, sir, not to shout," she shouted.

He glared down at her. "You do try my patience!"

Gabriella raised her chin. "Good," she said. "The day
is not wasted then!"

"Come," Dame Johanna interceded firmly, taking
Gabriella's arm.

"They called me a wench!" Gabriella protested, addressing both the nun and Morgan, as she was pulled away toward the door.

Dame Johanna smiled, but offered no comment on the exchange that had just taken place in the great hall. "I must look in on a new babe, in the village, and see to his mother as well. You are much distracted—pray, have a care, Gabriella, that you do not stray into the path of a charger."

Gabriella nodded distractedly, still smarting from the conflict with Morgan, and stormed off toward the lists.

Seeing the girl march across Chalstrey's courtyard, her color high around the bruise he had inflicted with his own hand, and the hood of her garment tumbling back to reveal her shining, honey-colored hair, Avendall felt the sting of regret. Nor was it the first time he had done so, since his rash actions in the night.

He dismounted and handed the reins of his stallion to one of his own attendants, his gaze following Gabriella's angry progress.

God's blood, Avendall thought, he had been a dunce's dunce, handling her the way he had. Worse than stupid.

Avendall strode after the chit, on impulse. He did not mean to apologize, never that; however alluring, the wench was soiled and therefore unfit to be his bride and the mother of the magnificent sons he would sire. Still, he wished he had not been so hasty in casting her off— she would have made a fine bed partner, for one night or a thousand, and how better to nettle Chalstrey than make the fullest use of his current favorite?

"Demoiselle," he called after her, somewhat hoarsely, like a nervous stable boy attempting to charm a comely kitchen maid.

She turned, and again he marveled at his idiocy—Gabriella had come to him, offered herself as his wife. And because he had been unable to control his rage—the shortcoming had caused him grief on too many other occasions to be casually dismissed—he had cost himself not only the exquisite pleasures of her body, but the opportunity to exact a dear price from his old enemy.

Avendall watched with veiled enjoyment as recognition, then disbelief, played in the minx's perfect features. "Good morning, my lady," he said, sketching a small but cordial bow.

Gabriella gave him a look fit to curdle the milk in a cow's udder, then whirled to walk away.

He stopped her by catching hold of her arm, but gently this time, despite the frustration that welled up within him, for he was only too aware that Chalstrey's men were everywhere, and surely looking on with interest.

"Pray, my lady, allow me to make my poor amends for the unfortunate events of our last encounter." Avendall spoke pleasantly, with what he hoped was a friendly light in his eyes, but in truth he was as outraged by the girl's insolence as before, and the yearning to give her the sound thrashing she deserved was a pulsing ache within him.

Gabriella glared at his gloved hand, still grasping her arm, until he removed it. "Pray do not lay hands upon me again," she warned. "I have only to scream, and you will be pierced with a dozen arrows before your knees buckle."

Avendall struggled wildly for control, and his hold on his temper was tenuous indeed. "You have a great deal of confidence in the abilities of your lover's men," he said smoothly. "But mind you, demoiselle—I have not come to Edgefield Keep alone, and my own soldiers are equal to my defense. Surely you would not care to witness more bloodshed than you will be called upon to see when Chalstrey and I meet in the lists hardly more than an hour from now."

She swallowed, though her eyes—her wonderful, ever-changing eyes—still flashed with the obvious and somehow enticing desire to put a dagger through his heart. "What is it that you want of me?"

Avendall smiled. "I think you know. And mayhap I will have it, if today's contests are decided in the manner I predict. Who will save you, sweeting, from becoming the spoils of battle when I have finished Chalstrey once and for all?"

Her shudder was visible, and Avendall delighted in it, as he delighted in the sensual promise of her high, full breasts, her supple, pliant body, her shapely hips. Taming her contentious spirit would be a difficult but most engaging task.

"There is every chance, sir, that Lord Edgefield will finish you," she pointed out, with a calmness he knew was feigned. "Then the spoils would belong to the devil, I should think."

Avendall wanted to slap her, to bruise the other side of her lovely, impertinent face, and yet his regret over tossing her aside so hastily was greater than ever. He would prevail in the lists—he must prevail—for then there would be no one to stop him from reclaiming the woman who belonged, by rights, to him. She would grace his bed as his mistress; she owed him that and more.

He committed no violence, but smiled instead, and continued. "I shall bed you before the moon rises," he promised, "but be warned, milady—you will not find my caresses so tender as Chalstrey's, nor my discipline so lax."

Gabriella spat at him, full in his face, and briefly Avendall thought he would throttle the little whore, right there, with most of the populace of Edgefield Keep watching, but he was restrained by the anticipation of subduing her. And by the weight of a soldier's hand upon his shoulder.

"Pray, my lord, do not be rash. You will surely have satisfaction in the lists."

Avendall did not need to look to know it was Withcomb, his most able archer and horseman, who had interceded. No one else in his company would have dared to step in.

"Aye," Avendall responded hoarsely, his eyes narrowed as he watched Gabriella's expression change altogether. "See to the others, Withcomb. I am recovered from my lapse."

Withcomb walked away, leading his horse behind him.

Gabriella spoke in an almost civil tone. "You still have the power to stop this," she said. "Chalstrey will not, but perhaps you are the wiser, for all your wretched temper."

Avendall folded his arms; he had somehow gained the advantage, and he meant to make the most of it. "What would you have me do?"

"Gather your men and ride back to Avendall Hall. Now. And let there be no fighting, no bloodshed—no death."

"And shame myself before my own men, not to mention my oldest enemy and all his vassals? What profit is there in such a grand but fatuous gesture?"

She bit her plump lower lip for a moment; her mouth

was chafed—probably from the roughness of Chalstrey's morning beard, or from repeated kisses. Damn the pair of them—they would answer for what they had done.

"I should go with you, to Avendall Hall," Gabriella said, in a small voice, and after an almost endless pause.

"As appealing as I find that idea, do you honestly think Chalstrey would countenance such a noble sacrifice for even a moment?" He could not resist touching her, running a light finger over the bruise he had left upon her cheek. Without waiting for her reply, he went on. "Mayhap you believe me to be a fool, my lady, but I know trickery when I meet it. You would rather lie with Lucifer himself, methinks, than go to my bed—alas, your preferences matter not, since you shall most assuredly part your thighs for me—but I am much offended that you hoped to deceive me. Did you not spit upon me? Did you not taunt me, only moments ago, with the threat of Chalstrey's victory on the field?"

"I was hasty," she said, with an effort at meekness.

Avendall laughed. "Oh, indeed," he replied. "Mayhap your young sister will be more tractable." He relished the spectacle of Gabriella's horror.

"What do you mean?" she demanded.

He smiled. "I have sent for the sweet, malleable one—I believe her name is—yes—Elizabeth. We will be wed upon her arrival—and this bride, I can promise you, will not be stolen before she reaches my side."

Gabriella was pale as death, and she swayed slightly on her feet. "Not Elizabeth," she pleaded. "She is but sixteen, and childlike in her ways—"

"As I prefer," he said. Out of the corner of his eye, Avendall saw Chalstrey striding toward them, and lowered his hand to his sword hilt in an easy, idle motion.

Should Edgefield challenge him, there in the center of the courtyard, he would gladly fight.

Heedless of Chalstrey, Gabriella clutched at Avendall's arm with both hands. "You must not take Elizabeth to wife," she cried. "She will surely perish—I will not allow it!"

Avendall ignored her, and shifted his full attention to his host and opponent,

Chalstrey, standing beside Gabriella now, glared at her hands, still curved around Avendall's forearm, and although she did not glance in his direction, it was as if she felt the heat of his anger. She sprang back, suddenly, trembling,

"I pray," she said, "that Chalstrey kills you!"

Avendall's gaze was locked with that of his foe, though he addressed his response to Gabriella. "You had best hope that God hears your petition, my lady," he said, "for you will pass the best of your days—the nights go without saying—as my whore. You might console yourself, I suppose, with the knowledge that when I am with you, your delectable young sister will enjoy a respite from her wifely duties."

Gabriella lost her composure completely then, as Avendall had meant for her to do, and she flung herself at him with a catlike shriek, a scratching, hissing, biting blur of furious woman. He laughed at the few blows she managed to land before Chalstrey grabbed her from behind, curving an arm around her slender waist, and hauled her off.

Edgefield held the struggling chit easily, sparing her hardly so much as a glance. "Be still," he told her, only to be rewarded with a shin blow from her heel and fresh attempts to break free.

Admirably calm, Chalstrey swore and then called out, summoning someone named Jocko. A wary-looking scoundrel came forward out of the small throng gathered about the three of them to gape and murmur.

"Take milady to the counsel chamber," Edgefield snapped, thrusting the twisting, half-wild woman into Jocko's arms, "and keep her there until I order her release."

"No!" Gabriella cried. "No, Morgan, please—you mustn't lock me up—"

"Another moment's delay," Edgefield said to the unfortunate Jocko, ignoring the wench and never looking away from Avendall's face, "and you will have cause for regret!"

Jocko needed no further convincing, and hurried away, grappling comically to contain the flailing girl, who continued to plead with Chalstrey not to imprison her.

"The lady made me an interesting offer," Avendall said, when the soldier and the girl had mounted the outside staircase and vanished into the keep. Her shouts echoed through the cold, sun-sparked air. "She offered me her virtue, such as it is, to leave Edgefield Keep without facing you on the field."

Avendall would have predicted that this announcement would infuriate his enemy, and Chalstrey's response proved him right.

Edgefield made to draw his sword, then evidently thought better of it. His tension, his will to fight, without delay, was palpable, but Chalstrey was a man of honor, for all his other faults, trained from infancy to be a knight of the realm. With a motion of one gloved hand, mocking in its grandeur, he invited Avendall to precede him to the lists.

The two men walked toward the field side by side, and no more words passed between them. Their armor was brought, and the ritual of donning each piece began. Their horses were led onto the field and they were helped to mount, and then the heavy lances were handed up.

Avendall took his position at one end of the lists, Chalstrey at the other.

The long-awaited reckoning was near at hand, and Avendall was much pleased.

Gabriella finally squirmed out of Jocko's tentative grasp in the upper corridor and, while he was still groping to regain his hold, she dashed out of reach and went hurtling in the opposite direction, holding her skirts high lest she trip.

Jocko was a soldier, and fit, but he was also stout and very muscular. Strength was his best attribute, not speed. Gabriella, always a fleet runner, slipped away and gained distance as she fairly flew down the main staircase.

"Hold!" Jocko yelled, almost pleading, as she shot across the great hall, down another set of steps, and back out into the courtyard. "Please, my lady—"

Gabriella was sorry to elude poor Jocko, for she knew he would be in sore straits when Morgan learned he had failed in his duty—should Morgan survive the folly about to take place on the field, that is. She could not prevent the conflict, and would not have done so, knowing what wickedness and cruelty Avendall planned for her gentle sister. Indeed, she thought herself capable of killing the man personally, had she the means.

No, Gabriella wanted to be present for only one reason: she loved Morgan Chalstrey, whatever his feelings toward her. If he triumphed, she would be there to share, if not to celebrate, the victory. And if he were struck down, she would run to Morgan's side—no one lived who could stop her—and gather him into her arms.

Avendall might drag her away, but not before she had pledged her heart and soul, for all of time and eternity, to the lord of Edgefield Keep.

11

⚜

The first clash of steel and wood struck Gabriella like a blow, reverberating through bone and muscle as she ran toward the lists; it was as though she herself had just met full speed with the point of a lance. Tears burned her eyes, and her breath grabbed painfully in her throat, but she kept on, fixed on her destination, heedless of anyone who might be in pursuit.

At last Gabriella reached the field and stood gasping at its edge.

Morgan's armor glittered like silver in the frigid sun, as did Avendall's. Both men wore visors, and carried their lances as though they weighed no more than a goose quill. Their horses were fretful, but not from fear, Gabriella thought; no, the stallions shared their masters' thirst for battle.

The insight displaced some of Gabriella's terror, and a certain disgust crept in. They were like stags in the forest, Morgan and Avendall, determined to clash at every opportunity, and with as much violence as possible.

The combatants took their places at opposite ends of

the list, paused, and then raced forward at a pace that chilled Gabriella's blood. She forgot everything then, Avendall's plans to wed Elizabeth and take Gabriella herself for an unwilling concubine, *everything* but the next deafening collision of men and horses.

When it came, it was so shattering to look upon that Gabriella gasped and covered her mouth with one hand. The lances met and parried, then engaged again, and upon that second impact Morgan's splintered like a twig against Avendall's shield.

Avendall held his seat, though the gray stallion quivered and flung its massive head from side to side. Gabriella, trembling, arms wrapped around herself to lend a poor comfort, had the strange, fleeting reflection that the horses might have done battle on their own, if they had been given that opportunity. It was as if they had been bred for this, and for nothing else.

Another pole was brought, with suitable solemnity, and handed up to Morgan. He hoisted it as easily as before, although Gabriella thought he must be nearly as shaken and bruised inside that spectacular armor as Avendall in his. She felt a brief, desperate flash of fury with Morgan, for risking so much, for risking *everything*. He might as well have carried her heart on the point of his lance, so vulnerable was she.

A signal was given, and once again the riders surged together, like the tides of two great oceans, long dammed and now suddenly flowing free. They met with a clash that seemed to jar the very heavens above, and set the earth shuddering to its very core.

Dust seemed to explode from the ground, a blinding curtain stirred by the hooves of the chargers, rising to swallow both the combatants whole. For several moments, there was an eerie stillness, an utter, pervading quiet, as though the world itself had stopped to listen, to wait.

"He's unhorsed!" one of the men in the crowd shouted. Gabriella could see nothing except a tangle of stallions and armor, amidst the slowly settling cloud of dirt, and thus did not know who had fallen—Avendall, or Morgan.

Without thinking, she began to run toward the middle of the field, slipping easily from the grasp of Dame Johanna who would have restrained her. She arrived to find Avendall seated ignominiously on the ground, with Morgan standing over him, sword drawn, visor raised.

Avendall shook off the men who came to help him to his feet, and stood on his own—a difficult process given the weight of his armor and the inevitable ache of a collision that must have rattled the roots of his teeth. He pulled his helmet off in an angry motion and flung it aside, revealing a head of bloodied and matted hair.

Gabriella drew a step nearer to Morgan, but did not quite dare to touch him. He, too, removed his helmet, with a deft motion of his left hand, and let it fall with a clank to the dirt. He did not spare her even a glance, let alone a word, though she suspected he would have plenty to say—all of it scathing—when privacy allowed.

Squires from both sides moved in almost on tiptoe to gather the reins of the lathered, nickering stallions and lead them away to be groomed and soothed and fed.

The look Avendall and Morgan exchanged was nearly as frightening as the mounted combat had been; Gabriella feared one or both of them would ignite into ravenous flames, baptized in the breath of an angry dragon.

Morgan still held his sword; Avendall was unarmed.

For all the blood in Cyprian's hair and the bruises already rising upon his forehead and chin, Gabriella knew the public defeat had done him greater injury than any of the physical buffets he'd taken. Because Avendall had declared himself an enemy to the most fragile and vulnerable of her sisters, as well as herself, Gabriella felt no trace of pity for him.

It was Morgan who broke the lengthy, blood-curdling silence. "Only the vows I took as a knight prevent me from running the length of this blade through your throat," he told Avendall, in a voice that was all the more harrowing for its quiet, measured pace. "Gather your men and get out, before I lay honor aside in deference to good judgment and kill you where you stand. There will be no further contests this day."

This pronouncement raised a collective cry of disappointment and dismay from the villagers and men-at-arms as well, and Gabriella was chilled by their reaction to Morgan's decree. Clearly they would have preferred an all-out melee, complete with splintering bones, gouged eyes, and a steady flow of blood. She gulped against a surge of bile, rushing into the back of her throat, and turned to glare at the crowd, her fists clenched at her sides.

They were undaunted by Gabriella's cold fury, of course, but Morgan turned his head and silenced them all, Avendall's people and his own, with a single look.

Avendall flung a poisonous glance at Gabriella, underscoring every foul vow he had made to her earlier, in the courtyard, without uttering a single word. Then he bent at the waist and, with only a slight grimace to betray that Morgan had indeed done other damage, took up his helmet.

There was naught he could say to Morgan, without appearing to grovel, so he simply walked away. His company
fell into a reluctant and low-spirited train behind him.
Horses were returned, and the day's foolery was over.
Morgan was alive, and very little blood had been shed.

Gabriella let out a long sigh of relief, and nearly
choked on it when Chalstrey turned his carefully controlled annoyance upon her.

"You," he said, in a low rasp.

Gabriella took a step backward. She knew Morgan
would never handle her roughly, let alone strike her, but
the wrath she saw glittering in his eyes foretold a lengthy
and possibly public scolding. The awareness that she deserved every stinging word afforded no solace, for
Gabriella was not one to take pleasure in penance.

"Did I not order you to the counsel chamber?" he
asked, pursuing her, step for step. For every retreat, he
made an equal advance.

Gabriella stopped and stood her ground, fists
bunched, deflecting the fire of Morgan's gaze with a
steady glower of her own. "It is not yours to order me
about, my lord," she said, and a faint wavering quality in
her voice revealed the trepidation her brave countenance belied. "I am neither wife nor servant, horse nor
hound, soldier nor vassal. No law or convention com-
pels me to leap whenever you pipe a tune."

Morgan sheathed the sword with a practiced motion
and, ominously, pulled off one heavy glove, then the
other. He flung them aside, and out of the corner of her
eye, Gabriella saw a youth scramble to gather the steel
and leather gauntlets up again. "You vex me sorely, my
lady," Chalstrey said, forcing the words through jaws
that looked as unbending as the helmet he'd worn ear-

lier. "I pray you, do not provoke me too far, for I have already exercised the greater part of what little restraint the Lord God saw fit to allot me."

To forestall absolute panic, Gabriella drew a deep breath and let it out slowly. "I merely wished to be present, lest you fall in battle and require my consolations," she said, believing the statement to be reasonable as well as truthful and prudent.

The expression on Morgan's face told her instantly that she had been mistaken. *"Lest I should fall in battle?"* he repeated, and looked, if possible, even angrier than before.

The crowd, though listening avidly, receded almost as one, as they might from a showering spray of sparks flaring suddenly from a bonfire.

Gabriella was irked and promptly forgot her previous efforts to placate Morgan until the worst of the tumult had blown over. "You are most arrogant, my lord, as well as ox-witted, if you think you are invulnerable to the skills and might of other men. Avendall would have departed in triumph instead of disgrace, but for a whim of fortune, taking me with him as the spoils!"

"Mayhap," Morgan said evenly, "I should call him back and offer you as my gift. I might then know the peace that has eluded me since first I encountered you!"

Gabriella's hands rose to her hips. Now she didn't care who was listening. Let her answer ring from the very walls of heaven! "You did not merely 'encounter' me, my lord—your memory fails you as easily as your temper. I was *abducted,* and held captive—"

Morgan halted the diatribe by grasping her arm and half flinging her in the direction of the keep. In the distance, the disconsolate echo of horses' hooves could be heard as Avendall and his company passed over the drawbridge. Gabriella spun to tell Morgan that he was a boar's rear—the most virulent insult she knew—just in time to see his eyes roll upward and close.

His knees buckled and he folded to the ground in a slow, oddly graceful motion, yielding no sound but the protesting clamor of his armor.

Gabriella was kneeling beside him in an instant, their differences forgotten, searching his pale face for any sign of consciousness. Others had gathered close, too, but Dame Johanna forced her way through and crouched in her plain gown to feel for a heartbeat at the base of Morgan's throat.

"Take him to his own chamber," the nun commanded briskly, rising again. "And be careful, I pray you."

Four strong men-at-arms hoisted Morgan's still and heavy form from the ground, hastening toward the keep with unquestioning obedience. Gabriella hurried along in their wake, her frustration with Morgan exceeded only by her fear for him. She had thought him safe and unscathed, a victor. Now she feared they would find grievous wounds beneath that now-dented armor of his, and she knew that if he perished, she would perish as well, as surely as if she'd been sealed inside his tomb. He was the breath in her lungs, and without the certainty that he lived, somewhere upon the earth, she would smother.

Using the back of one dusty hand, Gabriella wiped away troublesome tears. Would that she had remained at St. Swithin's, and taken vows, rather than open herself to the terrible defenselessness of loving another mortal as she loved Morgan Chalstrey, but love him she did.

There was no point in lying to herself.

Inside the chamber, Dame Johanna spewed orders. Remove Chalstrey's armor, quickly but gently. Heat water. Bring cloth for bandages. Build up the fire and gather braziers from all over the castle as well. Servants and soldiers alike rushed to do her bidding.

Gabriella hovered nearby, her gaze fixed, unwavering, on Morgan's still and colorless face. He looked almost like a corpse she had once glimpsed, at St. Swithin's, when a sojourner, begging refuge and a meal on a snowy night, had died in the wee hours, beside the infirmary fire.

She felt light-headed, and closed her eyes briefly in an effort to steady herself.

"Be calm, Gabriella," Dame Johanna told her, waving the frightened men-at-arms away from the bed that she might examine her patient. "You will be of no assistance at all if you dither and fret."

"Shall I fetch the leech, good dame?" one of the soldiers inquired anxiously.

"Most assuredly not," the nun replied tartly. "Now, take yourselves off, the lot of you, and let me tend to your master in peace."

Unwillingly, everyone wandered out of the room, except for Gabriella, who would not have been drawn away by the summons of Gabriel's trumpet. Her eyes were round with horror as she stepped nearer to the bed.

Morgan lay naked upon it, his entire midsection swathed in a hideous purple-green bruise. Dame Johanna examined each of his limbs, with an efficient but nearly holy tenderness, then ran her hands over his chest.

He moaned and moved his head upon the pillow, but did not rouse.

"As I thought," Dame Johanna said. "Edgefield has

taken cracked ribs for his prize. Mayhap he is injured within, as well, but I think not. Betwixt the battering he took from Avendall's lance and the rigors of his own temper, the master has plainly exhausted his physical resources."

"Fool," Gabriella whispered miserably, and immediately felt shame for her contentious tongue. "Will he die?"

Dame Johanna smiled at that, albeit somewhat sadly. "No, my child. Your Morgan can be likened to the ox for more than just stubbornness—he shares the young bull's stalwart constitution as well."

As if compelled by some deep part of himself to offer a defense, Morgan opened his eyes, looked from Gabriella to Dame Johanna and back again. Some of his color had returned, and Gabriella was suddenly exuberant, in spite of all the new trials that lay before her.

"Pray, do not tell me Avendall had the cowardice to return and strike me from behind," Morgan ground out. "I have regrets enough for letting him live as it is, and do not currently possess the necessary mettle, it would seem, to find the viper and make right my error."

Gabriella sat on the edge of the mattress and smoothed dusty brown hair back from his forehead. "Avendall is gone, my lord, rightly defeated. You swooned from spent fury, and one or two cracked ribs."

"Swooned," Morgan repeated tragically, and with an edge of ire. "God's blood, Gabriella, will you forever choose words that make me sound like someone's toothless grandmother?"

She bit her lip and looked down, much chagrined. She had not meant, on this occasion or the others that had gone before, to paint Morgan as weak.

"You must take up your quill, my lord," Dame Johanna inserted, tearing linens into strips, with which she would bind his unsteady ribs, "and list for us those words that will not offend your considerable pride. We shall post the decree upon the chapel door, that none may digress, unwary, into imprudent speech."

Morgan's dirty and bruised face was flushed from the nun's artfully delivered reprimand. "If you mean to chide me, good dame, pray have stout wine brought first, that I may drink, and buttress myself against your reproaches as well as the pain of my injuries. I fear the two together will be my finish, if I am to have no solace from either."

"Gabriella," Dame Johanna said without hesitation, "fetch wine for my lord. He shall require it."

Morgan laughed hoarsely, and submitted, between greedy draughts from the cup Gabriella brought and held for him, to the painful binding of his ribs. He was courageous, though the pallor in his flesh and the sweat on his brow betrayed his suffering. Dame Johanna, perhaps out of Christian mercy, did not plague him with more of her barbed observations, and when at last she had finished the long process of winding the torn linen tightly around his chest, she nodded in farewell and took her leave.

"If that woman had not been a nun," Morgan remarked, lying back on his pillows as Gabriella dabbed gently at his face with a cloth soaked in freshly drawn well water, "I would have made her a captain in my company." He frowned, gazing absently toward the window. "What do you suppose is keeping Sedgewick?" he muttered, as though addressing no one in particular. "Mayhap he's finally got enough of dealing with me. God knows he's oft threatened to give this place his back, and his old friend with it."

Had Morgan been looking at Gabriella, he would

have seen her wince at the mention of Gresham
Sedgewick, the man Dame Johanna had struck down
with a stone and, after it, stolen his horse. When
Sedgewick came to mind, she naturally thought of the
abbey, the place where he'd been bound, and of her sisters, Elizabeth and Meg. They were in terrible danger,
both of them, although Avendall had not actually mentioned Meg, let alone threatened her. Still, if poor little
Elizabeth failed to meet his expectations, he might well
summon Meg to serve in her stead.

No matter what losses she must suffer, no matter what
perils she would be required to face—and she knew now,
after her latest foray into the great world, just how grave
those perils might be—Gabriella could not allow such a
travesty to take place. She quite literally preferred death
to the torment of seeing Avendall destroy her sisters, and
she meant to do whatever she must to protect them.

She thought of her benefactor, surely a man of some
power and influence. Could she not turn to him for
help? Surely Dame Johanna would be willing to reveal
his identity now, given the threat to Meg and Elizabeth.

"I am certain my lord Sedgewick is well," she said be-
latedly, "and on his way back to Edgefield Keep even
now."

Morgan did not seem convinced. Indeed, his expression was troubled, and betrayed a sort of pain deeper
and more lasting than that caused by the fools' games in
the lists. "I should not have baited Gresham the way I
did. He was—is—my finest friend."

Gabriella extended a hand for the small wooden
bowl, containing an herbal sleeping draught, that Dame
Johanna had left on the bedside table. "Drink from this,
my lord, and pray do not fret yourself further.

Sedgewick will return, and when he does, then you may make your amends."

After a skeptical glance at the unappealing substance in the bottom of the bowl, Morgan grimaced and took a tentative sip. He immediately spat, spraying the bed-clothes with the noxious compound.

"God's teeth, wench, that stuff would cause a corpse to retch!"

Gabriella sighed. "My lord, you must accept your medicine, or I shall be forced to summon Dame Johanna to administer it personally."

Morgan gave her a murderous look, then grabbed the bowl in both hands and downed the contents in a single, strangled gulp. Upon swallowing, he sent the vessel clattering across the stone floor and simultaneously roared a new and much more colorful oath.

Suppressing a smile, Gabriella attempted to look stern. "I vow you could not have been half so troublesome as a wee lad," she scolded, tucking the covers carefully around him. "And here you are, grown to manhood, and throwing tantrums."

"Do not speak to me of tantrums, my lady," Morgan warned, before pausing to yawn greatly. The herbal was already doing its work. "Not when I had to drag you off Avendall this very day, like a lioness from a deer's carcass, lest you claw him to tatters and deny me the pleasure of unhorsing him before half the shire."

Gabriella frowned, recalling the scene in the lists only too vividly. "What stayed your hand, my lord? You were, for all the humiliation Avendall suffered, more than merciful when you had got him at a disadvantage."

Morgan closed his eyes. His lashes lay thick upon

his cheeks, and Gabriella smiled at the incongruity of
such a feature in such a man. "Honor prevents any
knight from killing an opponent who has been disarmed."

"He would not have done the same, methinks, in
your place."

Another vast yawn. "I need preserve no man's honor,
Gabriella, save my own. I was, I confess, as surely
tempted, holding that blade at Avendall's throat, as I
have ever been."

She caressed his bruised, abraded face with a light
pass of her fingertips. "Why do you hate him so much,
and he you?"

Morgan raised his eyelids and assessed her with an
unfocused gaze. "For Rebecca," he said, before Dame
Johanna's concoction shrouded his waking mind at
last. He struggled visibly against sleep and lost the
battle.

Rebecca. Gabriella repeated the name, in her mind,
and was stung by it. Morgan had been willing to risk
much, to avenge the lost Rebecca, whoever she'd been.
He had stolen another man's bride, had placed his life at
risk in the lists, at a foe's behest. Would he have done
the same, she wondered, if she, Gabriella, had been
wronged, as Rebecca surely had?

There was no point, she decided, in tormenting herself with such useless questions. She must put Morgan
and all she felt for him behind her, once and for all, and
set out for St. Swithin's abbey. There was no time to
spare—she must reach her sisters before Avendall's
men did. If indeed he actually *had* sent a company to
fetch the girl. Avendall might have been bluffing; mayhap he had guessed that Meg and Elizabeth were

Gabriella's greatest vulnerabilities, and sought to punish her by threatening them.

She knew she could not take the risk.

Dame Johanna did not seem surprised when, after vespers and the evening meal, Gabriella sought her out and calmly presented her plan. She would travel to St. Swithin's, get there any way she could, do whatever she had to do to keep her sisters safe. Mother Mary Benedict would surely help, once she understood the danger.

"You are willing to leave Lord Edgefield?" the nun asked, as they stood together in the privacy of a garden, now harvested and tilled to lie fallow until the spring. "Wounded though he is?"

"No, but I must." A tear tickled Gabriella's cheek, and she brushed at it with the back of one hand. "Morgan is most uncomfortable, but he is not grievously hurt. By the morrow, no doubt, he will rouse himself to play more silly, little-boy games upon the field of battle."

Dame Johanna's smile was kindly. "You are a noble creature, Gabriella Redclift, though a fey one, too. But you are right—there will never be a better time to leave Edgefield Keep than this night, when all the watchmen are distracted, wondering what will become of their lord, and when that lord himself lies abed, unable to pursue you." She paused, considered for a time, and sighed. "Very well. I shall journey with you, for you surely cannot travel alone. It is time I returned to the abbey to take up my old duties and, besides, I should like to find out how young Sedgewick fares. His delay in returning is a cause for much speculation and concern among the villagers and servants."

Gabriella felt a rush of gratitude and relief, for she

had not wanted to set out on her own. She and Dame
Johanna certainly had a better chance of reaching the
abbey safely, and at good speed, if they went together.
Still, she had one more question to ask. "Will you not
tell me my benefactor's name, now? Perhaps he would
intercede—"

Dame Johanna stiffened. "He is far away, my child,
and engaged in other things. No, we shall handle this ourselves." She turned thoughtful, and Gabriella knew there
would be no persuading the nun to break her vow of silence regarding the man who had paid for the Redcliff sisters' bed and board at the abbey through all these years.
"Alas, I fear I must stoop once more to thieving . . ."

"What?" Gabriella whispered, wide-eyed at the
prospect of taking part in a crime.

"Aye," Dame Johanna replied, with a sigh of cheerful
resignation and a certain twinkle. "We shall help ourselves to a horse, methinks. Should we both attempt to
ride Zacheus, he is certain to balk."

Gabriella nodded, warming to the idea, then the two
women put their heads together and, in cautious whispers, put the last masterful brush strokes to their plot.

Whilst Dame Johanna paid another visit to Morgan,
in the capacity of nurse, Gabriella hastily packed their
few belongings in the same cloth bag she had brought to
Edgefield Keep in the first place. When she had hidden
the sack behind the great chest in the room she had
been meant to share with the nun, Gabriella proceeded
to the master's chamber.

Morgan lay abed, as she had expected, his bound
chest rising and falling as he drew in the long, deep
breaths of a sleeper. Dame Johanna took her leave, and
though the old woman made no mention of it, of course,

Gabriella knew she was on her way to the stables, there to prepare the way for a truly daring theft.

Alone with Morgan, Gabriella sat upon the edge of the bed in which she had been so happily and thoroughly deflowered, and as silvery moonlight washed into the room, she laid her forehead against his. Her tears fell unnoticed upon his face; Gabriella was not even fully aware, in her sorrow, that she was weeping.

Finally, when she knew by the sounds in the courtyard and the corridor that it was time to act, Gabriella kissed him, pressing her lips to his with no more force than a midsummer breeze might have done.

"Fare-thee-well, Morgan Chalstrey, Duke of Edgefield," she said, so softly that her words did not rise to so much as a whisper. "Fare-thee-well."

Then, not daring to linger so much as a moment longer, lest she lose her desperate resolve, Gabriella hurried out of the master chamber, leaving the great door slightly ajar as she passed over the threshold and into the dark passage beyond.

He couldn't be sure how much time had passed since Gabriella had left him—an hour, a day?—at first, he'd thought he must surely be dreaming. Even Gabriella would not be such a fool as to set out for the other side of England, unprotected.

Morgan opened his eyes. "Damn it," he murmured. The encounter had been *real,* he knew it. With a grimace and a low hiss, through his teeth, he threw back the coverlets and sat up.

The effort was a costly one, for the lamps had not been lighted, and the chamber was pitch dark. He groped until he found his leggings, a tunic, a leather jerkin, boots. Dressing himself in such a state was an ordeal like unto the actual acquisition of his wounds, but he succeeded at last, and made his way over the stone floor, cursing when he rammed a strategically important toe into the doorjamb.

He was halfway down the main staircase, the lamp light from the great hall spilling at his feet, when he finally shouted a summons to the guards.

Gabriella and Dame Johanna left by the same postern gate the villagers passed through, morning and night, on their way to and from the nearby fields, where the pumpkins and gourds and late potatoes were still being gathered. The two women wore hooded cloaks, kept their heads lowered, and avoided the thin washes of cloud-strained moonlight as best they could. They were not inconspicuous, however—Gabriella rode the pristine white mule, Zacheus, a creature so sorely lacking in the simplest graces that he defied even Christian charity. Dame Johanna was in many ways even more noticeable, for her mount was an untried gelding, a striking dappled gray in color and only recently broken to the saddle.

For all her protests that a sturdy and fleet steed might mean the difference between escape and capture, Gabriella suspected, amused, that in truth Dame Johanna cherished a worldly appreciation of fine horseflesh. Certainly there were no opportunities to indulge such a fancy at St. Swithin's, where the redoubtable Zacheus served as the sole mode of transportation, aside from the ancient cart he could sometimes be persuaded to pull.

The nun had plotted a course across the countryside,

foreswearing the road, and when they had put Edge-field Keep well behind them—Gabriella allowed her-self a single backward look, despite the fear that she might turn into a pillar of salt like Lot's wife as just rec-ompense for her sins—they slowed their pace a little.

"Do you ever wish you had lived another sort of life?" Gabriella asked, after several minutes spent gathering her courage, lest Dame Johanna rebuke her for irrever-ence and brazen curiosity.

The older woman was a long time answering. "I sup-pose all of us do, now and again," she finally replied. "Make haste, Gabriella—if you allow that mule a mo-ment's indulgence, he'll lay himself down like an old cow and refuse to stir an eyelid until it suits his peculiar purposes to do so."

Gabriella kept her peace after that, pondering what might have been.

12

Gabriella and Dame Johanna traveled far into the forest, itself at some distance from Edgefield Keep, before the deepening darkness forced them to make camp in the shelter of a copse of birch trees. They gathered twigs and sticks by what light the fickle moon allowed to sift past racing clouds, and risked a small, feeble fire. The flames, though modest, might be glimpsed by anyone following, but wild animals, such as wolves and boars, presented greater and more immediate perils, as did the biting cold of an autumn night.

As she sat warming numb feet beside the tiny blaze, longing for the hearth in Morgan's room and, indeed, for Morgan himself, Gabriella reminded herself that the journey she had undertaken was one of great consequence. The welfare of her sisters, mayhap even their very lives, depended upon her reaching St. Swithin's Abbey before Avendall's emissaries did. When Mother Mary Benedict learned what sort of man he really was, she would surely refuse to surrender either Elizabeth or Meg to his keeping. If God willed it so, Gabriella further reflected, her sisters might choose to return home, with her, to Redclift Hall, there to look after their mother and hapless stepfather and possibly—by effort and trial and error—turn the ill-managed manor into a profitable enterprise once again. While there was certainly a great deal she did not know about raising crops and husbanding animals, she knew she would learn quickly, and her skill with numbers was sure to be of benefit.

The soul-chilling howl of a wolf interrupted these lofty thoughts, and Gabriella looked up with a gasp. On the other side of the quailing, flinching little fire, Dame Johanna tensed and reached for the large gnarled stick she had found in the woods earlier. It made a poor weapon, but it was all they had at hand, and would therefore have to suffice.

Gabriella spoke in a whisper. "Is the creature very close by?" she asked, as bloody images of dismemberment and throat tearing replaced the pretty dreams she had been entertaining only moments before. Zacheus and the purloined gelding, tethered to a fallen log nearby, offered an answer of their own, nickering and pulling hard at their bonds.

Dame Johanna laid the tip of the rod amidst the flames, squinting into the dense gloom that surrounded them. The moon, a generous beacon earlier in their expedition, sulked stubbornly behind a bank of threatening clouds. "Aye," the nun replied, speaking softly and rising to her feet with the nimble ease of a soldier. "There are several, methinks, and they draw nigh. Take up a stone or a brand from the fire, Gabriella, and prepare to wage battle."

Gabriella did not hesitate to obey; in fact, she'd already been casting about for a stick of her own. Rocks and burning switches made paltry substitutes, to her mind, when what was wanted was a sword or a mace. Or better still, a hundred archers with bows drawn and arrows ready.

The very worst thing about facing death, she thought fitfully, was the realization that she would never see Morgan again. Until that moment, she had somehow convinced herself that she was better off without him, but now she missed him with an ache that pinched her heart white and fair stopped her breath.

She grasped a long piece of wood from the fire and, wavering only a little, got to her feet.

The moon showed its face so suddenly as to startle Gabriella, but a much greater shock awaited her. Completely surrounding the little camp, eyes glinting yellow like those of demons in the night, was a pack of some half dozen wolves.

The gelding Dame Johanna had stolen at Edgefield Keep kicked and screamed in shrill panic, but Zacheus had recovered his fine, defiant nature, and stood with his long ears laid back, making a fearsome sound somewhere between a hissing grumble and a bray.

Moonlight spilled over the wolves, revealing their dull coats and slatted ribs, while the glow of the fire sparked a new and hellish red glint in their watchful eyes. The wolves took little or no notice of Zacheus and the horse; no, indeed, this night they wished to feast upon human fare.

"Do they not fear the fire?" Gabriella dared to inquire, placing herself between the slavering, snarling creatures and the log to which their mounts were tethered.

"These beasts are far past simple fear, methinks,"

Dame Johanna answered quietly, and with a note of pity in her voice, even as she braced herself to wield the wooden staff, with its blazing, crackling tip. "Do you see their ribs? They know a hunger beyond any we can fathom, poor creatures. Their bellies are fair consumed with emptiness."

One of the wolves turned toward Gabriella and, growling low, took a step in her direction. Her poor, bloodless heart quivered with terror, and then raced like a hare bound for a hole. She brandished the pitiful twig, all that stood between her and a monster that, for all its wretchedness and suffering, meant to devour her in pieces.

Dame Johanna spoke in soft, careful tones. "Stand your ground, Gabriella. If you turn to bolt, he will take you before you've gone two steps."

Gabriella shivered as still more gruesome images invaded her head. "Stay back," she said to the wolf, trying to sound commanding, and failing miserably. Her voice was no steadier than her knees, which threatened to give out at any moment.

The wolf halted, his pelt ruffled by a bitter wind, and he and Gabriella stared at each other, measuring, making private tallies. The other members of the pack did not move at all, but their growling seemed to fill the night.

"Move nearer to the fire," the nun counseled, in the same lulling, even way as before. "Go *very* slowly."

Gabriella held her breath and risked an almost imperceptible shift toward the faltering, inadequate little blaze. The wolf's gaze followed her, marked the motion, then, with no warning at all, sprang into the air in a sleek, horribly graceful arc. Gabriella screamed, in spite

of her best intentions, lost her balance, and tumbled to
the ground, coming within inches of the fire.

She sat, frozen, half blind with terror, fully expecting
the animal to land upon her, with all its wiry weight, and
she was surprised when it didn't. Instead of coming
after Gabriella, the wolf gazed upon Zacheus, greedy,
mayhap, in his terrible hunger.

Gabriella gasped in protest, certain the mule would
be ripped to tatters of hide and hair, but for once
Zacheus's redoubtable temperament proved to be a
blessing, rather than a curse. He brayed, fit to rouse the
dead from every graveyard in England and, breaking
free at last, in a burst of heroic strength, turned and
gave his attacker the full thrust of his hind legs.

The wolf yowled and went rolling, coming to his feet
so near Gabriella that she might have touched him,
had she dared to reach out. Had she dared even to
move.

"Over here!" Dame Johanna suddenly screamed.
"We are here!" Was she trying to draw the beast's attention, and thus protect her charge? Dazed, Gabriella
could not begin to guess; she could only sit trembling,
too horrified even to pray.

The pack receded a little way, into the shadows, but
Zacheus's personal wolf, though badly wounded, plainly
wanted restitution. He turned his great, gaunt head toward Gabriella, and she saw his teeth glint in the firelight. She felt his foul, fetid breath, hot upon her face,
like a gust from the furnaces of hell.

Only then did she hear the sounds, those blessed
sounds that Dame Johanna had heard first, of horses
and men, bursting out of the darkness. She did not look
for them, though, for her gaze was locked with that of

the wolf. If she so much as glanced away, she knew he would lunge for her throat.

She heard the pack scatter and flee through the underbrush, yipping and whining like hounds chased away from a scrap pile, but their leader remained steadfast, bloody and broken, yellow-red eyes fixed on her. He would die soon, this beast, but he meant for her to perish with him—she knew that as well as if he'd spoken the vow aloud. His sharp-boned haunches quivered as he gathered his still formidable powers to spring.

Gabriella heard the arrow slice, whistling, through the cold night air, and it seemed a long time before the shaft struck the wolf, plunging neatly into his heart and killing him with such dispatch that she saw the life leave his eyes before he fell.

She began to scream, hoarsely, gutturally, over and over.

Morgan appeared in the firelight, flung aside his bow, and crouched before her. "Gabriella!" he said, grasping her shoulders. When she continued to shriek, unable to help herself, he gave her a brisk shake. Her cries turned to sobs, and he wrenched her against his chest, holding her tightly, as if to shield her from every peril in all of creation, burying one hand in her hair. "You are safe now, sweeting," he told her. "Shhh. You are safe."

With great effort, Gabriella managed to cease weeping, but began to hiccough straightaway. "Dame Johanna?" she whispered, as a new fear found its home in her heart, raising her face from Morgan's leather-clad shoulder to look about. "Is she—?"

Morgan smiled, though there were creases in his brow and one of his temples throbbed visibly. "Your fellow horse thief is quite unhurt," he said.

She became aware of men moving about, like ghosts, dragging away the wolf's carcass, gathering up her belongings and Dame Johanna's, soothing the frightened gelding, murmuring gravely among themselves. At the edge of her vision, Gabriella caught a glimpse of Dame Johanna, stroking Zachcus's long white nose, smiling fondly, and probably praising him for his valor.

"We would have returned the horse," Gabriella said, as other dangers occurred to her. Mayhap the night's adventure had put a finish to Morgan's patience; should he surrender her to the sheriff and demand that she be tried for thievery, his petition was certain to be granted. "Eventually."

"Do you think I give a damn about the bloody *horse?*" he retorted. The smile was gone, and the look in his eyes rather reminded Gabriella of the wolf. "What possessed you to undertake such an addle-witted venture? Did you learn nothing from your last magnificent escape?"

Gabriella swallowed. "I had no choice, my lord," she said, as Morgan stood, drawing her with him and, almost in the same motion, swinging her up into his arms. Only a tightening of his jaw betrayed the pain he harbored in his ribs. "You heard Avendall, yesterday in the courtyard. He's sent men to fetch my youngest sister, Elizabeth. If she is brought to him, he will surely destroy her."

Morgan sighed and let his forehead rest against Gabriella's temple for a moment. "I sent a courier to St. Swithin's soon after Avendall arrived for the joust," he said, with grim and obviously hard-won forbearance. "He will not wed either of your sisters, now or ever." He hoisted her onto his charger, with a suppressed groan, and swung up behind her. "Pray you, my lady—when next you take up arms against the world, pause first, and consider if there be any need."

Gabriella was asleep in his bed, calmed by a sleeping draught, and that irksome nun had retired long since to her own chamber. The servants were settled on their pallets, no doubt, and the village lay sprawled below the keep itself, with not a single lamp burning. His men-at-arms slumbered noisily in the great hall, as was their custom, and even the mice had ceased their busy rustling in the rushes.

Only Morgan himself, it seemed, was unable to rest.

He turned from the window, crossed the room to the hearth, and stirred the blaze. The nagging pain in his rib cage was forgotten as he recalled the primitive fear that had encompassed him, swallowed him whole, when first he saw Gabriella on the ground, about to be torn asunder and devoured by a famine-crazed wolf.

Morgan had never felt anything like the terror he had known in those moments—not on the battlefields of France, not even in the Levant, where he seen atrocities so horrible that he would never repeat them to another human being. His hands had trembled with such violence that he'd barely been able to grasp his bow, let alone loose an arrow straight and true.

He slumped into a chair before the hearth and stretched out his legs, weary almost beyond bearing, yet unable to close his eyes. Each time he tried, he saw Gabriella lying dead, flesh torn and bleeding, her empty gaze fixed on an icy, starless sky. The vision, so narrowly deflected from becoming a tragic truth, was too real to endure.

"Morgan?" Gabriella's voice was husky with sleep

and comfort. The little minx had put the whole incident behind her, evidently, but he was still shaken, still half sick with residual fear. "Will you not come to bed?"

He did not look at her. To see her pale hair atumble, her eyes heavy lidded and sultry even in their innocence, her nipples showing through her chemise—all of it was more than could rightly be asked of a man in his condition. "No, Gabriella."

She yawned fetchingly. Sensually. He imagined her stretching, like a young lioness, and his loins tightened painfully. "Why not, my lord? Surely you are exceeding weary, and suffering from your injuries."

"Aye," Morgan answered, "I am both those things."

"Are you angry with me?" She sounded interested, but otherwise unconcerned.

"Oh, yes, milady," he said, in all truth. "Furious enough to take you across my knee. Fortunately for you, I probably couldn't manage that without cracking a few more ribs."

"I should crack them for you," she assured him, with sleepy spirit, "if you attempted such an outrage."

Morgan sighed, staring into the heart of the fire. "I would have your promise, Gabriella, that you will not leave this keep again without my knowledge."

"I am still a prisoner, then."

"No. Methinks *I* have taken on that role. I must keep you safe, Gabriella."

He listened as she sighed and shifted upon the thick feather mattress, stirring a sweet, violent tempest within him. "I cannot offer such an oath, my lord," she said regretfully, as he had known, and feared, she would. "If I should have cause to believe my sisters need me, I will contrive to go to them. And if—"

"If?" Morgan prompted, when she had fallen into a rueful silence.

"If you were to take a wife, I could not bear to stay. I will not be your mistress, my lord, and see my babes shunted aside for those of another woman, and named bastards."

He was so surprised by her words that he laughed. It was a bitter, rasping sound, entirely devoid of mirth. "Were I to take a wife, is it? I have neither wanted nor required one, before this."

"Before this?" she echoed, in a small voice.

Morgan turned at last to look at Gabriella, and it was as he had dreaded: she was a witch awash in firelight, a naked enchantress unaware of her magic, of her power. "Gabriella, I would wed no woman but you. And what babes you bear me will be reared with my name."

Her lovely, inviting mouth dropped open, and her eyes went wide. For once, she was utterly speechless. Morgan himself was surprised by the announcement he'd just made, for he had never consciously planned it. All he knew was that Gabriella, trial though she was, brought something elemental, something vital, to his life. Without her, he would be alone as he had never been before, for all his independence.

He had lain with legendary courtesans, with the tempting, neglected wives of men much like himself. He had passed pleasant hours with harem girls, eager to please him and skilled in the art, and with the spoiled, adventurous daughters of wealthy merchants. But none, not even Rebecca, had touched the core of him in the way this hardheaded, convent-bred, horse-stealing wench had done.

"Shall I fetch the priest to spare us from inevitable

and imminent sin, Gabriella, or will you refuse my suit?"

She blushed deeply, and thereby rendered herself, still without knowing, all the more desirable. "I cannot refuse you, my lord."

Morgan thrust himself from the chair. "Very well, then," he said, with earnest resolve. "Get up and clothe yourself decently while I rout the holy man from his pallet."

Gabriella knelt in the middle of the mattress, the sheet clutched to her chin, her eyes shining. The sight of her stabbed Morgan in a part of his being that he had never before laid bare, for he could guess at her girlish hopes. And he knew that he did not love her—with Rebecca's passing, nay, even before that, he had lost all capacity for such sentiment.

"Mayhap it is improper, to wed in the middle of the night—"

He crossed to her, cupped a hand under her chin for a moment, found it trembling. "It is yet more improper, my lady beloved, to do the things I yearn to do to you, without the sanction of the Holy Church."

Gabriella lowered her eyes shyly, and he kissed her forehead.

Then, wondering what fey and fickle spirit had taken him over, Morgan left the bedchamber to fetch back the priest.

Gabriella had barely managed to don suitable raiment, a plain woolen gown of blue, brush her hair, and waken Dame Johanna to serve as a witness, before Morgan returned. Father Aloysius, the diminutive cleric who offered matins, mass and evensong at Edgefield

Keep and slept in a tiny cell behind the chapel, followed, yawning, at the master's heels. His white hair was rumpled and his robe a little askew, but his manner was kindly and there was no condemnation in his pale blue eyes when he squinted at the bride.

"Ah, yes," he said to Gabriella. "I remember you, though I must say, not because I have seen you at mass." He looked blurrily at Morgan and spoke frankly, for he had served at Edgefield for many years. "Avendall will not like this at all," he warned fretfully. "My, no, not at all."

"Get on with it," Morgan said, with charitable impatience.

Gabriella glanced at Dame Johanna, whom she'd expected to be scandalized, and saw to her surprise that the other woman was smiling, with her eyes, if not her lips.

They stood facing the hearth, Morgan and Gabriella, while the little priest took a measure of mortal comfort by placing himself betwixt them and the fire.

Gabriella, who had expected for a twelvemonth to become Lady Avendall, who that very night had nearly been attacked and torn to pieces by a wolf, was befuddled to find herself vowing obedience, devotion, and fidelity to Morgan Chalstrey, Lord Edgefield. And she actually *meant* to be devoted and true, though obedience, she reflected sorrowfully, was not in her nature and therefore doomed to fall by the wayside.

She might not have known when the ceremony was over, except that Morgan bent his head and kissed her as thoroughly as if a nun and a priest were not present. The contact left her swaying, at least inwardly, like someone drunk on ale or barley beer.

While Morgan was pumping Father Aloysius's hand,

Dame Johanna came forward and gently kissed Gabriella's check.

"He will be a difficult husband, your Morgan," the nun told her quietly, "but he will look after you, and certainly give you cause for great happiness, methinks."

Gabriella blushed, thinking of what remained of the night, and the pleasures it would hold. She replied with a little nod, since no sensible words came to her. So much had happened, so quickly, and she was still struggling to catch her balance.

Dame Johanna took her leave, soon followed by the priest, and Morgan bolted the door. Then he turned and stood looking at Gabriella in silence for a long time, wearing an expression of mingled mischief and bewilderment.

"Comfort me, wife," he said, neither commanding nor pleading. "I pray you, chase the image of that wolf, devouring you, out of my mind."

Gabriella was touched that he had been so frightened for her. Mayhap he loved her, as she knew she loved him. "But what of your ribs, my lord—"

Morgan smiled. "Mayhap you will cause me to forget that hurt as well."

She undid the laces of her gown, allowed it to fall in a pool to the dark timber floor, worn smooth by the feet of the generations of Chalstreys that had gone before— making love in this room. Arguing, no doubt, and laughing together. Weeping betimes, surely. Siring and bearing children, and finally dying, in their appointed times and manners.

Gabriella hoped she would die in that same chamber, when she was old, and her hair was like snow, and her heart had stored up memories enough to last throughout eternity.

"What are you thinking about?" Morgan asked, frowning, as he came to her, looked at her body, bared for him, with a flattering expression of awe in his eyes. She might have been new to him, the way he weighed her breasts in his hands, ran his fingertips down her sides, let them linger at her waist, and then clasped her hips with a strength that said he meant to take full command very soon.

"I was hoping I would die in this room," she said, and when his gaze, heretofore fixed on the bounty of her breasts, flew startled to her face, she smiled. "When I am very, very old," she added. "So much will happen here, Morgan—can't you see it? Our children will be conceived and born within these walls. We will laugh together, and disagree at times, and surely we shall weep, as well. But we will be so happy."

She ignored the fleeting look—was it chagrin?—in his eyes, in that way of new and guileless brides, who will not yet allow themselves to recognize that love opens the heart, not only to riotous joy, but also to the profoundest of sorrows.

He fell to her, kissed her deeply, and with a hunger that stirred her blood. She felt him, pressed against her belly, and longed to take him inside her, keep him there, a part of her, forever.

"Your ribs, my lord," she whispered, when he gave her a moment to catch her breath.

"My ribs be damned," he replied, nibbling now at her earlobe, now along the length of her neck.

Instinctively, she tilted her hips upward, in brazen invitation, and he groaned with an agony she knew bore no connection to the injuries he'd sustained in the lists, doing battle with Avendall.

"Wench," he whispered, with an anguished chuckle. "Angel."

"Teach me to please you," she said, and upon those few words he was broken, a man not merely ship-wrecked, but entirely lost.

Lady Edgefield, for her part, proved an apt and willing pupil, and was richly rewarded for her efforts. She surrendered, when that was required, and took charge, in her turn.

The first pinkish-lilac light of dawn was just beginning to outline the windows when, at last, the lovers slept, utterly sated.

In point of fact, Avendall did not give the threatened marriage to Elizabeth Redclift another thought, after the humiliation he'd suffered in the lists of Edgefield Keep. He took horse, before the sun's setting, for London town, with some twenty of his men riding grimly behind.

Obsessed, Cyprian rode until the horses were stumbling with weariness, and could go no further. He passed the ensuing nights sleepless and brooding, while his men snored in bedrolls on the ground, in the common room of some roadside inn, and once in the barn of a crofter. He could think of naught besides the shame he had endured upon the field, the betrayal of the woman who should have been his to do with as he pleased, the terrible wounds to his pride. Naught but the singular charms of one Gabriella Redclift, that is.

She was but a treacherous, backstabbing tart, and yet he could not put her out of his mind. He wanted her with all that he was, bone and muscle, soul and mind. Only getting Gabriella under him, breaking her, and through her, breaking Chalstrey, would relieve him of the consuming rage that plagued him with every breath, every heartbeat. He was losing his mind, he knew it full well, and could do nothing about it.

He was under no illusion that he loved the little strumpet. That was an emotion for fools and poets, and Avendall was neither. It was revenge he desired, more than the Redclift chit, revenge against Morgan Chalstrey. He had seduced the lovely Rebecca, wooed her with words and flowers and wine—Chalstrey had never been able to accept the truth of it, though Sedgewick had cause to know—but the inevitable bed-sport with Gabriella would be something altogether different. He would teach her to cast him aside for any other man, least of all his old enemy.

After five days and as many nights on the cold, rutted roads, Avendall came at last to London town. Like the Chalstreys, the Avendalls had served the king faithfully and well. He knew he would be made welcome in the royal household.

On the banks of the River Thames, he paid a bargeman to carry him and two of his best men downriver to Sheen, where he might seek audience with an aging and beleaguered ruler. Things were not going well in France, Avendall had heard, and the king's health was failing.

The river stank with a pungence that brought water to the eyes, and was thick with vessels, reminding the country-bred Avendall of a stream of sewage, flowing through a gutter and choked with foundering rats. He said nothing to his companions, who had learned well, over past days and nights, to put whatever questions they had to each other, and not to him. They were not his friends; he tolerated their company only because London was an evil place, full of cutthroats and thieves, whores and deceivers. There was no predicting when he might need good swordsmen to guard his back, and these men, though barely more than vagabonds themselves, were able fighters.

Avendall marked, without interest, the spectacular Savoy Palace, home of the Duke of Lancaster, a younger son of the king and a formidable opponent on the battlefield, though John of Gaunt would never be the equal of his elder brother, the ruthless and ingenious Black Prince.

After what seemed to him a long and trying journey, following five sleepless nights and as many days of hard riding as it did, Avendall reached his destination. The legendary White Tower, once the residence of William the Conqueror, in his time the most ferocious lion in all of Europe, rose against a sky smudged with smoke.

At Sheen, Avendall led his horse over the barge's ramp to the shore and quickly found a lad to look after the stallion, as well as his men's mounts. As he pressed a coin into the boy's grubby palm, he also put the blade of a dagger to his throat. "Mind the task well," he warned the churl, who had gone pale even beneath a lifetime of filth, "or I'll leave you with nothing holding your head to your neck but a splinter of backbone. Have we a bargain?"

The boy nodded, babbling that he would take such good care of the horses that they'd mourn for him after their master had taken them back.

Trailed by his silent escort, Avendall turned and strode unchallenged through the outer gates of the palace. His proud name and coat-of-arms got him past numerous guards. Cyprian's family was known for loyalty, fierceness in battle, and the wisdom to support the needs of the realm in whatever coin might be demanded of them.

It did not trouble Avendall that the Chalstreys stood in equal or greater favor with the Crown. He had a legitimate suit to press, and the king would listen and sympathize, he was sure of it.

Confidence notwithstanding, Avendall was kept waiting in an antechamber for the better measure of an hour, during which time he seethed and paced and silently berated himself for letting matters reach this turn in the first place. He had made some serious errors, beginning with that rash encounter on Chalstrey's drawbridge, when he'd tossed Gabriella to Morgan in a fit of fury, and thus betrayed the depths of the passion her treachery had roused in him. God in heaven, what a weapon he had laid in his enemy's hand that night!

In due time, a servant materialized at Avendall's side, clad in court livery. "My lord?" he intoned, respectfully. "His Majesty will receive you now. Pray, do not weary him overmuch, for he must bear great trials of his own."

Avendall nodded, caring little for the sorrows of a rheumy-eyed and bewildered king, fixed his men in their places with a single glance, and followed the servant down a long corridor, up a flight of stone steps, and through the great double doors of the king's private quarters. The king's longtime mistress, Alice Perrers, was present as usual, looking after her own interests, no doubt.

Even as he dropped to one knee in obeisance to his ruler, lowering his head humbly at the same time, Avendall remarked to himself that His Majesty looked especially wan and haggard. Edward was a mere sketch of the man he had been—once imposing in height, he was now stooped, with a frail aspect to his countenance. His broad shoulders and gaunt face belied his reputation as a giant, something greater than a mortal.

"Avendall," the king greeted him, from the carved

wooden throne on which he sat, wrapped in shawls and a cloak like an old and ailing woman. "Come forward and let me have a look at you."

Cyprian obeyed, of course. Feeble and distracted though Edward was, he was yet king, and by his order an impudent subject, whatever his rank or station, could be brought to heel in a host of truly unsavory ways. "My condolences, Your Majesty," he said, with cultivated gentleness. "I was most grieved to learn of the passing of your sainted queen." Avendall made the sign of the cross with a deftness meant to convey reverence and inclined his head again.

Edward did not make a reply, and for several moments, the air seemed to thicken with the aging king's despondency. Alice, for her part, looked irritated at the mention of her lover's late wife, not liking, Avendall suspected, even to acknowledge that such a personage had ever existed.

"Leave us," Edward said to his mistress.

Avendall stole a precautionary look at the ruler of all England before meeting the tired blue gaze head on. Indeed, His Majesty was plainly finding the crown a heavy burden, these days. Cyprian spared Alice a brief nod when she left the chamber. "How fares the Black Prince?" he asked, when he and Edward were alone, except for the ever-present guards. "Surely he has brought France to her knees by now."

Edward smiled, but the expression was thin, like his once-lush mane of fair hair, his wasting body, his quavering voice. "My son carries on valiantly, in the manner of a prince, despite the many crosses that are his to bear. Mayhap you have come to offer your services, Avendall?"

"I have brought you twenty men, Your Majesty,"

Avendall said smoothly. He would tell the company the news later. "I can do more for you here, I vow, by recruiting and training soldiers."

"Speaking of soldiers," Edward said, brightening, "how does Edgefield acquit himself these days? He was of no small use to the Duke of Lancaster, in our strife against the Gaul, and has been sorely missed since his leave-taking."

Avendall's jaw tightened; he relaxed it by force of will. "It is because of Edgefield that I have come to you, Your Majesty," he said. "I fear he has done me a grave injustice, and I must ask for your advice and consolation."

Edward raised a bushy, faded gold eyebrow. "If it is that old business, concerning the Sommerville wench—"

"No, Your Majesty," Avendall interjected, though only when it was clear that the king did not mean to finish his sentence. "It is a fresh and melancholy injury." With that, carefully, and with a restraint and a degree of imagination he seldom employed, Cyprian related the tale of his stolen and ill-used bride. "I would have recompense for this wrong," he finished, with an artfully subtle display of humility, considering how little peace he'd had of late, and no rest at all.

The king considered for a long time. Then, with an echo of his old authority and force, he made his pronouncement. "I shall summon Edgefield to court, and hear his account of this matter," he said. "If I determine that you have indeed been ill treated, though I confess I have little heart for the prospect, Chalstrey will be duly punished. Your bride, if such proves fitting, will be restored to you, by order of the crown."

Avendall suppressed a smile of satisfaction and

bowed deeply, and with grace. "Oh, aye," he affirmed, under his breath. "I want Gabriella. Indeed, I do." Let the king take from those words whatever he might. Avendall was not fool enough to tell him the simple truth: that Chalstrey had bested him with the wench and the knowledge was driving him mad.

13

❧

"I can delay my return to the abbey no longer, my child," Dame Johanna told Gabriella gently, on a bitterly cold afternoon a fortnight after their adventure with the wolves, as the two women sat by the fire in the great hall of Edgefield Keep. "Winter is but days away, and I have far to travel."

Gabriella, though wildly happy as Morgan's wife, had not yet mastered the more public and, in many ways, more demanding role of Lady Edgefield. She had no friends in her new home, and when Dame Johanna finally departed for St. Swithin's, there would be no older woman at hand, to lend wise counsel. Counsel Gabriella desperately needed.

She laid her stitchery in her lap and suppressed a contemptible desire to break down and weep. "I shall not like to see you go," she confessed, forcing herself to smile. "There is so much to learn—the keeping of accounts, managing the kitchens and servants, planning which garden plots should be seeded in the springtime and which are best left fallow, devising whether to plant more beans or more grain, and seeing to the needs of the villagers. I fear I shall not be a worthy mistress, either to my household or to those who look to me for herbals and midwifery."

Dame Johanna smiled fondly and extended her sturdy legs, wriggling her feet, in their oft-mended stockings, before the fire. "Nonsense," she said. "You will do all that is required of you, and surpass every expectation. I have never doubted your fitness for the tasks that lie ahead, Gabriella, nor should you."

As Morgan's bride, Gabriella was bound by the laws of heaven and earth to serve as his helpmate, in addition to bearing his children and bringing him solace when he sought her comfort; she had known that. But nothing could have prepared her—she who had seemed destined, until a year before, to languish in a nunnery for the remainder of her life—for the other myriad and largely overwhelming duties that were also her lot. All the same, a part of her thrived upon those very challenges.

"I heard a kitchen wench say my lord could be summoned away to war, if the king so wishes," Gabriella confided, in a brave and at the same time tremulous voice. "When I asked Morgan if the girl spoke true, he said she did. And that he was a knight, and thus pledged to honor His Majesty's requirements, whatever they might be."

The nun assessed her with a firm but kindly gaze. "Did you not know this, Gabriella? You, whose father was a king's man? Your husband is a soldier, through and through. And as Lord Edgefield's wedded wife, you must learn to take charge of all his holdings, in case he should be absent."

It wasn't without appeal, the thought of wielding so much power, and yet Gabriella oft lay awake at night, once the glorious fervor of her lovemaking with Morgan had ebbed a little, to dread the day he would leave her side, because he had been beckoned by the king.

How long might she be parted from him, this man she loved more devotedly, more passionately, with every beat of her heart? Months—years?

Always?

She shuddered as a draft swept down the chimney, nearly quenching the fire. "It is most costly to love," she whispered. "I might not have undertaken to care so greatly, nor so deeply, had I known."

"Aye," Dame Johanna affirmed. " 'Tis dear indeed, such rapture as I suspect you know with Edgefield, but well worth the price. Be of good courage, child. You are a fit wife for your husband, and an able mistress for his household. But you must set your thoughts upon the demands of each day as it comes, and let those to follow unfold as they will. To poison the present with fear of the future is not only foolish, but wasteful."

Before Gabriella could reply, there came a stir upon the stair, and Morgan appeared, accompanied by several of his men. She caught Sedgewick's name once or twice, and noted that it was uttered in uneasy tones. She was well aware that there had been no word of Morgan's friend, and no sign of the riders sent, these many weeks past, to find him.

Catching sight of Gabriella, however, Morgan put aside his worry to favor her with a smile that warmed her to her toes, dismissed the several men with whom he had been conferring in secret for many hours, and approached her chair.

When Gabriella would have risen, as was proper, he laid a light hand to her shoulder to forestall her, and let it linger there. Still, it was Dame Johanna whose gaze he sought and held.

"I have chosen six good men to see you safely back to the abbey, good dame," he said, in a courtly, even cordial fashion. Although Morgan and the nun had certainly had their differences, Gabriella knew her husband liked and respected Dame Johanna for her resourcefulness, her calm spirit, and her daring, among other reasons. The two of them oft played chess of an evening, and Morgan found the woman a formidable opponent. "Will the morrow suit, at first light?"

Gabriella flinched at this, though involuntarily; Morgan's fingers tightened reassuringly on her shoulder.

"Yes, my lord," Dame Johanna replied. "I am grateful." She rose and, after one searching look at Gabriella, left the chamber by way of the staircase.

Morgan drew a stool up close and sat square in front of Gabriella, bending a little to peer mischievously into her eyes. "What troubles you, my lady?" he asked. "Are you plotting to leave me again?"

No idea could have been further from Gabriella's mind. She blushed with indignation at the realization of that, because it was such irrefutable proof of Morgan's power over her. When had she come to need him so much, to care so vastly? Misliking him had been easier and, she ofttimes feared, not merely wiser, but safer as well.

"No, my lord," Gabriella answered, with dulcet irritation. "I shall not leave you, for you will only follow after, and drag me home again." She could not sustain her annoyance long, however, in the face of Morgan's reprehensible charm, and her voice was unsteady when she went on. "You spend your days upon the field, as though training for war."

Morgan did not flinch from the faint note of accusation she had not meant her words to carry. His expression turned solemn, though his eyes were gentle, and he took both Gabriella's hands in his. "These are harsh and treacherous times, my lady. It is only prudent to maintain the skills of soldiering."

"You believe that he will summon you. The king, I mean."

Morgan sighed. "I believe," he replied, "that I am a knight, with a knight's obligations to his sovereign and his realm." He leaned forward, raised Gabriella's hands, and brushed his lips across both sets of knuckles, sending a sweet, fiery shiver spearing through her. "Can it be, lovely Gabriella, that you fear for me? You who have so often blackened my shins and jibed at my manly pride?"

She blinked back tears and wrenched her hands free; indeed, she would have risen and stormed away, had he not been sitting so disturbingly close. "Of course I do, you fool," she cried, though in a raw and despairing whisper, rather than a shout, lest the servants should overhear. "Would that *you* had common sense enough to be afraid as well!"

He leaned forward and planted a teasing kiss upon her nose. "Gabriella," he reprimanded, but with a tender affection that melted much of her ire. "I am a practical man, and when there is aught to fear, I shall engage myself in as much trembling and whimpering as may be required of me. In the meantime, I should prefer to enjoy the singular gratifications of domestic peace."

Gabriella gave a great, shaky sigh and let her forehead rest against his. "I could not bear to lose you," she said.

He kissed her mouth, lightly, lingeringly. "Pray, my lady—do not mourn my death while I yet live," he told her, upon drawing back, his eyes bright with that mix of spirit and earthiness that was his alone.

Gabriella was dizzy from the kiss, and her cheeks burned with passion and the knowledge that he could arouse her to wantonness with such ease. "You go amiss, my lord," she protested, "to speak frivolously of so great a sorrow."

He touched her mouth with the pad of one thumb. "You care for me," he said, "at least a little."

She swallowed hard. "Aye, my lord," she said, near to weeping for love of Morgan Chalstrey. An idea occurred to her, and she brightened. "Might I not go soldiering, too? Other women have surely done so—"

Morgan withered the suggestion with a frown. "If I am summoned," he told her sternly, "you will remain here, at Edgefield Keep, until I return. And that, sweeting, is the end of the subject."

Gabriella settled back, and tried to believe, if only for a few shining moments, that there would be no parting, no farewells, for her and Morgan. And even then, behind the teetering facade of her conviction, lurked the certainty this was too much to believe in, too much to hope, for kings were fractious creatures, and gave little thought to the wives left behind to wait, to watch, and pray, and, all too often, to mourn.

The small party of sojourners gathered in the courtyard, before sunrise the next morning, the breath of human beings and horses alike making cloudy plumes in the misty air.

Dame Johanna stood beside Zacheus, facing Gabriella in the unsteady light of torches borne aloft by sleepy servants. The nun smiled. "You have found your place, child. You will thrive here, like a seed that has fallen upon good ground. Say your prayers, as you've been taught, and go often to mass."

Gabriella blinked back tears and stepped forward to kiss her friend's cheek and press a small leather packet into her hands. "Aye, good dame," she said. "I will do as you say." She drew a deep and unsteady breath. "May God bless and protect you, Dame Johanna. I shall miss you greatly."

"And I shall miss you," Dame Johanna replied, her eyes shining with affection, "though I think we are better parted, since each of us seems to inspire the other to mischief."

Gabriella made a sound that was part laughter, part sob. "Yes," she agreed, and trusted herself to say no more.

Dame Johanna placed the packet in the deep pocket of her plain cloak. "I will give your letters to Elizabeth and Meg as soon as I arrive at St. Swithin's," she promised. "Is there another message you would like me to pass on to them?"

"Aye," Gabriella said, with a sniffle. Morgan stood close by, and his support was almost palpable, for all that they were not touching. "Tell my sisters that I am very happy at Edgefield Keep." Among other things, Gabriella had told Meg and Elizabeth, in the painstakingly written letters Dame Johanna carried, that she and Morgan would send for them, in the late spring, when the roads were passable again. Morgan had agreed to provide not only generous dowries, but suitable husbands into the bargain, if both girls still wished to wed.

"I shall tell them," Dame Johanna agreed. Then she turned and, politely waving aside the help of a groom, hoisted herself up into Zacheus's saddle, ready to depart on the arduous journey back to the abbey.

Morgan, standing behind Gabriella now, closed the folds of his cloak around her, cocooning them both, lending her strength as well as warmth. Even in her sadness at bidding farewell to her dear friend, she felt a powerful wrench as her body instinctively responded to his. Oh, yes, he would distract her from her sorrows, in the solace of their bedchamber, and thoroughly so.

Confirming this, Morgan held her tightly against him, and bent his head to speak into her ear. "Come, my lady," he said, low enough that only she could mark his words. "Our bed awaits. Let us return to it, before it grows cold."

Gabriella watched as Dame Johanna and her armed escort vanished into the enfolding shadows of the darkest hour of the waning night, heard the distant creak of the great gates as they were drawn back. She turned in her husband's embrace and rested her head upon his shoulder. He stroked her hair, brushed light kisses over her temple and, finally, led her back to their chamber, there to console her tirelessly until, exhausted, boneless with contentment, she finally slept.

Dame Johanna had been gone only two days when the courier arrived from London, on a sunny but frigid morning, shouting from the drawbridge that he brought a message from no less a personage than His Majesty, King Edward, ruler of all Britain and parts beyond.

Gabriella had expected just this, of course, and had

filled herself with as much joy as she could contain, storing it up against the despair she had sensed was approaching, like a reeve laying aside extra grain, in anticipation of a desolate winter. Had not Morgan been trying to prepare her, however gently, by word and deed? They had talked far into the night, many times, after making love, of what it meant to be a knight of the realm.

She was in the village, spooning one of Dame Johanna's carefully memorized herbal remedies into the mouth of a feverish little girl, when the sight of a rider was heralded from the front gates. As soon as she decently could, Gabriella left her patient in the care of Mab, the midwife, and hurried out, heart pounding, to find out what was happening.

Morgan was descending the steps from the guard tower when she arrived at the gates, and they both heard the newcomer announce his business in a ringing voice.

When the portal was opened, the man rode in, arrogant in his royal livery.

Gabriella was filled with dread, but she followed close behind Morgan as he went to greet the visitor.

"Lord Edgefield?" the messenger asked, and only then did Gabriella see that he was hardly more than a boy. He had spots on his face and an air of uncertain authority about him, as though he were trying to play a part without first learning the required lines.

Morgan nodded. "Get you down from that saddle, lad. You surely have time for a meal and a few hours rest, and your horse looks ready to fold beneath you."

Reluctantly, the courier swung a leg over the gelding's back and slipped deftly to the ground. He pulled a pouch from inside his tunic—not an ample garment, in

Gabriella's judgment, against the bitter coastal chill—
and thrust it toward Morgan.

Gabriella drew nearer and read the message as soon
as Morgan unfolded it. *By order and command of His
Majesty, Edward III . . .*

What followed was a terse summons to Sheen, near
London, on a matter of "honor and expedience." Edgefield was to set out at once, and to bring his lady wife as
well.

Gabriella's apprehension was eased somewhat by the
latter part of the royal missive. Morgan could not ignore
the king's wishes, but there was no mention of the
ceaseless warfare in France, and she wasn't to be left
behind—not yet, at least. She was expected at court,
and a frisson of excitement spread through her.

Morgan folded the sheepskin and regarded the
youthful courier calmly, but in a way that disconcerted
both Gabriella and the boy all the same. From his expression and his bearing, she guessed that her husband
was not particularly pleased by the king's command that
she be brought along to Sheen, and she wondered why.

Morgan issued several swift orders. The lad's horse
was to be stabled, curried, and given oats and water.
The messenger was consigned to the kitchens, in the
company of one of Morgan's men, and he went eagerly.
The ride from London town had surely been long, cold,
and rigorous, and probably lonely, too.

Gabriella stood watching her husband, waiting, as
everyone else drifted away, taking their time about it.
She had wanted all her life to visit London, though even
she, in all her natural boldness, had never dared hope
for so much as a glimpse of the king. Now that she was
faced with the prospect, she found herself wishing

she could have been spared the encounter altogether.

"Avendall is in this," Morgan said, as much to himself as to Gabriella, when a long, awkward interval had passed.

"Surely not, milord," she said, though she felt a distinct uneasiness at the mention of her husband's enemy and her own. She slipped her arm through Morgan's, watching his face closely, practically holding her breath, lest he decide to defy the king and leave her behind. "We will make the journey, then? Together?"

Morgan made a bitter sound, the hoarse parody of a laugh. "We have no choice, my lady," he replied grimly. "Edward has long been a great friend to the Chalstreys, but he will countenance disobedience from no one. Even the Black Prince and the Duke of Lancaster would not dare to challenge him."

"When shall we go?" Gabriella asked, in a mild tone. Like Morgan, she had misgivings, but they were making the trip together, after all, and she was to see London. She would have preferred almost any ordeal to being separated from her husband, left behind to wonder what was happening to him.

At the same time, a icy wind buffeted the walls of her heart.

Avendall is in this, Morgan had said. On at least one level, she feared he was right.

"We will set out at first light," Morgan decreed, with distracted resignation. "Go inside, Gabriella. The wind is sharp."

"I am not delicate," she reminded him, "and I'm wearing my warmest cloak."

"And I, my lady, am not prone to husbandly indulgence just now," he countered. "Go." His countenance was grim, and his thoughts seemed far away.

Gabriella's better judgment won out over her pride, and she went into the keep, as Morgan had bidden her to do.

At dawn the following morning, they set out, with Morgan at the head of the caravan of horses and carts, and Gabriella tucked away in the middle of the procession, like some frivolous trinket, fashioned of the thinnest glass and wrapped fit to smother in thick batting.

She had no chance, all during the interval between the rising and setting of the sun, to escape her circle of guards and spur her black and white-spotted palfrey forward, that she might ride alongside Morgan, or at least keep him clearly in her sight. He had been summoned to court by the king, after all, and war raged across the narrow sea, in France. She misliked spending so much time apart, even at a short distance.

They traveled at a hard pace, stopping only briefly to rest and water the horses, and ate a midday meal of cheese and brown bread in their saddles. The sky was harsh, an unkindly blue, and the wind, laced with salt from the nearby sea, had an edge that cut through muscle and bone to lodge like splinters in the marrow.

Gabriella was grateful, though she would not have admitted as much, when twilight overtook them at last and Morgan called a halt beside a brook, where a few bare-limbed birch trees traced grim patterns against the clouds. He dismounted, gave orders to everyone in general, and was in private counsel with a half dozen of his best men until well after the moon had risen. Gabriella, eager to be useful, worked at the varied tasks of setting up camp.

When the fire had been built to a comforting roar and

a single tent of plain, sturdy cloth had been erected, the party supped on trout speared with sharp sticks and roasted crisp over the blaze. Guards had been posted, and the horses, all hobbled, nibbled at the autumn grass and drank from the clear stream. Those soldiers who had not been assigned to keep watch talked around the campfire, played dice, and told stories in tones chivalrously crafted to elude Gabriella's ear. The remaining men spread their bedrolls on the ground and stretched out to sleep.

Only when Gabriella had taken refuge inside the tent, there to lie, fully clothed, upon a pile of deer hides, half buried in blankets and still cold enough that her teeth were chattering, did Morgan finally appear.

"Alas," Gabriella teased, in an effort to lighten his mood, watching as he unbuckled his sword belt and laid it within reach of the pallet they would share, "I thought to have this tent all to myself tonight. Did you have supper, my lord?"

Morgan mumbled something, lost in thought, kicked off his leather boots, and crawled into the improvised bed beside her.

Gabriella was stung. In recent days, she had become accustomed to the attentions of a lover and husband. This man was a soldier first and foremost and, as such, a relative stranger. "Morgan?"

He sighed, slipped a desultory arm around her, and drew her against his side. "The day was long and I am weary, Gabriella. Let us take our rest, and save conversing for another time."

She was silent for a long interval, knowing she should heed his words, and leave him to sleep in peace, but something inside compelled her to put the question she had rehearsed a thousand times in her mind before that night, the question she had not yet dared to ask.

"Who was Rebecca?"

For a few moments, the atmosphere inside the tent was charged, like the rumble of soundless noise that precedes a particularly violent clap of thunder. Then, after a fierce sigh, Morgan answered. "You would ask me this *now?*" he retorted, and he sounded a little too reticent for her comfort.

"Now," she said, very gently.

"And if I refuse?"

"Neither of us will get so much as a wink."

Morgan waited until Gabriella's nerves were on edge. Then, incredibly, he gave in. "Rebecca Sommerville was my father's ward. She grew up at Edgefield Keep—those gowns you've been wearing were hers. We were raised together, Rebecca and I—I had no brothers or sisters—none that survived infancy anyway, nor did she. We were inseparable, everything to each other. My mother became an invalid when we were eight, and my father took himself off to London, to serve the king. Rebecca and I gradually fell in love, and meant to marry when we were of age."

Gabriella's throat was thick with sorrow. Morgan had loved Rebecca, and she suspected from his tone that he had never gotten over that sentiment. Even worse, she, Gabriella, had been wearing the other woman's garments all this while. Had Morgan wanted her to resemble the wife that fate had denied him?

"And did you—marry, I mean?"

Another silence, pulsing with such dangerous emotions that Gabriella wished she had never spoken.

"No," Morgan said, finally. "My father summoned

me to London, and by the time I returned to Edgefield Keep, Rebecca was gone."

"Gone?" Gabriella whispered, struck by a horrible premonition.

"Dead," Morgan told her, in a merciless undertone. "She was out riding one day, as the tale goes, and met with Avendall. He wanted to court her—we had ever been rivals, Cyprian and I, at games and the like—and she spurned him. But he persisted, and wooed Rebecca quite prettily. Eventually, he convinced her that my father had called me to London for the purpose of marrying me off to the daughter of one of his friends, in order to gain some political advantage.

"Such alliances are common, of course—far more prevalent than love matches. Too, Rebecca was hardly more than a child, and she believed Avendall's story, despite all the sacred promises she and I had made to each other." He paused again, and the interval, though brief, was so ominous that Gabriella braced herself, as if for a blow. "She went to him at Avendall Hall, thinking to hurt me as she had been hurt, and he bedded her, none too gently I suspect. The shame proved overwhelming—Rebecca was not worldly, though a measure of guile might have served her well—and two days before my return, she hurled herself off one of the cliffs into the sea."

Gabriella pressed a hand to her mouth, her eyes burning with tears. She could only too easily imagine how a sheltered girl, reared in the country and unpracticed in the ways of deceit, might be led to such a desperate place.

"H-how did you learn all this?" Gabriella asked. She tried to hold Morgan, but the muscles in his side and upper arm hardened in resistance, until at last she withdrew.

"Rebecca left a letter, along with her pendant. I wore it round my neck until the day I took you captive."

Gabriella recalled the hard fury in Morgan's face as he had wrenched off the talisman, suspended on a faded ribbon, and flung it at Halsey, the man Avendall had sent to escort her to Cornwall. At least, she would have described the emotion as anger then. Now, knowing Morgan better, Gabriella realized that she had missed the mark. What she had seen was nothing so minor as rage, but instead a searing, relentless, and very private anguish, rooted in the depths of his soul.

"I am so sorry," she said, and she referred to many things.

Morgan did not speak, but lay rigid beside her, his profile like granite in the shadows.

Gabriella felt him trembling, and knew that he needed to weep and, further, that he would never permit himself such an unmanly release. So she cried for him, snuggling close even though he tried, by simple coldness, to repel her.

Gabriella would not be put off, but slid her arms around Morgan, and embraced him, and grieved bitterly, for Morgan, for the poor, lost Rebecca and, perhaps most of all, for herself. Gabriella had known from the beginning that Edgefield did not love her, but she had cherished the hope of winning him for her own, in time. Now, she feared that whatever pleasures she wrought in Morgan's body, she might never touch the essence of the man at all.

The years ahead looked bleak indeed, and Gabriella mourned the death of a thousand dreams as she lay there, sleepless and broken, until exhaustion finally claimed her.

Toward morning, Morgan awakened Gabriella with an urgent kiss, so full of despair, and the wanting of solace, any solace, that her heart shattered into fragments. It was only too plain, even to a new bride like Gabriella, that her husband came to her not for herself, but for need of the girl who had perished in the brutal surf, never knowing how much Morgan had loved her. How much he would have forgiven.

Gabriella could not turn him away; she loved him too much, wanted him too fiercely. Like a peasant invited to a royal banquet, she would take her fill, and more, for there were famines ahead.

She put her arms around Morgan's neck and, with a shift of her hips, urged him onto her. He poised himself over her, dragged her kirtle to her waist, parted her legs, and with a desolate, nearly unintelligible plea for her pardon, plunged deep into her body in a single, jarring thrust.

Gabriella had expected pain, had braced herself to endure it, for there was little tenderness in Morgan on this morning, and he had not prepared her to receive him. All the same, that first powerful conquering sent a jolt of lightning burning through her veins, consuming her like a spreading fire, and she had to bite down hard on her lower lip to keep from crying out, not in protest, but in passion.

Morgan raised himself on the palms of his hands and loomed over Gabriella, shuddering and yet refusing to surrender his seed. "Oh, God, Gabriella," he rasped, forcing the words out through barely parted teeth, "forgive me—"

She stroked his face, his hair, to let him know there

was no reason to seek exoneration. Then, with primitive strength, she grasped Morgan's taut hips and drove him back into her very core.

With a low groan, like a man suspended between heaven and hell, Morgan erupted, stiffening, moving frantically, and then stiffening again. Gabriella spasmed beneath him, her strong young body convulsing in a mingling of sorrow and pleasure that she knew had bonded her to Edgefield for all of time. When the last soft cry had been wrung from them both, he collapsed beside her, an arm and a leg sprawled across her in that abandon peculiar to satisfaction and surrender. Only then did Gabriella realize that they were both drenched in sweat.

"I'm sorry," Morgan ground out, after a very long time, raising his head. Although she could not see his face clearly, she knew that he was looking into her eyes. "My God, Gabriella, I had no right to force—"

"Shh," she said. "I received you, my husband, because I wanted you. Had I told you to stop, you would surely have done so."

He lowered his forehead to hers, still gasping for breath. "I am not so certain of that," he confessed. "And the fact remains that I used you, Gabriella, with no thought for your pleasure, your comfort—"

Gabriella kissed his mouth. She spoke with a smile in her voice, grateful that he could not see the tears in her eyes. "Did you not notice, my lord, that I was bucking beneath you until the last? It might be said that I used you in return."

Morgan gave a sort of grinding sigh and thrust himself away from Gabriella, and the parting was painful, in the way of a bandage ripped too soon from a wound. "You don't understand," he said, with a terse effort at patience. "I shouldn't have taken you to wife, Gabriella, let alone to bed. I ought to be damned to a thousand hells for what I've done, and there's no setting matters aright, unless I return you to the abbey."

Gabriella went cold as his meaning dawned upon her, for all the heat that still throbbed in her body. "You would put me away from you?" she asked, in a small and stricken voice. There could be no hiding that he'd dealt her a mortal wound. "But you cannot, my lord—I love you!"

Morgan cupped her face in his hands. "Don't say that, I pray you. I cannot bear to hear it."

"But 'tis the purest truth, my lord!"

"Then you must make a lie of it, Gabriella. I have loved once in my life, and badly, and I dare not do so again. For both our sakes, my lady, turn from me. Hate and despise and revile my very name, for I have earned your contempt. But by all the angels in heaven, *do not* ever utter such a vow again!"

Gabriella doubled up her fists, in frustration and terrible grief, and pounded at Morgan's chest until he finally took hold of her wrists, not in anger but in mercy, and made her stop. Breathing hard, he buried his face in her neck, and she would have sworn she felt his tears against her skin.

In the end, though, she decided they must have been her own.

14

❧

During the first part of their grueling journey, Morgan took great care to avoid Gabriella. He ate by himself, if at all, and even though the nights were cold, occasionally dusting horses and bedrolls with a feathery fall of snow, he did not return to the tent to lie with his wife.

Gabriella was beyond despair, though she was determined to let no one see her sorrow, her fractured pride, least of all Morgan Chalstrey, Duke of Edgefield. She rode with the countenance of a queen, chin raised, shoulders straight, back rigid. Inside, however, she was as shattered as the lost Rebecca must have been, standing upon the cliff's edge and gazing downward upon the rocks.

Of course, Gabriella had no intention of sacrificing her life for melancholy and regret, as Rebecca had done. Chalstrey did not love her, indeed, he was even now laying plans to send her back to the abbey, but she still had her precious hopes, and was sustained by them. Morgan's body burned for hers, and she knew it. In time, that burning might reach beyond his loins, into his heart and soul. Yes, he would come to her, wherever he'd tucked her away for safekeeping, and she would be ready. Waiting.

In the meantime, Gabriella meant to make her days count for something; she would return to Redclift Hall, if Morgan did not relent, but carried out his threat to put her aside, and find ways to occupy her hands and her mind. Neither would she allow Morgan to turn her out with nothing, though in truth his generosity was the least of her concerns. Gabriella knew her husband to be a fair man, for all his lack of sentimentality, and she trusted him to provide her with what she would require to carry out her plans: gold to buy sheep and horses, pigs and cows, looms for weaving, stone and timber for the repairs the manor so desperately needed.

John Robinson, Morgan's second in command after Sedgewick, who seemed the only one inclined to seek out Gabriella's company, reined in his stocky warhorse, slowing his pace to match hers. "You are undone, my lady," he observed, with gruff kindness. "There is an inn just over that next hill. Shall I advise his lordship that you want rest and sustenance?"

She turned aching eyes upon him, filled with fire. She would not be thought weak. Morgan was unlikely to leave her behind, she knew, but she refused to be the reason for cutting that day's travel short. "There is no need," she said. "I am as able as anyone else in this party."

Robinson looked rueful, but he was clearly not a man to be easily turned aside from doing a kindness, whether it was wanted or not. "Pardon me, my lady," he said, with quick humility. "I do not wish to offend. It is only that—well—" He glanced toward the front of the procession, and Morgan's impervious back, then went

on in a more constrained manner. "You do seem exceeding weary, and it will be dark soon."

With Dame Johanna gone back to St. Swithin's and
Morgan closing her off from him as surely as if she were
a leper, she was in sore need of a friend and confidant.
Not only would darkness be upon them before long, but
the wind was cold, and she was hungry. Her mouth wa-
tered at the thought of a savory stew, and mayhap a
spiced wine to ease her sore muscles. "I am as fit to
travel as anyone else in this company," she said mildly.

"Peace, my lady," the soldier protested, in a disarm-
ingly gentle way. "You look fit to tumble from your saddle. Allow me to speak to the master, I beseech you, if not
for your sake, then for that of the others, and the horses."

She assessed her husband, who might have felt her
regard; though it seemed Morgan stiffened in the saddle, he did not turn his arrogant head to meet her
gaze. "If you would make this plea, then name yourself
and the men and the horses as the cause. I will have
none of it."

Robinson raised an eyebrow. "I see that pride is your
pet sin, my lady," he teased. " 'Tis a common enough
failing. Alas, though, will Edgefield think you strong if
you collapse at his feet?"

Gabriella bit her lower lip. The exploits and misadventures of the day had indeed taken their toll on her,
and she yearned for something to eat, a warm wash at a
basin, and a soft, clean bed in which to sleep. For all of
that, she could not find it within herself to give in, for
pride truly *was* her greatest failing. "Methinks you concern yourself overmuch," Gabriella said and, with the
heels of her soft boots, nudged Sweetbriar, her little palfrey, to a speedier gait. The horse, a marriage gift from

Morgan, was spirited. But the graying soldier kept pace.

"He has the endurance of a young ox, our lord and master," the man persisted, indicating Morgan with a nod, "and will keep us all in the saddle until we swoon, hardened soldiers though we are."

Gabriella sighed. The inn was just coming into view, and she saw smoke curling from the chimneys, and a pleasant glow of lamp light at the windows. "Very well, then," she said. "But do not be too disappointed if Lord Edgefield finds my discomfort no cause for leniency."

Robinson reached over to touch her hand as a light snow began to fall. "The master is more solicitous than you know, my lady."

Gabriella said nothing, for already she was wishing she could call back the last words she had spoken. Morgan's spurning of her, as obvious as it must be to every man in the company, was still a private concern, and the thought of them all pitying her was nigh unbearable.

Her champion quickened his horse, that he might catch up to Morgan, and was gone before Gabriella could think of a graceful way to call him back. She watched, in a silent misery of numb feet, aching muscles, and disjointed pride as Morgan and his associate conferred.

Robinson pleaded an earnest though inaudible case, gesturing toward Gabriella, while Morgan looked as fierce and unyielding as a chieftain from one of the wild northern clans. Once, he glanced at her, his eyes angry and colder than any wind the forces of nature could unleash, and in that moment Gabriella wanted to do him some terrible and lasting violence, to scream at her husband that *she* had not been the one to begin their ill-fated union. He had.

She narrowed her eyes and glared at Chalstrey's back, now conspicuously turned to her again. Gabriella was reminded of a marvel she had once seen a peddler hocking at a fair, near St. Swithin's: a circle of glass that, when looked through, made small things large, and when positioned to receive the sun, sparked a smoldering blaze.

In the meantime, the snowflakes thickened, until they were the size of goose feathers, and fell with placid insistence upon a frost-hardened earth. They did naught, for all their chill, to cool Gabriella's growing wrath.

At last, Morgan relented, and granted the requested boon, though in a supremely ungracious manner. At the master's brusque command, his men reined their horses toward the welcoming inn, all of them trying, it seemed to her, not to look too pleased or to draw his attention in any way. Gabriella, taking a measure of solace in rebellion, fixed her eyes on Morgan and wished she had a snowball to fling at his back.

There were other travelers at the inn, due to the rapidly worsening weather, and only one room remained. Morgan's men were assigned places in the lofts of the stable, accommodations they were glad to get, and Gabriella was awarded the chamber. She assumed, given his decision to push her out of his life, that Morgan, like the others, would take his rest with the oxen and the milk cows. Or, better still, the pigs.

Telling herself she did not care *where* he passed the night, Gabriella took her supper beside the fire in the public room, and then retired to her chamber. If she was going to cope with the rigors to come—and she most certainly intended to—she needed her rest.

With the innkeeper's wife leading the way, lantern in

hand, Gabriella entered the tiny but remarkably clean room where she would sleep. A hearty fire crackled on the hearth, and the bedding looked not only innocuous, but inviting. As far as she could discern, after a careful examination, there were no vermin.

The proprietress made no comment on Gabriella's inspection of the mattress, but simply lighted the oil lamps on either side of the narrow bed, then went out. There was an enormous iron key in the door, and Gabriella viewed it with relief. Although she had never before stayed in such an establishment, she knew that inns could be most perilous places, with thieves and brigands and even murderers abounding.

Yearning for a hot bath, a luxury she knew would have strained the charity even of the innkeeper's wife, Gabriella resigned herself to none, stripped to her chemise, and crawled into bed. *Her* chemise indeed, she thought ruefully, adding another demand to the list she would present to Edgefield before he turned her out: bolts of sturdy wool, for gowns and kirtles of her own, and muslin for more private garments. Shoes, as well, and two warm cloaks, with hoods and linings of fur.

An end, at last, to wearing a dead girl's garments.

The key shimmied in the lock, making a clattering sound as it struck the floor that brought Gabriella bolt upright with a gasp. She pressed one hand to her heart, fingers spread, and called out, "This chamber is occupied!"

Dislodged, the key lay upon the timbers of the floor, and the door swung open. Morgan loomed in the chasm, looking rumpled and a little confused.

"How did you unlock that door?" Gabriella demanded, pulling the covers up to her neck.

He executed a bow, and she knew then that he had had one too many ales. "I didn't have to," he said, straightening again. "If you would have the door secured, my lady, you must turn the key."

Tears burned behind her eyes. She'd be damned to perdition if she'd shed them in this man's presence. Gabriella pressed her lips together and said nothing.

He shrugged and closed the door behind him. Then, stooping with less grace than he would usually employ, Morgan grasped the key, inserted it in the lock, and turned it with a deliberate motion of his hand.

"I do not desire your company, sir," she lied. "Please go."

He laughed, approaching the bed with a slightly unsteady step. Looking down at Gabriella, he unfastened his sword belt and laid it aside. Then, drawing a narrow-bladed dagger from his right boot, he put that on the crudely made night table. "Do not trouble yourself, my lady," he said, slurring his words a little, though Gabriella privately doubted if anyone would have noticed the lapse, besides herself, "for while I have much enjoyed divesting you of your virtue, thrust by thrust, I am repentant, and sworn to resist temptation in all its lovely—*lovely* forms." By then, he was looking at her with an interest that was, in the circumstances, untoward.

"Would that you had resisted the last several mugs of ale you must have consumed, as well," Gabriella remarked, with cultivated disdain. In truth, she knew that he was not nearly so drunk as he contrived to look and sound, though she could not imagine his reasons for this unbecoming pretense.

Morgan smiled, though his eyes glittered with something quite apart from happiness or mirth, and sat down on the bed to pull off his boots. "Aye," he said, with expansive and wholly unconvincing regret, "but I succumbed, and I am, I fear to confess, royally, spectacularly, *magnificently* drunk."

"If you think that reprehensible state excuses your intrusion, sir, you are sorely misguided. I do not want you in this chamber and I bid you take your leave." She was talking through her teeth by that point. "Go and sleep in the stable, where you belong."

Morgan let out an explosive yawn. "A cruel cut, my lady," he lamented, and hauled his tunic off over his head, revealing his muscular back. Gabriella felt a mortifying compulsion to touch him. "Alas, Lady Edgefield, it is a cold night, and I prefer your company to that of the oxen. Though barely, I must say."

"I will tell you only once more, *Lord* Edgefield: get out."

He laughed and tossed the tunic away, then divested himself of his trunks and hose. "If you so despise my company, sweeting, find another place to sleep. It was my coin, after all, that bought our night's lodging, and I'm not going anywhere." With that, Morgan leaned over, blatantly naked, and put out the lamp on his side of the bed.

Gabriella could not and would not sleep anywhere but in that room, and Chalstrey knew that, of course. She stretched awkwardly to quench the wick in her own lamp, trying to keep herself covered as she did so. "Just be sure you do not touch me, then," she said. This petulance did not serve the ends she had in mind, but she couldn't seem to get round her pride.

Morgan snored, loudly and in a manner meant to convey utter unconcern.

She snatched up her pillow and pounded him with it, again and again, desperately and furiously, until feathers filled the air and Morgan finally reached out to grasp her wrist and stay the assault.

"You have reason to hate me," he said, with a gentleness that was her undoing. "And I am so sorry, Gabriella, that I ever set foot in your life—it was an unconscionable trespass. May we not be kind to each other, until a proper parting can be managed?"

Gabriella's emotions reeled. What was it that this man wanted of her? Did he expect to bed her, until he could dispatch her back to the abbey—was that what he meant by "being kind to each other?"

"God's eyeballs," she spewed, "how I hate you! I would sooner part my thighs for blue-faced heathen than for you!"

Morgan sighed again, but she thought she heard an undertone of grim amusement in the sound. "Gabriella, I fear the nuns shall find great tribulation in the task of redeeming you. And I am not asking you to 'part your thighs,' as you so eloquently put it. I merely want to make a truce between us."

She was silent for a while, still spitting with rage, but aware that, once again, by raising her ire, Morgan had gotten the advantage. And she was damned if she would let him keep it.

"I will not be returning to the convent," she said, carefully, and after a long time spent tamping down her temper. "I intend to go back to Redclift Hall, there to take matters in hand. I should like you to provide sheep—a healthy flock, mayhap five and twenty in number. And I will require other things, too."

It was Morgan's turn to be silent. Ominously so.

"What in the name of God are you talking about?" he demanded, at last. Gabriella took a certain forlorn satisfaction in the awareness that he, too, was struggling to contain himself. "You will *not* return to Redclift, nor will you raise sheep. Those are not proper pursuits for a lady."

"I am not a lady."

"I must give you that. The nuns are probably your only hope of living an admirable and circumspect life."

"I do not intend to spend the rest of my days behind abbey walls," Gabriella said, with the greatest of clarity, using the same tone she might have taken with the mule, Zacheus. "Pray, leave off making demands, my lord, for you have chosen to put me away, have you not? I have my own plans, and they do not include moldering away in a nun's cell." She paused, purposely striving to irritate him now. "Mayhap, now that I am— besmirched, as it were, I shall take lovers."

She had succeeded beyond her greatest expectations.

Morgan rolled onto his side and even in the darkness, she saw the furious glint in his eyes. *"You shall lie with no other man for the rest of your days!"* he growled.

Gabriella felt a rush of triumph, soon followed by an equally dizzying sense of doubt. "Of course not," she said, with sweet idiocy. "I was planning to do that *at night*. In the daytime, I shall surely be occupied with sheep and fields and the like."

"Damn it, Gabriella!" Morgan roared, obviously unconcerned that they were not alone in the inn, that snowy night. "Are you trying to drive me mad? You know full well that I cannot bear the thought of any man touching you!"

"You shall just have to learn to bear it, then,"

Gabriella said moderately, enjoying the shift of power his anger had wrought. But an instant later, she was engulfed in sorrow, and when she spoke again, her tone was soft and unsteady. "Just as I must learn to go on, through one day and the next, and the one after that, while I wait for the hurting to stop."

Morgan lowered his forehead to hers. "I never meant to do you injury, Gabriella—I swear it," he said brokenly. "I cannot be the husband you need, the husband you deserve. I am a soldier, and I will never be anything more or less."

She smoothed his hair with tender motions of her hands. She could not speak.

Morgan folded Gabriella into his arms, and somehow, they slept, chastely, but without ease.

The next morning, the snow lay deep all around the inn, blanketing the countryside in a deceptive mantel of pristine and glittering white. The horses moved slowly through the stuff, and Morgan and all his men seemed especially watchful.

Gabriella urged her palfrey gently onward, pondering, as she went, the strange foibles of men. Morgan did not want her for a wife, or so he claimed, and yet the thought of her making her own way in the world, and taking lovers, had roused him to such a state that he had temporarily lost the inner control that had been the hallmark of his character from the first.

Gabriella permitted herself the merest and most fleeting of smiles. For the first time since Morgan had rebuffed her, she was truly hopeful. Mayhap, like the rest of the world, the master of Edgefield did not know his own mind and heart so well as he fancied he did.

As they progressed toward London, she occupied herself by choosing names for their children. There would be six, she decided ambitiously, three sons, and three daughters.

Morgan's mood was foul as he led his lumbering company of men, horses, and one impossible woman through the hard-crusted snow. His mind, always so orderly, so disciplined, was in chaos, and the aches in his body had naught to do with weather or hard travel. He had thought to insulate himself from Gabriella's charms by presenting himself as a drunkard, but he didn't think he'd fooled her, and lying beside her had been sheer agony.

He had not chosen to share her room out of any desire to test his will, or to torment himself, though he had surely accomplished both those ends. He had simply not trusted anyone else to protect Gabriella as he would. And the inn, for all its merry warmth and the decent fare that was served at its rough tables, was a known haven for thieves, smugglers, and all manner of outlaws.

With Gabriella beside him, warm and soft and fragrant, Morgan had nearly lost the small measure of honor that remained to him. He had wanted her, for all her snappish tongue and pillow pummeling, with a ferocity that frightened him, even then, hours after the fact. He had come close to repeating the travesty of that first night out of Edgefield Keep, when, like an animal in season, he had lost control and ravished a woman it was his duty to protect.

Gabriella's instinctive responses, her gentle protests, afterward, that she had wanted him, had in fact welcomed his lovemaking, afforded him no consolation. At the peril

of his own sanity, he had stayed away from her after that
night. He'd made up his mind to undo the marriage, and
thus leaving her alone was the decent thing to do.

Squinting against the glare of sunlight on snow,
seeing with mingled relief and dread the smudged
and smoky horizon that meant they would reach London within a few hours, Morgan let his thoughts turn
to Gresham Sedgewick. A weight, chilled and honed
sharp at its edges, settled deep into the pit of his
stomach.

Something was wrong there, for Gresh was long
overdue, and so were the men dispatched to find him.
There had been no messages, though ample time had
passed, and Morgan found the echoing silence more
troublesome than anything else. Had it not been for Edward's imperious summons, which even he dared not ignore, Morgan would have escorted Gabriella back to
the abbey himself, and confronted his friend, if he was
still there. With every passing day, it seemed more likely
that Gresham had decided upon a parting of the ways;
God knew, he'd been angry enough when last Morgan
had seen him.

He set his jaw, impatient with the unaccustomed,
rambling nature of his thoughts. One task at a time,
Morgan reminded himself, counting them off in his
mind. Make his appearance at court, along with whatever obeisances the king might subsequently require.
Restore Gabriella to the safety and, yes, the *sterility* of
the nunnery. Last of all, find Gresham and settle their
differences, for good or ill.

He risked a look back over his shoulder, and saw
Gabriella riding through the deep snow with an expression of sublime competence on her face. No, Morgan

thought miserably, as his groin tightened with an intensity of desire he feared no other woman could quench, he was wrong to suppose that anything would ever be the same for him. Even if he did not set eyes upon Gabriella Redclift again, in all the time God might have allotted him, she had conquered him, and in some ways, he would always belong to her.

Gresham might have been riding beside him, so clearly did Morgan hear his friend's voice then, ringing in his head. *Mayhap you love the woman—has that not occurred to you?*

Morgan raised a silent argument. *I have loved once, and once was more than sufficient.*

He saw Gresh's smiling face in his mind's eye. *You are not only a coward, my friend, but a fool. What you had with Rebecca was naught but the frolic of children—poor Becky was too fey by half to make a real wife, and you were a mere pup, with about as much understanding of the heart and its ways. Now, here you are, with this spirited woman, capable of bringing the same fire to your life that she brings to your bed, and you haven't the courage to step into the flames.*

In those moments, Morgan missed Gresham's counsel desperately; knowing what his friend would have said, had he been there, was no substitute. *God in heaven, Gresh, don't be dead. Be furious. Name me your enemy, for now and always. But, please, don't be dead.*

There was no response, silent or, of course, otherwise, to Morgan's plea.

Presently, Chalstrey wheeled his horse about and waited, while his men flowed around him, avoiding his gaze, until Gabriella reached his side.

She was blue-white with cold, and the hem of her gown, brushing over the snow, was sodden and frayed. For all of that, she held her head at an angle befitting a Plantagenet and merely looked at him.

"We will reach London before sunset," he told her, holding Nimrod to the palfrey's delicate but steady pace. "Sheen lies but a short way beyond."

Gabriella indicated the sooty horizon with a flick of her eyes. "Aye," she said. "Mayhap you will give me gold, that I might buy cloth for gowns of my own. I would not shame you at court, my lord, even though you plan to abandon me."

She was baiting him, Morgan knew that and fell into the trap anyway. Mayhap because it was a most alluring snare, where the struggle to be free, although hopeless, was pleasurable as well.

"The gowns I have given you *are* your own."

"They are Rebecca's," Gabriella said, in implacable challenge. "I would have others, made only for me."

"Fine," Morgan snapped, but he was not just irritated, he was also entertained. Enchanted. "Will silk and velvet serve, your ladyship?"

"Only if studded with diamonds and pearls," she said smoothly. There was a new fragility about her, Morgan noticed then, and he was more troubled than before.

Gabriella's beautiful eyes were faintly glazed, and her skin, though pale as the snow around them, felt hot when Morgan wrenched off one of his gloves to touch her face.

She did not withdraw from him, and that was a mercy, for he would not have been able to bear it. Not then.

"You are fevered, my lady," he said, almost accusingly.

Gabriella's smile, always saucy before, was now wan and somehow tattered, like a bit of brightly colored cloth, fluttering in a thornbush. Robinson had been right, then, when he'd implied that the rigors of this new journey might be Gabriella's undoing.

"Mine is a minor ailment," she said, "requiring no more than the brewing of the proper simple and a warm bath. I see by the look in your eyes, Edgefield, that you credit yourself with far too much influence over my well-being."

Gabriella's words stung, as they had no doubt been calculated to do. And Morgan knew he deserved a jab or two.

"If you want gowns of velvet and silk," he said, "and jewels of every hue, you shall have them."

"Such generosity serves your own interests more than mine, methinks," Gabriella replied coolly. "I shall accept your largesse, though I cannot grant the absolution you seek."

God's blood, but her aim was better than good. "You are not my priest," Morgan retorted, though he was at a loss and did not trouble himself to disguise the fact. "I make no confession to you."

"And I ask none. It is cloth I want. Seeds and horses. Pigs and sheep. Looms for weaving."

"You are but a woman, with no knowledge of husbandry. And did you not complain to Dame Johanna, hardly more than a fortnight past, that you were not trained for such practicalities as planting and keeping accounts?"

His reward was the look of surprise that hesitated so briefly in her eyes.

"I am intelligent—mayhap your equal or even your better in that respect—and I learn with wondrous ease.

In no time at all, I shall find a way to turn Redclift to a profit. All I need is the chance to try."

"No doubt your mother and stepfather will have opinions on that subject."

"My mother is not a spirited woman, my lord, and my stepfather, while equally harmless, is indolent to a fault. As long as there is barley beer and leisure to enjoy it, he will be content to surrender the running of the manor to me."

"You are very confident. And how is it that your mother, if so feeble, has made such a troublesome and contentious chit as you?"

Gabriella smiled, though she looked more fragile than ever. "Good fortune, I presume," she said, and then, swaying, clung to the pommel of her saddle with both hands.

Muttering a curse, Morgan hooked an arm round her slight waist and hauled her off the palfrey and onto his own horse. He enfolded her in his cloak, as well as his embrace, and felt the searing heat of her flesh even through his jerkin and tunic.

"Why did you not tell me you were ailing?" he demanded, driving the stallion to move faster through the deep snow.

Gabriella sagged against him, small, for all her bluff and bluster, and hardly more substantial than a sparrow. "The journey has been a trial for everyone in the company," she said.

" 'Everyone in the company,' besides you, of course, is a seasoned soldier. You cannot expect to have the same stamina, Gabriella. That is either madness or the pinnacle of arrogance."

"I know, I know," came the taunting and oddly tender reply, as she nestled against him, deep within the folds of his cloak. And, mayhap, those of his heart. "I am but a woman."

Despite his fear for Gabriella, his desperation to reach Sheen and thus the shelter and sustenance she needed, Morgan laughed and tightened his arms around her for a moment. "Aye," he agreed. "As a tigress is but a tigress." At the same time, he was wondering how he could ever give her up, either to death or to honor.

15

❧

Gabriella first saw the great, bawdy spectacle that was London through a haze of fever, torchlight, and acrid smoke. They boarded a barge at twilight, Morgan and Gabriella and all their soldiers, to travel down the River Thames, through the heart of the city, and beyond.

Throughout the morning and afternoon, Gabriella had ridden on Nimrod's back, cradled in Morgan's arms. The one time she had stood on her own foot, on the bank of the Thames, she had come perilously close to swooning, and Morgan had immediately gathered her up again. He had not let her go since.

They arrived at Sheen, where the king was presently holding court, just as twilight resolved itself into full night. Gabriella was both excited and fearful—no one she knew, except for her long-dead father, had ever been to the royal palace, let alone met the king—but the illness compelled her to sleep.

She fought it with all her strength, an effort which only exhausted her further.

Morgan carried her directly into the fortress, his

strides long, his jaw set in a way that indicated carefully contained outrage. Plainly, he did not wish to pay homage to the king, on that evening at least, and just as plainly, he had no choice in the matter.

It was, mayhap, a mercy that Edward had anticipated their appearance, and so did not keep them waiting long. Entering the rustic, well-lighted room where the king received petitioners and members of court, Gabriella was dazzled by the brightness of the torches and lamps, but not so blinded that she did not notice Avendall, standing below the dais, just to one side of the throne. His hands were folded, his head lowered in a mockery of humility. His manner was one of circumspection.

Morgan had been right, then, Gabriella thought fuzzily. Avendall *was* involved; he had surely provoked the king's summons.

"Chalstrey!" Edward boomed, with undisguised delight, from his magnificent seat upon the dais. Then, taking in Gabriella, still being borne in Morgan's arms, like an invalid, the once-great warrior drew his brows together and frowned. "What ails the lass?"

Morgan bent his knees slightly and inclined his head in obeisance before replying. "She is unwell, Your Majesty, and much in need of comfort and sustenance."

Edward gestured to one of his attendants. "Gibbon, fetch a litter, and find my physician."

Gabriella tightened her arms round Morgan's neck. "Pray, my lord," she whispered anxiously, "do not leave me in the care of a leech. Dame Johanna says the letting of blood is an evil medicine—"

"I thank you graciously, Your Majesty," Morgan said, in a clear voice, "but I should prefer to look after my wife personally." His gaze sliced sharp as a new-forged blade to Avendall, whom he had surely caught sight of before, then returned to the king. The slight but unmistakable emphasis Morgan had placed upon the phrase "my wife" did more to restore Gabriella than any potion could have.

"As you wish, then," Edward replied, somewhat distractedly.

Avendall cleared his throat.

"Oh, yes," the king continued. "There is the matter of your marriage, Chalstrey. Avendall has raised a charge against you—he maintains that you stole the woman from him. Is that so?"

Before Morgan could frame a reply, Gabriella spoke up. "I went willingly to my lord Edgefield."

The king glanced at his petitioner. Avendall's color flared, and his eyes glittered with malice as he stared at Gabriella.

"What say you of this, Avendall?" the king demanded.

"The lady was to be my bride," Avendall said, quite calmly, though his expression betrayed the intensity of his fury. "You yourself promised her to me, Your Majesty."

"I?" the king asked, and sounded befuddled.

"You've been her benefactor these many years," Avendall prompted. "The decision was yours to make."

Gabriella felt as though the floor had opened to swallow her. Edward, the king of England, was her benefactor?

"Ah, yes," Edward reflected. "I promised Redclift I would provide for his daughters, should he perish in my service." He leaned forward in his massive chair and touched the tips of his long fingers together.

"I knew Redclift," Avendall offered smoothly. "He was a knight, a gifted soldier, with an honorable name and a worthy heritage, and he served you faithfully. You did the right thing by placing Gabriella and her sisters under your protection. When I petitioned for a wife from that family, you granted my request. I ask only that you honor that pledge."

Gabriella, though still light-headed, struggled out of Morgan's embrace to stand teetering on her own feet. "I am not a piece of property, to be pledged and protected," she said, addressing the king. She would have gone sprawling, for the weakness in her knees, had it not been for Morgan's swift grasp and subsequent support. His arm was like an iron band around her waist.

Avendall smiled. "As you can see," he said to the king, "she is a fiery wench." He drew a folded parchment from inside his blue silk tunic and extended it to Edward. "Here is your own decree, Your Majesty, bearing your seal."

It was Morgan, not Edward, who leaned forward and snatched the worn missive from his enemy's hand. "Those of us who know you, Avendall," he growled, "do not find it in the least odd that you should fail to obtain a bride by your own merit."

Avendall went white, but recovered his composure very quickly. Gabriella could see that he wanted her back, though God only knew why, and he expected to win. What frightened her was his reason: he wanted to punish her for loving Morgan, punish Morgan for interfering with his plans. "Apparently you have forgotten Rebecca Sommerville," Avendall said in a level voice.

"I will not have that business raised again!" Edward interceded, with force. "We've settled that, long since."

"Mayhap you have, Your Majesty," Morgan said

evenly, his gaze never leaving Avendall's face. "For my adversary and me, I fear it is otherwise."

"It was Sedgewick Rebecca wanted," Avendall persisted.

Morgan said nothing, but Gabriella felt the heat of his rage as surely as the fever blazing within her.

"Give her up, Chalstrey," Avendall said. "Gabriella is rightfully mine. I will look after her and, in time, she will come to care for me."

Gabriella, though still depending upon Morgan to remain upright, was incensed, and turned a fiery gaze upon the king. "This man is mad!" she cried. "Am I to have no say about my own fate, Your Majesty? By God, I would name *neither* of these men husband—one has already decreed that I shall live out my days in a nunnery, and the other wants me only to spite his foe!"

"Did you not say you went to Chalstrey freely?" Edward challenged Gabriella, leaning forward. "You would deny him as a husband, and refuse Avendall as well?"

"Yes, my lord."

The king frowned. "I see," he said, though he plainly did not.

Morgan let out his breath but said nothing. Avendall merely folded his arms and waited, certain of victory.

"I have no wish to live out my life in an abbey," Gabriella added, using the last of her strength.

Edward leaned forward thoughtfully, brow crumpled. "By God and all the saints, Chalstrey, are you blind or simply stupid? This young woman is of the best and sturdiest stock, ripe for bedsport, and in no way fitted for the veil!"

Gabriella felt Morgan's fury flow through him, like contained lightning, but his hold on her did not slacken, and his voice betrayed no emotion at all. He spoke, in fact, with cool reason.

"I misspoke, Your Majesty, when I told my lady I would return her to the convent. She is well and thoroughly bedded." At this, Morgan again turned to glance at Avendall. "Ours was a lovers' quarrel, nothing more, and soon settled upon my pallet."

Gabriella was dizzy with fever, but she held her tongue, for she had already said too much.

Edward laughed wistfully at Morgan's boast, no doubt recalling conquests of his own. He was still a most impressive man, for all his failing health and innate sadness of spirit, and it was not difficult to imagine him surrounded by women.

"Aye, then," agreed the king, with a jovial expression dancing in his faded eyes. "Your lady wife wants taming, Chalstrey, as well as rest, for her tongue is too ready and her temper too quick. See that you train her to be a credit to you."

Gabriella let out her breath.

Edward turned his gaze upon Avendall, and immediately grew somber. "I fear you have made an unfortunate bargain," he said. "Honor demands that Chalstrey compensate you in some way, but as the marriage has been consummated, it cannot be annulled, either by God's laws or by mine. Mayhap you will choose another bride, from amongst Redclift's remaining daughters."

At this last, Gabriella broke free of Morgan's grasp again, a feat that could only have been managed by surprise, since his strength was so much greater than hers. "Oh, no, Your Majesty!" she cried, in a pleading and distraught voice, slumping to her knees at the foot of the dais. "I beseech you—do not let Avendall take either of my sisters to wife! He is a brute, and will surely break their spirits!"

Morgan came forward and drew her gently up into his arms. His voice was quiet and earnest as he spoke to the king. "I will make redress to Avendall," he said, "not only for Gabriella's bride-price, but for the others as well." He looked at his old adversary, who stood only a few feet away. "In gold. In lands or horses. Whatever is necessary."

When Gabriella dared to look at Avendall, she saw that he was trembling with the effort to contain his outrage.

"Your Majesty," he protested, "is this to be my redress? To have not one bride but three taken from me? I have no want of gold! Will you allow your subjects to steal from one another, and go unpunished?"

Edward's expression altered in a way that chilled Gabriella's insides. He looked pensive. " 'Tis truth," he said, at long last, "that thievery of any sort, especially among knights, must not be permitted. Chalstrey, by your oath, did you or did you not take this woman from Avendall by force?"

"I did," Morgan said, with neither shame nor insolence.

Gabriella gave a little gasp—she meant to remind the king of what she had said earlier, that she had gone to Morgan willingly, but Morgan silenced her with a squeeze that nearly crushed her bones.

The king considered. "You will serve no less than a year in France, to make penance," he said, after a long pause. Even Gabriella, who had precious little understanding of political matters, understood that Edward's decision was not based on a desire for justice. No, it served his own ends to send Morgan back to the battlefields across the narrow sea; he was merely using the supposed transgression against Avendall as an excuse.

"What of my sisters?" Gabriella dared to ask.

Edward waved a hand. "I see no reason to deny Avendall his choice."

She gazed up at her estranged husband, sick with fear. "Morgan? Will you do nothing? Say nothing?"

He touched her face with the backs of his fingers but did not reply.

The worst of Gabriella's fears had come to pass. She tried again to make a protest, but Morgan spoke to her in a fierce whisper before she could find her voice. "Do not utter a single word," he warned, and Gabriella knew that he was deadly serious.

Avendall bowed to the king, in a manner that bordered upon contempt and, after begging His Majesty's leave, turned on one heel and strode out of the room.

"A chamber has been made ready for you and your lady," Edward said to Morgan, and he suddenly seemed twice his real age and half his normal size. His conscience, if he had one, must have weighed heavy that night. "Take her there, and see to her comfort."

Morgan inclined his head. "By your leave, Your Majesty," he said. And then he turned and followed the same path Avendall had taken, though with a considerably greater measure of decorum.

In the antechamber, servants waited to collect the ailing Lady Edgefield. Avendall was there, too, leaning indolently against the wall, with one foot pressed to its ancient stones. At Morgan and Gabriella's appearance, he pushed away to stand straight.

"If God is just," Avendall said, glaring into Morgan's eyes, which glinted with a ferocity of their own, "you will be cut down upon the field. And when that happens, Chalstrey, I swear by everything in heaven and everything in hell that I shall have your lady wife for a doxy!"

"I will kill you first," Morgan answered, without inflection. There could be no doubting that he meant exactly what he said. "Indeed, were it not for Lady Edgefield's indisposition, I would draw my sword now, this moment, and sunder you in twain, from your head to what passes for your manhood."

Two of Edward's guards stepped forward; so did as many of Morgan's men, and, with less enthusiasm, Avendall's.

"Peace!" commanded Edward's captain, a burly, pockmarked man bearing the scars of many a battle survived and thus successfully fought. "There will be no swordplay here, beneath the king's roof. Take notice of my words, my lords—if either of you dares to draw a blade, you'll both pass the night in the dungeons."

Gabriella clutched at Morgan's tunic, for once again she felt cold fury coursing through him, like some violent river on the brink of overspilling its banks.

"This way, my lord," one of the serving women said, in a small and pleading voice, touching Morgan's sleeve. "We've made a fitting bed for milady, and set out wine and victuals to restore her."

After glaring through the guards to Avendall for a long moment, as if the king's men were invisible, Morgan turned in silence and followed the servant up the wide staircase, still carrying Gabriella.

Above stairs, in their chamber, a fire blazed and the covers of a great bed were turned back, welcoming and warm. Morgan dismissed the servants and peeled away

Gabriella's damp and clammy garments with his own hands. When she was naked, he placed her upon the feather mattress and lay the blankets over her with a gentleness that made her throat draw shut.

He crossed the room, to the table the servant woman had mentioned. Using a ladle, Morgan filled a wooden bowl with broth and carried it back to the bed. Seating himself on the edge of the mattress, he set the fragrant, steaming brew down long enough to prop Gabriella up on a mountain of pillows. Then he held the rim of the bowl to her lips and commanded her to drink.

Gabriella had no appetite, and barely enough strength to sip and swallow, but she was no summer flower, to quaver and wilt in the face of adversity. She wanted to recover, and her body required food to mend itself, so she took nourishment.

When she had accepted all the broth she could, Morgan set the bowl on the floor and smoothed her hair back from her face.

"God's blood, Gabriella," he whispered raggedly, "when did I come to care for you so much?"

Her heart, deeply bruised and strangely sluggish since the arrival of the king's summons, back at Edgefield Keep, suddenly rallied to a steadier, faster beat. "You truly do not mean to send me away?"

Morgan shook his magnificent head. "I have been a fool and a coward to spurn you, Gabriella—you are my better in every way, and I need you."

She believed Morgan, and she trusted him. Mayhap it was the fever that caused her to ask the boldest question of her life thus far. "And do you love me, Morgan, as I love you?"

He leaned forward and kissed her moist forehead. "Aye, my lady. That is the right name for what I feel."

"Then hold me," Gabriella said simply. "Lie down beside me, here in this bed, and hold me, that I may forget the sorrows that await us both."

Morgan stood, stripped off his clothes, and joined her, gathering her into his arms. She rested her head upon his shoulder.

"I cannot bear it," she whispered, "that you must go away."

He kissed her temple. "Shhh," he said. "That is tomorrow, or the next day, or the one after that. For now, we are together, and that must be enough. I, for one, need nothing more than simply to be close to you."

"Do you not wish to possess me, as a husband possesses a wife?"

She felt Morgan's smile against her flesh.

"Always," he replied. "But I can wait until you are well enough to receive me again."

"Suppose the king sends you away to France before I am recovered? Will—will you take a mistress?"

Morgan turned, so that he could look down into her troubled face. "No," he said firmly. "I shall be faithful to you, Gabriella, no matter how long we are apart. I could not rightly require fidelity of you—and believe me, I *demand* it—were I not willing to offer the same promise in return."

Gabriella raised her arms, with some effort, and draped them round his neck. Her eyes swam with tears and, pride be damned, she made no effort to hide either her love or her despair.

"Could you not have come to such a place *before* the

king commanded you to leave me?" she asked, with not
a little petulance.

Morgan chuckled and kissed the tip of her nose. "For
that I offer you my sincerest regrets, my lady. I can do
naught save proclaim myself utterly chagrined and beg
your absolution."

Her sisters were safe. She was warm at last, and full
of broth and, best of all, Edgefield loved her. Gabriella
struggled to keep her eyes open, found herself defeated, and slept.

The window sills were mounded with fresh, bejew-
eled snow, and a raw draught pervaded the bedchamber. Gabriella shivered beneath the thick covers and
spent several muddle-brained moments trying to recall
where she was and how she had come to be there.

All of it came back, in an unkind torrent, when she
realized that Morgan was not beside her. She recalled
Edward's decree—her impending separation from her
husband.

With a gasp, Gabriella attempted to sit up, and found
herself too weak for even that paltry effort. God's blood,
she thought, what was happening to her? She had ever
been the most vigorous of women, and to lie abed, helpless, was a torment to her.

"Peace," Morgan said, from somewhere just beyond
the range of her vision. "I have not left you."

Gabriella was ridiculously relieved, and closed her
eyes for a long moment, willing her flailing heart to settle back into its normal meter. She heard Morgan take
an iron poker from its stand and prod the failing fire.

"I have spoken with the king this morning," he said
gravely, upon crossing the chamber and seating himself

beside her on the bed. He was clothed warmly, and in the practical, unadorned garments of a soldier.

Gabriella studied his face, attempting to memorize it, in case . . .

She turned her thoughts forcefully away from that dismal track. "His Majesty has not changed his mind, then," she said, and even though she was screaming inside, her voice came out sounding reasonable and calm.

Morgan shook his head. "No," he answered. "Edward is not given to fancies and moods—at least, not where warfare is concerned. I am to ride to Portsmouth within the week, with twenty of my best men, and there take ship for France."

She tried again to sit up, and this time it was Morgan, and not her infirmity, that forced her to recline. "Am I to lie here, with no more will than a boiled turnip, while you go off to this absurd and endless war?" she demanded.

"Apparently, yes," Morgan replied, with a droll set to his mouth and a sparkle in his eyes. "Come now, Gabriella. I am a soldier, and I have never represented myself to be anything else. It was inevitable that, sooner or later, I should be called to serve." He paused, tested her forehead for fever with the back of one hand, and frowned. "By the way—if I were you, I would not let Edward or anyone else in this place hear you refer to the strife in France as an 'absurd and endless war.' The conflict is of vital importance to him."

"It must indeed be so," Gabriella grumbled, "if he would sacrifice so much to prevail."

Morgan laid a finger to her nose. "Nevertheless, sweeting, it will behoove you to reserve such remarks for private conversations. Edward's disfavor is nothing you wish to court."

She sighed. "I do not want you to go."

"And I do not wish to leave," he confessed. "But I am a loyal if sometimes disagreeable subject of my king, and I will do his bidding in all that is right. Still, I shall return in a twelvemonth, Gabriella, and I expect to find you well when I arrive at Edgefield. We will make our first babe then."

Gabriella turned her head, in a hopeless effort to hide the tears that had sprung suddenly to her eyes. She wanted Morgan with her always, and damn his silly soldiering, but she would not use frailty to hold him.

Morgan took her chin in one hand and gently turned her head, making her look at him. "Wait in London, until you are fit to travel. Mayhap that will not be until spring. I am leaving Robinson behind to escort you back to Edgefield when the time is right, and several fine and worthy men with him. John will protect you and, if need be, advise you. I ask but one vow of you, Gabriella, and if you will not make it, I am sure to lose my reason long before I return to these shores."

"What?" she asked softly. "Surely you know I would never betray you—"

"Aye," he said, with a sad smile. "For all your talk of taking lovers—designed to taunt me, I know—I trust you as completely, in matters of loyalty at least, as any saint has ever trusted Almighty God. My greatest concern, my lady, is that you will take it into your head to set out on some grand and impetuous crusade—as you have done in the past—and leave Edgefield Keep on your own. Only this time, beloved, I would not be there to rescue you. I must have your most sacred oath that nothing—*nothing*, my lady—will lure you away from home without guards."

Gabriella hesitated, but then, seeing the suffering in Morgan's eyes, relented. Being faithful would be easy, for she wanted no man but him, ever. As for the rest, well, she would try, with all her might, to keep her word.

"You have my promise, my lord," she said and, taking his hand, kissed the calloused flesh of his palm.

Morgan gathered her up in his arms and held her close against his chest. Although he made no more avowals of love, there was no need, for the strength of his embrace conveyed everything.

"Lie with me," Gabriella whispered. "Give me a babe now, not in a twelvemonth, I pray you."

He kissed her forehead then pressed her back onto the pillows again. Ruefully, he shook his head. "There is no time, Gabriella. And you are not well."

"No time? But you said you would set out for Portsmouth in a week!"

Morgan attempted a smile, but fell short. "And I spoke true. But there are counsels, messages to carry to the Black Prince and mayhap to his brother, the duke, as well. I am obliged to spend all the day and probably half the night shut away with the king."

"Cannot scribes prepare these messages?"

"They are critical, Gabriella, and thus they cannot be set down in ink. I am to commit them to memory, and Edward will drill me until he is certain of perfection."

"You will be in even greater danger than I feared, with such secrets locked inside your mind!" She tried again to rise, and again she was thwarted in the effort.

A sharp rap sounded at the door of the chamber.

"Yes!" Morgan called, rather inhospitably. He was gazing upon Gabriella's face, as though to press her image into his brain.

"His Majesty grows impatient, my lord," a man's voice replied, from the other side of the door.

Morgan sighed, kissed Gabriella lingeringly, hungrily, and then left her to cross the chamber. At the portal, with his hand on the latch, he turned to look back at her. He started to speak, then stopped himself.

Wrenching the door open, he spoke to the intruding guard in less than charitable tones—Gabriella did not make out his exact words—and went out. A serving girl slipped over the threshold before the heavy portal fell to again.

"I bid you good morning, milady," the young woman said brightly. "I've come to give the fire a stir. Cold as a tomb, this place. And well it might be, crowded with ghosts the way it is. You look a bit better now that the sun's risen and you've had a nice rest. I don't mind telling you, last night we all thought you might be bound for the churchyard, feet first."

Gabriella couldn't help being amused by the maid's chatter, despite her own melancholy state of mind. "I should like a bath," she announced. "With very hot water and scented soap."

16

✦

Gabriella felt much restored, after her bath. She was scrubbed and wearing clean garments from the skin out when Morgan came into the chamber, frowning.

She knew he was thinking of some weighty issue, probably his forthcoming duties in France, and tried to bring him round with a small jest. "My lord, if you are undone by such simple matters as my taking a bath, you will suffer greatly in the years to come, for I indulge as frequently as possible."

Morgan's vast shoulders sagged a little as he bent over Gabriella, one hand pressed into the bed on either side of her. A somewhat sheepish smile curved his mouth, and he gave a great, resounding sigh. "You are better, then. Thank God and all the saints for that."

"Would that you could be so easily uplifted, my lord," she said gently, her arms curving around his neck, as if of their own accord.

He smiled, truly, and at last. "You are a tease," he said, and kissed her forehead lightly. "And while we are on the subject of your charming faults, my lady, may I say that you do not know your limits?"

"I prefer to ignore them, insofar as possible," Gabriella replied succinctly.

He laughed and kissed her again, this time on the mouth. His lips lingered, tantalizing, only a breath away from her own. "Impertinent wench. You will turn my hair gray long aforetime." He paused, his expression at once serious and tender. "Or stop my poor heart with your beauty."

Gabriella smiled endearingly up at her husband. Her hair was damp and curling, spread over the pillow in the way he liked. "Mayhap a babe would inspire me to acquit myself in a way that will not age you quite so rapidly," she suggested, and wriggled beneath him.

Morgan groaned. "You are a merciless little minx."

"I know," she replied. "Pray, fasten the latch upon the door, my lord, and tell me again, in great and exhaustive detail, how I should comport myself."

He laughed once more, but raggedly. His wonderfully blue eyes shone with passion, with love. "As if you meant to heed my admonitions, now or ever. Yours is the soul of a rebel, methinks."

Gabriella arched her back, teasing, reckless in her love for him and in her desire to make the most of every moment that remained to them. "Mayhap I shall obey you in *some* regards, husband," she murmured. "Certain very particular ones, I mean."

Morgan cursed, but with no real conviction, and the powerful muscles in his arms corded as he thrust himself onto his feet. Gabriella despaired that she had not been persuasive enough, until she heard the latch snap into place.

He returned shortly thereafter, and took off his boots and then his hose, trunks and jerkin, before sliding into bed beside her. "Tell me, my lady love, shall I perish for want of you, or for contrition because I have had you, knowing all the while that you were sickly?"

Gabriella wrapped her arms around his neck, weakened, yes, but still overjoyed when Morgan poised himself above her. A wanton thrill sped through her blood when she felt the proof of his desire pressed against her belly. "If you must perish at all," she teased, "let it be from exhaustion."

Morgan grinned, but then he lowered his mouth to hers, and claimed her with both gentleness and hunger. When the kiss ended at long last, Gabriella was dazed, and her need of him thundered in her pulses and ached sweetly and warmly in her center. In his eyes, she saw tender desperation.

"I fear to do you hurt," he told her hoarsely. "My need of you is great, wife, and no tame thing."

She raised her head to kiss him lightly on the mouth. "You do me hurt only if you force me to await you even a moment longer, my lord," she said. It was true that she was ready for him, and that there was no place in this coupling for hesitation or the leisurely mischief in which they usually engaged.

Morgan searched her face once more, as if fearing that it was delirium that caused her to speak thus, and when he saw the yearning she made no attempt to hide, he moved inside her in a single long stroke, delving deep.

She loved the fact that he closed his eyes in quiet ecstasy and, for all his legendary ferocity and might, shuddered upon and within her in a sort of preliminary surrender.

Gabriella began to raise and lower her hips, ever so slowly, and Morgan stiffened and then rasped, "God's blood, Gabriella, *lie still.*"

She obeyed and, for a brief, magical, time out of time, they were both suspended in a blissful state of anticipation and utter union, not unlike the aftermath of the fiery, violent climaxes they always reached together, except that urgency had not yet taken them over.

Gabriella moaned as a sweet, soft sensation quivered to life, far within her, but that barely audible cry marked the end of Morgan's control. With a low, growl-like sound, utterly masculine and utterly primitive, he withdrew and then drove into her again and then again. For all his power, though, there was a restraint in him, a governing of his power, born of a wish to handle her gently, and she loved him all the more for that.

Gabriella's body blazed, her need so hot and wild and imperative that she had to keep pace with him, meet him stroke for stroke. She made no effort to stifle her cries of insistence and pleasure, could not have quelled them if she had. When release overtook her at last, it was shattering, carrying her high and shaking her in benign teeth like some enormous, playful beast. She sobbed and called Morgan's name as one spasm after another seized her, and ran its course.

Gabriella was beginning to descend when Morgan let himself go at last and, with swift, demanding thrusts of his hips and a low, growling shout—it held both a warrior's triumph and a supplicant's plea, that cry—spilled his warm and fertile seed within her.

She lay blissfully happy, with her heart torn asunder, somehow knowing that this night was an ending, for her and for Morgan. They would not lie together again, would not hold each other, or even look into each other's eyes, for a year at the least. She dared not consider the very real danger that they could be parted forever.

She was floating in a fog of sleep, her energy completely spent, before Morgan withdrew from her—she felt him go, and opened her eyes.

"Farewell, Gabriella," he said.

She hardly dared touch him, for fear she would cling, or speak, for the fear that she would beg him to stay. Still, she caressed the side of his face and whispered, "Godspeed, my lord."

He kissed her once more, almost reverently, and then he was gone. Perhaps because of exhaustion, perhaps because of the lingering effects of her recent illness, Gabriella slipped mercifully into a deep slumber and wept, unknowing, in that place.

The bedchamber was dark when she awakened several hours later, but for the dim, dancing glow of the fire, and it came to her anew, and with shattering clarity, that she was well and truly alone. It was of no moment that the palace was burgeoning with people, or that London town, with all its populace, was just up the river. Nay, without Morgan at her side, even legions of angels would fail to console her.

He had bid her farewell; he was not just gone from her body, gone from her bed. He had left the palace, and by now he had surely put Sheen and mayhap even London itself behind him.

At first, the weight of Morgan's absence was crushing, and bore down upon Gabriella with such awesome force that she could not breathe, think, or even weep. She drew comfort, though, from the memory of his most eloquent good-bye, bidden in the languages of his body and of his soul, as well as his lips.

By sheer force of will, Gabriella began to breathe again. *I wanted more words,* she protested, as the first tear escaped and made a jagged path down her cheek. *Pretty, poetic words, worthy of the bards. Words that would have taken years and years to say. Nay, even forevermore.*

She brushed at her face with the back of one hand, and commanded herself to be reasonable. Edgefield was a soldier, not a bard. His poetry was pleasure, and courage, and love, and he had left his mark on her mind and heart in a way no mincing troubadour could ever have done.

Gabriella laid her hands lightly upon her flat, bare abdomen. Mayhap Morgan had left another gift, as well— the babe she longed to bear, for him and for herself.

That was her best hope, her reason, that bleak and bitter night, for pressing on, for making plans. For not turning her face into the pillow that still smelled pleasantly of Morgan and lying there like an invalid until spring came to her rescue.

When the serving girl, Bette, entered the room, perhaps an hour later, preceded by a small boy bearing a lamp, she found Gabriella sitting up in bed, running an ivory comb through her mane of hair.

Bette carried a tray and, keeping her eyes downcast, set it upon Gabriella's lap.

The fare was cold joint of venison, cheese, brown bread, and wine. Gabriella looked at it with resignation. For now, she would occupy herself with rebuilding her strength.

"Be gone with you, now," Bette said to the boy,

whose attention was fixed, rapt, upon Gabriella's meal. "There is naught for you here."

"Wait," Gabriella said firmly. She was, after all, Lady Edgefield, a true duchess, and she meant to act the part. The child paused and turned to look at her with wide, hopeful eyes and Bette, having accurately read her mistress's tone, held her tongue.

Gabriella gestured for the boy to draw nigh, and when he did, she smiled at him and indicated the tray with a nod of her head. "Choose what you would like most," she said.

The child hesitated, then snatched up the venison, stuffed it into his tunic, and fled the chamber, no doubt fearing that the lady would change her mind and send Bette chasing after him.

"Poor little mite," Gabriella said.

Bette made a huffy sound. "Little thief is more like it," she fussed, but she made a bad job of meanness, and was forced to smile. "You'll have every beggar in England at the door, milady, the small and big of them, if you carry on like that."

Gabriella assessed the food remaining on her tray and decided to force down the cheese first. "So be it, then," she said. "Pray, prepare my things for travel and send for John Robinson, my husband's man. I wish to return to Edgefield Keep before the weather grows any worse."

Bette had gone to stir the embers in the hearth, and at Gabriella's command, she dropped the poker with an ear-splitting clang. " 'Tis too far by half, milady—and in such snow and wind, why the king will surely forbid it!"

"I hardly think the king need be asked for an opinion at all. His Majesty surely has far greater concerns than the comings and goings of one woman."

Bette's eyes were shining with what seemed to be

amazed admiration. "Milady, you are too bold!" she cried, but then she covered her mouth with one chapped hand, reddened with chilblains, and giggled. An instant later, her face changed and she plunged a hand into a pocket in her coarse, undyed kirtle. "I near forgot, milady. His lordship left this behind, ere he went. A splendid man he is, if you'll pardon my mentioning such."

Gabriella had gone still; all her being was trained on whatever it was that Morgan had given the serving girl to keep for her.

Flushed, mayhap fearing a smart reprimand or even a slap for her memory lapse, Bette hurried to the bedside and held out her hand, offering a small parchment packet, bound with twine. Inside was a golden locket, set with a ruby, and Morgan's ring.

Gabriella barely kept herself from grabbing up the tokens in the same way the little boy had grasped the joint of venison. Her fingers trembled as she examined Morgan's signet ring, the very symbol of his authority as the duke of Edgefield. In all the time Gabriella had known her husband, she had never seen him without it.

She took the ring into her palm and closed her fingers tightly around it. For a moment, the light of the fire was but a crimson blur.

"There's more, your ladyship," Bette pointed out, anxious, no doubt, to make up for her earlier error of omission. "See? He's written something there for you—"

Gabriella blinked a few times; then, after placing the signet ring temporarily on her thumb, the locket safe against her palm, she spread the parchment wrapper and saw Morgan's firm, dark script within it. *My lady beloved,* he had written, *with this golden band, forged for my grandfather in Jerusalem, I offer you all that I am, and will ever become. Let it be the proof of your authority, as my duchess, to act in my behalf. Be wise, and firm in your dealings with those under our protection, dear Gabriella, and remember that discipline is not necessarily akin to unkindness. I trust my heart to your keeping, my lady, and pray you, wear this locket against your throat, where your pulse may warm it. Morgan.*

She sniffled once, and pressed the message to her own heart, which was bursting, just then, with a bittersweet ache.

"Tell John Robinson to make ready," she reiterated, when she'd recovered a little. Bette opened her mouth to argue, then saw the look on Gabriella's face and closed it again.

Gabriella ate what she could, then rose and donned a chemise and heavy woolen gown. Bette, returned from her errand red-eyed and saying little, plaited milady's hair and then tucked it up inside a simple cap, with ties at the chin.

Within the hour, Gabriella, unsteady on her feet and thinner than before her illness, was received in the king's chamber. He had been her host, as well as her benefactor, and she could not take her leave without bidding him farewell.

"You are not yet mended, my lady," Edward protested, gesturing for her to rise from a curtsy deep enough to leave her head spinning. "I promised your good husband that you would remain abed, until God Almighty had seen fit to restore you to your full might and spirit."

Gabriella executed a second, more graceful curtsy, wryly grateful for all the times she and Elizabeth and Meg had played at going to court. Naturally, none of them had ever expected to actually need such skills as an audience with the king of all England required. Nor, of course, had they once dreamed that they had a protector in Edward III.

"I am greatly recovered, Your Majesty," she said, lying only a little. "I should like to set out for Edgefield Keep on the morrow, before cock's crow—with your kind permission, of course." Should he refuse, she meant to take her leave anyway, but it would be reckless to say so outright.

Edward poised himself to deliver a lecture— probably a restatement of Morgan's wish that she go no farther than London and wait there until the roads were clear and the wolves were not quite so hungry. Then he stopped, smiled. "I see a glimpse of your fearless father in you," he said.

Gabriella's throat constricted slightly. "I thank you most sincerely for looking after my sisters and me whilst we grew," she said. "In my father's name, Your Majesty, I must ask one more boon."

"What is that?" Edward asked quietly.

"Do not let Avendall take either of them to wife, I pray you. Let them be brought to Edgefield Keep, along with a certain nun, Dame Johanna, of St. Swithin's Abbey. My husband has offered to pay their bride-prices, and I seek only to assure their happiness and safety, my lord king."

He considered for a long while. "Avendall has served me well," he said. "His wants carry weight with me."

Gabriella thought, for a moment, that she would swoon, or fling herself, pleading, at the king's feet, but

MY LADY BELOVED   293

she maintained her dignity by force of will. "Please, my lord," she said simply.

The king gave a great sigh. "Very well. Let my debts to Redcliff be paid. Lord knows, I have acquired new ones, to Avendall."

Gabriella lowered her head to hide tears of relief.

The king frowned as he pondered his personal dilemma. Finally, he spoke again. "Mayhap 'tis a wise thing for you to depart, Lady Edgefield. There is pestilence in London, and it might soon come to Sheen. I will have your sisters brought to you in spring."

Gabriella nodded in humble acquiescence. "I want only to do your bidding, Your Majesty," she said.

Edward looked patently relieved. He favored Gabriella with a beaming smile. "Edgefield left a dozen men, headed by John Robinson. No doubt you will be quite safe in their keeping."

"No doubt," Gabriella agreed modestly. "I am most grateful for your hospitality, my king," she added. "Pray, may I leave you now, with my kindest felicitations? I shall want rest before tomorrow's journey."

The king gestured with a wave of one hand and an almost fatherly affection. "I will not detain you. Farewell, my lady, and godspeed."

With one last bob, Gabriella turned and hurried out of the royal chamber without once looking back.

The ride to Portsmouth was long and cold, and Morgan's longing for Gabriella was as severe as any ordeal he had ever undergone. To keep from going mad, or turning around and riding back to fetch her home to Edgefield Keep, he went over the complicated dispatches he carried in his head.

The trick soon failed him, however, for the messages were already firmly fixed, and practicing them was no real diversion.

Mayhap, Morgan reflected grimly, he should have wakened Gabriella once more, and bid her a second farewell. The truth, however unflattering, was that he had been afraid that when she spoke his name, or touched him, or when he looked into her eyes, the last shreds of will he had managed to retain would desert him. The intensity of what he felt for and with Gabriella had unnerved him, and despite the pain of separation, he knew he needed time to come to terms with the situation, to measure these discoveries and put names to them.

He had spent years, he reflected, guarding his emotions, letting no one see inside him. Indeed, he had taught himself not to notice the charred timbers and scattered rubble of his own inner landscape, but now, by loving him, Gabriella had caused him to look, and look closely. There could be no turning away from the truth about Rebecca now for, having faced these long-secret wounds, he was no longer willing, no longer able, to ignore them.

Morgan wanted to heal, and Gabriella's love, combined with his own efforts, would be his tonic.

He imagined her in London, taking a house, buying cloth for the gowns she so wanted, and smiled. In the spring, Gabriella would return to Edgefield Keep, bearing his seal, and he had no doubt that she was capable of managing his holdings—*their* holdings—with the help of Ephriam and John Robinson, among others.

The thought of Avendall served as a swift and potent reminder that life was not idyllic. Although Morgan trusted the men he had left to look after Gabriella, especially John Robinson, who had served him long and well, and his father before him, he was aware that no one else could protect her the way he would.

And Avendall was a very dangerous foe.

Morgan glanced heavenward, to assess the snow-burdened sky, mayhap to offer at least the intention of a prayer. He had not been on good terms with the Holy Church since Rebecca's death, despite his service in the Levant, and little had changed in that regard.

He sighed. He would have to trust that Gabriella had learned her lesson, on her one and only visit to Avendall Hall, if not from subsequent encounters with its master. Though impetuous, Morgan knew that his wife was, as she claimed, as quick-witted as any man—and that probably included himself.

Where Avendall was concerned, Morgan had kept his bargain. A sizable amount of gold had been delivered to Cyprian's lodgings in London, as agreed, and he had dispatched a courier to St. Swithin's, with a similar sum, for the bride-prices of Gabriella's two sisters. Surely by midsummer, Elizabeth and Meg would be at Edgefield Keep, plotting mischief with Gabriella.

The image restored at least some of Morgan's former good humor, and he set his mind once again upon the tasks awaiting him in France.

Gabriella was well aware that her husband's men disapproved of her decision to return to Cornwall without delay, but she carried his seal, and in Morgan's absence, they had no choice but to obey her.

The sky was a clear and brittle blue by the time they had put Sheen and then London behind them, and many difficult and dangerous miles lay ahead, yet to be traversed. The snow had mostly melted away, and lay in rags and shards upon the frozen ground, like bits of soiled cloth.

Although Gabriella was still frail, her determination made up for that and a great many other weaknesses, and she gave orders as confidently as if she had been born to her title.

The rumpled and somewhat fretful John Robinson took up his usual place at her side, and would not be moved from it, save when night came, and they rested at some inn. Even then, Robinson slept on the floor outside her door, his dagger drawn.

The other men in the company rode afore and behind, keeping their own counsel, silent and alert. Good soldiers, all. Gabriella knew that some of their number, particularly the younger ones, resented being left behind, while their leader went to fight in France with the Black Prince and the Duke of Lancaster.

"You will find this journey hard going, milady," Robinson had warned solemnly, the first morn. "London, for all its failings, would at least have offered shelter and a few modest comforts."

Gabriella had fixed him with the look of a duchess, rather than a frightened girl kidnapped on her way to an arranged marriage. Oh, indeed, she had changed much since leaving St. Swithin's, and she cherished no wish to change back. "I want for no comfort besides my own hearth in Cornwall," she said, though it wasn't entirely the truth. Indeed, she could have borne any privation, if Morgan had been with her.

Lady Edgefield had thought she glimpsed a flicker of amused respect in Robinson's steady gaze. "As you say, milady," he had replied and, after that, nothing more was said of the matter.

Whilst they traveled, Gabriella occupied her mind by adding columns of figures in her head, and going over her plans for the future. She had a great many misgivings about her inexperience in the governing of lands and castles and men, but she was intelligent and confident that she would learn quickly. Too, she had good advisers in John Robinson and in Ephriam. By asking a great many questions, and heeding their counsel, insofar as it made sense to her, she could succeed. In the springtime, the king had promised, Meg and Elizabeth would join her at the keep, and mayhap Dame Johanna, too. Those three, with their varied talents and sharp minds, were sure to be of great help.

Yes, when Morgan returned from France in a year's time, he would find his wife, and his holdings, thriving.

17

❖

€dgefield Keep, ever a cheerful place to Gabriella,
seemed past empty upon her return, after seven trying
days upon a horse's back and as many nights sleeping in
inns and roadhouses. Indeed, the world itself was not
quite as it should have been, without Morgan, rather
like a body forsaken by spirit.

Weary and bereft, Gabriella nonetheless continued
in her resolve to gather her private forces and make a
fine showing as the mistress of Edgefield, for purposes
of her own self-respect and so that Morgan's heart
might safely trust in her.

By the same token, Gabriella was sorely fatigued,
and knew that she must restore herself before she could
be of any true value to the land and its people. Morgan's
home was her home, she belonged there, as his children
would belong.

Upon her arrival, therefore, Gabriella crawled into the
bed she had shared with Morgan, slept soundly for the
better part of a day, and ate heartily when she awakened.

She was in Morgan's counsel chamber, at midmorning, examining the exhaustive lists and records kept by Ephriam, when a maidservant came to tell her that a messenger was waiting at the castle gates. Because the boy came from Avendall Hall, he had not been permitted to enter, but waited upon the drawbridge for Gabriella's decision.

She glanced at Robinson, who had become her friend after a fashion, during the difficult journey from the king's palace at Sheen. "How much harm can one small courier do?" she mused. "Admit the boy, and have him brought to me."

Within minutes, a lad was escorted through the gaping doors of the chamber, with frowning guards holding him by either arm. The urchin, skimpily clad despite the savage cold, was no more than two and ten years in age, and ashen with fear. What tales had he been told, of Morgan Chalstrey and other residents of Edgefield Keep, to terrify him so? He looked as though he'd been commanded to bathe himself in the River Styx.

Gabriella smiled, in an effort to put the boy at ease.

"What is your name?" she asked, firmly but not unkindly, dismissing the guards with a slight motion of her head. Reluctantly, the soldiers left, although Robinson remained, leaning against the wall, arms folded and eyes watchful.

" 'Tis Cletis, milady," the small messenger croaked, clutching the battered leather pouch he carried.

"You will not be harmed within these walls, Cletis," Gabriella said, and pushed a wooden bowl, filled with dried fruit and nuts, forward upon the surface of Morgan's desk. "Take what sustenance you will, while I read the message you bear."

Cletis approached, after flinging one frightened and

questioning glance at Robinson, and laid the bag before Gabriella with a respectful bend of his knees and bob of his head.

Gabriella took the pouch while the lad reached tentatively for the bowl, filling his mouth slowly, and then, when no one cuffed him or offered a rebuke, filling the pockets of his patched tunic as well.

Meanwhile, Gabriella brought out the message, written on a square of sheepskin in Avendall's own script, hoping the trembling in her hands was not noticeable, and therefore sure to be reported upon Cletis's return.

> *Lady Edgefield—I trust this missive finds you well, and rested after what was surely a journey of significant hardship. I know my men and I found it trying, riding a day behind you.*
>
> *I write to request your permission to make a visit to Edgefield Keep, that I might discuss several matters of extreme importance, and await the kindness of your speedy response.*
>
> *Cyprian Avendall*

Was the man mad? Gabriella wondered, as a shiver wove itself along the length of her backbone, like bright ribbons round a May Pole. He wrote as though he were a trusted friend, not a sworn and fearsome enemy.

She bit her lip, pondering. No, these were not the words of a lunatic, but the cleverly crafted verbal darts of a true foe. Still, what could Avendall have to say to her, now that Morgan had relieved him of any responsibility or rights where she and her sisters were concerned? The king himself had witnessed the covenant between Morgan and Avendall, and Morgan had kept his bargain. It would not be prudent to scorn such a promise.

At the same time, Gabriella was well aware that the king had had obvious misgivings, and not wanted to offend Avendall.

"Tell your master," Gabriella said to Cletis, after a lengthy interval of consideration, "that he may come to Edgefield Keep when he chooses, provided that he is alone and unarmed."

A sidelong glance at Robinson showed no reaction whatsoever, either for or against this decision.

"Aye, milady," Cletis said, through a mouthful of dried apricots. After another bob, he turned and dashed out of the chamber.

Gabriella awaited comment from Robinson, but none came, and she let out a long sigh of relief. Her head was aching a little, and she felt mildly uneasy at her stomach.

Avendall presented himself at the gates at the setting of the sun, that very day, bearing no visible weapons, and unescorted. Gabriella watched from a window of the keep as he rode through the village, and never, even though she was well guarded, had she been more painfully conscious of Morgan's absence.

She went out to meet Avendall, in the center of the main courtyard, next to the well that served all the castle itself, standing tall in a gown she'd helped to stitch from cloth bought in London, hair unbound by wimple or cap. Robinson and several of his men lingered nearby, vigilant in the light of their torches, but remained out of earshot.

Avendall, clad in the warm, finely made garments befitting his rank, swung down from his horse and walked toward Gabriella with a casual gait, pulling off his heavy leather gloves as he approached.

"My lady," he said, in cordial greeting, though there was a predatory expression in his eyes that made Gabriella especially glad of Robinson's presence, and that of her own men, of whom she was admittedly less certain.

She stared at her visitor coldly, waiting, offering no word of greeting or welcome.

Avendall stood face-to-face with her now. He took in her guards with an amused glance, then turned what he undoubtedly regarded as his great charm upon Gabriella.

She was unmoved, and still refused to be the first to speak.

"I fear I bring most troubling news from St. Swithin's, milady," he said, with no small amount of satisfaction. He could not have missed the alarm his words wrought in Gabriella, although she did her best to hide it.

"What is this 'news?' " she asked, after a pause contrived to settle her nerves.

Avendall smiled again and took in their surroundings in a leisurely fashion, though she knew he had seen the internal environs of Edgefield Keep on at least one previous occasion. At length, his gaze returned to her face, and the look in his eyes was at great variance with the smile upon his lips.

"I have heard there is plague at St. Swithin's," he said. "Those occupants who were not infected have fled, and are now scattered to the four winds."

Gabriella drew in a sharp breath—her sisters, their friends, Dame Johanna! Driven out into a world disinclined to show mercy, let alone hospitality, to those who might carry the dreaded disease. With one hand, she grasped the rim of the ancient stone well, to steady herself. Then she braced up. "If you have invented this tale—"

Cyprian bowed his handsome head in acknowledgment of her remark, but made no comment upon it. "There are, I fear, other somber tidings as well. Your husband's esteemed friend, Sedgewick, was in the nuns' keeping, but has now vanished, your sister—Meg, I believe—with him. The younger girl has fallen ill. And I must lay upon you yet one more burden: an English ship has gone down in the narrow sea, and all but a very few of those aboard, men and horses, were lost." He paused, to let the words sink in, find their mark in the tender flesh of Gabriella's heart. "Morgan was among the unfortunate ones, milady."

Gabriella would wonder, long after, how she held herself upright. She was terrified for her sisters, and concerned for Gresham Sedgewick as well, but the possibility that Morgan might have perished in the cold and ofttimes turbulent waters between England and France caused her a sorrow of such proportions that she could barely contain it. "I don't believe you," she managed.

Avendall, well aware of the effect his words had had, reached out solicitously to take Gabriella's arms. The sounds of swords whisked from scabbards chafed the air, but when Gabriella held out a hand toward Robinson, palm first, the soldiers remained where they were.

"You are a liar," she told Avendall again, in a voice so calm that even she was not certain she could rightly claim it for her own. "I was a fool to admit you to Edgefield Keep, and I bid you leave before I must command my soldiers to put you out by force."

Avendall was undaunted. "Think what you like, my lady. When you learn the wretched facts, and thus know that I have spoken true on all these matters, come to

Avendall Hall. I may yet take you for a mistress, if not a wife."

Gabriella was ferocious in her terror and her fury. She spat at him, and struck his insolent face.

Avendall raised his hand, to wipe away her spittle, and might have retaliated with a blow, had Robinson not crossed the breach in barely more than an instant and pressed the tip of his sword to the other man's side.

"You have overstayed your welcome in this place and all others within the boundaries of Edgefield," the soldier said. "Pray, take your leave, sir, before my forbearance runs out."

Avendall smiled again, and raised his hands in a cheerful bid for peace. "I am going," he said. "You have done well, Gabriella, to win your late husband's men to loyalty, in so brief a time. But remember, when your bed grows cold, where you may seek a man worthy to lend you comfort."

Gabriella spoke briskly to Robinson. "See Sir Avendall to the gates," she said, in measured tones, although her head was spinning and she was about to be violently sick, "and make certain that he is never admitted again."

With that order, she turned and walked away, toward the sanctuary of the castle, praying all the while that she would not collapse short of its door, and disgrace herself before her foe.

Behind her, Avendall laughed, though she heard the sound of creaking leather as he mounted. "You would have made a fit partner for Edgefield," he taunted. "You are as ruthless as he was, and spout orders as readily. But you are still naught but a wench, made for bedsport, with no knowledge in the ways of war and no authority to command seasoned soldiers. They will turn on you, Gabriella, one or all, and give you cause to lament the foolhardy choice you make this day."

"May I run him through now, your ladyship?" Robinson inquired.

Gabriella did not look back; she had fixed the whole of her being on reaching the lower floor of the keep, on getting beyond Avendall's sight. "Aye," she answered strongly. "Skewer the knave, and roast him on a spit, for all it matters to me."

Inside at last, Gabriella sagged against a wall, ready to retch, and might have slid to the floor had not Ephriam been there to gather her up, verbally, and lend her some of his own fortitude.

"Here now, milady," the old man said, offering a hand that was gratefully grasped, "Avendall is a coward, a perjurer, and a scapegrace. Surely you have not taken these vile inventions of his to heart."

Gabriella held herself tightly with her free arm, lest she be torn asunder like a scarecrow beset by foxes. "Therein lies the soul of the problem," she said, when she could speak. "I do believe him, for I cannot credit that even Avendall would dare to utter such lies if he thought he would be challenged, and made to give an accounting to my lord husband. Or the king."

"He is mad," Ephriam counseled persistently, "and madmen do not fear accountings of any sort. They invariably believe themselves to be justified in even their most sordid transgressions."

Gabriella tried to take comfort from Ephriam's words, but she had a terrible conviction, in the deepest and most elemental part of herself, that Avendall knew his claims were true, at least in part.

Suddenly fearing to stumble again, Gabriella braced

herself against a chill, damp stone wall with one hand, while she fought for breath, for composure, for wisdom. Finally, she spoke. "I must learn for myself what has come to pass. Pray, Ephriam, ask Robinson to send a man to London and Sheen, to discover all he can of recent shipwrecks in the narrow sea, and yet another to St. Swithin's, to hear the fate of my sisters and my friends."

"But, my lady," Ephriam protested gently, "the winter is all but upon us, and I fear that we cannot spare even two soldiers for such a venture. There are other dangers to these holdings besides those Avendall presents."

Gabriella stood very straight. "Pray, Ephriam, do as I tell you. Lose no time."

Ephriam received this command with his customary equanimity. "Might I escort you to your chamber first, your ladyship? You do not look well. Mayhap you should lie down awhile."

"I am not bound for my chamber," Gabriella said, with gathering fierceness. "I will return to the ledgers. Make haste, lest I grow impatient."

Ephriam did not sigh aloud, though the desire to do so was evident in his countenance. "Aye, milady," he said, and went out into the blustery twilight.

Later, the elderly servant sought Gabriella in the room where Morgan had worked, to inform her that Robinson had dispatched two messengers, in accordance with her wishes, one to Sheen, one to St. Swithin's. He prevailed upon her to eat the light supper he brought to her, and left her to her work.

Gabriella found blessed distraction in the mechanics of numbers, as some women would have in prayer, and, for that reason, she spent many hours in the counsel chamber in the coming days and weeks, conferring with Ephriam and John Robinson and others, including Dame Johanna's friend, Mab, the village midwife. When not going over records, Gabriella insisted on learning other elements of the management of Edgefield Keep.

She inspected the dovecotes, the stables, even the fields, curious to know which were to be planted and which would lie fallow, and went with Mab to aid in the birthing of babes. While this was often grim business, and made an end to what remained of Gabriella's girlhood innocence, she found a strange solace and peace in the attendant tasks. When mother and child survived, she knew joy. When one or both were lost, a too-common occurrence, she mourned.

From dawn until the darkest hours of the night, when she finally tumbled into an exhausted sleep, more often than not with a tallow still burning upon the table in the master bedchamber, Gabriella worked, learned, examined, questioned, and pondered. She laid plans to acquire sheep and cattle when spring came, and to buy looms, and have village girls instructed in their use.

For all her efforts to keep her mind busy, as the weeks became months, and the winter deepened to a brutal whiteness that pervaded the bones and blinded the eyes, Gabriella never passed an hour without thinking of Morgan and of her sisters. She did not hear from Avendall, or see him, either, but she was always aware of his presence, just beyond the walls of Edgefield Keep, waiting and watching. She spent long intervals in the keep's small chapel, on her knees before the altar, begging the Blessed Virgin to restore her husband to her and to keep her sisters safe.

No messengers came, either from Sheen, in regard to Morgan's ship, or from Devonshire, where St. Swithin's held a modest and ancient place.

It was at Christmastide, when all the villagers came to dine in the great hall, as was the tradition of Edge-field Keep, that Mab gave her mistress a thoughtful look and then respectfully drew her aside. She, with Ephriam, had schooled "milady" well in the workings of the small community.

Mab was a small, stringy-looking woman, with sparse teeth and thin hair, but she was strong of spirit, like Dame Johanna, and made a good and steady friend. She had been watching Gabriella with unusual intensity lately.

"My lady," she began, frowning. "Are you well?"

Gabriella's first impulse was to lie, though she oft-times retched of a morning, in the privacy of her bed-chamber, and occasionally felt so light-headed that she feared she might be plague stricken. Knowing Mab to be much skilled in discernment, and worn out by the preparations for Christmas, however, Gabriella did not bother to evade the question.

"No," she said, reluctantly, while villagers happily consumed their special dinner at the trestle tables nearby, raising a pleasant din as they chattered. "I fear I have become spindly in the knees of late, and my stomach is most inconstant."

Mab's eyes sparkled in her gaunt, weathered face. "It is as I thought. And when did you last have the bleeding, mistress?"

Gabriella flushed, for the query was an unrelated one, in her opinion, and personal. Still, she measured the time carefully in her mind, and was surprised by the outcome of the exercise. "Not since the autumn," she said, marveling, "well before I journeyed to Sheen, with my lord husband."

Mab nodded, as though some theory had been confirmed. "Aye," she said, with a brisk nod. "Can you not guess the meaning of these signs, lady?"

Gabriella had no answer at the ready, and so shook her head in reply. No one had ever explained why women bled, although Meg had claimed the process was related to the phases of the moon. She herself had experienced the phenomenon as bothersome, and invariably irregular.

Mayhap this was a symptom of the plague, she thought fearfully, and clasped her hands together with a force that made her knuckles ache.

"Shall I perish?" she whispered.

Mab chuckled. "No, lady—not with Mab nigh to look after you. You truly have not guessed!" She lowered her voice to a confidential whisper. "Mistress, 'tis plain the master got a babe on you, afore he went asoldiering."

Gabriella felt a rush of terror and hope, and slumped onto one of the benches lining the wall just before her knees failed her. "A babe?" she breathed, laying both hands to her middle. Then, anxiously, she demanded, "When? When will it come, Mab?"

The midwife asked a few more questions, calculated, and said, "In summer, I should think. May or June."

Tears filled Gabriella's eyes—tears of joy because she so wanted a child of Morgan's blood, and of sorrow because her husband might never know he had sired a babe before setting out for France. If indeed he *had* perished, as Avendall claimed. Her heart denied the possibility with tremulous certitude—would she not have known, if a part of her own soul and being had truly passed into death?

"I must go to the chapel immediately," she cried softly, "and thank the Virgin for this wondrous gift!"

"The cold has teeth, milady," Mab protested, albeit good-naturedly, and with a little shiver, "and 'tis not much better inside. I'm sure the Virgin will accept your thanks as readily from beside the fire in your bedchamber."

Gabriella longed to be alone, where she might turn this unexpected news over and over in her mind, examining it from every angle, like a precious gem found in the midst of rubble and waste. Still, she was Lady Edgefield, and the night's festivities were much anticipated, throughout the year, by those souls now so merrily gathered at the tables of their lord and lady. She knew she could not disappoint them by taking her leave too soon, for her presence was reassuring, with Morgan absent and feared dead.

And so she lingered, to hear the tales and enjoy the music made by wandering minstrels, hired specially for the purpose. She personally presented every villager with a coin, as Ephriam had coached her to do, and wished each man, woman, and child joy and plenty as they filed out of the hall. This also was a tradition, honored in Morgan's family for a hundred years.

Only when the last celebrant was gone did Gabriella retreat to her private quarters, there to laugh and cry, wonder and weep, as she tried to absorb the knowledge that Morgan's babe surely thrived, even then, in the warm place just beneath her heart.

Just after dawn, the next day, the first of the two messengers returned at last, frostbitten and half starved, to say that St. Swithin's had indeed been taken by plague, and no one remained within but those who were stricken and those who attended them. Elizabeth was there, but Meg and Sedgewick had gone. No one seemed to know where.

Gabriella took this terrible confirmation as calmly as she could, for Mab had explained that agitation and worry might harm the babe. She was in the chapel, that same afternoon, praying upon her knees, when a great stir heralded the return of the second messenger.

Gabriella dashed breathlessly, heedlessly out into the courtyard, demanding to know what news the courier brought. She might have known before she spoke, however, by the rider's forlorn expression.

"A ship did founder and sink betwixt Portsmouth and the Normandy shore," the man said, his voice quavering as he related the news. "Naught can know who was aboard, or even which vessel it was, for matters go amiss for us in France these days and all must fix their minds on victory."

Gabriella, so strong since her parting from Morgan, felt her legs fold beneath her, and saw a spark-shot darkness rise around her like smoke before she toppled, insensible, to the paving stones.

When Gabriella came round again, she was lying on one of the long benches in the great hall, with Mab crouching next to her, clutching her hand in both of her own. Robinson hovered nearby, as did Ephriam, and everyone wore a long and dolorous face.

"Bear milady up the stairs to her bedchamber, if you will," Mab said to Robinson, who came forward hesitantly, with a question in his eyes. "She wants rest, or there might well be still another sorrow to grieve us all."

Such was Gabriella's despair that she did not protest. She nodded permission to Robinson, who raised her carefully in his muscular soldier's arms, and carried her up the broad staircase.

After that night, Gabriella wrested her despondency

into a private place, inside herself, and refused to let it show. Only when she was alone did she weep, and pray for her husband, and her sisters, one gone from the abbey, one within, mayhap dead or dying of the plague.

Gabriella's normally slender waistline began to thicken, day by day, and she made no secret of the fact that she was carrying a babe. The knowledge seemed to comfort the residents of Edgefield Keep, and it certainly helped her to go on. The stamina for which she was well known throughout the Edgefield holdings faltered only slightly as the winter went on. Gabriella found peace only in hard work, of which there was plenty, and in sleep, which was far more elusive.

The first, most intrepid wildflowers were just beginning to dot the meadows when a peddler came to Edgefield Keep, with fine sturdy woolens to sell.

Gabriella purchased a good supply, in plain colors, and set a village seamstress, glad of the wages, to the task of making gowns to fit her rapidly enlarging figure. Although Mab begged her to choose a cheerful blue or a pretty rose color for these garments, Gabriella would wear naught but black and gray.

One rainy spring night, when the roads and fields were awash in mud, yet another messenger appeared at the gates, drenched to the skin and shivering with cold and fever. The news he bore distracted Gabriella, at least temporarily, from her other sorrows.

The rider claimed he had been sent from Redclift Hall, and he brought Gabriella's mother's only treasure to serve as proof—a narrow golden band, set with a single, modest purple stone. Lady Mainwaring, he related, teeth still chattering as he huddled before the great fire in the kitchen, sipping broth from a gourd and soaking his poor feet in hot water, had fallen grievously ill. She implored Gabriella to come to her, as did Hugh Mainwaring, Ariel's husband.

Gabriella never considered refusing; Lady Mainwaring was her mother, and she needed her—Hugh would be of no use at all—and besides, further word of Meg and Elizabeth might have found its way to Redclift Hall.

Over the protests of Mab, and of Robinson, and of the little priest who had married Morgan and Gabriella that long-ago night, before the hearth of their bed chamber, Lady Edgefield began preparing in earnest for an expedition longer and more arduous than any she had attempted before.

"You gave his lordship your promise that you would not leave this castle," Robinson reminded Gabriella tersely, as she checked the storerooms to make sure there would be food enough to sustain the residents of keep and village alike until the new crops came in. "Edgefield told me so himself."

"Nay," Gabriella said. "You are misguided. It was his wish that I secure a suitable escort before I undertook to travel. You shall go, of course, along with a half dozen men of your own choosing. We will require at least one mule for carrying things I wish to give my mother. And plenty of warm blankets, for I have no love of sleeping upon bare ground, especially now."

Robinson looked panic-stricken. "You cannot be far from your time, milady!"

"We shall bring Mab along with us," Gabriella said, marking items off on a mental list. There were lentils aplenty, and ample grain remained from the autumn harvest as well, although the supply was dwindling.

Gabriella's lower back had begun to pain her of late,

and she pressed a hand to it now, and stretched uncomfortably. She was very large, and the babe had long since quickened within her, constantly moving, serving as an ever-present reminder that spectacular fires grow from a single spark. "Do you think we should take a cart, lest my babe should prove himself hasty, and decide to be born along the way?"

Robinson shuddered and went pale as whey at the prospect. "My lady, this is madness—surely your poor ailing mother has servants to look after her, until a more fortuitous time—"

"My mother, with servants?" Gabriella scoffed, tossing her head.

"Then surely your stepfather—"

Gabriella uttered another impatient sound. "Worse than useless, when there is sickness or trouble of any kind in the house. Pray, do not harangue me further, Robinson, for I have made up my mind and you will not change it."

Mab's powers of persuasion were no better than Robinson's, but the midwife made an admirable effort that evening, while assisting Gabriella with one of her much-discussed baths, next to the fire in the master bedchamber.

"Look at you—not more than a month from bearing that babe, and him sure to be the size of Adam's best ox. You must be moonstruck, just to think of such a thing!"

Gabriella smiled sadly. She hoped her babe would be a "he," not because she would have loved a girl any less, but because a male child could carry on the Chalstrey name, and one day assume Morgan's title. No matter what it took, she would keep the holdings safe for her children. "You need have no fear for my little one," she said. "He will be strong, like me, and like his father."

"Strong headed is more like it," Mab replied, disgusted. "God has something to answer for, giving a mortal babe a dam as bone stubborn as you are, and a sire the likes of Morgan Chalstrey."

"Did you bring him into the world, too? Morgan, I mean?"

Mab's countenance softened, and she lapsed into a rare reflective mood. "Aye," she said. "A strapping lad, he was. I was there when Sedgewick was born, too, and Avendall." She sighed, thinking, perhaps, of all that had happened since. " 'Tis the nature of flesh, I fear, to be frail, and too soon returned to the clay."

Gabriella straightened her backbone as she stood before the hearth, almost in the spot where she had been married, gazing into the flames. "I do not choose to be frail," she said, and for the briefest of moments, in the very center of her heart, she felt Morgan's touch.

18

❧

Months before . . .

"Will you have a wench to warm your bed, Edge-field?" asked the legendary Black Prince, firstborn and greatly favored son of Edward III, as he entered the large field tent where Morgan lay, feeling as though his blood had dried up within him and his muscles had turned to stone. "Mayhap a woman's favors will restore your wits!"

"It has been my experience, Your Highness," Morgan replied foggily, attempting to rise from his pallet and promptly failing, "that such attentions have precisely the opposite effect."

The prince laughed, and Morgan winced at the sound. The atmosphere was close and hot, and had it not been for the braziers placed all around, he would not have known the season. Except for himself and his legendary commander, the place was empty.

A flask was offered, and Morgan took it, and drank— wine, potent and raw, but still not so bad as the English stuff. "France, then," he said.

The prince, crouching beside the pallet, took a

draught of wine for himself. "Do you remember nothing at all of your journey?" he asked.

Morgan thought with an effort that produced a knot of pain at his nape and fell back upon his pillow with a grimace and a hoarse expulsion of breath. "The ship," he said.

Sudden, horrific images overwhelmed him, as if from nowhere: the vessel, cracking, splintering, sinking into the frigid, briny waters. Men screaming, flailing, drowning, all around him, with the shore in sight, yet hopelessly out of reach. "I confess, I believed it to be a long, ugly dream."

"I am told you were hauled from the sea, as were a few others, by fishermen, though not before a piece of wreckage struck your head. Count yourself blessed that your skull is evidently fashioned of good English oak." The prince seemed agitated, and began to pace. "I have waited weeks, Edgefield, for you to rally your scattered senses. First you lay still and gray as a corpse, never opening your eyes, barely breathing. A sweating fever followed that, during which you ranted and raved and called out for your lady wife. Quite touching, that. Now, tell me, pray, that the dispatches my father tucked away in your brain have not been lost amidst all this magnificent misery!"

Gabriella. The thought of her washed over Morgan, bringing joy and hope with it, displacing the earlier visions of terror at sea. Beautiful, intrepid, stubborn, avenging Gabriella. He wondered if she had heard of the shipwreck, and worried over his fate. Doubtless, no messenger had been spared to carry the news back to England; every able man was needed in France.

"No," Morgan said, stifling a groan and wishing heartily for more wine. And, more, for Gabriella. "I re-

call the king's messages well enough. Shall I recite
them, or will you fetch a scribe?"

The fabled warrior ceased his tramping to and fro to
step outside and speak to a guard. Soon, he was back,
and once again crouched beside Morgan. "I want no
minion to overhear," he declared.

Morgan closed his eyes; he had to concentrate, in
order to override the pain in his head, though the words
Edward had entrusted to him sprang easily from the
depths of his mind. For more than an hour, by his own
reckoning, he recited strategies, the names of men
thought to be spies, the locations where supplies and
gold were to be brought ashore and hidden.

"You have done well," the prince allowed, somewhat grudgingly, when Morgan at last fell silent
"When you have regained your stamina, I will send you
to spy for me, in Paris. Time will pass quickly, and in
less than a twelvemonth, you shall return to your own
lands for good, and the lady who awaits you." He
paused, smiled. "Mayhap I shall make her acquaintance myself, one day. She must be more than passing
pretty, the way you spoke of her while you lay here,
mending."

Morgan could only nod; he was exhausted, and his
throat was dry as grave dust. Beneath the aching weakness that permeated muscle and bone, however,
coursed a jubilant river of anticipation.

He was going home, to Gabriella, for good. To England. This campaign was to be his last time to go asoldiering; the prince had decreed it so. Surely the months
remaining would pass quickly; he would have much, in
the way of strategy, to occupy his mind whilst he was in
Paris.

He slept in complete peace, and dreamed that he was home, at Edgefield Keep, with Gabriella.

Five days later, gaunt and unsteady on his feet, but much recovered nonetheless, Morgan set his jaw and took horse for Paris, though his heart had already boarded a ship bound for Portsmouth. He had written to Gabriella—she was surely still in London, for the summer, though imminent, had not yet come. In spring, English roads would be mired in mud, and the weather most intemperate for traveling.

Morgan's mind, like his heart, lived in the future.

He would go first to Edward, at Sheen or Woodstock or Windsor, as duty demanded, in order to relay the Black Prince's good wishes and personal reports. Then, at last, Morgan would find Gabriella, tell her forthrightly and in all truth that he loved her, and take her straight to bed.

The thought sustained him through a difficult and turbulent assignment, during which he managed to do considerable damage to the cause of the enemy. He worked tirelessly, met periodically with the prince's emissaries, and he waited. He dared not write to Gabriella, lest his missives be intercepted and his identity discovered; he could only pray that she was well.

Blessedly, and after a number of interminable delays, Morgan's duties had been fulfilled. He spent a week with the prince, going over new battle plans, then made the crossing to Portsmouth. During the passage, vivid recollections of the shipwreck surged, full-blown and violent, into his mind, causing his heart to quail with a fear he would never confess, even to a priest.

At Portsmouth there were gray threads of snow upon the hard ground, and the winds were bitter. Morgan bought a gelding, silently mourning the stallion, Nimrod, who had been lost, with so many of his men, in the first crossing. London was still some distance away.

Although less than strong, Morgan stopped only when he knew the horse required rest, subduing his own needs in the interest of haste. His will, formidable even before the disaster at sea, had been forged, in the fires of his long exile in France, to a new intensity.

Upon reaching London, after three days of travel, Morgan proceeded to Sheen.

As he had hoped, Edward's flag flew from the towers; the king, who might have been at any one of a half a dozen places, as his whim decreed, was in residence.

Morgan was received graciously, and food and drink were pressed upon him. Even though he wanted naught but to see, hear, and touch Gabriella, he endured the royal welcome and, when courtesy allowed, made an attempt to steer the conversation with Edward in a more serious direction.

"You do not ask after your pretty wife!" remarked the king, when all the news had been exchanged, exhaustively. "Have you become enamored of the women of France, then?"

Morgan felt his jaw tighten and relaxed it by force of will. He was impatient to be gone, to be through with soldiering. "No, my lord," he answered. "I am a faithful and devoted husband. And I do not ask about Lady Edgefield because I know she has taken a house in London, as I instructed her to do."

Edward frowned. "Then you will be surprised, methinks, to learn that she has long since left us for Cornwall," he said. "Aye," he went on, recalling. "Went the day after you took horse for Portsmouth."

Morgan was stunned, disappointed, and quietly furious, but he hid these emotions behind a stony smile. "I fear milady is headstrong to a fault, and requires a word of correction."

Edward laughed. "That," he said, "shall do no good. No good at all."

Though Morgan was not dissuaded from his intention to rebuke Gabriella in a loud, pointed, and memorable fashion, he made no comment on the king's remark. Inside, he was reeling—he had sustained himself, these many months, by anticipating his reunion with Gabriella in every splendid, groin-tightening detail. Now, more time would pass before they were together—mayhap a great deal of it, if Edward decided upon some other errand he considered uniquely suited to the duke of Edgefield.

Patiently, Morgan repeated the Black Prince's messages, on the king's demand, and listened to his sovereign's lengthy discourses on matters of marriage and war. One and the same subject, Morgan reflected ruefully, when one was wed to Gabriella Chalstrey.

Duchess or none, he vowed, Lady Edgefield would have an upbraiding fit to sour everything in the buttery and singe the tapestries in the great hall the moment he arrived.

He smiled to himself, and gave an inward shrug. Mayhap he would not undertake his wife's chastisement *immediately* upon his return. Soon after, though. Very soon after.

Several days following their departure from Edgefield Keep, on their way to Redclift Hall, by way of St. Swithin's, during which they had plodded through mud deep enough to reach their horses' knees, suffered the importunities of spring weather, and slept with their eyes open because of wolves and outlaws, Gabriella and her party reached the village of Upper Gorse.

A small and wretched place, with only a chapel, an inn where even a discerning rat would disdain to pass the night, and a few dozen wattle-and-daub huts, Upper Gorse was nonetheless the midway point in their journey. In another day, if they were fortunate, they would reach St. Swithin's.

Redclift Hall and its own pitiful village were a day beyond the abbey.

Gabriella would have pressed on, so anxious was she to reach the gates of St. Swithin's and inquire after Elizabeth—mayhap there would be word of Meg, too—but neither Mab nor John Robinson could be persuaded to agree. Both of them were tiresome, in their insistence that milady travel slowly and carefully.

She and Mab had just taken refuge in the stable beside the chapel when a hard spring rain began, turning swiftly to hail. Robinson and the men were battered as they rushed the horses under a stand of birch trees in an effort to protect them.

"Madness," Mab said, as she had numerous times throughout the trip, standing at the window of the stable, with her back to Gabriella and her hands on her hips. "All of it madness. Why, if Lord Edgefield could see you now, he'd take a switch to you, sure as the Lord God commanded Noah to build his ark."

Gabriella, settled cozily in the straw, smiled and rubbed her enormous belly. "Morgan may be stern, and shout he surely would, fit to straighten a pig's tail, but he'd never raise a hand to me." She sighed. "Methinks this child has four legs and as many arms, the way he carries on."

Mab turned, her gaze kindly and even fond, despite her earlier scolding. "You are uncommon big, milady," she conceded, and her expression became thoughtful. "Mayhap you carry not one babe, but a pair. Did you not tell me that your mother bore a sister, with you?"

Gabriella swallowed, saddened. She and Meg had indeed shared Ariel's womb, and they had seldom been apart after. She missed Meg sorely and, for the thousandth time, wondered if the messenger had spoken true, when he claimed Meg had long since left St. Swithin's with Sedgewick.

"My mother suffered greatly for bearing as she did," Gabriella confided.

"Aye," Mab said reluctantly. Gently. "There will surely be pain, but when it passes—"

Gabriella shook her head. "I didn't mean that," she said, "although I'm sure childbirth was as much an ordeal for Mother as for any woman. I was speaking of the slander—people said she must have lain with two men, to bear two babes, and my father believed them. He—" Gabriella swallowed, for she had not thought of those days in a very long time. "He shouted at her until she wept, and begged him to stop, and he named her whore."

"Then he was a superstitious fool, as well as a cruel one," Mab sputtered angrily, coming to sit beside Gabriella in the straw and pat her hand.

"The villagers were no better," Gabriella recalled, gazing off into the distance as she recalled the stories that had circulated round Redclift Hall, albeit in whispers, throughout her childhood. "They taunted her, and even threw stones."

Mab said nothing; there was naught to say. She just continued to pat Gabriella's hand.

"Then Elizabeth was born," Gabriella went on, and smiled because her younger sister would always be a child to her, at least in memory. "Mother was not redeemed, in our father's eyes in any event, because Elizabeth was female and therefore a grave disappointment. But then he went away, and was killed in service to the king. The villagers left Mother alone after that, no doubt thinking the loss of her husband to be punishment enough."

Mab stood, removed her cloak, and spread it over Gabriella. "No more talk now, milady. You must rest while you may."

Gabriella stretched out, too sleepy to resist, and sighed. After hours in the saddle, the musty straw seemed as welcoming as a featherbed. "Two babes," she said dreamily. "Mayhap a boy *and* a girl—"

"Aye," Mab replied tenderly. "We shall soon see, methinks."

Gabriella gave a great yawn. Her eyelids were too heavy to lift, and she was warm, so deliciously warm. "Morgan is nothing like my father," she said.

"No, milady," Mab agreed gently. "Now, rest."

The rain was still pounding down when Gabriella awakened, sometime later, to find lanterns burning in the stable, bringing forth a flimsy light. John Robinson was there, quietly conferring with Mab, and their conversation ended abruptly when they realized their mistress was no longer asleep.

"Robinson has brought you bread, milady, and a bit of boiled bacon from the inn," Mab said, and came to Gabriella's side carrying a small basket. "How do you fare, child? Is there pain?"

"Pain?" Gabriella echoed, mystified. "Only the sore-

ness one expects after days upon a horse's back. Here—
let me have that food, for I am empty."

Mab surrendered the basket, watching her charge
with concern.

Gabriella turned her attention to Robinson even as
she took the bacon from its wrapping of cloth. She had
already decided that it was better not to look too closely
at the food.

"Tell me," she said, "have you and the men a dry
place to pass the night? And what of the horses?"

Robinson smiled, though he looked no less troubled
than before. "Aye, milady—the horses are safe in a
crofter's barn, and the men with them. Except for
Cullen and myself, that is. We're keeping watch here."

Gabriella studied him, chewing hard because the
pork was tough. "Think you the rain will stop us traveling?" she asked.

He sighed. "It will be bothersome," he admitted.

"But we could still reach St. Swithin's on the morrow?"

Robinson thrust a hand through his thatch of rain-
dampened hair. "Aye," he said. "But there is plague in
that place, milady. The men are afraid, and some have
sworn to leave the company if we insist upon stopping."

"I would not make them court the plague," Gabriella
replied. "You may tell them that for me. But I must go,
at least to the gate, and beg news of my sisters and my
friend, Dame Johanna."

Mab's plain face contorted with worry. "But milady—"

"Do you not see that the wondering is as great a peril
to me as the plague itself?" Gabriella interrupted. "I
must ask if Meg is truly well away from St. Swithin's—I
pray she is—and learn Elizabeth's fate, too. If one or

both have perished, I want to know, and make my peace with the matter."

Neither Mab nor Robinson raised an argument after that and, at dawn, in a drizzling downpour, the company was moving once again.

When St. Swithin's came into view, at long last, Gabriella was wet to the skin, but her heart leaped with a hope the worst of tidings had not quenched. While the others hung back, Gabriella, Mab, and John Robinson rode toward the convent. Once bustling with enterprise, the abbey was now strangely still, and no smoke curled from the chimneys, despite the dreary weather.

Gabriella held her head high as she rode, and barred her heart against the fear that pounded in her throat and thundered beneath her temples.

Reaching the gates, which were fastened with a great iron lock, Gabriella dismounted without waiting for help from John. The rain was unrelenting, and cold as sleet.

Grasping the dangling bell rope, Gabriella pulled hard, and the once merry peal, so familiar and beloved, sounded forlorn to her now, and hollow. She peered through the metal railings of the gate and saw a cloaked figure dashing across rain-polished flagstones to answer the summons.

She barely recognized Dame Johanna, so thin and gaunt was she, and so solemn. "Oh, Gabriella—why has your lord husband permitted such a foolish errand?"

Gabriella grasped the bars of the gate in frantic hands. Her hood had slipped onto her shoulders, and her hair lay in sodden ropes down her back. "In the name of God, good dame, let me in—let me see Elizabeth! Give me news of Meg!"

Dame Johanna closed bony fingers over Gabriella's,

which were still wrapped, like those of a prisoner bound for the gallows, round the bars. "Meg is not here," she said gently. "She left us months ago, with Gresham Sedgewick. And Elizabeth cannot see you, child, for she lies ill."

Gabriella felt as though she would swoon, and pressed her forehead to the icy metal for a moment, breathing deeply. Someone—be it John or Mab she did not know, at first—came to stand behind her, and place a restraining hand upon her shoulder. "Tell me!" she cried, baring her teeth like an animal in her desperation. "If ever you were my friend, tell me!"

Tears stood in Dame Johanna's eyes. "Elizabeth does not suffer from the plague, but simple exhaustion—she has toiled so to aid those who suffer. It is bad, Gabriella. We have sent for a priest."

"Peace, milady," pleaded a male voice. It was John, then, who restrained her.

Gabriella might have attempted to climb the gates had his strong arms not prevented her. Supported her.

"No!" Gabriella screamed, struggling. "No!"

"Be on your way, child," the nun begged. "I cannot permit you to see Elizabeth. She would not know you, though I have given her the letter you put in my care, and she has kept it close by her all the while. Gabriella, heed me—there is great danger here. Think of your babe, I pray you."

Gabriella cried out again, from deep in her belly, and tried to fling herself against the impenetrable barrier.

"Take her away from this place," Dame Johanna said, gazing imploringly at Robinson. "We have pestilence here, I tell you, and will not open our gates to anyone save the priest."

John held Gabriella firmly, or she would have slipped to her knees and curled in upon herself, sobbing and beating at the paving stones with her fists. "My lady," he pleaded, nigh to weeping himself, from the sound of his voice, "remember the babe, I beseech you. Remember the babe!"

Gabriella calmed herself, for she felt the child moving restlessly inside her, and feared to bear it afore time. Trembling, she kissed the tips of her fingers and reached through the gate to press them to Dame Johanna's forehead, which was hot with fever, even in the rain.

"God be with you," Gabriella whispered brokenly, "and with my beloved sister."

"I will tell Elizabeth that you live, my lady, and that you are breeding, and sure to bear a sturdy child. Mayhap her spirit will hear, if her mind does not, and she will take comfort." With those words, Dame Johanna turned and hurried away.

Gabriella uttered a soft sound of protest and of sorrow, but allowed John to carry her back to her horse, and lift her into the saddle. She wept, in utter silence, and took no note of the ride, or of the house of a peasant farmer, where they stopped for the night. The landholder, though a kindly man, would not allow Gabriella and Mab to enter his home, lest they bring the plague with them. Still, he gave them leave to rest in his barn, which was ample in size and possessed of a good roof, and offered four of his chickens out of Christian charity.

Inside the stable, Mab undressed Gabriella and wrapped her in a blanket brought along from Edgefield Keep. The midwife knelt in the stale straw, cradling

Gabriella's head upon her lap and assuring her, in a raspy voice, that all would be well.

All would surely be well.

Morgan was ready to fall from his saddle by the time he finally reached Edgefield Keep. The place looked gloomy, in the rain, and even from a distance, he sensed some great despair within.

Fear struck him, and it was not the first such blow. Had the plague come here, in his absence, to claim Gabriella, to strike down his friends and vassals?

He spurred the exhausted horse forward, and shouted a command from the foot of the drawbridge.

One of the two towering gates swung open, groaning upon its hinges, and Morgan rode through. "What is amiss here?" he demanded harshly of the guard who greeted him. It was midafternoon by his guess, though he could not see the sun for rain clouds, and yet the whole place was idle, almost empty.

The man smiled up at him, pitifully happy at his return. "We thought you dead and gone, milord," he snuffled, and wiped his nose on the sleeve of his tunic.

"And you're all in mourning, is that it?" Morgan snapped, afraid to ask whether he would find Gabriella fit or ailing. He leaned down to look the guard in the face. "Spread the word, lad—every man within these walls will present himself in the main courtyard within the hour or be flogged for his negligence. Is that clear?"

The guard beamed stupidly. "Aye, milord!" he responded, and snuffled again. " 'Tis good to find you so unchanged, after all this while!"

Morgan rolled his eyes. "Where is everyone?" he demanded.

"Most are busy with the planting and the tilling, milord," came the earnest answer.

"My soldiers are in the fields? And what ails the villagers?"

"We've all been sharing the work, milord," the guard said proudly. "Lady Edgefield took a good many of the men with her when she left, you see."

Morgan tensed. "*What* did you say?"

"I guess you wouldn't have known about her leaving, would you, milord? You being dead and everything."

The last of Morgan's patience evaporated in a venomous mist. "Tell me where my wife has gone, and when, or I shall draw my sword and relieve you of your ears!"

The man clasped his hands over said appurtenances, presumably to protect them. "Lady Edgefield has gone to St. Swithin's, and then to Redclift Hall!" he spouted. "She's been away these ten days past!"

Morgan left the guard at last, and when he reached his own courtyard, Ephriam was standing in the rain, long faced. No doubt he had observed his lord's approach for some time, and guessed the gist of Morgan's exchange with the unfortunate guard.

"*You let her go?*" Morgan shouted at the old man, dismounting and flinging the shivering gelding's reins at a stable boy, who cowered nearby, gnawing at his lip.

"You are alive and well," Ephriam said, as though Morgan had greeted him cordially. "God be thanked."

Morgan started to speak again, but a surge of weakness rushed from the soles of his feet to the crown of his head, and he swayed. Ephriam steadied him, grasping his shoulders in both hands.

"Come inside, my lord, and take sustenance. I will explain everything."

"You let her go," Morgan repeated, this time dully, though his disbelief had not lessened.

"Aye," the retainer confessed. "There was no reasoning with Lady Edgefield, once she'd set her mind on making the journey." He gave Morgan a discreet shove in the direction of the castle's nearest entrance. "I suppose there is no explanation of your absence and heroic demise forthcoming?"

Morgan entered the keep thankfully, although the knowledge that Gabriella was not safe within, waiting for him, was as crushing as if the place had collapsed on top of him. He explained, while Ephriam gave him wine, and ordered food, and sent the housemaids rushing to build a fire upon the master's private hearth, how the ship had struck from Portsmouth and sunk, how the majority of his men had perished in that disaster, and the magnificent charger Nimrod with them.

When Ephriam would have steered him up the staircase, however, he halted.

"I cannot set foot in that bedchamber," Morgan said. "Not without Gabriella there to greet me."

"My lord," Ephriam said, by way of comfort, and sympathy.

"Save your soothing words," Morgan ordered, spearing his old friend and trusted confidant with a furious glare. "I expected to find my wife in London town, and did not. I then trusted that she would be here, within the walls of Edgefield Keep, where she most assuredly belongs, yet once again I am disappointed. I would be told, before I take another step, why she left!"

Ephriam let out a long breath. "She received word that her mother, Lady Mainwaring, is ailing, my lord. Earlier, we heard that one of her sisters was lost, and the other in danger of plague. Fearing that you were drowned, as we all did, I suspect her ladyship could not bear the prospect of another loved one's passing, and raced off in the hope of preventing that."

Morgan felt the blood drain from his face. He grasped the stone railing of the staircase, solely to hold himself upright. "Plague?" he said, for, in an instant, his whole being had locked onto that single word.

"Aye, my lord," Ephriam answered. "It is rumored that there is pestilence at St. Swithin's, as there is in London."

"God in heaven," Morgan muttered. "And Gabriella has gone there? In search of her sister?"

"I believe so," Ephriam said, and took his master firmly by the elbow. "If you take no rest, my lord," he reasoned, as he guided Morgan up the stairs, "you will be of little use to your lady wife, when you reach her."

Morgan longed for the luxury, the release, of weeping, but he dared not indulge the yearning, for the other man was right. If he was to find Gabriella and bring her home unharmed, he must not harbor the slightest weakness.

At the top of the stairs, Morgan entered the chamber he had occupied as a youth. Magically, a fire was already blazing on the hearth, and servants were turning out the bed, putting fresh sheets and blankets upon it, fluffing pillows.

Morgan stood before the fireplace, staring blankly into the flames, until he and Ephriam were once again alone. Then he turned to search the old man's face. "What is it that you have withheld from me?" he asked raggedly. They had known each other too long, Morgan and his most trusted adviser, to keep secrets.

Ephriam brought a cup, brimming with wine, and held it out, saying nothing.

Morgan took it, drank. "Well?" he demanded, wiping his mouth with the back of one hand, in the uncouth manner of soldiers too long in the field.

The old man gestured toward a nearby chair. "Sit down, my lord. You are right—there is yet one bit of news you have not heard."

Gabriella passed the rest of the journey to Redclift Hall in a daze—Morgan, vanished. Elizabeth, shut away within the walls of St. Swithin's, dead or dying, and with no one of her own blood to soothe her. Meg gone, God knew where, with Gresham Sedgewick. Had Morgan's long-absent friend been bringing Meg to Edgefield Keep, and been set upon by thieves and murderers? Or had he kidnapped her, as Morgan had kidnapped Gabriella herself?

Meg was strong. That thought was the only solace Gabriella could find, amongst her immediate circumstances. Behind her lay St. Swithin's, ravaged by pestilence, and before her, her childhood home, where her mother waited, sick unto dying. If indeed Ariel, too, had not already succumbed.

The rain had ceased, somewhere along the way, and the sun dazzled the eyes with its brightness, greening the meadow grasses and resurrecting bluebells and buttercups from their winter graves. It was May, Gabriella realized with a start, and her unwieldy belly, stretched taut as the rind of a ripened melon, indicated that her babe, or babes, would arrive sooner than she had thought.

As they passed through the small village, dogs barked and children chased each other between the tiny, hut-like dwellings. At the top of the knoll rose Redclift Hall, its low garden walls crumbling, its thatched roof sagging. Even then, with the spring so recently come, weeds and prickly vines threatened to engulf the house. The orchards, much in need of pruning, gave forth spindly blossoms.

Hugh was there to help Gabriella down from her horse when they reached the gate. He looked old and stooped and affably defeated.

"My mother?" Gabriella asked, and the words came ragged from her throat, for she had not wanted to ask them.

Tears welled in Hugh's sunken eyes, and his hand tightened on Gabriella's as she stood beside him, great with child and weary beyond the point of collapse. "I am sorry, child," he said. "You are too late by a sennight."

19

⤌❦⤍

Gabriella stood beside her mother's grave, awash in belated sunlight, whilst the birds sang a cheerful requiem. *I am alone, but for my babes,* she thought, as she had oft done, in the three days since her arrival at Redclift Hall.

Morgan, Meg, Elizabeth, Ariel—all of them were gone, in one way or another, and in that moment, Gabriella did not want to go on. Only the thought of her unborn children sustained her; she had lost all else.

The grass was warm and sweet and dry around Ariel's resting place, and Gabriella sat down, smoothing the skirts of her rough woolen gown. The grave was new, not yet marked with a stone, and covered in raw earth, recently turned.

"I wish I had been here to help you," Gabriella confessed to her lost mother. She did not weep; her trials had driven her beyond tears, beyond sorrow, into a state of numbness, though she knew the grief would return, in time, with crushing force.

A soft breeze ruffled Gabriella's fair, free-flowing

hair, and reminded her of Ariel's chiming laugh, her love of games and stories, her fey and childlike spirit. She had been more like an elder sister to her daughters than a parent, but that, Gabriella knew now, had been enough. She and Meg and Elizabeth had drawn their strength from other sources—from the good nuns at St. Swithin's, from their own imaginations, from each other.

Her mouth curved into a soft smile, and she laid both hands to her belly, as if to calm the babes, and reassure them that love awaited them, outside the confining safety of her body. That there were two, and that they would burst into the world, already set upon changing it to fit their own vision, she had no doubt.

Her greatest hope, just then, was that the birthing might go well. Gabriella did not expect the experience to be an easy one; simple logic decreed that the task must be difficult and painful for the mother. It was the babes she worried about—were they large enough, and strong like herself and like Morgan? Had they all their fingers and toes, arms and legs, eyes and ears?

A shadow fell across the grave, and Gabriella knew that it belonged to Hugh Mainwaring, her stepfather. She did not look up at him.

"Did my mother suffer?" she asked. It was a question Gabriella had had no opportunity to raise, for upon their arrival, and Hugh's immediate announcement of Ariel's recent death, Mab had put her to bed and dosed her with potent herbs that caused her to sleep.

Hugh crouched on the other side of the narrow mound, touched it fondly, tentatively, with his hand. "No," he replied. "She lay abed for many weeks, but there was no pain to speak of, though I know she

grieved for her daughters. That is why I sent a message
to you, by way of St. Swithin's."

"Did you know that the king himself was our benefactor?" Gabriella asked, gazing directly at Hugh now.
She had not expected to speak of that, but the words
were out, unplanned and stark in the glittering sun-
shine.

Her stepfather sighed but did not flinch or look away.
"We had no means to provide for you, Gabriella, or for
Elizabeth and Margaret. We believed the king would
make fine matches for you all, when the time came, and
we were heartily grateful to know you would suffer no
true privation."

Gabriella expelled her breath. "Aye," she muttered.

"Your handmaiden, Mab, is fretful, thinking you will
be too long in the spring air, and tire yourself," Hugh
said gently, offering a hand. "Won't you come back to
the manor house now, and break bread with us?"

Gabriella allowed herself to be raised to her feet,
though she had no appetite.

"What will you do now, Gabriella?" Hugh asked. "Remain here at Redclift Hall, to bear and raise your babe?"

She shook her head. "My place is at Edgefield
Keep," she said. "My children belong there, for one day,
it will be theirs. If we make haste, and the good weather
holds, we can return there before the birth."

Hugh looked truly stunned. "But it is so far, child,
and you are close to your time!"

Gabriella tucked her arm through his as they walked
toward the rear garden of the manor house. Once a
playground for three fanciful and spirited little girls, it
was now naught but a spiky thicket, haunted by beloved
ghosts.

"I have a month before my confinement," Gabriella reassured her stepfather. "And it is important to me that my children be born on the land that will one day be their own."

"Children?" Hugh asked. "You anticipate more than one?"

Gabriella nodded, and gave him a shy smile. "Aye—I am certain there are at least two. Sometimes I feel as though I carry a troupe of traveling acrobats, constantly at practice."

Hugh laughed, though the sound was hollow, made more of habit than of amusement. His grief at losing Ariel was plain to see, and a burden he struggled visibly to bear. "Suppose they are both boys, then," he said. "Which will become the duke of Edgefield?"

Gabriella had not considered the question of ascendency, for she, like her stepfather, was a conquered land, occupied and ofttimes ruled by heartache. "The elder, I suppose. There are people at Edgefield who will advise me." They had almost reached the rear door of the manor house, which gaped open, as it had on other fair days, the better for three exuberant girls to dash in and out. "What of your plans, Hugh? Will you remarry?"

Hugh looked away, and Gabriella did not follow his gaze, for she knew he hoped to hide his tears. "I cannot bear the thought of another woman," he said. After a brief silence, he turned back to his stepdaughter, attempting to smile. "It is my plan to return to London, where I have a brother. Marcus owns a modest shipping concern, and he has offered many times to take me on. I might have accepted earlier, but that Ariel could never have left Redclift."

"She spent all her life here," Gabriella confirmed softly. Her mother had been a distant cousin to Gabriella's father, and betrothed to him at an early age. Fostered at the hall from her fifth birthday, that she might be properly trained in the mores, manners, and tasks that befitted a future Lady Redclift, Ariel had found a degree of happiness as a child that eluded her later on.

Hugh leaned forward to kiss Gabriella's forehead. "You were made for better things than a tumbledown manor house," he said. "Your mother and I always knew that. Therefore, it is right and fitting for you to undertake the journey back to Cornwall. Pray, make haste to go, for 'tis sure your babes will take after you, and have ideas of their own about everything, including where and when to be born."

Gabriella smiled. "I will send word to you in London, when the times comes, that you may know all is well."

The following day was as sunny and mild as the one before it, and Gabriella departed Redclift for good, with Mab and Robinson and the small company of men. Mayhap because they knew it would be useless, and because they, too, wanted to return to their own homes, neither John nor the midwife had bothered to protest the decision.

The second and third days were fair also, and the nights, though chilly, were no hardship. It was on the fourth morning that the skies grew dark and ponderous and finally threw down hail and rain with a fury that drove the travelers to take shelter at Upper Gorse.

They had planned to pass that village by as well as St. Swithin's, but the storm made that impossible.

On this visit, Gabriella and her entourage found the village slightly more accommodating than before. The men-at-arms were given habitable, or at least tolerable, quarters at the inn, and a monk called Brother Percy, taking note of Gabriella's advanced pregnancy, gave her his cot in the cell behind the chapel.

She was agitated as she paced back and forth beneath the church's one stained glass window, a grisly representation of St. Paul's crucifixion, upside down and singing praises until the end. Mab, meanwhile, was seated on a pew, her lips moving rapidly as she offered private prayers.

Gabriella could imagine only too well what the midwife begged of heaven's mercy and grace. She herself was the object of these fervent petitions, along with the babes she carried, for though she had tried to hide the truth, the infants had dropped low in her belly, and her back ached so that the pain leeched the blood from her face.

"With the favors you ask of God and the Blessed Virgin," she said to Mab, somewhat testily, because she was so weary, and so sad, and so heavy in front that she could barely keep her feet, "pray, make one plea for me—that my babes might be born in Edgefield Keep, as their father was, and his before him. Aye, Ephriam said there have been Chalstreys there since the time of the conqueror—"

Mab gave her a look, but did not interrupt her swift and secret entreaties. Until a ferocious pain gripped Gabriella, that is, with such suddenness and force that she cried out and bent double.

"John Robinson!" Mab shouted, rushing to support Gabriella and lower her onto one of the rough-hewn benches where worshipers gathered, if indeed Upper Gorse had any left to it. "Come hither!"

John dashed inside and past the rows of humble pews with such expediency that Gabriella knew he'd been waiting for just such a summons. Another pain, more vicious than the last, tore through her, and she called out, falling helplessly forward into Robinson's steady hold.

"Take her to the priest's cot," Mab ordered, calmer now than before. "Then find me a serving woman, a tavern wench, a whore. It makes no matter to me what she is, as long as she's got clean hands and a stout stomach."

Gabriella was seized by a sharp and unrelenting agony, blinded by it, and because of the suddenness of her suffering, and its intensity, she guessed that her travails were not normal ones, something was very wrong. "My babes," she gasped, groping for Mab's hand and finding it, strong and calloused as a swordsman's.

"Hush," the midwife soothed. "Hush now, and listen to me, Gabriella. You must do as I say!"

Gabriella could only nod; a low, whimpering sound came from her center as her belly contracted again, this time with such violence that she nearly pitched off the side of the little cot. The pain was shattering, as hot and sharp as a dragon's teeth, bearable only because it could not be escaped.

"Aye, you're a brave thing, fit for the name of duchess," Mab said.

Gabriella had found her voice, though only briefly; even as she spoke, some force in her throat was already shaping itself into a scream. "My babes—oh, Mab—see that they are not hurt, I beg you—"

"Hush," Mab said again, but gently. "All will be well."

But Gabriella knew by the other woman's tone that she was not so certain.

After that, the ordeal got progressively worse. Gabriella was bathed in sweat, yet chilled to the marrow of her bones, and the pain was beyond bearing. She slipped in and out of consciousness, and cried out when she was awake. As the hours passed, agony upon agony, she suffered the realization, over and over again, that she had been wrong and foolish to push herself so hard, through the rain and the cold and the everlasting, grinding fatigue.

Mab and some other woman tended her, and talked between themselves in low, careful voices, keeping their words and their worries just beyond Gabriella's reach.

Finally, the pain rose up like some great, slack-jawed beast, ground her between bone-crushing teeth, and swallowed her in pieces. Gabriella sank deeper and deeper into an inner abyss, never explored before, a place so hot and dark and terrifying that she truly believed she had been cast into hell.

Only a few scattered words floated down to her, like feathers, from the lost world: *fever . . . priest . . . pray . . .*

Had Ephriam not had the effrontery and, yes, the compassion, to drug his wine that first night, Morgan would have bolted from the keep, mounted the first horse he came to, set his course for Redcliff Hall, and ridden the beast until it dropped.

The elderly servant had foreseen the possibility, however, and taken steps to intercede. He was conspicuously absent when Morgan finally regained his full senses, and burst from his bed shouting with rage and vowing to strip the skin off everyone who had had a part in the plot to render him insensible.

He had dressed and gained the stables before he learned that three days had passed since his return, and once he knew that, his fury was so cold and so violent that no one dared come near him.

Morgan flung his saddle onto the gelding himself, and the main gates stood open wide when he reached them. The horse's hooves hammered on the thick timbers of the drawbridge and yet Morgan drove the beast harder, and harder still.

He supposed it was the consummate irony when, after only an hour or so on the road, he and the horse struck some unseen barrier and went rolling, the both of them, end over end.

When, finding himself upon his stomach, Morgan regained his breath, not to mention his senses, and raised himself onto his elbows, he saw that the gelding stood a few yards away, nibbling sweet grass and evidently unhurt.

Morgan cursed and moved to rise, only to feel the point of a sword at the back of his neck. Years of hard training and gruesome experience stood him in good stead; he spun to his feet, and his own blade leaped into his hand just in time to strike its counterpart with a jarring *clang*. The force of it reverberated through Morgan's arm and shoulder and caused his sturdy teeth to quiver at their roots.

Avendall laughed, wild eyed and ruffled, and as fine a swordsman as he had ever been. "Methinks that love has tamed you, Edgefield," he taunted. "Once you would have known to watch for a snare such as I laid this day."

Their blades struck again, and the sound echoed.

"I have no time for this, Cyprian," Morgan warned.

"Step aside or this time, by God's breath, I *will* kill you!"

Another blow, equal in force from both sides.

"Ah," said Cyprian, undaunted, "you cannot have forgotten, even in your agitation over your lady wife, that I am, in this one game at least, as good as you are?"

Clang.

"You have a spy in Edgefield Keep. Did you think I would be surprised?"

Another clash of steel against steel, and a shower of blue sparks.

Avendall pulled a face. "I have more than one."

They parted to assess each other, and it came to Morgan that he would have enjoyed the conflict if it hadn't been for his desperate need to find Gabriella.

"Aye," Morgan allowed. "A kitchen wench, I would guess, and mayhap a stable hand. Do you think I give a damn? Get out of my way, Cyprian, before I'm forced to ram this blade through your withered little heart."

Avendall raised his sword and brought it down hard, as if to split Morgan's head; and Edgefield intercepted it. "There is one thing I want to say to you, before I take horse for Portsmouth," Cyprian said. "It seems His Majesty has decided to press me back into service."

"Imagine that," Morgan replied. Under other circumstances, he would have given the words a smug turn as he uttered them. As it was, he had no inclination to waste time and energy on such frivolous luxuries.

"I did not mislead Rebecca." Avendall struck again, and the blades sang a discordant chorus. "It was you, Edgefield, who played the fool."

Morgan had worked all that through, during the long months in France. He knew that Rebecca had loved Sedgewick, and when he spurned her affections, she had turned to Avendall, for whatever reason. He no longer cared. "A role I have ofttimes assumed," he admitted, and his sword met Avendall's again, and seemed to tangle with it. For a moment, the two men were so close that their breaths mingled. "Pray, impart your revelation, for I grow weary of letting you live."

The muscles in Avendall's face worked spasmodically; he had ever been slow in verbal exchanges, if not battle games. "She had been practicing for marriage, Chalstrey, with a stable boy, whilst you were learning to be a soldier. And she leaped to her death because she was breeding, and could not bear for you—or her precious Sedgewick—to know."

Morgan's next blow was born of urgency, not passion or fury. Avendall's sword flew into a thicket, and Morgan pressed the point of his own blade to his opponent's throat. He felt only pity for Rebecca now, not fury. She had been a child, confused and far from her true home. And what a burden it must have been for Gresham, all these years, knowing that his closest friend's betrothed had wanted only him.

Avendall stood breathing hard, but unrepentant. "Put an end to me; you've earned the right. But know this, Edgefield: I die innocent of Rebecca's blood."

It was true, all of it, and Morgan knew that. Still, he was not ready to forgive Avendall's more recent transgressions, those involving Gabriella. "Have a care in France," he said, "for other enemies will not be so merciful as I." With that, he struck Cyprian hard alongside the head with the flat of his sword, and the other man crumpled unharmed and probably no wiser than before, to the soft, cushioning grass.

Long before he stirred, Morgan would be well away, leaving behind, with Avendall, the grudge he'd cherished for too many years. In some part of himself, he realized now, he had always known of Rebecca's deceit. It had simply been easier, and far less painful, to blame his lifelong rival.

He rode without pause, and at breakneck speed, all that day and well into the evening, stopping only because the gelding was stumbling beneath him. While the horse rested nearby, hobbled, Morgan himself slept sitting upright, with his back pressed to the rough trunk of a tree.

A light rain awakened him, sometime in the depths of the night, and he unhobbled the gelding, mounted, and set out again.

At midmorning, the beast would go no farther, and Morgan traded it for a crofter's plow horse, in a rain-splattered field. The second animal lasted until he was just short of the village of Upper Gorse; he gave it to a peasant woman and bought a bay stallion from a tinker for ten gold florins. It was robbery, but Morgan, by then covered in mud and wet to the skin, did not care that he had made a poor bargain.

He might have ridden straight through Upper Gorse, if he hadn't seen John Robinson, his own man, sitting forlornly on a bench outside the village's tiny church, watching the rain fall.

A strange sensation moved in the pit of Morgan's stomach, and he reined the tinker's horse in that direction.

"Robinson?"

John leaped to his feet, looking gleeful and stricken by turns. "My lord—I can't believe it—surely there's a miracle here—"

Morgan swung down from the stallion's bare back—
he'd lost his saddle in the first trade—and handed the
reins to his friend. "What is it?"

It was then that a woman's anguished cry rent the
air, and somehow Morgan knew that it was Gabriella,
that he'd been led to this place because she needed
him.

"In the back," John said woefully. "She's had a hard
time of it, my lord—very brave she is, though—there's
fever, and she's yet in terrible pain—"

Morgan shoved the church doors open with both
hands, stormed through the chapel, drawn by a second
tormented cry. *Jesu*, he pleaded, and entered the small
room behind the altar.

Gabriella was there, abed, with a priest standing
over her, murmuring and making holy signs. Morgan
was seized with a terror so deep that there was no name
for it.

"Gabriella!" he rasped, and the sound was half a sob.

The priest barred his way; only the sight of two
babes, squalling in a basket next to the fire, kept him
from flinging the man out of his way.

A woman, Mab, took his arm. "Pray, my lord, do not
interfere, and cause your lady wife to die unshriven.
Come and look upon your sons."

Morgan wrenched free, and warned the priest aside
with a look. Then he knelt at Gabriella's side and took
one of her hands in both of his, and kissed it. It was like
touching his lips to a horseshoe still glowing from the
forge.

"Gabriella," he whispered. "Sweet Gabriella."

She stirred, but her skin was gray and bloodless, yet
strangely translucent, and she did not open her eyes.

The priest laid a hand on Morgan's shoulder. "If you would serve your lady wife, my lord, go hence, to the chapel, and pray."

Morgan rose, dazed, and made his way to the basket where the babes lay. Two lads, small but sturdy-looking, with fair hair. Their feet and fists pumped furiously, tiny though they were, and they screamed fit to wake the dead.

Morgan touched them, each one, with a tentative pass of his fingertips. Then, after one more glance at Gabriella, he stumbled into the chapel and fell to his knees at the altar.

He did not know how to pray; indeed, he had forgotten. At first, he merely knelt there, numb, unaware of the tears that caught in the stubble of his new beard. Somehow, he had to find words—words that would please God, that would save Gabriella.

Covered in mud as he was, wearing chain mail over a coarse tunic, leggings, and filthy boots, it came to Morgan that here, before this altar, he was not a knight, not a noble, but a mere beggar. He drew his sword from its scabbard and laid it where he was certain God would see. Then he put his palms together and interlaced his fingers.

"I know not what You would have me say," he said, eyes upraised to the crude wooden cross and its crucified Christ, affixed to the wall above the priest's chair. "That is my wife, behind yonder door, closer now to heaven, methinks, than to earth. I love her more than my own life. We need her, Lord, my babes and me. That is my prayer, that You will spare Gabriella. I am a sinful man, and have naught to offer save my sword, and my vow to serve no other king, from this day forward, but for You."

He bowed his head and then rose, awkwardly, and returned to the room where Gabriella lay, a single heartbeat from death.

The priest and woman conferred in a corner, each of them cradling a sleeping babe in their arms. Their eyes followed Morgan as he approached the cot where Gabriella lay, still and fragile, but neither spoke to him.

Morgan knelt again, and rested his forehead lightly upon Gabriella's breast, and his great shoulders shuddered with grief he made no attempt to stem or disguise. He did not know how much time had passed when he felt her hand brush against his hair with no more weight than a butterfly's wing.

He raised his head and saw that her eyes were open. Well aware, after years of death vigils on battlefields all over the known world, that people often rallied before they gave up the ghost, he found and clasped her hand.

"Stay with me, Gabriella," Morgan pleaded, in a rough whisper. "I love you and I need you. Stay—" he kissed her knuckles frantically. "Stay."

Her lips moved; she breathed his name. And then she closed her eyes.

Morgan pressed his ear to her chest, hardly able to hear over the pounding of his own heart, and found a faint, steady beat, struggling to grow stronger.

In the coming hours, it was Morgan who bathed Gabriella's fever-dried flesh with cool water, Morgan who murmured to her, almost without a breath, anchoring her to him as best he could with poems and prayers, promises and pleas. He told her tales, some true and some not worthy to be called a lie, and soldiers' jests, bawdy though they were. He recited what he knew of astronomy, and Latin, and the ways of horses. In the small hours, he fell asleep, still kneeling, his head resting on her chest.

The light stroke of her fingers, playing at his nape, brought Morgan out of the depths and into the pinkish-gold light of a summer dawn. She smiled at him and, at first, he feared he was dreaming.

"Gabriella?"

Her voice was weak and raspy, but mischievous as well. "You thought to find someone else making a pillow for your head, my lord husband?"

Morgan laughed; the sound was strangled and hoarse. "I love you." He couldn't say it fast enough, or often enough. He kissed her forehead, then her lips. "I love you!"

"Be still, husband," Gabriella said tenderly, her fingers in his hair now, pushing it back from his face. "You'll wake our children."

"Sons," Morgan marveled. "Two of them!"

"Aye. What names shall we give them? Apollo and Zeus, mayhap?"

Morgan grinned. "Try again, my lady wife, but do not depend upon me to choose. I favor any name save my own."

She frowned. "Can we not name one Morgan?"

"Nay," he said. "My father was called Steven. Mayhap that would do."

"Steven Morgan," Gabriella said.

He could not refuse her. Indeed, he would have given her all he owned, and never known a moment's regret. "What of the other son? Is he to be nameless?"

Gabriella pondered that. "Michael Alexander," she said presently, and with triumph. "For the archangel, and for my late father, who was the opposite."

Morgan chuckled. "Aye," he agreed. "Being your son and mine, methinks the boy will be a devil instead. Mayhap such a fine name will be his salvation."

That afternoon, Steven Morgan Chalstrey, the first-born, and Michael Alexander Chalstrey, the younger by several minutes, were properly christened. After a week, Morgan took the upper floor of the inn, disreputable as it was, and had the whole of it stripped to the walls, scrubbed with lye soap, and furnished with goods sent by cart from Redclift Hall. Then, when Mab pronounced Gabriella strong enough, he moved his family into their temporary quarters and proved himself insufferably proud of all three.

Morgan slept beside Gabriella all night, and hovered over her all day, until she became ungrateful and impatient and told him to go below stairs and drink ale with John Robinson and the others. At first, he was injured, but Mab explained to him that it was a good omen—Lady Edgefield was recovering, and would soon be herself again.

They had been in the inn at Upper Gorse for more than six weeks when Gabriella demanded that they pack up the few belongings she wanted to take along and set out for Edgefield Keep. It was bad enough that Steven and Michael had been born so far from home, she proclaimed, with her old, delightful audacity. She would not raise her children in a tavern!

And so, with all the pageantry of an army going to war, Lord and Lady Edgefield, with their babes, their soldiers and their midwife, along with the four or five servants they had acquired during their stay, struck out for Cornwall.

For a month after their return to Edgefield Keep,

where they were received with jubilation and much sloshing of ale, Morgan did not come to Gabriella's bed. He was a devoted father to the babes, and a great favorite with their nursemaids, but he treated Gabriella as though she had taken the veil.

One day, she donned a green gown to confront him, and braided a matching ribbon through her hair. She touched the pulse points behind both her ears with scent, and peered critically at her reflection in the looking glass.

"Where, pray tell," she began, an ironic note dancing in her tone, "is my lord and master?"

Mab smiled, shrugged, and went on humming.

Gabriella moved her heavy plait from one shoulder to the other, then marched to the door with resolution, only to sigh and rest her forehead against the panels. "Dear heaven, what shall I say to him?"

Mab looked cheerful, and full of knowing. "That you are ready for him. Methinks he has been waiting quite anxiously to hear it." The midwife chuckled, then a tender solemnity filled her eyes. "The man adores you, but he witnessed the worst of your ordeal—aye, the worst— when you had the babes, and I'm sure milord is afraid to get you under him again, lest he sire another child, and see you die abearing."

Gabriella's mouth fell open. "He can't possibly think such a foolish thing!" she cried, when she'd recovered. "It was the riding and the sorrow and the rain that brought me to my deathbed before, not the birthing!"

Mab shrugged and went on folding. "Tell his lordship that, for your wisdom is wasted on me, my lady."

Gabriella stormed out and, aided by a nod from Ephriam, found her husband in his boyhood chamber, where he had taken to sleeping upon their return. He was standing at one of the windows, looking out upon some scene in the courtyard.

"My lord," Gabriella said, somewhat imperiously.

Morgan turned, surprised. "Gabriella," he replied.

She drew a deep, tremulous voice. "I have missed you in my bed, husband."

He gazed at her, at once hungry for her, and frightened. Mab had been right, then. "Gabriella—"

"I had not thought you a coward, sir."

In one motion, he slammed the door behind Gabriella and trapped her against it, between his hands. His eyes flashed with temper, amusement, and passion. "What did you call me?"

"A coward," Gabriella said fearlessly, pressing a fingertip lightly into the hollow of his throat. "Furthermore, if you think to fill my place by taking a mistress—"

"A mistress! What nonsense is this?" he demanded.

Gabriella swallowed. She did not seriously think he had resorted to trysting with other women; she had merely been baiting him. She said nothing, but simply looked up at him, casting her singular spells.

"You have just given birth—" he reminded her.

"That was more than two months past," Gabriella pointed out. She knew her chin was quivering, but she couldn't help it. "You said you loved me, Morgan."

His nose was nearly touching hers, and his eyes glittered with emotion. "And I do, Gabriella. Too much to see you suffer that way again—"

"Fool," Gabriella said, but she slipped her arms round his neck. "Tell me true, my lord. Do you still lust after me, as you once did?"

"You know damn well I do!"

"Then take off my clothes, and your own, and make love to me. Here. Now."

This time it was Morgan who swallowed. "Suppose we make another babe?"

She smiled saucily. "I should be delighted."

"Are you mad? You nearly perished the last time!"

"Not from bearing our sons, my lord. I was sick with exhaustion and grief. I did not rest when Mab and Robinson begged me to do so." Gabriella stood on tip-toe, and touched her mouth to his. "I still have my sorrows—I know not what has befallen my sisters, and both are precious to me—but you are my comfort, my lord. You are my joy. It is heartless of you to spurn me."

Morgan groaned, tasted her lips, drew back as if struggling to control himself. "Gabriella—"

She laid one hand to him, boldly. "You do desire me. That is most encouraging."

"God in heaven—"

"God is most certainly in heaven," Gabriella teased, "but we are yet on earth, my lord, and must make our own paradise."

Morgan kissed her then, pressing her hard between his body and the door, parting her lips with his tongue and conquering her mouth in the same way he would soon conquer her body. Without breaking the contact, he unlaced Gabriella's gown and pushed it down over her arms and hips, into a pool on the floor. Then he lifted her into his arms, carried her to the bed, and flung her down upon it.

His eyes blazed as he stood over her, shedding his own garments as rapidly as he could.

She crooned and arched her back, purely to tempt him.

He laughed, a low and manly sound that she loved, and arranged her for a conquest of another kind. "There is a price for playing the temptress," he warned, and he bent over her, and took his due.

Gabriella's cry of surprise and surrender filled the chamber, and mayhap the corridor, too. As Morgan tamed her, she tossed upon the bed, as if to escape him, begging senselessly, joyously, for the attentions he was already giving her. When he teased her, she sobbed with tension, and when at last he poised himself over her, and plunged inside, she called his name, gathering him closer with her arms and legs, and closer still. They moved together, in glorious celebration and reunion.

"What of my sisters?" Gabriella fretted, some time later, when she and Morgan lay entwined, having dressed again, after that first bout of lovemaking, found their way to their own bed and lost themselves in each other once more. "What of Sedgewick?"

Morgan kissed her temple. "We will learn what happened to all of them," he promised, "if I have to send messengers to every corner of England."

Gabriella settled against her husband. "I fear that Elizabeth has left us," she said, crying a little. She had missed him, not only in bed, but as her confidant. "I have waited for word from the abbey, but no letter has come—"

He turned, kissed her under each eye, drying her tears in that most tender way. "Shhh," he said. "You were as near death as anyone could be, and still you came back. Do you expect less from your little sister?"

She smiled, sniffled. "Elizabeth *is* strong."

He grinned. "Of course she is," he said. "And so is

Meg. As strong as you, methinks." He slipped downward, took suckle at one of Gabriella's ripe nipples, then the other. "Now, then," he murmured, and circled her naval with his tongue, setting her flesh aquiver all over again, "there is the matter of making a sister for our sons."